D1575399

COMMITMENT
HOUR

Other Avon Books by
James Alan Gardner

EXPENDABLE

COMMITMENT
H O U R

JAMES ALAN GARDNER

AVON • EOS

AVON BOOKS
A division of
The Hearst Corporation
1350 Avenue of the Americas
New York, New York 10019

Copyright © 1998 by James Alan Gardner
Published by arrangement with the author
Visit our website at **http://www.AvonBooks.com/Eos**
ISBN: 1-56865-687-4

First Avon Eos Printing: April 1998

AVON EOS TRADEMARK REG. U.S. PAT. OFF. AND IN OTHER COUNTRIES, MARCA REGISTRADA, HECHO EN U.S.A.

Printed in the U.S.A.

To Linda:
Here's another novel you don't have to finish
if I get hit by a bus.

ACKNOWLEDGMENTS

Thanks to the usual gang of writers (LINDA CARSON, JOHN MCMULLEN, DAVE TILL) for providing initial feedback as chapters came hot off the printer, and to ROBERT J. SAWYER, RICHARD CURTIS, and JENNIFER BREHL who read the whole thing in one chunk. Thanks too to SHELLEY GOETZE who told me the name of that little bump at the back of your neck (while she was giving me ultrasound for a broken leg . . . but that's another story).

Finally, thanks to CHRIS BLYTHE, ERIC BRISTOW, DUNCAN BRISTOW, and LARRY HACKMAN who first walked with me from Tober Cove to Cypress Marsh. Death to quill pigs forever!

ONE

A Net for a Duck

The night before Commitment, I was down in the marsh with the frogs and the fish, sitting out the time on a mud-crusted log and waiting for the gods to send me a duck.

I'd spent hundreds of hours in that marsh when I was young, practicing my violin. Elderly mosquitoes may still tell their larvae about the human child who was so busy rehearsing arpeggios he didn't have time to swat. Our village doctor claims I forced her to work daily from dawn to dusk, gathering and grinding the herbs I needed for skin ointment when I came home each night. But back then, Cypress Marsh was the only place the Elders of Tober Cove let me practice; they said if they let me play in town, the noise would curdle milk.

Now that I was twenty, they'd stopped complaining. I'd become our cove's most gold-getting export: shipped down-peninsula to weddings, harvest festivals and spring struts, earning five times as much as any fisher or farmer. My foster father told me the Elders sometimes fought over which of them could take the most credit for my success; but the real credit should go to the dragonflies who discovered that where there's a violin, there are all the mosquitoes a bug can eat. They saved my blood and bone . . . and even today, Cypress Marsh dragonflies come buzzing at the sound of violin music, like children hearing the dinner bell.

As I sat on the log that night, I considered taking up my bow and giving the dragonflies a thank-you serenade. Of course, I'd brought my violin with me—I never left the cottage without it under my arm, even when I set out to my "day job" hauling nets on the perch boats. The violin made my work easier: in the middle of the afternoon, someone would always say to me, "Fullin, we could sure use a tune." Then I passed a couple hours playing "The Maiden and the Hungry Pigboy" while the other men bent their backs.

We all thought it was a fair exchange.

I had taken the violin out and was softly tuning the strings when a song drifted to me from the far end of the marsh.

> *I will come to you in winter.*
> *Though we lay us down in snow,*
> *It cannot chill us.*

Cappie, waxing romantic. In the years she was a man, her voice was a fine bass, a rough-edged rumble like Master Thunder's lament for his fallen son. Many times I'd told her she could polish that voice into a real money-maker, if she just made the effort. But in the years she was a woman her voice was scabby—thin as a reed and apt to wobble on anything longer than a quarter note. The pity was, she liked to sing as a woman; as a man, she was the silent type who stared moodily into campfires.

> *I will stay with you through spring.*
> *Though the wild Nor'westers blow,*
> *They cannot spill us.*

Lately she'd taken to singing every day: drippy sentimental songs that she directed toward me with a delivery she'd picked up from a throb-woman who passed through Tober Cove with a troupe of traveling players. By popular request I'd gone to the platform to accompany the singer in a tune, and this woman had chosen a moist little ballad designed to set men drooling. You know the kind of song I'm talking about—performed with so many hip grinds, you can't tell whether the woman is singing actual words or just bed-whinnies. Because I was on the stage with her, most of the bump'n'hump was aimed at me . . . not that I noticed it much. While the woman was trying to rub up against me, I was working hard just to make sure the pointed end of my violin bow didn't poke out her eye. Still, Cappie got the idea I'd been aroused by all that slinking and strutting, and had taken to doing her own torch routines for my benefit. Let me tell you, Cappie was no South-city seductress—it was all I could do not to cringe every time she began to shimmy.

> *I will dance with you through summer.*
> *Though the heat makes rivers slow,*
> *It cannot still us.*

Cappie had also started to ask what sex I was going to Commit to. The laws of the Patriarch expressly prohibited discussing the choice, but that didn't matter; when Cappie was a woman, she disregarded any law that didn't make sense to her.

"I have to know what you're going to be," she'd say. "It would be a disaster if we both chose the same sex and could never be married."

More and more, I didn't think that would be a disaster at all. It was too cruel to say out loud, but that response clattered around in my brain every time she asked how much I loved her. She asked the question a lot; I thought my unspoken answer just as often.

I'd outgrown her. I was famous throughout the Bruise Peninsula, and well paid for my music: a goat for an evening, a sheep for a day, a cow for an entire weekend. When Cappie wanted to tag along on my out-of-town performances, I discouraged her. Being seen with her embarrassed me. Her love songs and attempts at being wanton stirred nothing in me but pity—the pity you feel for a crippled old dog that still tries to catch rabbits.

> *I will hold your hand through fall.*
> *Though the sun damps down its glow,*
> *Our love will fill us.*
> *Our love will fill us.*

The song ended. I wanted to scream back, "Stop lying to yourself!" . . . but of course I didn't. It would only bring Cappie thrashing through the marsh to ask what I meant, or to demand that we talk about our future before it was too late. That was the last thing I wanted. Every talk about our future forced me to invent new ways to dodge her questions.

On top of that, we were both on Commitment Eve vigils and forbidden to see another human being till dawn. Cappie might ignore the law if it didn't suit her, but I wanted to do things right. I had to avoid confrontation, and that meant playing up to Cappie for one more evening.

She would be sweat-trickling now in the darkness, waiting for me to answer her song. I had no stomach for singing back to her, but I could always play my violin. Its sound would carry clearly to her, and I wouldn't have to worry about her hearing the lack of enthusiasm in my voice. A simple tune would do: "Stars in the Hottest Black" came to mind, a song that felt dreamy and romantic but never actually mentioned the word "love." Besides, it was appropriate—the stars were out in abundance, smeared across the summer sky like gems in Mistress

Night's hand. I lifted my bow above the strings, inhaled before the downsweep, and . . .

. . . heard another violin begin to play somewhere deeper in the marsh.

I was so startled I dropped my bow. It bounced against the strings with a soft twang and fell to the dirt at my feet. I snatched it up again quickly, as if someone might steal it.

The player out in the marsh was good.

A stranger.

The violin is a Southern instrument. I inherited mine from my lamented mother, who inherited it from her father, and so on, back seven generations. No one else on the peninsula owned one, let alone played with any skill. I assumed this new player was some out-of-place Southerner, a traveling performer who'd wandered off the road and camped in the marsh for the night. But the tune was native to Tober Cove itself, an unfaithful lover's ballad called "Don't Make Me Choose."

I cursed loud enough to send nearby frogs plopping hastily into the water. There was no telling how an outsider had learned that song, but no tune on earth could bring Cappie running more quickly. She would run straight to me, not the unknown Southerner—she knew where I was keeping vigil, and she would never guess there was a second violinist out in the night. I had to get away before she arrived. As a matter of fact, I had to find the Southerner as evidence I wasn't the one playing the song.

For a moment, I debated whether to take my violin with me. I didn't want to leave it on its own, but if I slipped on mud while slinking through the midnight marsh, I might tumble into some scum-covered pool, instrument and all. Hurriedly I put the violin away and slid the case into the hollow of the log where I'd been sitting.

Instead of the violin, I took my spear. Tober Cove already had all the violinists it needed, and I intended to make sure this Southerner got the message.

From childhood days practicing in the marsh, I knew the best shortcuts and the most solid trails. As expected, I slipped several times anyway, soaking my pants to the knee. A dunk or two didn't bother me, but I wanted to avoid stepping on a stone that was really a snapping turtle, dug into the mud to lay her eggs. I cautiously approached every rock that lay in my path, knocking the top with the butt end of my spear, waiting to see if a mean little head would appear and bite off a chunk of the shaft.

The music continued to play strong and clear. "Don't Make Me

Choose" is a long piece with a dozen choruses and variations, as the singer details the virtues of the two men who want to share her bed. She's twenty years old, and therefore about to choose her sex permanently. She believes one of her lovers will become a woman while the other will stay a man; whichever gender she chooses for herself, she'll be shutting the door on one person and committing to the other. It's a frequent Tober Cove dilemma, which makes it a song of enduring popularity . . . except for people like Cappie who find it strikes too close to home.

I soon realized the music was coming from the heart of the marsh, probably the patch of open mud known as the duck flats. Despite the name, you seldom find ducks on the flats—they avoid the place because the people of Tober Cove set so many traps for them there. The tradition is this: every year on Commitment Eve, each candidate for Commitment sets a snare on the flats. If the gods want you to choose a particular sex, they'll send a duck of that sex to tangle itself in your net; if the gods don't have special plans for you, your net stays empty and you can choose whichever sex you like. Two decades had passed since the last divinely inspired duck was netted. The Mocking Priestess attributed this to a growing intelligence on the part of ducks . . . but of course, it was her job to say things like that.

As I neared the duck flats, it occurred to me I was close to violating the rules of my vigil. I wasn't supposed to set eyes upon another human being till sunrise . . . and a Southerner probably counted as human, even if the laws of the Patriarch sometimes hedged on the issue.

What was the penalty for breaking vigil? I couldn't remember, but the Elders were forever looking for excuses to grab a bigger share of my music income. Earlier that very day, the Patriarch's Man had imposed a "monetary penance" on me for suggesting our village should build a roofed dance pavilion like the one in Wiretown—as if I were the only Tober who thought it wouldn't hurt to borrow ideas from down peninsula. I *was* the only Tober who got fined for saying so . . . which meant I had to observe every little rule carefully, including the one about not setting my eyes on anyone else during vigil. Instead of facing the stranger directly, I pulled up with only a stand of bulrushes between me and the duck flats, then shouted, "Hey!"

The music stopped.

"This is Tober land," I said. The Patriarch had used the same words to repel the Pagans during the Harsh Purification—saying the words made me feel like I wasn't just carrying the spear for show. "Take yourself and your ways," I recited, "and slink back to the pits of iniquity. You are damned, and your smell offends me."

"The gracious welcome I expected," a voice sneered back. "Thank you." I couldn't tell whether the speaker was male or female, and there was none of the nasalness of a Southern accent.

"Who are you?" I asked.

The only answer was a loud thrashing of reeds. I covered my eyes quickly, expecting the stranger to burst through the wall of rushes; but the noise plunged off in the opposite direction. I held my breath as I listened to it recede.

The stillness of the night seeped back in: no sound but crickets chirping, frogs chugging, and hundreds of dragonflies buzzing around the flats. Cautiously, I parted the bulrushes, ready to avert my eyes if the stranger returned.

In the middle of the flats, a fire sputtered on the muddy ground. By its light, I could see footprints everywhere: boots with leather soles that left sharp outlines—city boots, unlike the moccasins worn by everybody local. Judging from the quantity of tracks, I guessed the unknown violinist had been here for hours, but I saw no sign that he or she had intended to stay the night. There was no tent, no gear, nothing but the fire . . . as if the stranger had been ready to pick up and run as soon as someone came to investigate the music.

"I'm not going to play hide and seek!" I shouted into the darkness. Immediately, I regretted the noise—Cappie might hear me. If she was close enough, she'd know I was on the flats, and technically speaking, my presence here was another violation of vigil. Once we set our traps we were supposed to stay clear until . . .

Uh-oh.

I didn't know how long the stranger had lingered here, but it wouldn't have taken much to spot my snare. Maybe it was a good idea to amble over that direction—not to break the rules by checking my trap before dawn, but just to see if there were bootprints close to it. Sure enough, the prints were there, lots of them . . . and my trap had caught something.

There was a duck tangled in the net, a motionless duck. I felt a perk of excitement—me, the first person in twenty years who warranted the attention of the gods.

But gloating was childish. As chosen favorite of the gods, I had to comport myself with dignity. Gingerly, I picked up the net by the slack at one end, expecting the bird to quack itself into a frenzy.

It didn't move. A fat drip of liquid fell from the duck's body to the mud.

Slowly I untangled the bird. The netting was wet, even though I had set the trap on land, two paces from the edge of the water. I looked at my hands; by starlight, the wetness on my skin seemed black. Lifting my fingers to my nose, I smelled blood.

The duck's body was cold.

When the bird was completely unwrapped, I let the net fall from my hands and walked back with my catch to the stranger's campfire. The flames were almost out; I yanked some dry cattails off the nearest bulrushes and threw them onto the embers. They flared into a fizzing yellow blaze that gave more than enough light to examine the duck.

It was a mallard, its coloration male. Under its tail, however, was nothing but a mess of bloody guts dangling where a knife had cut off a chunk of flesh.

Coloration or not, the duck wasn't male. Not anymore.

I grabbed the bird by its neck, swung it twice around my head, then threw it with all my strength. Its wings fell open limply as it traveled, and dragged against the air; it barely cleared the reeds before it splashed into open water. For a moment I stood there panting. Then I kicked at the cattails I'd thrown on the fire. They scattered in a flurry of sparks, some hissing as they hit water. Methodically I walked around the flats, stamping on burning cattail fluff and grinding it into the mud.

The stranger had castrated my duck. The duck sent to me by the gods. The duck telling me what sex the gods wanted me to choose.

The duck had been cut neuter. Made a Neut.

I'd seen a Neut once. It was my earliest memory: a pale face, fat and blubbery, close to mine; and hands lifting me up, heaving me off the ground. I screamed, terrified—I knew this monster wanted to kill me. Then I was torn away from the thing and there were other people there, throwing stones at the Neut, thrusting at It with the butts of their spears. The Neut howled as a sharp rock opened a cut across Its forehead. It looked back at me once, hungrily, then fled.

That was how we Tobers treated Neuts: immediate exile, and death if the monsters ever returned. Neuts were renegades, malcontents, heretics. Untold generations of our people had chosen a permanent sex in their Commitment Hour, accepting that they had to abandon either their male or female halves . . . but Neuts refused to let go of either side. Neuts claimed you didn't have to reject half your life, that people could follow both male and female ways. So Tober Cove hated Neuts with the fierce burning hate you always aim at someone who says your pain is stupid and self-imposed.

To suggest that I should turn Neut—that the gods *wanted* me to turn Neut—the thought was poison. An evil so disgusting, my brain could hardly grasp it.

"Fullin?" It was Cappie calling, very close—on the other side of the bulrushes, not far from the place where I'd called to the stranger. Perhaps she'd seen the fire I'd made with the cattails. "What are you doing on the flats?" she asked, her voice whetted sharp with anger.

"There's someone else nearby," I said as quietly as I could. "Someone dangerous. Don't make any noise."

"How could there be anyone else here?" she asked, softer but not soft.

"I don't know what's going on; I just know there's trouble, all right? Go someplace safe and stay there."

"Don't talk to me like that!"

"Cappie, please . . ."

But the rushes parted and she stepped out to join me. I sighed. So much for vigil.

Surprisingly, she wore pants, bleached cotton pants. Perhaps I shouldn't have been taken aback—pants are more practical than skirts when spending the night in a mosquito-filled marsh—but I had never seen her in pants, not in the years she was female. She must have sneaked the clothes from her father's closet: they were much too big for her slender frame. Held sloppily at waist level by suspenders and stuffed firmly into socks at her ankles, the pants billowed in the middle like the sail of a perch boat. Her shirt billowed too, a man's shirt so large and loose there was only a hint of her compact breasts under the cloth. And her hair . . . no billowing there. Her long black beautiful hair was gone. Just a few hours earlier, it had draped fluidly over her bare shoulder as her daughter Pona sucked sloppily at supper. But now Cappie's lovely thick hair was chopped off raggedly, as short as mine.

Cappie the woman was dressed and barbered as a man. I wondered if this could be some new ploy to arouse my interest. If so, it hadn't worked; I found it unsettling and unnatural. Commitment Day tradition allowed candidates to wear whatever they liked, but the town would still be scandalized.

"What have you done to yourself?" I blurted.

"Think about it," was her only answer. "What are you doing here?"

Under normal circumstances, I would have lied or brushed her off—it was a reflex I'd acquired over the preceding months. Since winter, I hadn't had the stomach to share anything with her, certainly not events that confused or disturbed me. Now, however, she looked so unlike herself that the reflex didn't spark. I told her everything, all the while glancing furtively at her hair, her clothes. She snorted in outraged disbelief when I swore there was a second violinist; but she had figured out the music came from the duck flats and she could see I didn't have my instrument with me.

When I finished my story, she headed immediately for her own duck trap. The brisk way she stomped off intimidated me; I didn't go after her. In a moment I heard her curse with a phrase no woman should ever use, and something heavy splashed into the water.

She walked back slowly. In the darkness I couldn't identify the expression on her face.

"A duck for you too?" I asked.

"Part of one. Are you going to use that spear for anything?"

"If you think I should track down the stranger, you're wrong," I said. "I don't want to break vigil any more than I have already."

"Then give *me* the spear." She held out her hand.

"Don't be ridiculous. You're a woman."

"I'm better with a spear than you are."

I had to laugh. In her male years, yes, Cappie was an absolute master with the spear, both in target throwing and hand-to-hand fighting. If she Committed as a man, she would surely be offered initiation into the Warriors Society. But this year she was a woman and unfit to wield a weapon. Her clothes must have gone to her head.

"Go hide someplace safe," I told her. "Down by the dead tree where we once saw the owl, remember? I'll stay close to that tree too; if the stranger comes back, you can call for help and I'll be right there."

She stepped in close to me, and I thought she was coming for a hug of reassurance. I started spreading my arms. Then her fist ploughed hard into my stomach and she kicked my feet out from under me. I crumpled to the ground and lay there dizzily, the smell of mud under my nostrils.

The spear was no longer in my hand. Somewhere far above me, Cappie said, "Go hide someplace safe."

I lay on the flats several minutes, my head spinning. Eventually I managed to flop over on my back and stare up at the stars as they reeled like drunken fireflies. My stomach fluttered on the edge of vomiting, but I had no strength to fight it down. I simply waited to see what happened . . . and my stomach settled, the stars slowed to a stop, and the murkiness in my brain cleared.

Cappie had breast-fed Pona at supper. She had been a woman then; I saw all the evidence anyone could need. The mood during our own meal was strained, but we were used to that. Then we had gone our separate ways to prepare for the vigil, she to her parents and I to my foster father.

Sometime after we parted, she must have been possessed by a devil. Or a legion of devils. When devils possessed a woman, they often made her think she was a man. Hakoore, the Patriarch's Man, claimed that

Commitment Eve was too holy for devils to leave their burrows, but the Mocking Priestess said it was the devils' favorite night of the year: the air was alive with power that they sucked up with toothless mouths in their skin.

For once, it looked like the Mocking Priestess was right.

I rose painfully to my feet and looked around. Cappie was gone, my spear was gone, and I was alone in the dark.

Toward the south, somewhere near the spot where Cypress Creek smoothed over Stickleback Falls, a violin began playing again: "Don't Make Me Choose." The stranger obviously wanted to catch our attention. I took a deep breath, then started toward the sound.

I knew the marsh trails well. I had walked them many times as a child, violin under my chin, pretending to be a wandering troubadour. These trails taught me the power of music—my playing scared utter hell out of wildlife. Many of the marsh landmarks I'd named in honor of animals I'd frightened there. A patch of stinging nettles I'd christened Turtle Terror; a stretch of puckered mud was Heron Horror; and an OldTech horseless cart half-swallowed in bog I called the Frenzy of Frogs.

The OldTech machine was now no more than a stepping-stone across sucking muck. Four hundred years earlier, before the collapse of OldTech culture, there must have been a road running through this marsh; but it was gone now, swallowed by mud and time, just as everything else of twentieth-century Earth had been swallowed. When I was young, I sometimes like to scare myself with the image of a skeletal driver trapped inside the swampbound cart, fingers clutched on the steering wheel, bony feet still pressing the pedals. More likely, he simply abandoned the vehicle—stepped out and called to the sky, "I want to leave!" Then he was carried off to the stars by the so-called League of Peoples, just like all the other traitors who turned their backs on Earth in the Great Desertion.

Good riddance.

As I clambered onto the cart's grille, the music ahead of me stopped in mid-phrase. I paused and listened. Silence . . . then a shout followed by the splash of something hitting open water. I raced forward, swiping my way through head-high reeds till I came to a clear area on the bank of Cypress Creek itself.

Cappie stood waist-deep in the water, her spear held over her head and ready to plunge downward, as if she were going to jab a fish. I couldn't see what she was aiming for, just black water lapping around her. She waited, holding her breath, watching the stream in front of her.

On shore near my feet was a violin bow, and a few paces off, the violin itself, lying facedown in the mud. I hurried to pick it up. It looked like a fine instrument, lighter than mine, with the scroll more ornately carved. The strings weren't gut, but metal wire. Wire strings must last a lot longer than the gut ones I made myself; I wondered where I could get a set.

As I wiped muck off the violin's bridge, water surged loudly behind me. I turned in time to see a stranger erupt from the creek a stone's throw away from Cappie.

The stranger was a Neut. No doubt of that. Its homespun shirt hung wetly over full breasts that sagged slightly with age; but Its face was thickly bearded and lean as a man's. In Its hand It held a huge knife, a machete dripping water and glinting in the starlight.

"You'd better hope my violin isn't damaged," the Neut said to Cappie.

"It's all right," I called out.

Stupid. Neither of them had noticed me yet. Cappie half-turned at the sound of my voice, and in that moment, the Neut lunged. If that lunge hadn't been slowed by the water . . . but it was, and Cappie dodged in time, knocking the Neut's machete aside with the butt of her spear. She tried to follow through with a cross swing that brought the spear point around to attacking position, but she was off balance and slow. I shouted, "Quick!" but the Neut was gone, vanished beneath the water again. Cappie stabbed out once but hit nothing.

"Watch that It doesn't grab you underwater!" I yelled.

"Shut up," she yelled back. But she retreated toward the riverbank, all the while holding the spear ready to drive downward. When her thighs touched the bank behind her, she stopped and waited, in fishing position again.

I set the violin on a clean bed of reeds and approached Cappie, saying, "Get out and give me the spear."

"No."

"You can't fight, you're possessed. Women are very susceptible . . ."

The Neut geysered up a short distance to our right. Cappie turned to meet the attack, spear held high. The spear was within reach, perhaps my only chance to get it away from her. I seized it with both hands, just as she was stabbing out.

I think I saved her life. If she had followed through, she would have run straight into the blade that the Neut thrust at her, stomach height. But my hold on the spear brought her up short, twisting her body out of the path of the knife. She grunted with pain, but it was only the pain of wrenched muscles, not metal piercing flesh.

There was no time to congratulate myself. Cappie's weight and the force of her jab jerked me forward to the edge of the creek bank. My feet slid on mud like sleigh skids on snow; for a heartbeat I stayed up, dancing for balance, then I furrowed into the water with a deep plunging sound, directly into the gap between Cappie and the Neut.

Water stung in my nostrils as my head went under. A body bumped against me; I'd lost my grip on the spear, so I punched out blindly, hoping it wasn't Cappie. My fist was slowed by water and connected without force, but it still spooked my opponent. The body surged away from me with noisy splashing.

Good—someone was afraid of me. If it was the Neut, I was pleased; but if it was Cappie, the Neut was still out there somewhere, ready to impale me on Its knife. Without coming up for air, I kicked out into the night-black water, just trying to put distance between me and the Neut's blade. A few strokes, and my outstretched hand collided with the opposite bank of the creek. Cautiously, I lifted my head.

The Neut, Cappie and I stood dripping in a widely spaced triangle: me against one bank, Cappie against the other, the Neut in the middle, several paces downstream. Cappie no longer held the spear; I assumed she'd lost it when I fell into the creek.

Keeping Its eyes on both of us, the Neut asked, "Is either of you named Fullin?"

The question startled me. I said, "No," immediately, the same reflex that automatically lied to Cappie whenever she asked what I truly thought.

Cappie said nothing.

"This makes things easier," the Neut said with a dark smile. "Two against one isn't so bad when I have the knife."

The Neut waded down the center of the creek, until It stood on a direct line between Cappie and me. That particular stretch of the Cypress isn't wide—from the middle it was only a few steps to either bank, where Cappie and I waited to see which of us the monster would attack. Behind my back, my hands scrabbled for any sort of weapon: a stone I could throw, a stick I could jab at the Neut's eyes. I found nothing but a dirty piece of driftwood, shorter than my forearm and light as a bone with the marrow sucked out. It would break into tinder with the first strike of the Neut's knife . . . but I swung it up smartly and hoped that in the dark, the Neut couldn't see how flimsy my defense was.

I must have looked intimidating—the Neut lunged for Cappie instead of me.

She still had the spear. Just below the surface of the water, she must have held it pressed between thigh and bank so that her hands would seem empty. I marveled at the ingenuity of the devil that possessed her. Now she snapped up the spear in the face of the Neut's charge and thrust forward. The Neut managed to parry the attack with Its knife, but not entirely. Cloth ripped. In the dark, I couldn't tell if the spear point had torn flesh as well as shirt.

The Neut wasn't fazed by whatever damage It had taken, and now It was inside the arc of the spear. Cappie had no room to swing her weapon around for another attack, and the Neut was raising Its blade. Without hesitation, Cappie let go of the spear and grabbed the Neut's knife arm with both hands.

I plunged forward to help as the two of them wrestled. Cappie was at a disadvantage: pressed up against the bank, she had no space to move for better leverage, while the Neut had a weight advantage. Slowly, the knife descended toward Cappie's face. I wished I had time to find the spear, but it had sunk into the creek as soon as Cappie released it. The only weapons I had were my bare hands, my vulnerable musician's hands. I delayed another second, trying to decide how I could save Cappie without risking injury to my fingers. At last, I grabbed the Neut's shoulders and dragged sideways, the two of us slamming against the bank beside Cappie.

For the second time that night, I had saved Cappie's life. My move had thrown the Neut off balance; with groaning strength, Cappie angled the knife point away from her body and over the ground. A split second later, she let go of the blade. The Neut's momentum stabbed the knife deep into the mud. Immediately, Cappie leaned over and punched the Neut in the face, bare knuckles into soft cheek. I shouted to her, "Run!" and grappled to pin the Neut's arms.

At that moment, a boot stepped onto the bank beside my head—a boot surrounded by violet fire. I began to lift my eyes to look at the newcomer; then a metal canister struck the ground and exploded into smoke.

The smoke stung like a hundred campfires and stank like the marsh's worst rot. My stomach was already fragile from Cappie's gut punch out on the flats; now, I bucked up my supper, vomit splashing warmly on my hands, the Neut, the mud. I tried to keep my grip on the Neut's shoulders, but my muscles felt as slack as string. Cappie made one more swing at the Neut's jaw, but her fist had no strength behind it. The Neut slumped, not from the punch but the smoke, and all three of us collapsed helplessly onto the mud, tears streaming, bile dripping down our chins.

With my last remaining energy, I dragged myself to one side, away from the mess I had gagged up. Part of me wanted to let go of the bank, and sink into the creek to clean the stomach-spill from my hands; but

I was afraid I'd drown retching, too weak to keep my head above water. My eyes turned back to that fiery boot; and slowly I followed the boot upward, to leg, to body, to helmet.

It was a knight in full armor. Not metal armor, but something glossy—OldTech plastic. The helmet was completely blank, no holes for mouth or nose, only a smoked-glass plate in front of the eyes. The violet fire surrounding him gave off no heat, but hissed softly like a sleeping snake.

Through the smoke, I saw Cappie weakly pull the Neut's machete out of the mud. Before she could use it, the knight kicked the knife lightly from her hand. " 'Keep up your bright swords, for the dew will rust them,' " he said. "That's from *Othello*, Act One, Scene Two. Not that I expect anyone to care. Centuries ago, my ancestors could impress the peasantry by quoting Shakespeare, but now it takes tear gas. Oh, well—time marches on. Hello."

TWO

A Finger Exercise for Master Disease

 "Damn it, Rashid," the Neut croaked to the knight, "this isn't funny." It coughed deeply and spat.

"Don't fuss," the knight said. "You're perfectly all right."

The three of us in the water lifted our heads to stare at him, tears streaming from our eyes and vomit crusting our clothes.

"Some people should cultivate a sense of humor," the knight muttered. "Two days from now, you'll be stopping strangers in the street to tell them this story."

I heard a soft click and the violet fire around his armor winked out. Sighing, he slipped into the water beside us. I shied away, dragging myself farther along the bank though my arms were weak as twigs. The knight wasn't interested in me; he put his arm around the Neut's shoulders and helped the creature wade to the middle of the creek, away from the smoke near shore. There, he bent the Neut over and scooped water into Its weeping eyes.

"Let's get you washed up," the knight said. "You'll feel a hundred times better when you're clean."

The words jarred me worse than the choking smoke. A woman had said almost the same thing to me a year before, in circumstances that still made me cry out "No!" suddenly, day or night, when the memory came unbidden.

I had been down-peninsula in Sobble Beach, playing for a wedding dance. It was a good spring for weddings; I'd played three already and was scheduled for two more before solstice. The men of the town attended my performances enthusiastically—as a woman, I wasn't beautiful but I behaved as if I was and that fooled most people. One man in particular, a young carpenter named Yoskar, was always in the front row whenever I coy-smiled my way onto the podium. Between songs, Yoskar and I flirted. On my break, we even slipped out a side door and spent a tasty few minutes teasing flesh to flesh on the beach. Mouth and hands only, of course—I was always faithful to Cappie, even when he was far away.

It turned out that Yoskar had someone else in his life too. I met his other woman after the dance, as I walked under a shadowy aisle of cedars on my way to the boat that would take me home. The woman moved quietly and she had a knife.

Her first stab took me in the back, but high and off center, stopping itself against my shoulder bone. I nearly passed out; if she had immediately tugged back the knife and gone for my throat, Master Day would have welcomed a new violinist in the Fields of Gold. Luckily for me, the woman was as surprised as I was that she had actually plunged a blade into my body. She stood there stupidly, staring at me as I staggered about. By the time she had recovered enough to consider another attack, my head was clearing too. I had just enough time to squirm the knife from my back and throw it into the darkness before the woman was on top of me, clawing at my throat and scratching for my eyes.

I don't know if we fought for minutes or seconds. I remember heat: my body, hers, and the sweaty suffocation of clothes over my face as we grappled. At some point, the pain and screaming woke my male half, where he slept far off in Birds Home; carried on the wings of crows, his spirit raced in to take over my body. The moment it took possession I felt stronger, more in control. As a man, I knew how to fight and no woman could beat me. I began to punch instead of bite, to grab the woman's softest parts and twist.

Then people were separating us, Yoskar among them. He went to her, not me, babbling apologies and love. The male spirit in me vanished as quickly as it had come and I was left a discarded woman, weeping in rage. I wanted to start the fight again, just to rip Yoskar's pretty face with my fingernails, but the onlookers held me back. They carried me to a private room of the wedding pavilion and a woman wearing the purple scarf of a doctor stripped off my clothes to bathe my wounds.

"You'll feel a hundred times better when you're clean," she said.

She was in her early forties, a woman with confident voice and hands. Those hands ranged over my body, sewing up the stab wound in my back ("Very shallow—you're lucky") and tending multiple bites and scratches. All the while, she spoke of her admiration for my performance that night. "You have fire," the doctor said. "I've never seen such passion."

Gradually the pain and heat remaining from the fight changed. The doctor's hands were still at work. My head was growing dizzy; I could no longer remember wounds in the places she touched, but I let her continue. She kissed me on the right breast and whispered, "Passion." I felt my body twist toward her, wanting more.

I remember heat: my body, hers, the sweaty suffocation . . .

At dawn I woke alone, in the same room and lying under a thin blanket on the floor. Surprisingly, my male soul had come back to take charge of my female body; and I barely had time to roll onto my side before I threw up, appalled by what I had done. Obviously, the doctor had drugged me—that was the only explanation for how I could participate in such perversion. Two women! How could my female half have been so weak as to yield to such . . . no, I'd been drugged. Otherwise, I would never have . . .

I ran outside to the beach, frantic to scrub my flesh raw, to clean the doctor's smell from my face; but when I splashed on water, I stopped immediately. In my mind I could still hear the woman whispering in my ear, "You'll feel a hundred times better when you're clean."

Leaning against the bank in Cypress Marsh, I watched the knight tenderly washing the Neut's face. He whispered softly in the creature's ear; their faces were close and the knight's touch gentle.

I knew lovers when I saw them. If I'd had anything left in my stomach, I would have thrown up again.

What kind of man could bring himself to bed a Neut? One incapable of shame. A man who could openly wear OldTech plastic. The one and only time I'd worn plastic, I was eight and a group of us kids had found an OldTech dump in the forest, just off the Feliss City highway. We spent the afternoon digging through it and ornamenting ourselves with junk: bracelets twisted together from greenish wire and capes made of plastic sheets. I was proud of a plastic collar I found, shaped like a horseshoe but big enough to go around my neck like a yoke. We came back to the cove wearing our finery and huge grins, expecting the adults to praise our finds. Instead, they slapped us till our cheeks burned and promised we would be struck ill by the diseases that OldTech trash always carries.

A knight wearing plastic OldTech armor had to be a walking plague. The smoke bomb that made us sick was only the beginning—everywhere he went, he must leave behind poxes and pestilence. In fact, he might be Master Disease himself, god of evil, hater of life.

The thought chilled me . . . but the Elders told many tales of Master Disease walking the earth. To face him, you needed courage; to banish him, you needed the magic of the heart.

Painfully, I dragged myself out of the water onto the shore. The breeze had thinned the stink he called "tear gas"; my eyes were nearly swollen shut, but my strength was coming back. Off to my right, Cappie furtively gestured toward the knife, lying on reeds where the knight had kicked it. I ignored her—a mere knife couldn't hurt Master Disease. Even if it penetrated his armor, the blade would simply release a tornado of sickness to ravage our village.

Instead of the knife, I crawled toward the violin. Music has boundless purifying power, and I knew my playing was our only defence against this evil. The Patriarch taught that a song can banish devils of fear, and a war chant can summon angels of victory. Defeating Master Disease might take more than a simple tune, but I could do it. I was the only person in the village who could.

The violin and bow lay where I'd left them. Both were dirty. I ran my fingers lightly along the bow-hairs, trying to clean off the sludge without removing too much rosin as well. I don't know if it helped—my fingers were gritty with mud—but I brushed off the worst clots, propped my back against a nearby log, and prepared to play.

A smack of muck hit me in the leg. Cappie wanted my attention—she gestured again toward the knife. Ignoring her, I readied my bow over the strings.

I intended the first sweep of the bow to sound a strident challenge: E flat minor, the most challenging chord I knew. The chord didn't have quite the attack I wanted because the dirt on the bow weakened the rosin's grip on the strings; but the sound was loud enough to grab the knight's attention. He shoved himself in front of the Neut and turned to face me, his hands raised and pointing toward me like a wrestler waiting to grapple.

"Ha!" I said.

"I beg your pardon?" he replied.

"Ha!" I said again and played a B flat arpeggio.

The knight lowered his hands and half turned to the Neut. "What's he doing, Steck?"

"Playing my violin," the Neut answered.

I played another E flat minor chord.

"Sounds like an E minor chord," the Neut said.

"E *flat* minor!" I shouted.

"Oh. That's a lot harder," the Neut told the knight. "He's trying to impress us."

"I'm trying to *exorcise* you," I said.

"Me?" the Neut asked.

"Him," I said, pointing the bow at the knight. "Master Disease."

The Neut laughed and put Its arm around the knight's waist. "He thinks you're Master Disease!"

"Who's Master Disease?"

"A god."

"I see." The knight sloshed a few steps toward me. "Young man, I'm not a god, I'm a scientist. We're like gods, but more irresponsible."

"You're lying," I said. "The Patriarch killed all the scientists." I began a finger exercise in C. No point playing in a difficult key if my enemy had a poor sense of pitch.

"Steck!" the knight said sharply, rounding on the Neut. "Why didn't you tell me they think all scientists are dead? You know I don't want to offend local sensibilities."

"I forgot."

"How stupid do you think I am?" the knight asked. Without waiting for an answer, he turned back to me and said, "Your Patriarch, though his wisdom encircled the globe, overlooked a tiny enclave of scientists far away on the other side of the planet. We survived, and were duly chastened by the just retribution wrought by the Patriarch on our fellows. Now we have changed our ways; we pursue only the good."

"How stupid do you think we are?" Cappie said quietly.

"I didn't know till I tried," the knight answered cheerfully. "Experimentation is the essence of science."

"You aren't a scientist," I said. "You're Master Disease." I played the finger exercise louder, all the while trying to decide what kind of music was best suited to drive off a god. Right then, my repertoire for weddings and barn-raisings seemed a touch feeble.

"Rashid *is* a scientist," the Neut replied in Its male/female voice. "The Patriarch only killed one scientist in his entire life, and that was a poor anthropology student who wanted to study Tober Cove for her thesis. Bad luck for her—if she'd come a few years earlier, before the Patriarch seized control and perverted everything, she could have studied us to her heart's content. As it was, she was welcomed with the full hospitality ceremony; but two nights later, the Patriarch and six warriors attacked while she was sleeping, raped her, then burned her in the usual place on Beacon Point. Every person in the village was forced to watch her bubble and pop. At dawn, they were told to smear themselves with her ashes in order to share the triumph. Then the Patriarch declared he had rid the world of scientists and demanded that the Hearth and Home Guild make a quilt to commemorate the deed. Something to keep people warm and toasty in the dark."

I'd seen the quilt, of course, in the Patriarch's Hall at Mayor Teggeree's house; I'd even been allowed to sleep under the quilt one night, after I won first prize in a talent contest at Wiretown's Fall Fair. But that proved nothing. Devils can always twist a glorious truth to make it seem sordid. "I don't believe you," I said, starting the finger exercise again and hoping Master Disease would evaporate into greasy black smoke pretty soon. I was accustomed to the gut strings on my own instrument, and the wire strings of the Neut's violin were chewing into my fingers.

"Quite right," the knight said, "don't believe everything you hear." He gave the Neut a not-so-light push toward the opposite bank. "I'm going to wash out Steck's mouth with soap for telling such lies."

"You know nothing about Tober Cove," the Neut muttered resentfully to the knight.

"I know that we haven't made a glowing first impression." The knight turned back and said, "We'll be leaving now. Sorry to have caused a fuss. Next time you see us, I trust the circumstances will be better."

"The circumstances will be better if you stay away," Cappie said tightly.

The knight turned to her. She gazed in silence at that faceless helmet for many long seconds. Finally, it was the knight who gave up the staring contest. "I come in peace," he shrugged. "If trouble starts, I won't be the cause."

"You'll be the cause, no matter who strikes the first blow," Cappie told him. "Remember that."

"Don't be such a mope," the knight said, as if briskness would win the argument. "Everywhere I go, people are so deathly serious. I don't see why they always work themselves into a state. Just once I'd like to visit a town where my arrival doesn't precipitate some crisis."

He turned away and sloshed to join the Neut on the far shore. Without a word, he grabbed the belt of the Neut's pants and heaved up solidly. The Neut nearly flew onto the bank, scrabbling forward on hands and knees to avoid landing on Its face. "Rashid!" the Neut cried, "be careful, damn it. Just because the girl annoyed you, don't take it out on me."

"You're the one who annoyed me," the knight answered in a sharp whisper that carried across the water. "What were you doing out here? We have other business."

"Just let me get the violin . . ."

"No. Stop your whining." The knight turned back to me. "Take care of that instrument. We'll expect it returned in good condition."

"Begone, Creature of Darkness!" I shouted, as I began the finger exercise yet again.

"Fine. I'm gone."

Suddenly, the water around the knight roiled with bubbles, as if every twelve-year-old boy who'd ever gone swimming was farting under the surface. The knight shot upward, clouds of smoke billowing from his boots as they broke clear of the creek. I quickly held my breath and spun away from the smoke, anxious to avoid more vomit-gas. This smoke, however, was nothing like the previous kind; its smell was foul but its effects harmless.

When I turned back toward the creek, knight and Neut were gone, leaving only broken reeds to show their path. Slowly I lowered the bow and violin, as quiet awe filtered into my mind.

I had defeated Master Disease.

True, he hadn't been reduced to a stinking pool of lava, but what could you expect from a finger exercise? Especially one in the key of C.

I wished I'd stayed with E flat minor. He might have burst into flames.

THREE

A Shoulder for the Mocking Priestess

Cappie dove under the water. When she surfaced, her face was cleaner and she once again held my spear. She laid it on the shore and clambered out beside it, water pattering off her clothes onto the soft mud bank.

Men's clothes or not, she was clearly a woman now: her nipples pressed tautly against the wet fabric of her shirt. I thought of the feel of them, in my fingers, my mouth, and was suddenly more hungry for her than I'd been in months. With Master Disease banished, I was keen to celebrate my triumph.

"Cappie . . ." I started.

"No."

"You don't know what I was going to say."

"You're so obvious," she said, walking over to the Neut's knife and picking it up. I liked the way she walked—bold as a man, but with a woman's hips. "When you want to grope and fumble," she continued, "you always get the same tone in your voice and put on a moronic expression. Is that your idea of a sly grin?"

"What *is* this?" I cried. "Half an hour ago, you were singing "Our Love Will Fill Us," and now you're made of ice. Not to mention that you're dressed like your father. Have you been smoking dizzy-weed with the Mocking Priestess?"

"We have to go home and warn people," she said, jamming her shirttails back into her pants. There was a swipe of mud on her nose; I was furious with her, but I badly wanted to dab that nose clean with kisses.

"It's Commitment Eve," I reminded her. "We can't go back to the cove tonight. We're in isolation."

"Check your priorities, Fullin," she snapped. "A Neut and a scientist show up in the marsh, and you don't want to tell people?"

"We can tell people," I said. "Later. After. Come lie down."

"Do it with the damned violin," she replied. "You aren't doing it with me."

Tossing me an angry glare, she picked up the spear and ran. A sleek and easy run. A warrior's run. I opened my mouth to demand that she wait for me, but stopped myself in time. She wouldn't wait, no matter what I said, and a man loses face when his woman doesn't obey orders. Finally, I called, "You better not break my spear!" but not loud enough for her to hear.

Now I had no choice but to go back to the cove, Commitment Eve or not. If Cappie showed up and I didn't, the Elders would say I'd sent a woman to deliver a message I was too timid to deliver myself. Not to mention that she'd surely give a distorted version of what happened. She was, after all, possessed by a devil. I kept forgetting that.

But I knew how to take care of devils. I tucked the Neut's violin under my arm and started for home.

Soon I regretted letting Cappie get away with the spear—every stone in my path looked like a snapping turtle. I thought of rapping those rocks with the violin bow, but I couldn't bring myself to do it: I kept thinking of the crunch a snapper would make biting off a mouthful of wood and horsehair. Just imagining the sound gave me the shakes. I told myself it wasn't *my* bow, but that didn't lessen my queasiness. Musicians are sensitive people.

I took to veering away from every rock that could possibly be a snapper in disguise, with the result that I strayed off the paths that led directly to the cove. No one could claim I was lost—I retained my bearings by keeping an eye on the dead tree rising high above the reeds in the center of the marsh—but when I finally reached the turtle-free safety of the forest, I was far from the frequented trails.

You can measure the distance from town to any part of the forest by the age of the people who use that area as a hiding place. The youngest children make their forts just deep enough into the trees to be out of sight of the Council Hall steeple. As they grow older they venture beyond, in search of OldTech dumps and collapsed buildings they believe have never been seen by Tober eyes. Teen-aged couples steal out even farther, past the haunts of tattletale siblings, to beds of scratchy pine needles where they share love poems and ghost stories. (Ghost stories are the best aphrodisiac a fourteen-year-old knows.) Past the nesting areas of new lovers are the glower-bowers of the jilted, the solitary clearings where older teens brood over the unfairness of life and tell themselves how sorry everyone would be if they were found dangling from an oak. Soon, most of the brooders return to the coupling grounds, but a few proceed to higher degrees of restlessness, ranging farther and farther until their connection to Tober Cove snaps and they are propelled down-peninsula to the cities of the south.

Avoiding turtles had brought me to those outermost regions, a part of the forest seen only by solitaries and the occasional hunter. It was still Tober land, however, and a clear trail led back in the direction of the cove. No doubt the trail would reach more familiar regions soon enough.

I had barely walked twenty paces when I caught sight of a yellow-orange campfire in the forest on my left. Common sense said to avoid it—no honest traveler wandered so far from the main road. More likely, it was some fugitive from Feliss City. Each year, a handful of thieves and murderers came up-peninsula to hide in our woods; each year, the Warriors Society tracked them down and turned them in for bounty at the Feliss army outpost in Ohna Sound. It was a lucrative business: for fifteen years, the bounty money had completely paid for Tober Cove's "Fish-on-a-Bun" booth at the Wiretown Fall Fair. (We used to call the booth "Perch-on-a-Bun" . . . but cityfolk who didn't know perch were a type of fish got the strangest ideas.)

The thought of tangling with a criminal so soon after the last fight turned my stomach. On the other hand, Cappie would have reached the village already and given her version of our battle. She'd likely paint me in a bad light . . . and people in the cove envied my success so much, they'd love an excuse to look down on me. I could use something to counteract Cappie's spite, to explain why I was late getting home. Reporting the whereabouts of a big-bounty outlaw was perfect for redeeming myself.

As quietly as I could, I laid the violin under a bush and stole through the forest toward the fire. Soon I heard the sound of wood burning, popping and snapping loud enough to cover any noise I made. I managed to get very close, down on my stomach behind a fallen spruce where I could peer through the cover of dead branches toward the lighted clearing.

The fire burned high and bright, set on the edge of one of the many limestone shelves layered throughout our woods. By its light I could see old Leeta, the Mocking Priestess, huddled on a rusty wrought-iron bench. (The woods are full of such things—the whole area was once an OldTech nature park, but the OldTechs liked to see nature made presentable with benches and signs.)

Leeta was dressed in green, with daisies threaded through her loose gray hair and crusty-dry milkweed pods dangling from a fringed band at her waist. Her face was hidden in her hands; I couldn't hear over the crackling of the fire, but from the way her shoulders shook, I knew she was crying.

No man in the world likes to ask a tearful woman, "What's wrong?" You tell yourself, "She hasn't seen me yet; I can get away before she notices." But a true man, a *gentleman*, shows compassion no matter how hard it is to pretend you care. Taking a deep breath to nerve myself, I stood and said, "Hi Leeta, how's it going?"

She screamed. Not much, just a little shriek, and she cut it off so quickly I couldn't have startled her badly. Still, she made a big show of it, putting her hand to her heart and sagging as if she were going to faint. "It's only me," I said, not hiding my annoyance at her histrionics.

"Fullin," she groaned. "You scared me half to death."

"You're fine," I said. To calm her down, I added, "That's a nice dress."

She looked like she was going to snap at me; but then she put on a dithery smile and said, "It's my solstice robe. Do you like it?"

"The milkweed is a good touch," I told her. "Very earthy." I nodded sagely, trying to think of something else to say. There was no way I'd ask why she was crying; I didn't have the patience to listen to some tale of woe. "Nice night, isn't it?" I said. "Not as crushing hot as last week."

"There's a chance it could get hotter," Leeta said.

"You think so?"

"This is the solstice," she said, falling into the tone of voice she always used for storytelling. "The height of summer, when Master Day is at his strongest and Mistress Night is languishing. Do you know what that means?"

"Mistress Night has time to catch up on her lapidary?" (During the day, Mistress Night searches the earth for precious stones, which she then polishes and puts on display as stars.)

"It's time to enact the solstice ceremony," Leeta said. "To dance the dance that tips the balance back in Mistress Night's favor. Otherwise, the days will keep growing longer and hotter until there comes a time when the sun doesn't set and the earth catches fire."

"That would be bad," I nodded. Cappie's father had taught me about planetary rotations, revolutions, axial tilts and all, but now was not the time to discuss celestial mechanics, especially since Leeta had stopped crying. Now was the time to pat her on the shoulder and leave, before she remembered whatever brought on the tears in the first place. Duly, I patted. "Enjoy the ceremony. I'll get out of your way."

"Wait, Fullin," she said. "I need a man."

I looked at her in surprise.

"Don't be ridiculous," she grimaced, giving my arm a mock-slap. "The solstice dance has to be performed by a woman and a man. The sacred duality—I taught you that, I know I did."

If she taught me that, she must have done it when I was female. There were a lot of things about my female years I couldn't remember when I was male . . . or rather, there were a lot of things I couldn't be *bothered* to remember. In the years I was female, my male soul slept soundly in Birds Home; trying to fish up my female self's memories could be like trying to pin down a dream. Nevertheless, I had to humor Leeta. "Oh yes, the sacred duality," I said. "Man and woman."

"And I need you to be the man." She put her hand on my arm and said, "Please."

Our Mocking Priestess was a short woman with misty green eyes, and she had been wheedling her way around men for forty years before I was born. I don't consider myself weak for giving in to her. Besides, I could tell the Council of Elders that I tried to rush home with news of the strangers but had to stop to help the priestess with a life-and-death ceremony.

And Leeta looked like she might start crying again if I said no. "What do I do?" I sighed.

"You dance," she said. "It's easy. Find some leaves and put them in your hair."

I looked at the ground, then up at the spruces and pines surrounding us. "Will needles do?"

"They're leaves too."

I scooped up a handful of red, rotting needles and sighed again—it would take weeks to wash them completely out of my hair. Trying not to wince, I sprinkled the debris on my head and patted it down. "Will this dance take long? I have to get back to town."

"I thought you were on vigil," Leeta said. "Aren't you Committing tomorrow?"

"Something came up."

"Something involving Cappie too?"

I looked at her warily. "Why do you ask?"

"Because I wanted Cappie to play the man for this ceremony," Leeta answered. "She was quite enthusiastic. I know she borrowed her father's clothing to look the part."

One mystery solved. And as soon as Cappie had put on men's clothing, she'd have been ripe for possession by devils. I dimly recalled dressing up as a man when I was a teenaged girl: I hid behind closed doors and jumped at every creak of wind, but I put on a complete outfit, pants, shirt, jacket, sheath. When I finally stood in front of the mirror, fully dressed, both man and woman . . . yes, I was excited by the sight, by the weight of the jacket against my breasts. Easy to see how a woman dressed as a man was ripe for possession; I had been strong enough to resist, but Cappie was not.

I felt myself growing aroused at my memories of secret sin and quickly cast about for a distraction. "If the duality is so sacred," I said, "isn't it wrong to use Cappie as a fake man? I mean, when the fate of the planet depends on the ceremony."

"In any ceremony, appearance is more important than reality," Leeta replied. "And Cappie *wanted* to take part. She really did."

"Instead of vigil?"

"In addition to vigil," Leeta corrected. "Just for an hour or so." She gave me a glance, as if she was weighing whether to say more. "The thing is," she finally murmured, "a girl who wants to become the next priestess is *required* to break a few rules. Especially the Patriarch's ridiculous rules about vigil."

"Cappie?" I said in disbelief. "The next Mocking Priestess?"

"Why not Cappie?"

"Because . . . because . . . "

I couldn't say it to her face, but the female religion was nothing but a hodgepodge of silly rituals—the Patriarch had only tolerated it to avoid a backlash among the women of his day. He often said the female religion amused him; he sanctioned the office of Mocking Priestess with the same joviality he showed when he appointed a Town Drunk and an Official Fool. The cove had been fond of its priestesses over the years, but the fondness stopped short of respect.

Cappie couldn't take on such a ludicrous calling. It would reflect badly on *me*. True, I didn't intend to stay with her after Commitment, but the other men would still talk. They always do. "Cappie's not right for the job," I said. "Isn't there someone else?"

"I've left it too long," Leeta answered. "Doctor Gorallin . . ." She cleared her throat. "Gorallin has suggested I put my affairs in order. And it's traditional to choose the next Mocking Priestess from the current candidates for Commitment. I can only pick Cappie. Or you."

"So why pick her over me?" I asked, affronted.

"Would you do it?"

"Not a chance!"

"There's your answer." Leeta bent over a burlap bag lying on the ground and pulled out a red sash decorated with animal claws. The claws ranged from a huge yellowed bear talon with a raggedly broken tip, to a gray fleck that might have come from a mouse or chickadee. "Hold still," she said, and put the sash over my shoulder.

She fussed for a while trying to get the claws sitting straight. I held my breath, uncomfortable that she was so close but treating me like a sewing dummy. I didn't like women concentrating so intently on my clothes—it was as if the clothes were real and I wasn't. To pull her attention back to me, I said, "If you had to choose a successor, why did you wait so long?"

She looked up with those watery green eyes. I couldn't read her expression. "I chose a successor once before," she said. "It didn't work out."

"Why not?"

"She wanted to use the position as a weapon, to pressure for change. I tried to convince her that being priestess was a spiritual office, not a political one; but Steck wouldn't listen."

Steck? Uh-oh.

"The office could be political in the right hands," a voice said behind my back. "You're too afraid of rocking the boat, Leeta."

The voice was neither male nor female. I cringed as I turned around.

"Thanks for taking care of my instrument," the Neut said, holding up the violin I'd left back in the bush.

The knight was there too, both of them standing behind the spruce tree where I'd hidden earlier. " 'Once more well met at Cypress,' " the knight said. "*Othello*, Act Two, Scene One. That's a *bon mot* actually, because Shakespeare meant Cyprus the island, as opposed to Cypress, the swamp. You see? It's a pun. Clever, if I say so myself."

We stared at him. Blankly. For a painfully long silence.

"Oh sure," he finally muttered. "You're just jealous you didn't think of it first."

FOUR

A Dance for Mistress Night

Leeta said, "You shouldn't be here, Steck."

The Neut, Steck, shrugged. "I'm here anyway."

"You shouldn't be." Leeta took a few shuffling steps forward, the milkweed pods on her belt clacking against each other. I looked away, embarrassed. A dress decorated with weeds was all very well when Leeta and I were alone in the forest; as soon as outsiders arrived, she looked pathetically shabby. It didn't matter that the outsiders were a Neut and Master Disease. Visitors like that must have seen city women dressed in finery, with their hair just so, and their bodies tall and elegant. Now to have these outsiders see me in the company of dumpy little Leeta, all milkweed and daisies hanging haphazardly around her ears ... I was mortified.

Leeta showed none of the shame I felt. She pointed a pudgy finger at the Neut and said, "Don't you remember what I taught you, Steck? I taught you to ask questions, I know I did. *What good will this do?* That's the first question, that's always the first question. And *What harm will it do?* That's the second. Did you ask those questions, Steck? You didn't, I know you didn't. Because if you asked those questions, you'd see why you should have stayed away."

"Steck is here as my assistant," the knight said, stepping more clearly into the light of the campfire. With a flick of his hand, he twisted off his helmet and shook out his hair—thick coal-black hair, as long as a woman's. He had a droopy pencil mustache and heavy-lidded eyes: a foreign face but human, not crawling with maggots and sores like Master Disease's should be. Maybe, just maybe, this *wasn't* Master Disease after all; but a scientist was almost as bad, and he'd admitted to that.

For a moment, the knight waited in the firelight, as if he thought we might recognize him now that the helmet was off. Then he shrugged and spoke again. "My name is Rashid and Steck is my *Bozzle*. Do you know that word?"

"Of course," I answered. Even children knew a "Bozzle" was the aide of someone important: a mayor or a noble, maybe even a Grandee like a Governor or a Spark Lord. Did Rashid think we were bumpkins, not to know such a thing? Or maybe he was hinting he was special enough to rate a Bozzle; I guessed he might be an Earl or a Duke from Feliss Province. He should have known that didn't matter up here—Tober Cove held a charter of independence from the Sparks themselves, and within our boundaries, even a day-old Tober baby was worth more than a thousand Dukes.

"We all know what a Bozzle is," Leeta replied. "Do you think that makes a difference?" She didn't spare a glance in Rashid's direction; she kept her gaze glued on the Neut, not in a stern way, but soft and pleading. "Coming here will just stir up trouble, Steck . . . you know that. What good can you do after all these years? Leave before it's too late."

The Neut stared back, saying nothing. It was one of those moments when you know unspoken undercurrents are flowing all around and you don't understand a turd of what's really going on. You want to shout, "I deserve an explanation!" But sometimes, when you see faces like Leeta begging and Steck gazing back as dark as lake water at midnight . . . sometimes you decide you don't care about their stupid problems anyway.

Rashid, however, wasn't the kind who stayed out of other people's staring matches. "Look," he butted in, "there's no reason for Steck to leave, because *nothing is going to happen.* I'm a scientist and I've come to observe your Commitment Day ceremonies. That's all. Nothing sinister, nothing intrusive—I just want to watch. Steck is here, first as my Bozzle, and second because she can help explain your customs."

"Don't call a Neut 'she,' " I muttered. "A Neut is an 'It.' And if Steck is supposed to explain Tober customs, why not start with our custom of killing Neuts on sight?"

" 'A custom more honor'd in the breach than the observance,' " Rashid replied. He looked around at us expectantly, then exploded, "Oh come on, that was from *Hamlet*! Everyone knows *Hamlet*!"

"What I know," I said, "is that every man in the cove will try to kill your Neut if It comes to our village. A few women may try too," I added, thinking of Cappie.

"Barbaric," he muttered. "Just because someone is different—"

"Neuts *choose* to be different," I interrupted. "They know Tober law, but they Commit as Neut anyway. The Patriarch said that choosing Neut is no different than choosing to be a thief or a killer. But Neuts get off easy compared to other criminals. No whippings, no chains, no execution . . . they just get sent away and told not to come back.''

"How generous!'' Steck hissed. "Driven down-peninsula to cities we don't understand, where we're despised as freaks. Shunned by friends, separated from my lover and *child*—''

"Steck, shush!'' I'd never heard Leeta raise her voice so sharply. Mostly I thought of our priestess as a mumbly, self-effacing woman; but now she rounded on Rashid and poked a finger into his green plastic chestplate. "You say you don't want to interfere, Mister Rashid, Lord Rashid, whoever you are . . . but you're interfering right now. At this very moment, I'm supposed to be dancing a dance for the solstice. I'm supposed to be doing some good for the world instead of wasting time with outsiders who are only going to upset everybody!''

"A solstice dance!'' Rashid said, wrapping his gauntleted hands eagerly around hers. "Wonderful! Steck, step back, give them room. Yes, I should have noticed—the milkweed, the daisies, whatever that young man has in his hair . . . very nice, very *vegetal*. A 'romping through the groves' motif. Neo-paganism can be so charming, don't you think, Steck? Such a homespun, *agrarian* feel to it. I assume this dance celebrates your instinctual attunement to the ebb and flow of the seasons? Or is there some other purpose?''

I said, "No,'' at the same time Leeta and Steck said, "Yes.''

"Really,'' I insisted, "we shouldn't talk about this, should we, Leeta? The women's religion must have some prohibition against sharing secrets with outsiders.''

"No,'' Leeta replied. "Secret handshakes only appeal to men.''

And she proceeded to tell Rashid the complete story of Mistress Night and Master Day, and how Earth would burn up if she didn't dance to shift the balance from light back to dark. Rashid produced a notebook from a compartment on the belt of his armor and scribbled excitedly; now and then he would murmur "Charming!'' or "Delightful!'' in a voice that was far too amused. Steck just made it worse by offering background commentary, speaking with condescension about Master Wind's dalliance with each year's Mistress Leaf, or Mistress Night's continuing misadventures that always begin with someone saying, "If you want that pretty stone, you'll have to do me a favor . . .''

I wanted to crawl into the campfire and burn to ash. It's bad enough to hear your priestess claim she's personally responsible for the solstice. Then to have a mealy-mouthed Neut give such sneering versions of the good old stories . . .

Listen: everyone knows it's not hard to make the gods sound ridiculous. It just takes sarcasm, exaggeration, and a determination to be vulgar. Instead of saying, "Mistress Leaf donned her brightest finery in a vain attempt to rekindle Master Wind's passion," you say, "Mistress Leaf tarted herself up like a red-powdered whore and still Master Wind stayed as limp as lettuce."

But that's kid's stuff. You do it as a thirteen-year-old girl, when you want to show the boys how daring you can be. After a while, as with most things at thirteen, the memory of how you behaved makes you squirm; even if you know that seasons come from a tilting planet whirling around the sun, the old stories still *mean* something to you. Why not confide in Mistress Night when you can't understand why love gets so screwed up? She's not wise, but she never breaks secrets. And when you're out on the perch boats, how can you *not* talk to Master Wind a dozen times a day . . . respectfully, of course, because he has a temper, but if you ask nicely, he might give more breeze, or less, or another half an hour before he lets the storm break open.

The gods aren't jokes; they're people you walk around with every day. Insulting them is like insulting family.

"Don't let me delay you any longer," Rashid said at last. "Carry on with your dance."

By that time, I was sitting with my back to the three of them, trying to pretend I couldn't hear their conversation. Why was I still there when I should have been running to tell the cove about this Neut? If anyone asked, I'd say I didn't want to leave Leeta alone with the outsiders . . . that I intended to watch and listen until I learned what they were up to. But the truth was that Cappie had stolen my chance to do anything spontaneous and noble; now I was floundering, lamely hoping another opportunity might arise. So I frittered away the minutes by poking the fire with a stick. I'd watch the stick burn, then I'd snuff it out in the dirt, then set it on fire again. As a pastime, it didn't have much to recommend itself, but I kept doing it anyway.

A hand settled lightly on my shoulder—Leeta. "We have to do this now. Please?"

Rashid waited for my answer, his pen poised over his notebook. Half of me wanted to stomp off into the forest while telling them all to go to hell; the other half said I would damned well do what Leeta asked, just to show these outsiders that Tober people stuck together. "Sure," I told her. "What do I have to do?"

"Dance. Really, that's all."

She held out her hand to help me up. I took it, but stood up on my own—she was such a little woman, I would have pulled her over if I let her take my weight. When we were standing side by side, the top of her head scarcely came to my chin: a short, dingy-gray-haired woman, only a few years away from being a great-grandmother. But she kept hold of my hand and wrapped her other arm tight around my back, the way Cappie did at weekend dances when I set aside my fiddle and took to the floor with her. A moment later, Leeta rested her head against my chest.

In recent months I'd managed to avoid dancing with Cappie; it felt uncomfortably odd to have Leeta settle next to me in such a warm-bodied way. Ceremonial dances were supposed to be different from weekend dances, weren't they? Ceremonial dances were supposed to be . . . chaste. The way Leeta snuggled against me had a lot more of the sacred male/female duality than I'd expected.

"Come on," Leeta said, squeezing me tighter. "We have to dance."

I put my arms around her guardedly. With her elbow, she shoved my right forearm downward, so my hand was only a hair's breadth from touching her rump.

"Now I assume," Rashid called to Leeta, "you represent Mistress Night and the boy represents Master Day?"

"That's right," she called back over her shoulder. "Come on, dear," she said to me, "you aren't going to break me. We're *dancing* here. You have to hold me like you mean it."

Reluctantly, I squeezed a little tighter. She leaned into me . . . the way a woman leans into a man when she doesn't have patience for preliminaries.

"And this dance," Rashid called out again, "somehow transfers energy . . . cosmic force . . . some mystical something . . . from Master Day to Mistress Night, to redress the balance of light and dark?"

"You're talking like the Patriarch," Leeta said. "This dance goes back to the saner days of Tober Cove, before the Patriarch came along. There's no doubletalk; it just fixes things."

"How does it fix things?" Rashid asked.

"Talking won't help," she said, annoyance creeping into her voice. "Keep still now. Words only get in the way."

Rashid shrugged and settled himself on the edge of a low limestone outcrop. Steck sat at Rashid's feet and leaned against the knight's armored legs—an intimate pose, probably intended to offend me. I ignored it; my attention was dominated by the jab of milkweed pods on Leeta's belt, now crunched tight against my crotch.

We began, slowly, to dance, holding each other like lovers. No music; no sound at all but the crackling of the campfire. For a while I kept my eyes open, staring at the dark trees beyond the firelight so I wouldn't have to look at Rashid and Steck. But Leeta had her eyes closed, with the shadow of a smile on her wrinkled face . . . dreaming of other dances, I suppose, other men, or maybe other women from her long-ago male years.

I tried to get dreamy myself: to think of past dances with Cappie and others, to think of anything besides the smell of wilted daisies curling up from Leeta's hair and the prickle of animal claws digging into my chest.

Slow rocking, shifting back and forth from one foot to the other . . . not really a dance at all, no steps, no explicit rhythm, just that slow movement. I wondered if I should lead: I was the man, I should lead. But when I tried directing our motion, toes got in the way of toes and Leeta's hand clenched into a fist where it rested against my back.

I gave up steering.

Time passed. The fire faded to coals. Gradually, the claws on my sash, the milkweed pods, everything else prodding between our tight-locked bodies tweaked into more comfortable positions and drifted out of my consciousness. Leeta and I danced together in the quiet dark, alone among the trees. Distracting thoughts about Rashid, Steck and Cappie slipped away, as I stopped worrying about what I was supposed to do. I stopped thinking much at all—time blurred and thought blurred, but the dance went on.

Two people in the sleeping forest.
Back and forth in the quiet dark.

At some point, we stopped. Neither of us made the decision; the dance was simply over, and we clung motionless to each other for a time that might have been seconds or minutes. Then we parted, blinking in slow surprise, like children awakened from sleep. I wondered if I should do something—maybe bow and say, "Thank you." But a leaden awkwardness weighed me down so strongly I couldn't speak. I turned away, looking off into the forest . . . away from Leeta, away from Rashid and Steck whose presence I had just remembered. Despite the warmth of high summer, I felt chilled and naked.

Leeta poked the fire with a stick. Maybe she was stirring the coals; maybe she just felt as awkward as I did, and needed time to draw in on herself. After a moment, she muttered, "That's it. It's done." She kept her head bent over the ashes.

"That's *it*?" Rashid asked. "That was the whole ceremony?"

"That's all it had to be," Leeta replied. Her voice sounded choked; for some reason, I worried she was angry at me.

"But nothing happened!" Rashid protested loudly.

"Things happened," Leeta answered, still not looking at anyone. "You can't put two people together without things happening. Maybe folks on the outside can't see the change, but it's real. When you're quiet and tired enough, you stop posing and you stop worrying. For a few seconds, you aren't trying to be something other than what you are; for a few seconds, two people are *real*, and balanced. Me and the boy, Mistress Night and Master Day. Then, of course, we go back to posing again, because reality is terrifying; but we made the balance, and we made the difference."

At that moment, I admired her: her faith. She was clearly embarrassed to defend the ritual in front of Rashid—Leeta probably knew about rotations, revolutions and axial tilts too—yet she'd come out here to dance anyway, because that's what a priestess did. The only magic in the entire universe might be inside her own head; but that could be enough.

Maybe it *had* to be enough.

Rashid opened his mouth to ask another question, to dissect the moment, to explore our quaintly absurd "superstitions" . . . but he was interrupted by an arrow speeding out of the darkness and an explosion of violet flame.

FIVE

A Bribe for Bonnakkut

A second arrow followed on the nock of the first and this time I had a better glimpse of what happened. The arrow shot straight for Rashid's unhelmeted skull; but before it penetrated his temple, the arrowhead struck an invisible barrier and vaporized in a crackling burst of violet light. That arrowhead was made of flint, flint which blazed like straw falling into a blacksmith's forge . . . and the flame burned so hot, it incinerated the arrow's shaft and fletching with the same gout of fire. The flash left an afterimage of purple streaked across my vision, but in the ensuing darkness, I could blearily see a violet outline surrounding Rashid from head to toe.

The outline extended around Steck, still cuddled against Rashid's knee.

Another arrow brought another eye-watering explosion as the barb struck the violet fringe . . . and it occurred to me, Leeta and I should hightail it out of the target area before we regretted not having violet fringes of our own. I looked around for Leeta, intending to shield her with my body as we crawled away—it's a man's duty to safeguard the women of his village. Leeta, however, had already scurried into the darkness on her own initiative; so instead of making a strategic withdrawal as the heroic protector of a vulnerable woman, I scuttled into the bushes like a raccoon caught stealing garbage.

I found a place to crouch behind a bigger-than-average birch and waited as a flurry of violet flashes speckled the blackness. How many archers were out there? Probably the whole Warriors Society. Cappie must have dragged them out of their beds when she got back to town, and they'd followed Steck's heavy-booted tracks from the marsh to this clearing. The first few arrows were aimed at Rashid, so Cappie must have told the men about his stink-smoke weapon; now the shots split half and half between knight and Neut, trying to pierce the violet barrier that shielded the two.

"Is this really necessary?" Rashid called over the crack and sizzle of arrows burning. "My force field was designed by some very smart beings in the League of Peoples. Unless you're carrying laser rifles or gas bombs, you don't have a chance of touching us."

As far as I could see, he was right: the barrage was a waste of arrows. Then again, men of the Warriors Society weren't famous for developing new strategies. If something didn't fall down when they hit it with a stick, they'd try again with a bigger stick. If they emptied their quivers on Rashid and Steck, the Warriors would probably whack away with spears, and swords, and that big steel ax our First Warrior Bonnakkut always bragged about.

It put me in a quandary, that ax. Did I want to close my eyes when Bonnakkut swung it at Rashid, so I wouldn't be dazzled when the ax exploded? Or did I want to watch, so I'd see the expression on Bonnakkut's face when his precious baby turned to smoke in his hands?

Tough choice. A flash that big might permanently blind me, but it could be worth it to see Bonnakkut reduced to steamy tears. Why did I hate him so much? Let's just say Warrior Bonnakkut was not a music lover. He was five years older than me, and had always been jealous of the attention I got for being talented. Bonnakkut wasn't talented; he was only big and strong and mean. Apparently that was enough to win his way to the top of the Warriors Society in record time.

You had to worry about the safety of Tober Cove, if this ineffectual volley of arrows was typical of Bonnakkut's "tactics."

Rashid did nothing despite the commotion. He continued to sit on the ledge where he'd watched the dance, one arm wrapped around the Neut's shoulders. With his other hand, he shielded his eyes from the bursts of violet flame that flared a finger's width away from his face. I had to admire his composure; if I were the target of so many archers I'd be flinching constantly, no matter how protected I was by diabolic fires.

The arrows were still flying when Leeta stuck her head from behind a nearby tree and called, "I'm only a foolish woman, but perhaps you might humor me." Those words always started a Mocking Priestess homily, and Tober custom dictated that people stop what they were doing to let her speak. I figured it was fifty-fifty whether Bonnakkut would let the other warriors quit shooting; but maybe he thought Leeta would suggest a more effective way of killing the outsiders, and he was ready to listen. The forest fell silent: no thrum of bows, no cracks of flame.

Leeta cleared her throat. "I just wanted to say perhaps you should save your arrows for when they might be useful. It's exciting to watch them go pop and make pretty lights . . . but suppose a wildcat or bear shows up in the pastures before Fletcher Wingham has a chance to make more ammunition. We'd lose sheep and cattle, wouldn't we? People wouldn't like that."

"They don't like Neuts either," a deep voice shouted back. Bonnakkut, of course.

"That's true," Leeta agreed, "but your arrows aren't solving the Neut problem, are they?"

"There is no Neut problem," Rashid said, rising to his feet. Steck stood quickly too, wrapping an arm around Rashid's waist; I could just make out the violet glow surrounding both of them. "Steck and I won't harm anything," Rashid went on. "We just want to observe your ceremony tomorrow."

"You can't," Bonnakkut snapped. "Steck was banished twenty years ago, legal and proper. And Cappie said you claim to be a scientist. That's against the law too."

"All these laws against *being* something," Rashid grimaced. "Don't you have any laws against *doing* things? Like trying to kill visitors who come in peace?"

Steck said, "The Patriarch was not noted for his hospitality."

"I'm prepared to be lenient," Bonnakkut said in an unlenient tone of voice. "If you leave immediately, we'll let you go."

"Oh, very generous." Rashid rolled his eyes.

"Otherwise, we'll kill you here and now."

If those words had been said by anyone but Bonnakkut, I might have held my tongue; but I'd hated him ever since he was a twelve-year-old girl who shoved my sheet music down an outhouse hole. I couldn't pass up the chance to rub his nose in his inadequacies, even if it meant siding with outsiders. "Come on, Bonnakkut," I shouted from the cover of the bushes, "you can't make a dent in these two. Stop pretending to be effective and escort them back to the cove. Let the mayor and council sort out this mess."

Bushes rustled on the far side of the clearing and Bonnakkut stepped out. In the darkness, I could only make out his silhouette: massive shoulders, massive chest, massive ax held in one hand. "So," he said, pointing the ax-head at me, "look who's become a Neut lover. Why doesn't that surprise me?"

"It surprises me," Steck said, craning Its Neut neck to peer at me. "Where'd you find this sudden streak of common sense?"

"The solstice dance breeds common sense," Leeta answered, saving me the trouble of an excuse. "The dance puts things in perspective."

"And while we're brimming over with perspective," Rashid said brightly, "shall we go to Tober Cove?"

"Taking you to the cove would start a riot," Bonnakkut replied, planting himself and his ax squarely in front of us all. "We don't want riots."

"Neither do I," Rashid assured him. "I'm one hundred percent in favor of tranquility. You're some kind of local town guard?"

"I'm Bonnakkut, First Warrior of the Tober Warriors Society. I protect the peace."

"Hence, the repetition of 'warrior' in your official title," Rashid murmured. Then in a louder voice, he said, "I happen to be carrying an official peace offering for the leader of the local constabulary. This seems like an excellent time to pass it on."

Without waiting for a reply, Rashid reached into a pouch on his thigh and pulled out something I couldn't see in the darkness. "This," he told Bonnakkut, "is a classic Beretta Model 92F automatic. You know what that is?"

"A firearm," Bonnakkut said. "A pistol. It shoots bullets."

"Indeed it does. It holds fifteen 9mm Parabellum cartridges, and Steck has another sixty rounds in her luggage. The powder and primer are guaranteed fresh. You could probably sell each bullet for twenty crowns on the black market in Feliss City. As for the gun itself . . . what would you say, Steck, five thousand crowns for a mint condition 92F?"

"It depends whether buyers in Feliss know anything about guns," Steck replied. "A lot of so-called collectors can't tell the difference between a perfectly maintained pistol like this, and some rust-eaten thing that will blow off your hand when you try to fire it."

"You're giving me the gun?" Bonnakkut asked, not quite tuned up to pitch with the conversation yet.

"No, he's not," Leeta said fiercely. "The last thing Tober Cove needs is a new way to hurt people. Shame on you, Lord Rashid, for bringing it."

"A responsible man like the First Warrior will only use the gun for reasonable ends." Rashid held out the weapon to Bonnakkut, butt first. "Here you go."

"Is this a bribe?" Bonnakkut asked.

"Yes," Leeta replied.

"No," said Rashid, "it's a peace bond. To show I support the laws of Tober Cove and those who enforce them. Go ahead, take it."

"Don't you dare," Leeta ordered.

But cautiously, Bonnakkut shuffled forward, holding his ax at the ready in case . . . well, I don't know what he expected Rashid or Steck to do, but whatever it was, they didn't do it. They stood placidly while Bonnakkut reached out, took the pistol, and hurried back away.

"This gun actually works?" he asked.

"Just point and click," Rashid answered. "I left the safety off because I knew you'd want to try it."

To no one's surprise, Bonnakkut fired at Rashid.

The bullet made a blindingly bright flash and an exceedingly loud bang at both ends of its trajectory. The flash coming out of the gun was yellowy orange. The flash on Rashid's end was violet: a huge mauve-tinted blaze that fizzed and crackled after the initial impact, spitting molten drops of the bullet's lead. Casually, Rashid reached out a booted foot and tamped out the flames where the red-hot spatter had lit the pine needles on the ground.

"Before you try that again," Rashid told Bonnakkut, "I'll remind you, each bullet is worth twenty crowns, and when they're gone, they're gone. So make up your mind: do you keep stinking up the forest with pricey gunpowder, or do you escort Steck and me to Tober Cove?"

Bonnakkut stood still for a moment, weighing the gun in his hand. I could guess what was going through his mind. Tober Cove's patron gods hated firearms. It was said (by both the Mocking Priestess and the Patriarch's Man) that Master Crow and Mistress Gull might boycott Commitment Day completely if any gun lurked within a day's ride of the cove. On the other hand, Bonnakkut must have wanted that gun the way a beetle wants dung. He wanted to strut with it. He wanted women to show fear and men to pucker with envy. He wanted word to pass down-peninsula all the way to Ohna Sound: First Warrior Bonnakkut of Tober Cove has himself a Beretta.

And he's not afraid to use it.

"For heaven's sake," Leeta said, "put that wicked thing down."

"It scares you, does it?" Bonnakkut asked.

"Of course it does. And on Commitment Eve too! Give it to your fastest runner and rush it off Tober land before Mistress Gull and Master Crow get angry."

"It would be faster to put it on a boat," Bonnakkut replied. "If the mayor decides it's necessary."

"Ah," smiled Rashid, "we're going to let the mayor decide. I love the chain of command. By all means, let's see this mayor of yours. I've brought something for him too."

"No good will come of this," Leeta said darkly.

"Stop muttering," Bonnakkut told her. "You were the one who chewed us out for wasting arrows; you should be happy we've stopped. We're going back to town so the mayor can sort everything out. Discussion and negotiation . . . aren't you always saying we should solve problems through discussion and negotiation?"

"I'd prefer less negotiation," she answered, glaring at the pistol in his hands.

"Why expect consistency from a woman?" Bonnakkut asked no one in particular. Then he turned to face the bushes and called, "Fall in, men. We're taking them back to the cove."

As members of the Warriors Society emerged from the darkness, Bonnakkut made a show of shoving the pistol into his belt. Rashid winced. "Steck," he whispered, "show the First Warrior how to put on the safety before he does himself an injury."

SIX

A Maiden Speech for Cappie

Leeta led the way home, milkweed pods clacking. Bonnakkut's three warriors followed her—Kaeomi, Stallor, and Mintz, all of them bullies when I was growing up—then Rashid and Steck.

Rashid kept his arm around Steck's shoulders as they walked, even in places where the trail was narrow enough for them to be knocking heels. He obviously wanted Steck close enough to be covered by that violet glow that grew out of his armor. Rashid was wise to take precautions—if Steck ever stepped out of the glow's safety, Bonnakkut would certainly pump bullets into the Neut's back. Since I was walking behind Steck, and Bonnakkut marched behind me, I was just as happy that Bonnakkut never got an opening to use his bang-bang: I was straight in the line of fire. When the trail widened enough to walk three abreast, I caught up with Rashid and Steck, so I wouldn't be sandwiched between the Neut and that gun.

"Hello again," Rashid said cheerfully. "How are you feeling? All recovered from the tear gas?"

"I'm all right." In a lower voice, I added, "It's too bad you used that stuff on me instead of Bonnakkut."

"Back at the creek," he replied, "you and your lovely companion were close to perforating my Bozzle's liver—I had to take drastic action. But in the clearing, Steck was safely under my force field, so we could afford to wait things out. Besides, I have my helmet off. If I started playing with gas, I'd gag with the rest of you."

"It would serve you right," I said.

"Don't grouch," Rashid chided. "You just said you're feeling fine. Now tell me more about yourself and Tober Cove. How old are you?"

"Twenty," I answered.

"So you'll Commit to a permanent sex tomorrow?"

"That's right."

"And have you really alternated sex every summer since you were born?"

"They don't change sex their first summer," Steck put in. "Mistress Gull is too tenderhearted to separate babies from their families. Infants aren't taken till after their first birthday."

"Fair enough," Rashid shrugged. Turning back to me, he asked, "Were you born a boy or a girl?"

"A girl," I answered.

"So you became a boy in the summer when you were one year old, a girl when you were two, a boy again when you were three . . ."

"That's how it works," I said, trying to sound bored. This wasn't the first time I'd had this conversation. In all the world, our little secluded village was the only place where the gods allowed children to switch sex each year . . . so whenever I went out of town to play, I could expect questions on the subject several times an evening. Yoskar, the carpenter with whom I had that dalliance—he had asked me again and again. Had I really been male the year before? Would I really be male again after the solstice? When I stopped being a woman, did I stop liking men? Or did I like men all the time, or both men and women, or what?

I couldn't decide if such questions were indecent or just trite. No one asks a woman, "Hey, how does it feel to have breasts?" or a man, "Isn't it weird having a penis?" The questions don't make sense—you don't think about yourself on that level. In Tober Cove, only a person's current gender mattered. Whatever happened before or after was irrelevant.

On the other hand, Rashid wasn't the type to stop asking questions just because I showed disinterest. "And," he continued, "Steck tells me that all residents of Tober Cove bear a child when they're nineteen or twenty."

"In one of their last years before Commitment," I nodded. "Tomorrow at noon, several male teenagers will go off to Birds Home with Master Crow, and when they come back at sunset, they'll be female and pregnant. The baby is born five or six months later."

"Of course," Steck put in, "Master Crow is said to be the baby's father . . . even though the child often grows to look strikingly like someone else in the village."

I glowered at the Neut. As a former Tober, Steck must know that

Master Crow made such children resemble other people in the cove so the kids would fit in with their peers. The offspring of Master Crow had enough prestige already, compared to children with human fathers. They didn't need to *look* special too.

But I didn't have the patience to bandy words with a Neut. I just told Rashid, "Master Crow fathers the babies to make sure every Tober experiences childbirth, nursing and such, before Committing to one sex or the other. We have to know everything about being a woman, and everything about being a man, so we can make the right choice."

"You give birth to children . . . and I assume you're encouraged to have sexual relationships . . ."

"Doesn't take much encouraging," Steck snickered.

I glared. My stomach clenched to hear a Neut talk smut.

"So every Tober," Rashid continued, "gets to make love as both a male and a female—"

"Not *every* Tober," Steck interrupted. "Some find they can only get lucky when they're women . . . and then only with men who are really hard up."

I gave the Neut a curious look.

"Or it might work the other way around," Steck added hurriedly.

"Either way, I can see it's important information to have," Rashid said, "when you're trying to decide how to spend the rest of your life. You must be thankful if you have a strong reason to choose one gender over the other. Like, uhh . . . if making love is more enjoyable as a woman or a man?"

Every Tober in the party groaned. Even Kaeomi, Stallor and Mintz, blessed with the collective intelligence of pine sap, smacked their foreheads and grimaced. Behind us, Bonnakkut muttered something that was probably obscene and even Steck mumbled, "Come on, boss, you're embarrassing me."

"What'd I say?" Rashid demanded.

No one answered. We'd all been asked that question a thousand times, by peddlers passing through town, by Wiretown merchants buying our fish and grain . . . even by a half-dead Mishie pirate who once washed up along our coast. Was making love better as a man or a woman? The first time you hear the question, you feel smug; outsiders envy us for knowing both sides of the bed. But after you hear the question over and over, asked with drooling leers or fervent sincerity, you want to hide your head and weep.

It's better with some men than other men, okay? It's better with some women than other women. And it's better with a Tober than with anyone else, because we've been both sexes, so we know what is and isn't fragile.

While the rest of us cringed at Rashid's question, Leeta took it upon herself to give an answer. "If sex were better as a woman, Tober Cove would be all female, don't you think? And if it were better as a man, we'd all be men. But the cove population is half and half, give or take a handful, so that should tell you something. Not just about who likes bedding whom, but about men things in general versus women things in general. Cove people are free to choose, and they choose half and half. Think about that."

"And think about it quietly," Bonnakkut growled. "No more talk." Clearly, our esteemed First Warrior didn't want Rashid asking any of the other foolish questions outsiders always foist upon Tobers . . . and for once, I agreed with him.

We finished the walk in silence. High clouds had drifted in from the lake over the last hour, but we still had plenty of starlight to travel by. From time to time an owl hooted at us, and once Leeta called a halt while a porcupine waddled across the trail. On a normal night, one of the Warriors would have put an arrow through the beast, just on principle; the damned porcs love eating salty wood, which means they're forever gnawing on our outhouse seats and leaving loose quills behind. Most Tobers get rudely spiked at least once in our lives, and that means most Tobers *hate* porcupines. But the bullies must have spent all their arrows on what Rashid called his "force field," and Bonnakkut was saving his bullets for more prestigious targets.

In time, we reached the lake shore: Mother Lake we called it, though the maps in Wiretown labeled it Lake Heron. The Tober name was better—herons are marsh birds who never put a toe into the deep waters of Mother Lake. Even at summer solstice, the water was cold enough that your lungs could seize up if you dove straight in. Parents made children wear ropes when they went swimming, and once or twice a season, we used those ropes to land someone who'd stopped being able to take in air. Men working the perch boats had their ropes too, and bright orange OldTech life jackets retrieved from the Cheecheemaun steel-boat that ran aground in Old Tober Harbor four hundred years ago.

Even with all that protection, men died. My mother . . . I'd been born when she was twenty. The Elders told me she'd Committed male when the time came, had gone to work on the perch boats and run afoul of a fierce flash storm . . .

Which is another reason I liked to call it Mother Lake.

But the lake was calm that Commitment Eve, lapping the rocky shore with regular rhythmic waves. Water stretched out forever, dotted by flowerpot islands and off to the north, a long low outcrop called the Bear's Rump . . . I don't know why. I've never made a detailed study of bears.

In another ten minutes we rounded the eastern headland and sighted Tober Cove itself. At that distance in the dark, I couldn't see more than the OldTech radio antenna on Patriarch Hill, but I could smell the village with all the fondness of home. Wharf odors predominated—fresh perch, salted perch, and the rotting pile of junk fish waiting to be minced for fertilizer—but the air also carried fragrances from the farms that ringed the edge of town: sheep, cattle, hundreds of chickens, and the sweet perfume of clover.

Above all that ran one more smell, usually tamped down on summer evenings, but thick tonight because it was solstice: woodsmoke, coming from every chimney. Tomorrow was Commitment Day. Cook stoves would burn all night long, roasting meat and baking bread, warming potatoes and simmering white bean/crayfish chowder, all in preparation for the great feast that celebrated . . . well, that celebrated *me*. And Cappie, of course. We two had reached the age of Commitment. For one day, we were the cove's official darlings.

The door of the Council Hall opened and someone stepped onto the wide cement area at the top of the steps. Lamplight spilled from inside the hall, silhouetting the figure: a man's clothes, but not a man's body.

"That's Cappie," Bonnakkut said from behind me.

I nodded.

"Hard to decide," Bonnakkut went on softly, "whether I'd rather see her Commit as man or woman. If she decides to be a man, she'll make one hell of a warrior. Strong as a bull, but fast . . . she could win half the sports trophies at Wiretown Fall Fair."

I knew that; Cappie's muscles had got me out of several down-peninsula scrapes, in the years when she was male and people were jealous of my talent. Still, I wondered why Bonnakkut had chosen this moment to rhapsodize about her prowess.

"On the other hand," Bonnakkut said, "if she decides to be a woman . . . well, I like her as a woman, just fine."

I stared at him. He smirked back. "Cappie's mine," I said.

"You're sure of that?"

"What do you mean?"

Bonnakkut kept smirking. "Maybe I just mean that tomorrow is Commitment Day. If you both Commit female . . . you and Cappie can still be good friends, as the saying goes, but she'll be looking for a man. Maybe that's all I mean."

"And maybe it isn't?"

"Nearly every weekend, you go down-peninsula to play your little fiddle," Bonnakkut said. "Maybe Cappie likes company when you're gone."

I would have punched him in the mouth if I hadn't been afraid of hurting my fingers. Bonnakkut's gun didn't scare me, and neither did his huge arms and shoulders . . . but a violinist has to think of his hands first, no matter how badly he'd like to thrash someone. I could only say, "You've always been a lying asshole, Bonnakkut. It's nice when you provide new proof."

Then, before he got ideas about retaliation, I hopped in front of Rashid to get that violet light between me and Bonnakkut's anger.

When Cappie caught sight of us coming up the beach, she called into the Council Hall and several more people joined her on the steps. In the darkness, all I could see were silhouettes—silhouettes with the tousled hair and skewed clothing of folks just roused from their beds. The women of Tober Cove might spend much of Commitment Eve cooking, but the men (especially the Elders) slept like slugs, wisely saving their energy for the next day.

Though I could only see the Elders' silhouettes, I could still recognize Mayor Teggeree: a balloon of a man as wide as a door and as heavy as a prize heifer. Perhaps there's some secret law of the Spark Lords that all mayors have to be fat; in my travels down-peninsula I've never met a mayor who didn't bulge at the seams, even in perverse towns where women held the office.

Another person came out to the steps, this one holding an oil lantern. Teggeree snatched the lantern and held it above his head . . . as if it would help him see better, instead of interfering with his night vision. He stood for some time, the lantern glow lighting his squint as he tried to identify who was approaching him.

I could tell the exact moment when the lamplight touched our party—everyone on the steps gasped and started babbling. Well . . . not everyone. Cappie stayed silent, wearing a grim look on her face. Sometimes she had no sense of humor. Personally I couldn't help but chuckle at the flabbergasted expressions on the Elders' faces; it isn't every day you walk up to the Council Hall with a knight and Neut on your heels.

Mayor Teggeree soon composed himself enough to call in his sonorous voice, "Bonnakkut . . . what do you think you're doing?"

"The situation is complicated," Bonnakkut replied. "Very complicated." With a false air of casualness, he lowered his hand to stroke the Beretta on his belt. "This is a matter for the full council to decide."

Teggeree called over his shoulder into the council building. "All in favor of killing the Neut, say, 'Aye.'"

A dutiful chorus within answered, "Aye."

"Motion passed." He turned back to the First Warrior. "Carry out the sentence . . . and try not to break the noise bylaws, there are children sleeping."

"It's not that easy, mayor," Bonnakkut insisted. "The council should discuss this."

"He's right," Leeta added. "You don't appreciate the nature of our visitors." She cast a glance at Rashid.

"Still sticking up for Steck, are you?" Teggeree said to Leeta. Then he sighed. "All right, Cappie woke us all anyway. We can afford to talk about this for the thirty seconds it deserves." He held up the lantern and gestured toward the door with his free hand. "Everyone into the hall."

One by one, we mounted the steps. I let Rashid and Steck go ahead of me. They climbed the stairs awkwardly, Rashid's arm still around Steck's shoulders. As the Neut passed Teggeree, It nodded Its head and smiled. "Dear little Teggie. Mayor now, are you? I knew you were bound for great things."

The mayor's face curdled in exasperation. "What do you want me to say, Steck? Welcome home?"

Steck only smiled and passed into the hall, squeezing tight under Rashid's arm. I made to follow, but Teggeree put a fat hand on my chest. "Not you, Fullin."

"Fullin?" Steck hissed, turning to stare at me. "Back at the creek, you said you *weren't* Fullin."

But Teggeree pushed into the hall and closed the door in my face before another word was said. Confused, I gazed at the blank door for several seconds.

Its paint was cracking. It needed a new coat.

"Something wrong?" asked a voice behind me. Cappie.

I turned slowly. She stood two steps down the stairway, leaning against the wooden rail that served as a bannister. With her arms propped back against the railing, her breasts pushed out against the man's shirt she wore.

At that moment, I realized there *was* something about a woman in man's clothing. Something *arresting*. I couldn't take my eyes off her. Cappie, of all people, looking *desirable*. I could hardly believe it.

"Nothing's wrong," I said, gazing at her. "Nothing at all."

She rolled her eyes. "You're being obvious again."

"What's wrong with that?"

"The past few months you've barely looked at me. As soon as I dress like a man, you start drooling. What does that say, Fullin?"

"Nothing." With an effort I tore my gaze away from her, turning instead to look at the shadowed fishing boats rocking on the dark lake water. "Bonnakkut was suggesting some ridiculous things about you."

"What things?"

"Stupid lies." I checked her face for signs of guilt. Nothing. It was a thin soft face, attractive in its way, but at this moment very guarded. Maybe I should have asked outright if anything had gone on between her and Bonnakkut, but I couldn't ask Cappie anything outright anymore. I turned back to the darkness and mumbled, "Bonnakkut is such a turd."

"He's not that bad," she said. I couldn't tell if she was defending him or just contradicting me. Lately she'd got into the habit of disagreeing with me, purely for spite. "What did Bonnakkut say?" she asked.

I shook my head. Offended as I was at Bonnakkut's insinuations, I didn't want to discuss them with Cappie. I didn't want to discuss anything with her. But I couldn't help saying, "Leeta claims you volunteered to take over as Mocking Priestess."

"Someone has to," Cappie replied. "Doctor Gorallin found lumps in Leeta's breasts. Both of them. This is her last solstice."

"That's too bad," I said, in that immediate, automatic tone of voice you always use when you speak of death. But a moment later, I thought about the slow dance in the woods, and said again, "That's too bad."

"So Leeta asked if I'd be her successor," Cappie continued. "I'm tempted, Fullin, I'm really tempted. Tober Cove needs a priestess, as counterbalance to the Patriarch's Man. Besides," she said with a half smile, "the wardrobe suits me. If you think I look good in suspenders, just wait till you see me wear milkweed."

I had a vision of Cappie and me on a bed slathered flank-deep in milkweed silk . . . which could be interesting . . . if she wore the suspenders too.

"So you're going to Commit as a woman?" I asked.

She grimaced. "I've tried to talk about this for months, Fullin, and you've just avoided the subject."

"You've been after me to say what *I'll* do. You never mentioned what *you* want."

"Because you never asked!"

"I figured if you'd made a decision, you'd tell me," I said. "Why would you keep asking what I intend to do, when you really wanted to tell me what *you* intend to do?''

"Men!" Cappie flumped down on the top step and made a show of burying her face in her hands. The too-big sleeves of her father's shirt dangled around her slim wrists like puffed cuffs. It's odd how something as simple as dangling sleeves can make you want a woman, when everything else makes you invent excuses to avoid her.

I sat beside her on the step. "Do you really want to become the next Mocking Priestess?"

She lifted her head. "We holy acolytes describe the job as just 'Priestess.' The 'Mocking' part is more of a hobby . . . when the Patriarch's Man says something so boneheaded, you can't help but hit him with a dig."

"So you're going to do it?"

"Why shouldn't I?"

I shrugged. My first reaction had been to oppose the idea. It wasn't just that the priestess was a figure of ridicule among the men in town. The priestess also had a lot of errands to run—consecrating babies, attending to the dead, telling stories for children, teetering on that uncomfortable wooden stool in the back of the Council Hall while the male Elders held their meetings. Cappie wouldn't have time to do the chores a wife should do . . . and despite everything, I still pictured myself married to Cappie after we Committed.

Everyone in the cove expected us to get married. They said we were the perfect couple.

But when I thought about it, Cappie becoming priestess had its good points too. For one thing, it would be an excuse not to marry her, an excuse the rest of the cove would understand—the priestess wasn't allowed to take a husband, since that might create a "conflict of interest." On the other hand, the priestess wasn't expected to be celibate either; Leeta supposedly had a sex life, judging by the way people occasionally winked when talking about her. With Cappie as the next Mocking Priestess, I could bed her if I wanted (say, when she wore men's clothing), but never have to tie the unforgiving knot.

Another good thing about Cappie taking over from Leeta: it would shut Bonnakkut out of her life. The women of the cove would hate to see their oh-so-serene priestess associating with the First Warrior, just as the men would hate their manly First Warrior spending time with a puddinghead priestess. Even if I dumped Cappie, I could be sure the cove would never let her take up with Bonnakkut.

Then too, if Cappie wanted to be priestess, she'd have to Commit as a woman. That left me the option of Committing as a woman too, an easy way out of any "obligations" people might think I had toward Cappie. I'd often thought about Committing female—if nothing else, I wouldn't have to work much. Dabble around the house, take care of my son Waggett . . . and make buckets of money playing violin on weekends. Of course, if I were a woman and Cappie the priestess, she'd think she could lord it over me; but I wouldn't be the first woman to distance herself from the Mocking Priestess.

Cappie was still waiting for my answer: did I want her to take over from Leeta. "If it's what you want," I said, "it's okay with me."

She looked at me curiously for a moment, then nodded. "Thank you. Very generous."

Frankly, I expected more gratitude. Enthusiasm. Showering me with kisses of appreciation for giving her permission. Of course, then I'd shrug her off in annoyance, but I wanted her to make the gesture.

We sat in silence for several minutes, side by side on the steps. The time was about two in the morning, but I felt too tired to turn and look at the clock on the Council Hall steeple. Would the Elders expect Cappie and me to go back to the marsh when this was all over? Or could we just head for the house we shared on the west side of town?

Cappie must have been thinking along the same lines. "If they really want us to stay out here all night," she muttered, "they could at least lend us a deck of cards. Leeta says most council meetings are five minutes of business followed by three hours of poker."

"That would be Leeta living up to the 'mocking' part of her job."

"But why are they taking so long to discuss this?" Cappie growled, glancing at the closed door behind us. "Ask anyone what to do if a Neut comes back from exile, and you'll get a real short answer."

"It's different if the Neut comes bearing gifts." I told her how readily Bonnakkut took the Beretta and how he sucked up to Rashid thereafter. I may have exaggerated a bit; who said I had to cast Bonnakkut in a favorable light?

By the time my story was done, Cappie was scowling fiercely. "So they're in there right now," she said, "and Rashid is handing out presents to the Elders."

"Probably," I agreed.

"But the Elders wouldn't take bribes, would they?" She paused. "Well, Leeta wouldn't."

"Depends what the bribe is," I answered, in what I hoped was a worldly-wise voice. "Leeta might turn down gold . . . but suppose Rashid has some high-grade medicine from down south. Vaccines or antibiotics straight from the Spark Lords, something that could save lives for years to come; perhaps even get rid of those lumps in Leeta's own breasts. And all Rashid wants is to watch the ceremonies tomorrow, then go away. Do you think Leeta would refuse a deal like that?''

"Leeta wouldn't take medicine just for herself," Cappie said, "but for other people . . . for children . . . do you think Rashid really brought something like that?''

"Rashid is a noble," I replied. "At one point Leeta called him 'Lord Rashid,' like she recognized him or his name. If he's an aristocrat from Feliss, he might have access to the medical supplies that the Sparks give to Governors. Or he might have enough money to afford something just as good as medicine. Seeds for a strain of wheat that can survive a spring snow. OldTech equipment for fishing or farming. Or a refrigeration machine for the perch-packing plant. My foster father said they had refrigeration machines in Feliss, OldTech inventions that ran off sunlight . . ."

The Council Hall door swung open. Laughter ho-ho'd its way out to the porch. Cappie gave me a look that made it clear what she thought of people who laughed after taking bribes from Neuts.

Three seconds later, Teggeree and Rashid swaggered out, the mayor's arm around Rashid's shoulders in much the same way that Rashid had walked so long with Steck. Teggeree was saying, "If you really want to keep your identity secret, Lord Rashid, we'd better . . ."

The mayor's voice died away as he saw Cappie and me sitting on the steps.

"We can keep secrets," Cappie said coldly.

"Good," Rashid smiled. "The council and I have come to an agreement, and it would be better for all concerned—"

"Better for the prosperity of the cove," Teggeree put in smugly.

"Yes," Rashid continued, "better for everyone if we don't spread rumors about Neuts and other complicated issues."

"Then why not leave, and take Steck with you?" Cappie asked.

"I'll leave tomorrow, after I see Master Crow and Mistress Gull," Rashid replied. "In the meantime, we can disguise Steck—conceal the nature of her gender, at any rate—so we won't upset the rest of the village. I want you to swear you won't tell what's happened here tonight, till after I'm gone."

"You have to swear on the Patriarch's Hand," Teggeree added.

Cappie rose to her feet. "Why should I?"

"Cappie!" That was me, shocked. People didn't talk like that to our mayor.

But Cappie gave me a dark look and turned back to glare at Rashid and Teggeree. "I'm only a foolish woman," she said in precise tones, "but perhaps you might humor me."

The mayor's jaw dropped open. He stared at her, then let go of Rashid and craned his neck toward the open hall door, where Leeta stood amidst the Elders. Leeta took a shy step forward, lowered her eyes, and mumbled toward the ground, "I've invited Cappie to become the next Mocking Priestess."

"It seems to me," Cappie said loudly, "that if the council has good reason to permit strangers to observe Commitment Day—the most central event in our lives and the thing that makes us unique from everyone else on Earth—it seems to me if the council has good reason for this decision, there's no need to keep it secret from other Tobers. If it's the right thing to do, everyone will agree when you explain. They'll say, 'Yes, it's a good thing you're allowing a Neut to mingle with our children. It's a good thing you've welcomed a *scientist*.'"

"Rashid is more than a scientist," Leeta sighed. "He's *the* scientist. King of all other scientists on Earth. He's the Knowledge-Lord of Spark."

SEVEN

An Oath for the Patriarch's Man

Leeta's news set me back a pace. As far as I knew, we'd never had a Spark Lord within a hundred klicks of Tober Cove. Spark law only allows fourteen Lords at most, and an average generation has just five or six—way too few to visit every little village on Earth. On top of that, the Lords are too busy to worry about peaceful places like our cove, because they spend their lives stopping wars and fighting demons in more complicated parts of the planet. Between battles, they have their hands full with other important work, making medicines, organizing food shipments in time of famine, and leaning on provincial Governors who get too uppity for the good of their people.

Tober Cove had never had the sort of trouble that warrants a Spark Lord's attention. It made me wonder what kind of mess we were in, to get the Knowledge-Lord now. But at least I knew why the Elders had welcomed Rashid with open arms. All the stories about the Sparks drive one message home: they get their way in the end, so you might as well give in right off.

I wasn't the only one unsettled by a Spark in our midst. Cappie's stern expression wilted and she whipped away to face out into the dark. Anyone would feel crestfallen to deliver her first homily as Mocking Priestess, then have it swept aside by the intervention of a Lord; still, I fussed that Cappie had just put me into that toss-up situation all men hate. Was I supposed to go over and say comforting there-there's? Or should I leave her alone till she'd recovered from the disappointment?

Leaving her alone finally won out. If I tried to comfort her and she pushed me away, I'd be embarrassed in front of important people.

"All right," I said, pretending to ignore Cappie's sulk, "we'll swear not to tell anybody about tonight . . . at least till Lord Rashid leaves the cove.''

"Then let's finish this," yawned one of the Elders—Vaygon the Seedster. "We're losing sleep here."

People chuckled. Vaygon had a reputation for sleeping twenty-two hours a day. Any time you ventured into the seed storehouse, you'd find him sprawled across burlap bags of wheat and corn, snoring as loud as a sow. Someone (maybe his wife Veen) had spread the rumor it was good luck to have Vaygon sleep on your seed. People would bring all kinds of unlikely things for him to use as pillows—sacks of potatoes, vines of hops, even bundles of cuttings from apple trees—all in the hope that a night under Vaygon's head would make the plants flourish. A normal man might find it a challenge to sleep on apple branches, but Vaygon was a master at his trade. If we didn't let him get back to bed, some poor farmer's strawberry crop might come up sour next year.

Elders at the back of the crowd murmured, then parted to let someone shuffle through: old Hakoore, the Patriarch's Man. He was three-quarters blind and sickly with arthritis, but still a rattlesnake, spitting venom at the slightest deviation from the Patriarch's Law. I wondered what Hakoore thought about giving permission for a Neut to return to the cove . . . but the Patriarch's authority had come straight from the High Lord of Spark, so the Patriarch's successors could hardly oppose Spark now.

Hakoore had his arms wrapped around a golden box the size of a newborn baby: a tawdry sort of box, scratched and tarnished and dented. Even in its prime, the box couldn't have been much to look at. Its surface was only imitation gold, maybe imitation brass, and the four sides were embossed with indistinct reliefs of stiff men and women in pleated robes. Down-peninsula, I'd seen better looking window planters; but the box still held the greatest treasure in all Tober Cove. As Hakoore opened the lid, even Rashid leaned over to get a better look of what lay inside.

The box held a human hand—said to be the Patriarch's hand, doused with salt and herbs to keep it from crumbling to dust a hundred and fifty years after its owner's death. As children, Cappie and I made up stories about the hand: that it crawled out of its box at night and strangled you if you said bad things about the Patriarch; or that the original hand had rotted years ago, and a succession of Patriarch's Men kept replacing it with hands chopped off thieves or Neuts. I could list a dozen such tales . . . but you know the stories children whisper to each other on blustery afternoons when there's thunder in the distance.

The hand was a central part of Tober life. Couples getting married had to kiss it to seal their vows; newborn babies got it laid across their chests as a blessing, and it was laid there again at their funerals. The hand would even play a sideways role in the Commitment festivities; when Mistress Gull came to take Cappie and me away to Birds Home, we each had to carry a chicken foot, symbolizing the hand, symbolizing the Patriarch.

Hakoore thrust the box toward me. I reached inside to touch the hand with my fingertips; the skin felt like paper. My foster father always said he cringed to see Tobers touch "that dirty old thing." He worried about us contracting an illness . . . although I doubted anyone could get sick from contact with the Patriarch, the pure antithesis of Master Disease.

"Swear," Hakoore hissed. Hakoore *always* hissed, and seldom more than a few words at a time. Some folks claimed he had a festering growth in his throat; others said he just spoke that way to make your skin crawl.

I shrugged to show I wasn't intimidated, then said, "I swear I'll conceal the true identities of Lord Rashid and Steck until they've left the cove. Okay?"

"Fine by me," Rashid answered.

"The girl must swear too." Hakoore got a lot of hissing into that sentence—even the words without S's.

"Do you really want a Mocking Priestess to touch your precious relic?" Cappie asked. "Aren't you afraid I might contaminate the hand . . . say, with common sense?"

"Oh, boy," I muttered under my breath. A few Elders groaned stronger oaths; some glared at me, as if I were responsible for what she said. I tried to look innocent, the picture of a reasonable man, and said, "Cappie, aren't you taking this priestess thing too far?"

Okay—I should have known Cappie wasn't prepared to listen to reason. In fact, she suddenly looked prepared to claw my eyes out; and she might have done so, if Steck of all people hadn't stepped protectively in front of me. I wanted to tell the Neut I could look after myself . . . but I decided to save that for a less public moment.

Leeta hurried into the middle of everything, dithering vaguely to Hakoore, the mayor and Cappie. "Now, now," she said. "Now, now. It's true a priestess doesn't swear on the hand. If necessary, she swears on a stone or a tree, you know, something real. Which is not to say the hand isn't real. Anyway, it's not an illusion. But the point is, Cappie, you aren't priestess yet, are you? To be priestess, you have to be a woman, and you aren't fully a woman until you've Committed. People change their minds at the last moment, you know they do. They *promise* they'll Commit as a woman, and then at the last moment . . ." Leeta cast a glance at Steck. "At the last moment, they get other ideas," she finished. "So I'm not rejecting you, Cappie, I still want you to be my successor, but claiming the rights of office tonight . . . that's premature, don't you think?"

Whenever Leeta went into her wooly-headed old woman act, it became impossible to stay angry. Annoyed, yes—especially if you had pressing business. But even Cappie in full temper couldn't blaze hot enough to burn through Leeta's dampening babble. Cappie sputtered and guttered and shrank down to sullen coals of resentment. Lowering her eyes, she mumbled, "All right. Let's get this over with."

"Swear!" Hakoore hissed, and thrust the mummified hand toward her.

Cappie reached out to touch it; but as she did, Steck bent, picked up a small stone, and dropped it into her other hand. "Nothing says you can't hold a stone the same time you touch the hand," Steck told her. "Who knows which you're really swearing by?"

Hakoore's face twisted with hatred. Rashid, however, clapped Steck on the back. "Excellent compromise!" Cappie smiled a fierce smile. Touching both stone and hand, she quickly recited the same oath I had.

"That's fine," Mayor Teggeree said, taking a step back from the furious Hakoore. "Now, shall we wend our separate ways to bed? We don't want to fall asleep in the middle of tomorrow's feast." He favored us with a mayoral chuckle.

"Do Fullin and I have to go back to the marsh?" Cappie asked. I was glad she'd spoken up; otherwise I'd be obliged to, and I didn't want to draw Hakoore's wrath.

Hakoore didn't answer immediately. When his rage really caught fire, he didn't snap; he took his time, thought things over, then attacked you in cold blood. "So," he hissed at Cappie, "you think you're exempt from vigil? That it's beneath you?"

"I think it's pointless," she replied, with no apparent fear. "We aren't going to catch any ducks—Steck sabotaged our nets. And I'm sure you don't want us to set out new ones, considering how you insisted we use specially consecrated netting, purified and attuned to our individual essences over three months. Without nets, there's nothing useful we can do in the marsh; if we stay in town, at least we can help cook pies."

Again, Hakoore paused before replying; not the pause of a man thinking about the question, but a pause intended to make you fear the answer. "Vigils," he hissed, "are not for catching ducks. They're for *reflection*. Reflecting how you can best serve the Patriarch: as a man or as a woman. But if you've set your feet on the downward road . . ." He jerked his hand dismissively. "What you do with your life doesn't interest me."

"Good," Cappie answered, just as dismissively. She threw a glance in my direction, and said, "I'm going back to our cabin." She meant the cabin where the two of us and our children had been living for the past year; but I didn't know if she wanted me to go with her or was warning me to stay away. She didn't stick around to clarify the point—she just plucked up the spear at her feet (*my* spear) and strode off into the night.

Leeta smiled weakly at the Elders around her, curtsied to the Spark Lord, and hurried off behind Cappie. I guessed Cappie was due for some tutoring on the niceties of being our cove's priestess.

The crowd on the steps dispersed. Elders slumped toward their homes; Hakoore shuffled off, trying to look fierce while clinging to Vaygon's elbow. Mayor Teggeree wrapped an arm around Lord Rashid and propelled him toward Mayoralty House, with Steck trotting behind. Bonnakkut and the other Warriors went off in the other direction, arguing whether Kaeomi, Stallor and Mintz would get a chance to fire the Beretta.

I stood on the steps, watching them go. Then, with a deep sigh, I started back to the marsh to continue vigil. Cappie might defy the Patriarch's traditions, but I was above cow-headed contrariness. Besides, my violin was still stashed inside that hollow log. I wouldn't relax till I knew it was safe.

Just one problem: now that I wasn't tied up in thoughts of Cappie and the Neut, I couldn't help taking a deeper sniff of the woodsmoke in the air. Was it my imagination, or could I smell baking bread too? Roast pork. Raspberry mash. All the things women would spend the night cooking in preparation for tomorrow.

My stomach wasn't growling, but it would start any second. If I went straight to the marsh without getting food first, how could I possibly concentrate on fostering a spirit of proper sanctity?

I couldn't go to my own home—Cappie was there, and probably Leeta too. They might spend the whole night talking priestess talk: Leeta with her milkweed pods, and Cappie in her man's shirt, perhaps with the top few buttons undone because the night was hot and because with Leeta she didn't have to worry about exposing the occasional flash of bare breasts if she leaned over . . .

Food. I needed food.

So I headed to my foster father's house.

*   *   *

In OldTech times, the house must have been amazing: two stories tall plus basement, with enough space to squeeze half the population of our village inside. It had been rebuilt many times over the last four hundred years, losing much of its upper floor, having walls reinforced or reassembled, getting its living room replaced with a woodshed. A lot of the original construction materials were still at the back of the property, where they'd been dragged after they were pulled off the house. Dirt had accumulated over the mound of junk, but you could still see the occasional roof shingle or metal eaves trough sticking out. I'd dug up plenty myself, no matter how much my foster father had shouted, "Leave those dirty things alone!"

Unlike the other houses in town, this one showed no lamplight in the kitchen. No one was cooking for tomorrow's feast; no one was embroidering the final stitches on Blessing outfits for children. My foster father, Zephram O'Ron, left that to other people . . . partly because he wasn't native to the cove, and partly because he could afford to pay others to do whatever had to be done.

Those two facts went hand-in-hand to tell everything about Zephram's life in our town: he was an outsider, but he was rich. He'd made his money as a merchant in Feliss, selling everything from soap to cinnamon. Sometimes he claimed to be one of the wealthiest men in the province; then he'd turn coy and dismiss himself as "middle of the pack." No one in Tober Cove knew enough about the Southlands to tell one way or the other. All they could say for sure was that he had barrels more gold than anyone local.

Not that he lorded it over people. A lot of Zephram's success in business came from his ability to be likable. He charmed folks without being charming—you know what I mean. Zephram didn't ooze or enthuse; when he talked, there wasn't a flea's whisker of putting on an act. I'd often watched him striking deals with people in town, to buy fish or to hire someone to help with repairs on the house. He had the friendly reasonable air of someone who'd never take advantage of you: the other person always walked away with a smile. I'd tried to imitate him many times, especially when working to make Cappie see things my way . . . but I guess Cappie was more pig-blind and willful than the people Zephram dealt with, because I could never dent her stubbornness when she got into one of her states.

Zephram came to the cove almost twenty years ago, not long after his wife Anne died in the South. "She got sick," was all he would say; and no one ever found out more. Whatever the circumstances of Anne's death, Zephram turned half corpse himself. He sold his business, left Feliss City, and wandered in mumbles until he ended up in Tober Cove.

"Come to see the leaves," he muttered . . . and it's true, our region is famous for its autumn colors, enough to draw a dozen sightseeing boats up the coast each fall. Zephram stayed late, maybe because the falling leaves suited his mood or maybe because he didn't have the energy to think of somewhere else to go. Then winter broke with a surprise blizzard, he got snowed in, and by the time spring budded back, he was alive enough again to invent excuses why he didn't want to leave.

I was his best excuse. He adopted me in the middle of that summer, and then he *couldn't* leave. I figured he might have known my mother and felt he owed her something. Then again, maybe taking on a toddler was his way to make a new connection with life; maybe he wanted to stay in Tober Cove and used the adoption to cement himself into the community. I didn't know why Zephram wanted me . . . and the thought of asking made me balk, because I couldn't imagine any answer it wouldn't embarrass me to hear.

The kitchen door was unlocked. I counted myself lucky; even after all these years, Zephram sometimes reverted to city ways and turned the key before going to bed. He claimed it was just old habit, but I knew there was more to it. When I was young, I'd tell him, "This is Tober Cove. You don't have to worry about burglars." Many nights, he locked the door anyway.

At age fifteen, it occurred to me maybe his wife hadn't really died of sickness. Down south, rich men are targets.

I walked into the larder, found bread and cheese, and cut off hunks of each. Now that I'd moved out, Zephram stocked the sharpest, oldest cheese he could find—he loved giving his teeth a workout, chewing up cheddar that was halfway to becoming landscape. The bread was hard too, with handfuls of cracked barley heaped into the normal flour. I swallowed enough to take the edge off my hunger, then tucked the rest into my pocket until my jaw regained its strength.

Feeling better, I was heading for the door when my ears caught a gurgly sound from the next room. It made me smile. On tiptoe, I walked through the dark kitchen into the side parlor, its air filled with the leather-dust smell of books. The room also had a creeping aroma of something less dignified and more dear: my son Waggett, one and a half years old, with a habit of making that chucklelike gurgle as he loosed himself into his diaper.

Waggett's crib stood close to the far doorway, where Zephram slept in the bedroom beyond. That made me smile too. Since Cappie and I were required to spend the night in the marsh, Zephram had volunteered to babysit his "grandson" . . . and even though my foster father adopted me when I was younger than Waggett, Zephram behaved as if he'd never had charge of an infant before. Where to put the crib? If it went right in the bedroom, maybe Zephram's snoring would keep the poor lamb awake; but if the crib sat too far away, maybe Waggett would cry and cry without his grandfather hearing. I could imagine Zephram moving the crib a hair, running into the bedroom to see how sound carried, then hurrying back to move the crib a freckle in the other direction. He fussed over things like that.

When I'd left Zephram, I wondered if he'd sleep at all during the night. His worry and exhaustion must have worn him out, because I could now hear him snoring peaceably in the next room. There was no point in disturbing him. Since I happened to be here, I'd deal with my son on my own.

Carefully, I lifted Waggett, picked a clean diaper from the stack beside the crib, and moved quietly to the kitchen. After so many months of baby-tending, I didn't need a lamp to work; the movements came automatically as I laid my son on the kitchen table and changed him in the dark. All the while I whispered soft, "Shh, shhs," and, "Be quiet for Mummy." It was only when I hugged him to my chest afterward that I realized I didn't have breasts . . . that like Cappie, I was now a woman dressed up in a man's clothes.

Physically, I was still male: the same body I'd been wearing since the previous summer. But internally . . . my male soul was gone, and my female one was snugly in control.

If you're not a Tober, it's complicated to understand.

The Patriarch taught that all souls have a gender: males have male souls and females female. The exception is a newborn child, possessed of two souls: baby girl and baby boy in one body, often swapping dominance back and forth every few minutes . . . not that it makes much difference at that age.

The first time a child travels to Birds Home, Master Crow and Mistress Gull gently remove one of the child's souls, leaving only the male soul in a boy's body or the female soul in a girl's body. From that time forward, the gods take one soul out and put the other one in, each summer when they change the body's sex. Boy bodies get boy souls; girl's bodies get girl souls. This is how the gods ensure that mortals think and act according to the ordained inclinations of their gender . . .

. . . or so the Patriarch preached in his fatuously uninformed way a hundred and fifty years ago. Since then, a series of Patriarch's Men had quietly admitted it wasn't as simple as that.

In times of great need (so the current wisdom went), the gods might permit your opposite-sex soul to fly from Birds Home to take temporary possession of your body. I've already described how this happened when that woman knifed me: my male soul arrived to help my female soul win the fight. A pity my male soul then stuck around and got in a tizzy about my harmless tumble-fumble with the doctor woman: it was no big deal, certainly not the "perversion" he was forever moaning about. But then, whenever I became a woman, I always felt mystified by the things my brother self thought were important.

Don't get me wrong—it wasn't common for my female soul to take over my male body, or vice versa. This was only the third cross-gender twist in my life. And everyone agreed these flip-overs never happened after Commitment . . . only to younger people who hadn't yet chosen a permanent sex. Still, almost every Tober had experienced a gender swap at least once, no matter what the Patriarch said; and now that I was my woman self, I had no trouble accepting that once again, the Patriarch hadn't had a clue what he was talking about.

(Men and women tend to disagree whether the Patriarch was a sacred prophet ordained by the gods, or a vicious old windbag who should have died from the clap.)

Hakoore had lectured us that temporary gender flips sent by the gods shouldn't be confused with possession by devils. Devils could make a woman think she was a man (and occasionally vice versa); but there was a crucial difference between opening up to your own brother or sister self, versus the troublemaking invasion of a fiend. Our Patriarch's Man summed up the situation this way: the gods are quiet, devils are noisy. If someone acts like the wrong sex to the point of disturbing other people, you know hell must be involved.

Like Cappie dressing up as a man. That was deeply disturbing—I could remember being deeply disturbed.

And yet, as I cuddled my son in the darkness of Zephram's house, I couldn't understand why Cappie's clothes had affected me at all. They were only clothes . . . and it was only Cappie, my oldest and dearest friend, who hadn't been possessed at all—just helping Leeta with the solstice dance.

Generous, dependable Cappie.

I smiled fondly. As a woman, I still loved Cappie—no resentment of her neediness, no suffocation if she wanted to talk about *Us*. In fact, words like "neediness" and "suffocation" felt alien in my mind: cast-off sentiments left behind by someone else. The gritty tension that had grown between Cappie and my male half, the silences, the avoidance, the evasions and lies . . . I could still remember all that, but the memories were like stories I'd heard secondhand, or thoughts I'd read in an OldTech book.

The past year had left its mark on my brain, but not my soul. As a woman, I wasn't mad at Cappie, or afraid of a future together. I loved him.

Her.

No, him. I loved him. In a way, I barely knew *her*.

That's the odd thing about having two souls. It's fuzzier than being two separate people, with no sharp division between boy and girl. My consciousness was one long, uninterrupted line: I was always me, Fullin, a continuous thread stretching back to my earliest days. It was just that some parts of the thread were dyed red, and others dyed blue.

When I was Female-Me, I felt differently; I thought differently; I seldom felt the emotional impact of events that had happened to Male-Me . . . his obsession with snapping turtles, for example. When I was boy of six, I had been dangling my feet off the docks with several other children, when the girl beside me got bitten by a snapper. The turtle took off two of her toes, and the girl screamed, and the blood spilled . . .

Both Male-Me and Female-Me remembered that moment. But when I was male, the memory crackled with immediacy, very vivid, very real. Now that I was female, the memory was like something I'd seen in a dream—still meaningful enough for me to be wary of turtles, but not the overwhelming concern my brother self felt.

I had said all this a year before, to my pretty carpenter Yoskar . . . who wanted to be sure that whatever he was doing, he was doing it with a woman. The best way I found to explain it was this. Suppose twin children are born, a boy and a girl; and suppose that every day, one twin goes out into the world while the other stays home in bed. The first day the girl goes out, the second day the boy goes, and so on, back and forth. At the end of each day, the twin who's been outside tells the twin in bed everything that happened—every new thing learned, every emotion felt, every daydream that happened to sift down under the afternoon sun. In this way, the twins know the same things and have the same experiences to remember . . . but the experiences have different weight. Half your life is real, and half just comes from stories at the end of the day.

Is it any wonder the two children grow up with different outlooks? And of course, there are other differences. In time, the girl will take a shine to boys, just as the boy puffs himself in front of girls. (At least, that's how it works with most girls and boys.) And your boy self has only heard about the principles of hem-stitching while your girl hands have actually done it . . . just as your girl self observes spear practice, but your boy self is the one who wakes with tired muscles.

A single line of memories, but two different experiences.

So, when one of my souls took over from the other, the world quietly shifted. Different things became important. Different things caught my eye. Different interpretations occurred to me for the same set of facts.

Even though I happened to be in my male body—even though I could feel a penis pushing against my pants, still wet from Cypress Creek—I knew with unquestioning acceptance that I was a woman.

I could feel my absent breasts like weightless phantoms.

I could squeeze crotch muscles this body didn't possess.

I even had a sense of humor. Male-Me didn't possess one of those, either.

And it all felt completely natural . . . just as it must have felt natural for Cappie to dress like a man in the swamp, and fight like one too. Now that I was a woman, the Patriarch's words about separate male and female souls struck me as the kind of dogmatic oversimplification you always expect from men.

The priestess had explained it better, in one of those "girls only" sessions that Male-Me never made an effort to remember. "Yes," Leeta had said, "you have two souls, male and female. And they've gone through different upbringings, haven't they? You girls live fully in your female years, but experience your male years at arm's length. Of course your two halves will see things differently—you've had different lives. But what the Patriarch lied about is that a female soul can be *anything*, just as a male soul can. It's not like only one half is capable of cooking, and the other can shoot a bow. You girls can be whole universes, just as your brother selves can be whole universes. You can't help but be different people . . . but you can both be whole. You *know* you can."

"You're going to be whole, Waggett," I whispered to my son. "If Daddy Fullin says the Patriarch will only let you be half a person, you tell him Mommy says that's a load of horse-flop."

My boy didn't answer—if he wasn't completely asleep, he'd drifted three-quarters of the way. Carefully, I carried him back to the crib and tucked him in. As his little fists relaxed open, I kissed him lightly on the cheek, then silently left the house.

The night was quiet as I walked through the hundred paces of forest that separated Zephram's house from the rest of the village. Twice, I caught myself staring at my feet because they weren't the proper distance away. My male body was three fingers shorter than my female, and it took some getting used to.

Still, it was a minor adjustment compared to some of the changes I'd gone through. On Commitment Day when I was thirteen, I went from a prepubescent boy to a fully-blossomed girl, almost a head taller, rounded above and below, and just starting my first period. I stared at more than my feet, let me tell you . . . at least when I wasn't tripping over doorsteps, bumping into furniture, and wondering what the hell the gods had been thinking when they invented menstruation.

The one saving grace was Cappie, who'd gone through his first period a few months before. He sat me down so earnestly and tried to explain . . . but he'd gone all male and shy and mortified, with a stricken expression that made me laugh myself wet and forget about my cramps. . . .

Never mind. You had to be there. And you had to be thirteen.

When I reached the village square, I paused for a moment. Turning right would take me to the path leading into Cypress Marsh . . . and I could remember how Male-Me thought it crucial to resume our vigil for the rest of the night. He'd always had inexplicable priorities. Surely it was more important to patch things up with Cappie, to make sure he—no, *she*—wasn't ratcheting herself into a resentment that would poison our Commitment and the rest of our lives. Cappie had a tendency to brood if you didn't chivvy him out of it fast. The last thing we needed was either of us fuming and sullen when we finally reached Commitment Hour.

Our house lay close to the water, one of four identical cabins set aside for pre-Commitment couples. By the time you reached age nineteen, you were expected to be living with someone, getting a taste of how your later life might go. That gave you one year as master of the house and one year as mistress, so that you'd see both sides before Committing. When you chose your final gender, the gods wanted you well-informed.

Not that a short time playing house could really prepare people for the long haul . . . but the little cabin we were allotted by the Council of Elders had a pressure-cooker quality that helped simulate the intensity of decades living in each other's laps. The cabin was cramped; it was damp; it reeked constantly of fish; and when spring thaw raised the lake level, water sometimes oozed up through the floorboards, puddling in the north corner where the carpenters had skimped on support joists. If a couple could laugh together, and solve problems together, the hardship drew them closer to each other. If not . . . well, that was useful information to have before Committing, wasn't it?

As I approached the cabin, I could see dim light shining through the window's mosquito net: light from our only oil lamp, burning on our only table. Of course, Leeta would still be talking with Cappie—explaining the full duties of priestess while there was still time to back away. As if Cappie really had the temperament for such a job! I loved the man, I truly did, but he was hopeless when it came to interacting with people. Whenever I tried to talk about feelings, his or mine, he'd think I was asking for *advice*! He'd completely miss the point, or squirm uncomfortably, or . . .

I kicked myself for thinking of the male Cappie again. The female version was almost an unknown quantity; I'd only seen her through my male half's eyes, and I knew better than to trust *his* judgment.

Still . . . Cappie as priestess? *I'd* make a better priestess than she would. Wouldn't I?

Would I?

Hmmm.

It would be a good position for me: prestigious, but not onerous. I'd still have ample free time to practice violin and jaunt down-peninsula to earn gold at festivals. I wouldn't be allowed to marry Cappie, but I could still keep him as a lover . . . a live-in lover, and not cooped up in a tiny fish-smelling cabin: the priestess's house was quite spacious. And because I wasn't *married*, I'd still be free for any sweet-smelling Yoskar I might meet when I went south to play.

You didn't expect me to be more of a saint than my male self, did you?

Since I was in my male body, I had to pretend to be Male-Me . . . and as I reached the cabin porch, I stopped to ponder if he would knock on the door or just barge in unannounced. He prided himself on being a gentleman, but only on those rare occasions when it occurred to him there was more than one way to behave. I decided to knock, then tromp inside without waiting to be invited—it seemed like an appropriate combination of surface courtesy and self-centered entitlement. Being such an obvious lout made me queasy, but I didn't want Cappie to think I was anyone more than my unsubtle male self.

I knocked. I tromped. I said, "Hi."

Leeta was rocking in the chair by our fireplace; Cappie sat on the floor a short distance away, knees hugged up to her chest. They had the air of people talking about such important things that they hadn't spoken for several minutes. When they turned to look at me, their expressions were more surprised than annoyed at the interruption.

"Weren't you going back to the marsh?" Cappie asked. Her voice almost whispered; I suppose she was reluctant to speak any louder.

"No point to vigil anymore," I replied. "Like you told Hakoore, we aren't going to catch ducks, not the way Steck ruined our nets. And when I thought of sitting out there doing nothing, versus coming back to talk with you . . ."

Leeta shifted in the rocker. "If you two want to talk . . ."

"No." Cappie put a hand on Leeta's knee so the priestess stayed in the chair. "I doubt if Fullin has talking in mind." With her gaze fixed on me, she closed up the top few buttons of her shirt.

"Oh, *please*," I told her with wounded dignity, "when I say 'talk,' I mean 'talk.' If Steck hadn't interrupted us in the marsh, I would have done it there."

"Do you expect me to believe that? You've avoided things for months—"

"And I don't want to keep avoiding them until it's too late. Look, Cappie, I've been telling myself for weeks that tonight's the night to settle everything. I thought we'd be alone on vigil and we wouldn't have any distractions . . ."

"We're alone every night, Fullin. We have this cabin all to ourselves."

"No we don't—the kids are always here. But tonight Waggett's with my father and Pona's with your family . . . this is our chance."

"Don't worry about me," Leeta said, placing her plump little hand on Cappie's shoulder. "We can talk about being priestess another time."

"But . . ."

"I'm not going to die before you get back," she told Cappie with a reproving smile. "And it's important for you and Fullin to clear the air before tomorrow. You know it is."

"Definitely," I agreed. "We shouldn't be mad at each other tomorrow."

Cappie stared at me, obviously wondering if I was up to some trick. I met her gaze with all the sincerity I could muster, warning myself to be careful—she might wear men's clothes, but this Cappie wasn't the male version I knew so well. I couldn't take anything for granted.

"All right," she sighed. "I'll let you talk."

"Don't just talk," Leeta said, getting to her feet. "You have to listen too—both of you." She took a step toward the door, then turned back to Cappie. "And if you decide in the end that you want to Commit male, do what's right for your life. There are other women in the village who could become priestess."

"Sure," I nodded. "For all we know, *I* might end up Committing female. Then I could be priestess."

I laughed lightly, in the hope they wouldn't think about that too seriously; but both of them gave me a look, as if they were far from sure I was joking.

"Okay," Cappie said. "Talk."

I took a deep breath. She was standing beside the door, having just closed it behind Leeta. I leaned against the cold stone fireplace, directly across the room from her—I had the impression that Male-Me did a lot of leaning against things. Men do.

"Well?" Cappie asked.

"Okay," I told her, "it's just . . . it's been a bit of a bad year for us, hasn't it?"

"That's like saying a tornado is a bit of a bad wind."

"It hasn't been *that* horrible," I protested. "We've stumbled along. Still . . . this is hard on my pride, but when I'm a guy I'm colossally stupid. Self-centered. Obnoxious even. I have no idea why any woman would . . . never mind. Things were better last year, weren't they? When you were the boy and I was the girl?"

"We just hadn't had as much time to get on each other's nerves," Cappie replied. Her voice was sharp with bitterness. "Last year we were still fresh, that's all."

"No it isn't. We felt right together. We loved each other."

"And you don't love me now?"

"Cappie . . ." I wanted to plant my hands on her shoulders and burn my gaze into hers, but we were still far apart, on opposite sides of the cabin. "Listen, because I mean this: I want to throw away this year and go back to the way things used to be. You a man and me a woman. As a woman, I love you deeply. As a man . . . I'm all screwed up."

"Amen to that last." She took a step toward me. "You aren't just saying this to keep me quiet, are you Fullin? Or because you're horny?"

"I'm not horny." I had a feeling Male-Me would have been—aroused by her clothes, and the quiet solitude of the night. But I felt no sexual passion for the Cappie before me . . . at least nothing beyond a certain curiosity of how it would feel to make love inside a male body.

"And I'm not up to any tricks," I went on quickly. "I'm being honest. I love you, Cappie, I really do; but so much crap gets in the way when our sexes are wrong."

"Fullin . . . such strong language!" She gave the ghost of a smile. "I suppose it means you're sincere."

"Don't laugh at me." I pushed myself off the wall and moved toward her. "I'm telling the truth."

"And not just what I want to hear." She slipped behind one of the wooden chairs arranged around our table, so that the chair came between her and me. "You haven't asked yet how *I* feel."

"Don't you feel the same way?"

"About us? Yes and no. Yes, it was better last year; but considering how bad it's got this year, that's not saying much. I just don't know if our sexes had much to do with it, ever. We started out happy; now we aren't. Maybe the novelty of being together just wore off."

"Cappie," I said, "we've been together longer than two years. We've been together all our lives. After my mother died, we nursed together—so your mother constantly reminds me. And we played in the same henyards, hung our coats side by side in school, froze our toes together that night when you were trying to work up the nerve to kiss me . . ."

She rolled her eyes and gave a rueful chuckle. "That was my male half. I've never understood what was going through my head."

"But I *like* your male half," I said. "I like you this way too," I added hurriedly, "but we work better the other way around."

"And what about me being priestess?" she asked. "I can't just drop that—not after making such a fuss in front of the council."

"Leeta said she could get someone else."

"But suppose I *want* to be priestess. If Leeta can't pick me, she'll have to pick one of the older women—someone who's already Committed female. And when I think of the older women, they're all so *conventional* . . . or else completely crazy."

"If you're worried about it," I told her, "*I'll* volunteer to be priestess. Okay? And I'll consult you on everything—we'll make decisions together. If you have changes you want to make, I'll make them. You can be the power behind the throne."

She looked at me suspiciously. "Is that what this is about, Fullin? You've decided you want to be priestess?"

"I've decided I can't live without you," I answered. "It kills me when we can't look each other in the eye, and I want to fix that. If you don't want me to fill in as priestess for you, fine—let one of the older women do it. They aren't all so bad. And at least we won't be as closed off to each other as we've both been the past year."

Cappie's eyes glistened in the lamplight as she searched my face. "Usually I can tell when you're lying," she whispered. "It *has* been rough, hasn't it?"

Slowly I walked around the chair she'd been holding between us. Her hands gripped the wooden back tightly; I laid my own hands gently on hers, then lifted them to kiss her fingertips. She closed her eyes for a moment, as if shutting off everything but the touch of my lips. Then she let out a sigh and pulled reluctantly away.

"You've lied to me a lot, Fullin," she said. "You've hurt me and ignored me. I've almost drowned in loneliness."

"That was this year," I told her. "When I'm a woman, I—"

She put her fingers against my mouth to silence me. "Don't make me mad with excuses. I don't want to be mad. I just . . . you wouldn't lie about something as important as this, would you? No, forget I said that—you've never been deliberately cruel. You can be so *damned* thoughtless, but you've never hurt me intentionally."

"I love you, Cappie," I said. It wasn't a lie—when I thought of the male Cappie, my heart shone. "Do you love me?"

Silence. Then she answered, "I'm so lonely, I can't tell."

Her arms came around my neck and she pulled herself tight to me, as desperate as all the devils in the world.

EIGHT

A Call for the Weasel

I awoke male. Male-Me in Male-me.

The cabin was dark and the sheets beneath me damp with sweat: mine and Cappie's, slick for each other. When I licked my lips, they tasted of her.

Oh, boy—I was in deep, deep donkey dung.

I could remember everything my sister self had done . . . as much as you can ever remember what happens when you make love. It had been a novelty for my female half—she had taken her time. That had been what Cappie wanted too: she whispered that she longed for comfort. Tenderness. No inventive athletics, just melting into each other, touching and being touched.

Ooo, yuck.

My sister self, gurgling lovey-dovey sentiments to another woman . . . what had I been thinking?

And I couldn't quite reconstruct the exact sequence of events. Had Female-Me been aroused before the touching began? It didn't bother me if my male body had responded physically to physical stimulation; but if my female half had been excited purely by *looking* at a female Cappie, before the strokes and caresses . . .

Well, at least our bodies had been male and female. At least we had that. Last summer down-peninsula, when I had been female and the woman doctor had . . . no, I didn't want to remember. That had been a perversion: two physical women. But this time, Cappie and I had been in male and female bodies, and that was all that mattered.

In sex, souls didn't count. Did they?

Cappie lay sleeping beside me. I couldn't see in the dark, but I imagined she had a smile on her face.

Yikes.

I'd made love with Cappie . . . promised to become Mocking Priestess on her behalf . . . formed a pact that I'd become female and she'd become male, even though that sort of arrangement was *strictly* against the Patriarch's Law . . .

And speaking of the Patriarch's Law, I was supposed to be on vigil. Yikes again.

I had to restrain myself from leaping out of the bed. How soon was sunrise? Could I get back to the marsh in time?

With agonizing caution, I pulled away from Cappie's sleeping body, holding my breath so I wouldn't smell the cowbarn sweat and sex that oozed off her skin. She was naked, of course, no longer wearing her father's clothes; plain old Cappie now, except for the short-chopped hair. In the darkness, that haircut made her look disturbing—I didn't like seeing her scalp so easily, or the raw shape of her skull. It was like one of those terror tales the old men told around the campfire: the hero embraces a beautiful woman and when he pulls away, finds that she's turned into a worm-eaten corpse.

No. That wasn't fair. Cappie may have looked scrawny and underdeveloped as she lay uncovered in the darkness, but she was no horrible monster. She was just . . . ordinary.

Didn't my female half realize that?

My life had progressed beyond this unsophisticated girl in my bed. I was famous the whole length of the peninsula. Admired by far more interesting women.

I couldn't let myself get trapped by mediocrity when I was just coming into my own. This was no time to make senseless commitments.

I managed to find my clothes—scattered over the floor and furniture, but thank heaven the cabin was small—and I took everything outside so there was less chance of waking Cappie while I dressed. No one saw me. Only one of the nearby cabins was occupied, and that belonged to Chum and Thorn: a pair of nineteen-year-olds who lived together like crashing thunderheads. One second they'd be screeching over who should empty the chamberpot, and the next they'd be passionately a'moan with rough lovemaking that smacked against their cabin walls and knocked out chips of mortar. Since tomorrow would be their last sex switch before permanent Commitment, I was sure they had battered themselves into raw-chapped stupor hours ago. They would never open their eyes long enough to notice me on my own porch, pulling on my pants and hurrying off into the darkness.

Hurrying off, then hurrying back again. A gentleman doesn't abandon a woman in the middle of the night, without at least leaving a note. Just inside the door, Cappie and I kept a white pine board and a stick of charcoal for leaving each other messages. Holding the charcoal with a feather touch to avoid making noise, I wrote GONE BACK TO VIGIL ... then added, LOVE, FULLIN.

Anything else would have been rude.

The black sky was just beginning to lighten over Mother Lake as I reached the trail to the marsh. Dawn was still a good hour away. I slowed down and tried to force myself to relax, to keep an eye out for snapping turtles, but I didn't have the concentration. My mind kept going back to Cappie.

What had I done?

What had I promised?

What would she think when she found me gone?

This mess was my sister self's fault. If she hadn't showed up, I could have fobbed Cappie off forever. Evaded conversation. Avoided promises.

A gentleman doesn't break his promises—a *smart* gentleman doesn't make any.

Now what was I going to do?

I didn't want to hurt her; that would just cause trouble. Cappie wouldn't hesitate to make an embarrassing scene in public, even on Commitment Day. My only choice was to play along with what my female self had tied me to, at least until we reached Birds Home. Then ... well, if Cappie was going to Commit male, I could go male too, making a relationship impossible.

Or maybe I could Commit Neut, get myself banished, and escape everything.

Not funny, Fullin.

My violin was safe where I left it, inside the log near the duck flats. I took it out of the case, tuned up, and played ... not exercises or any specific song, just playing, soft or loud, sweet or savage, whatever came from second to second. It helped. Music doesn't solve problems, any more than daylight eliminates stars; but while the sun shines the stars are invisible, and while the music sang from my bow, Cappie, Steck, Female-Me, and everyone else who choked up my life vanished into the breakers of sound.

In the sky, stars began to fade. Light seeped up from the eastern horizon, pasty-faced and watery as predawn usually is. (Zephram once observed to me, "Master Day is not a morning person.") In the wan yellow light, flies began to buzz and frogs to chug, while loons still called night songs to each other and fish splashed the surface of open water, on the grab for fluff and insects.

Buzz, chug, hoo-ee-oo, splash.

Buzz, chug, hoo-ee-oo, splash.

In time, I eased the violin off my shoulder and let the marsh sing without me. Or at least make noise. I couldn't tell if the sound was wholesomely relaxing . . . or getting on my nerves.

After minutes of sitting, my stomach rolled with a puma-like growl. I put my instrument back in its case, then pulled out the bread and cheese I had taken from Zephram's. As I worried the rock-old cheddar with my teeth, I considered what to do next. Officially, my vigil would end as soon as the sun cleared the horizon . . . not that I could see the horizon with bulrushes all around me, but if I climbed the dead tree near the duck flats, I'd have a clear view all the way to Mother Lake. I still might not see the sun directly, but I'd easily catch its glare spooning the water to sparkles.

When I reached the flats, they were still jumbled with footprints from Steck's boots, plus the occasional smudge of moccasins from Cappie and me. No sign of ducks. I crossed to the dead tree and tried to waggle it, just to check how securely it was set into the wet ground. As far as I could tell it was rooted like stone, though it had stood bare and sapless since I came to practice violin as a child. Back then, I could only reach the lowest branch if I stood on tiptoe and jumped; now, I scrambled up easily, as high as I wanted to go. That was just high enough to see Mother Lake—you can't trust old bleached wood to hold your weight, even when the tree feels solid. I intended to peek for the sun, then get down again before the branches snapped beneath me.

That was before I saw Hakoore coming in a canoe.

Cypress Creek runs down the very center of the marsh, a meander of clear water among the cattails. If you start at Mother Lake, you can boat up the creek as far as Stickleback Falls, and even then it's an easy portage to Camron Lake and points south. The duck flats don't touch the creek itself, but when the water is high enough you can paddle to the flats if you know the right route through the reedy mat of marsh . . . at least I assume that's true, because the canoe was doing precisely that.

Hakoore wasn't paddling. He sat stiffly in the front while his granddaughter Dorr stroked in the stern. Dorr was twenty-five years old and tyrannized by the old man. I found her intermittently attractive, or at least pretty-ish, but she had no idea how to put herself together for good effect. On hot days, you might see her wearing a sweater; on cold, she might wander barefoot around the town common, hair tumbled shapelessly around her face. If Dorr had been a violinist, she'd be the sort who played with the energy of a devil, but never bothered to tune up first . . . and would always be slashing her way through a scherzo when the audience wanted a ballad.

Dorr wasn't a musician, though—she made quilts and dyed blankets that were eagerly sought by well-to-do buyers down-peninsula. Her designs were striking: sad-eyed trees with blood dribbling down their bark; catfish leaping into bonfires; horses with human faces crushed under stone-weight thunderclouds. I often said to myself that Dorr desperately needed a man . . . but until Hakoore was gone she was chained to the old despot, like a heifer marked with her owner's brand.

By the time I caught sight of the canoe, Dorr had already spotted me in the tree. Our eyes met. Her face was expressionless and her mouth stayed closed—she wouldn't tell Hakoore I was there. (The more he treated her like a dumb animal, the more she behaved that way . . . at least when he was around.) I had hopes of scurrying back to the ground without being seen, but Hakoore must have possessed enough dregs of eyesight to notice me backlit against the brightening sky.

"Who's in that tree?" he hissed.

Dorr didn't answer his question. I forced myself to call down, "Me. Fullin."

"What are you doing?"

"Checking whether it's dawn yet."

"Is it?"

"Yes." Truth was, I couldn't make out any sunlight shining on Mother Lake, but I decided to feather the issue. If the sun hadn't risen, I was breaking vigil again by communicating with people; therefore, the sun had risen.

"Come down," said Hakoore. "It's time we talked."

I didn't like the sound of that—Hakoore's talks could shrivel a man's testicles at fifty paces. On the other hand, I had no choice. Moving slowly, trying to look the soul of cautious prudence when I was actually just delaying the confrontation, I descended from one branch to the next until my feet touched solid mud. By that time, Dorr had run the nose of the canoe onto the flats and helped her grandfather get out.

"So, boy," Hakoore said, hobbling toward me, "up a tree, were you? To see if it was dawn."

"Yes."

"Woman!" he snapped at Dorr. "Go do something productive. Don't you use these plants for dyes? Pick some. Don't hurry back."

Dorr said nothing. She brushed noiselessly through the nearest stand of rushes and disappeared. Hakoore peered whitely after her for a time, then turned back to me. "I climbed a tree on my vigil too . . . to see if it was dawn."

Some men would say that with a companionable smile of nostalgia. Hakoore didn't, but his hissing voice *did* seem less venomous than usual. That worried me—the old snake was setting me up for something.

After a moment he said, "Take me to the boat." He held out his bony hand, and reluctantly I let him take my arm, the way he always walked with Dorr. I couldn't remember him touching me before—he preferred to commandeer the help of important people like the mayor, or ignorable ones like Dorr. Then again, we were in the middle of a marsh. If he needed help walking, he didn't have a lot of choices.

His grip on my arm was tight and he leaned hard against me . . . not that he weighed enough to be a burden. Hakoore might be close to the same age as my foster father, but he looked several decades older: shriveled, gaunt and hunched. He had an old man's smell to him, a mix of ancient sweat and urine, rising from his clothes like a sad memory. As we walked toward the canoe, I could hear him clack his molars together every few steps, as if he were still chewing the ghost of some long-ago breakfast.

"So," he said as we walked, "your Cappie intends to be priestess."

"Not *my* Cappie," I answered quickly. "I don't control her."

"True." Hakoore nudged me knowingly with his elbow. "Cappie is just a girl you live with, right, boy? She's the only female your age, so it's natural you two would . . . be boy and girl together. But beyond that?" He made a rasping sound in his throat. "I don't suppose you have *feelings* for her."

The old snake said "feelings" with so much intensity, I clenched my jaw. Did he want me to agree with him, that she was just some meaningless convenience? Even if I'd outgrown Cappie, a gentleman doesn't talk about a lady as if she's something he wants to scrape off his moccasin. I couldn't tell Hakoore Cappie meant nothing to me, whether or not it was true. But the Patriarch's Man was waiting for me to speak—to deny her, to say something disloyal.

"There's feelings and there's feelings," I answered carefully. "Depends what feelings you mean."

Hakoore actually smiled—as much as a frown-lined face like his could ever support an amiable expression. He reached out with his free hand and patted my wrist almost fondly.

"You're a weasel, aren't you, boy?"

His thumb suddenly dug into my flesh, gouging the soft web between my thumb and index finger. There's a nerve there that hurts when it gets squeezed. Hakoore knew all about that nerve.

"You're a weasel, aren't you?" he said again.

"What do you mean by—"

The old man squeezed and the pain was enough to clot my voice silent. "I mean," Hakoore said, "that you'd kill your own mother under the right circumstances." He released the pressure and gave a fierce grin. His teeth were yellow and jagged. "You're a weasel, and one way or another, you see the rest of the world as your meat."

I didn't answer. He was wrong, but it seemed politic to hold my tongue.

Hakoore studied me for a moment with his milky eyes, then gave a soft snort of amusement. "Look in the boat, boy."

We had reached the edge of the flats where the canoe's nose was pulled up onto the mud. Snug in the middle of the boat, tucked safely under the central thwart, lay the battered false-gold box containing the Patriarch's Hand.

What now? I thought. Did the old snake want me to take another oath?

Hakoore released his grip on my arm. "Get it," he said, pushing me toward the canoe. "Take it out."

Mistrustfully, I reached down and wrapped my fingers around the brass handle on the nearest end of the box. One pull told me the container was heavier than I expected; it took several good heaves for me to drag it out from under the thwart and lift it into the air.

"Wait," Hakoore said. He leaned into the boat and pulled out a blanket that lay under the front seat—probably one of Dorr's own creations, but the blanket was too dirty for me to be certain. I noticed Hakoore didn't wobble as he bent over; our Patriarch's Man was only infirm when it suited his purpose. With a few dusty shakes, he opened up the blanket and let it settle onto the mud. "Set the box on that," he told me. "Be careful."

I gave him an aggrieved look. Did he think I intended to take risks with the cove's greatest treasure? But I held my tongue. Squatting, I laid the heavy chest on the blanket. "There," I said. "Now what is this—"

"Quiet!" he interrupted. "You're going to learn something." He lowered himself to his knees with the slow inevitability of an old dog taking its place by the fire. For a moment he just knelt there, stroking the tarnished gold surface with his fingers. Then he lifted the lid and exposed the mummified hand to the brightening light of dawn. It seemed smaller than it had looked last night, the skin rough and puckered. "Do you know what that is?" Hakoore asked.

"The Patriarch's Hand," I answered, wondering if this was a trick question.

"And I suppose you think it was cut off the Patriarch himself."

"It wasn't?"

He gave me the sort of look he'd been giving to lunkhead boys for forty years. "Who'd have the nerve to cut off the Patriarch's hand? I wouldn't. Even after he'd died, no one in the cove would dare."

"I always assumed the Patriarch left instructions for his successor to—"

Hakoore waved me to silence. "Why would a man want to be mutilated after death? Even the Patriarch wasn't that crazy."

I gaped at him. No one ever called the Patriarch crazy . . . except for all the women in the village, and they didn't count.

"The hand belonged to the Patriarch," Hakoore told me, "but it wasn't cut off his own wrist. It was just his property."

The old snake spoke dismissively as if the truth was self-evident; but all my life, I'd been told the hand was an actual piece of the Patriarch. When people swore oaths on it—when it was used at baby blessings and funerals—the Elders always spoke of it as the Patriarch's own flesh. If it was just one of the Patriarch's *possessions* . . . if he had hacked it off some criminal . . . or a heretic . . . or a Neut . . .

Hakoore actually chuckled at the expression on my face—his version of a chuckle at any rate, a toneless *hisk-hisk* sound. "Touch the hand, boy," he said. "I'll show you something interesting."

Reluctantly I placed my right fingertips on the hand's papery skin. Hakoore reached down too, pressing hard against a small protrusion on the box's metal side. The spot he touched looked like nothing more than a slight dent. I had no idea what he might be up to . . . until I heard the box give a soft click.

With a shudder, the hand squirmed under my fingers. Before I could flinch back, the hand had locked onto mine with an arm wrestler's grip.

I jumped back, shaking my hand frantically the way you do to shake off a speck of burning debris spat up by a campfire. The hand came with me, right out of its box, and clung like hot tar as I hopped around the flats trying to dislodge it.

"Hah, boy," Hakoore laughed, "if you could see the expression on your face!" *Hisk-hisk*: the sound of his laugh. *Hisk-hisk*. "If all those pretty girls who swoon at your fiddle-playing could see what a duck turd you look like now . . ." He stopped, still laughing, *hisk-hisk-hisk*. The sound put my teeth on edge, like a blacksmith filing iron.

"What's going on?" I demanded. "Is this some kind of magic?"

"Magic!" The word was a sudden angry bark. "What kind of superstitious fool are you, boy? The hand and the box are just machines, special machines. You think a real hand could last over a century without rotting to dust? Use your sense! And don't ask me to explain how it works: I don't know. But it's not sorcery or deviltry, just wires and things."

I couldn't imagine how wires and things could make a hand that moved as fast as a striking rattlesnake. Still, the mayor had an OldTech clock where a goldfinch came out and chirped every hour; if our ancestors could make mechanical birds, a mechanical hand wasn't out of the question.

"Well, you certainly gave me a start," I told Hakoore, "and I'm glad you had a good laugh. Now can you make the hand let go? It's holding a little tight."

"You think that's tight?" Hakoore's milky eyes glittered in the light of the dawning sun. "It can squeeze much harder. It can squeeze like iron tongs."

"I'm sure," I agreed. "But you've had your joke and I'm suitably impressed. Maybe it's time we both went home for breakfast."

"A joke," he said, still smiling. "You think the Patriarch's hand is a joke?"

"No, no," I corrected myself quickly, "the hand isn't a joke, it's a sacred artifact, but . . ."

I gasped. The hand had suddenly tightened its grip, wringing me hard around the knuckles—the way Bonnakkut had sometimes grabbed my hand and mashed my fingers together, back when he bullied me in the schoolyard.

"You don't believe it's a sacred artifact," Hakoore hissed softly. "Now that you know it's mechanical, you think it's just another piece of OldTech garbage."

"It's sacred, it's special, I believe that!"

The hand squeezed again. I felt one of my knuckles give under the pressure with an audible click. It wasn't broken—not yet. Just slipped slightly out of alignment.

"Stop doing that!" I shouted at the old snake.

"I'm not doing anything," he replied, all innocence. "The hand has a mind of its own. My old master explained it this way: when people lie, they sweat. Not normal summer sweat, but damp-palm-nervous *liar's* sweat. And the Patriarch's hand can taste that sweat in your palm, boy. It doesn't like the taste. Lies turn its stomach."

It's a hand! I wanted to say. *It doesn't have a stomach.* But I kept myself under control and told him, "I don't believe the OldTechs could make something like this. In all the OldTech books I've read, there's no mention of anything close."

Hakoore gave me a coy look. "Maybe not. Maybe the hand is older than the Patriarch, dating back to the founding of the cove." He grinned at me with those jagged yellow teeth. "The founders of Tober Cove were something special, boy—far beyond the OldTechs. There are secrets I could tell you, passed down from one Patriarch's Man to the next; but I can't share those secrets with you until . . ."

He let the last word hang pointedly in the air. I didn't want to give him the satisfaction of asking what he meant, but the hand was still pulping my knuckles. Even worse, there might be other hidden buttons Hakoore could press in the box, buttons that would make the hand clinch up on me even if I wasn't lying.

"Until what?" I asked through gritted teeth.

"Until you agree to be my disciple and become the next Patriarch's Man."

"Me?" My voice was almost a squeak—I blame that on the pain in my half-crushed hand. "Your *disciple*? Who says I want to be your disciple?"

"Who says I care what you want?" Hakoore rasped back, mimicking my tone. "I'm not choosing you for your opinions, boy."

"But why choose me at all?"

"Since Leeta told me she was making Cappie her apprentice, I've been thinking about a successor too. It appeals to me, easing back the same time Leeta does. Especially after seeing Cappie last night, trying to play priestess while dressed like a man. The girl's got fire; she'll hit the cove like a lightning strike. And she's smart—when women have problems, Cappie will solve them. Won't be long before men turn to her too . . . not for everything, but for important things. Show me the man who wouldn't rather talk to Cappie than to me. Present company excluded, of course."

He actually gave me a grin.

"So it got me wondering," he went on, "what man in the cove can handle Cappie and come out on top?" He poked a bony finger into my chest. "Guess whose name came to mind."

"But I don't want to be *anyone's* disciple . . ."

"Shut up!" he snapped, jabbing his finger into the pain-hub of nerves at my sternum. "I don't care about a weasely boy's personal preferences. All I care is whether you're suitable for the job."

"I'm not. The only thing I'm fit for is playing violin . . ."

"You won't be fit for that if you don't shut up! The hand won't let go till I want it to; you understand that, boy? And how are you going to play violin with crushed fingers?''

I choked back the retort that came close to spilling out of my mouth: *It's holding my right hand, you old fool; I play violin with my left.* But giving that away might be a tactical error. Besides, how could I hold the bow if my right hand got ground to powder? How could I pluck pizzicato? Without two good hands, I'd be just some kid who'd once had delusions of grandeur—condemned to work the farms or perch boats for the rest of my life, as if I'd never dreamed of more.

"All right," I muttered. "What do you want?"

"To ask some questions. To see whether you appreciate the cove's need for a Patriarch's Man."

"And if I lie, the hand will hurt me."

Hakoore nodded. "The Patriarch found it useful for getting at the truth."

"I'll bet."

"Don't go insolent on me, boy! I can always order the hand to grab a different part of your anatomy. Something you *really* don't want mangled."

I glared at him for a moment, then gave a defiant flick of my head. "Ask your questions," I told him. "See for yourself that I'm wrong for the position."

The Patriarch's Man just smiled, an ancient yellow smile.

"First question," Hakoore said. "Do you believe in the gods?"

"Yes."

"All the gods? Even Mistress Want and Master Disease?"

"Yes." After last night, I wondered if I believed in Master Disease too much, but I didn't say so aloud.

"Do you pray to the gods?"

"Sometimes."

He gave me a withering look. I expected him to ask how often was sometimes, but he must have presumed the worst. Instead he asked, "Is the cove important to you, boy?"

"Absolutely."

"And how far would you go in order to keep the cove safe?"

I hesitated. "That's hard to say," I finally answered. "It depends on the circumstances."

"Of *course*, it depends on the circumstances, you idiot!" Hakoore roared. "*Everything* depends on the circumstances." He gave me a steely glare. "Stop being such a weasel."

Easy for you, I thought. *You aren't the one whose fingers get mulched if you answer wrong.* Out loud, I told him, "Describe some threat to the cove and I'll tell you what I'd do."

"Don't give me orders, boy!" He closed his eyes for a moment, then opened them again. "Last year," Hakoore said, "a Feliss merchant came here, supposedly to see the leaves, but what he really wanted was to buy his way into the village. He had a lot of money, a pregnant wife ... and when the baby came, he wanted it brought up like a Tober, alternating sexes. Thought that would be healthy for the child."

"He was right," I answered.

"Of course he was," Hakoore agreed. "And he was willing to pay for it—donations to the Council of Elders, to the school, to me, to Leeta—not bribes, he insisted, but gifts to help the people."

"I hope the Elders spat in his face."

"You don't know the Elders," Hakoore answered. "They have a long list of projects they'd love to start if only they had the money ... and some of the projects are even sensible. Like paying to train a replacement for Doctor Gorallin; she's going to retire in ten or fifteen years, and it'll take that long to put one of our own through medical school. It'll take a lot of gold too. If the council took the merchant's money, they could guarantee the cove would have competent doctoring for the next forty years. That's a hard thing to turn down."

"I didn't think of that," I admitted. "But the council still must have said no in the end. We didn't have an outsider family move in."

"The council didn't reject the merchant," Hakoore told me. "I did. Started shouting threats and scared the nipples off every man there." He allowed himself the ghost of a smile. "One of the fun parts of my job."

"You think it's fun to make it harder for Tober Cove to afford a doctor?"

"No," he sighed. "*That's* one of the ugly parts of my job."

"So why did you do it?"

"Because if one merchant buys his way in, another will try too. Only the next one will just want a summer home—come up for solstice, let Master Crow and Mistress Gull *process* the kids, then go back to Feliss. A lot of Tobers would be outraged at such a proposal, but others would just say, 'Get a good price.' That way we could buy more books for the school ... or maybe some muskets for the Warriors Society so they can match the firepower of any gun-toting criminals who come up-peninsula."

"One gun is too many," I muttered.

"And one merchant is too many too," Hakoore replied. "Not that I have anything against merchants in themselves ..."

"No," I said, "you've always been so welcoming to my father."

The old snake glared at me. "You think I was hard on Zephram? There are times I still think I should have booted him out. With the money he's brought here, the cove has expanded its perch fleet, bought more cattle, improved the sawmill . . ."

I rolled my eyes. "How awful!"

Hakoore sighed. "I know they aren't bad in themselves, Fullin, but they're distractions. Tobers are starting to think prosperity is their due. That'll kill this town, it really will. Money is only smart about making more money; it's sheep-stupid about everything else. The cove is already sunk so deeply in materialism—"

"Come on," I interrupted, "why is it greedy to want your kids to have a doctor when they grow up?"

"Materialism isn't the same as greed," Hakoore snapped. "Materialism is reducing everything to an equation of tangible profit and loss. It's saying that a family of outsiders will cost this much for housing and this much for schooling and this much for ongoing annoyance factor, so if we get twice that many crowns back in payment, we should take the deal. Materialism is an uncomprehending blindness to anything that isn't right in front of your nose—believing that material effects are the only things that exist, and there's nothing else you'd ever think to put on the scales. Hell, boy, materialism is the belief in scales at all: nothing is absolutely right or absolutely wrong, but just something to be weighed against everything else."

"Okay, right," I told him, trying to calm his tirade, "I'll be sure not to let myself fall into materialistic . . . yoww!"

The Patriarch's hand had tightened again. When I looked down, my fingers had turned birch-white.

"Pity about your hand," Hakoore said without sympathy. "Still it was nice you tried to humor me. Respect for your elders and all that."

My voice came out in a strained whisper. "Can we skip the sermons from here on out? Please—just ask your questions and I'll answer them."

"That's what I like to see," Hakoore smiled. "Abject submission. And as for questions . . . if you had been Patriarch's Man, would you have said no to that rich merchant?"

"I don't know," I whispered.

"Do you need more information?" Hakoore asked helpfully. "Do you want to know exactly how much money he offered us?"

"That doesn't matter."

The old snake nodded. "At least you understand that much. So why can't you make a decision?"

"Because . . . because . . ." I closed my eyes and tried to find the most sincere, honest part of my heart. It wasn't all that difficult once I started searching. "Because," I said, opening my eyes, "because I have a son. Of course, I don't want Southerners barging in here, but I want Waggett to have a good doctor too. If it ever came to the point where we had to take Southern money or else our children got sick . . ."

Hakoore's expression wilted. "That's just it, isn't it, boy? That's where the knife cuts." His milky eyes stared at me for a moment, then turned away.

"A hundred and fifty years ago," he said, "the Patriarch rode on the backs of our people with spurs of iron. When babies grew famished, he blamed outsiders . . . Neuts . . . scientists. And he started a reign of terror that kept Southerners scared for a whole century after he died. But the fear seeped away eventually. In my lifetime, I've seen the Southerners start to get interested in us again. More tourists . . . more traders . . . more of their godless materialism rubbing off on us. Still, if I tried to choke the town the way the Patriarch did—if I said no trading with the South or I'd pronounce the Great Curse—who could I blame when children grew sick with starvation? People think I'm harsh, but I'm not the unbending man our Patriarch was. Once upon a time, I was a mother, just like you, boy. I nursed my little girl . . ."

He closed his eyes and lifted his hands as if holding an infant to his chest. I looked away. I don't know if I was embarrassed or just giving him his privacy.

After a while, he whispered, "Enough." He reached into the hand's tarnished metal box and pressed at another dent. Click. The grip around my knuckles suddenly went limp; the Patriarch's Hand slumped as lifeless as an ugly glove.

I'd have let it fall onto the mud, but I couldn't get my fingers to uncurl.

"Put the hand back in the box," Hakoore said quietly.

"You've run out of questions?"

"I was going to ask you everything my predecessor asked me," he replied, "but you'd just say you didn't know the answers and I'd say I couldn't blame you. Put the hand back where it belongs."

Carefully, I lowered my arm toward the box. Because my fingers had no feeling left in them, I had to use my other hand to pry my grip open. The mechanical hand-thing fell off me into the box and rocked a bit before lying still: flat on its back, fingers in the air . . . like a dead fly, legs up on your windowsill.

"So I suppose I failed your test," I said as I straightened up.

"Idiot boy," Hakoore rasped. "It wasn't a test you could fail. I told you, I don't care about your opinions. I've chosen you as my disciple, and that's that."

I massaged my fingers to try to get them working again. "Then why hurt me if you never cared about my answers?"

He gave me a look. "Had to get your attention, didn't I? Had to start you thinking. Had to let you know that a Patriarch's Man must be ready to be a ruthless bastard for the good of the cove."

"I knew that already," I growled.

He smiled . . . then suddenly slapped me flat across the face. It wasn't hard and it wasn't fast, but it stung like fire. "You haven't seen anything yet," he hissed. "After you've Committed, you and I will get together with the Patriarch's Hand day after day after day. I'll get the warriors to hold you down if need be; Bonnakkut would like that. My own master had to hold me down a few times before I accepted my fate. You'll accept your fate too. Patriarch's Man."

"I'll Commit female," I snapped. "You can't make me Patriarch's Man if I'm a woman."

"If you do that, boy, I'll make your life hell. You know I can."

"You can't. The most sacred tenet of Tober law is that we can each choose male or female, and *no one* can punish us for the choice."

"Just wait and see," Hakoore snarled. "When I say you're going to be my disciple, boy, it's not a request. It's a calling from the Patriarch himself. A vocation. A *command*. Whatever you may have wanted to do with your life doesn't interest me. You are what the Patriarch says you are."

With a last ferocious glare at me, he raised two fingers to his lips and blew a piercing whistle. "Dorr! We're leaving."

His granddaughter slid through the rushes immediately. In one hand she held a clump of bedraggled greenery; in the other was a knife nearly as long as Steck's machete. I suspect she had simply cut off the first bunch of reeds she'd seen, then hidden in the bulrushes to eavesdrop. She must have heard everything, Hakoore's sermon and his threats . . . but her face was devoid of expression. Without looking in my direction, Dorr gave Hakoore her arm and helped him clamber into the canoe.

"Your vigil is over," the old man snapped as he settled in the prow. "Go home. And even if the gods didn't send you a duck, you know what sex they want you to Commit."

Dorr lowered her eyes. She must have felt ashamed for her grandfather, trying to influence my free Commitment choice. With a stab of her paddle, she pushed the canoe off the mud and stroked quickly out of sight.

NINE

A Hush for Mistress Snow

So first I swore loud enough to panic every frog, duck and muskrat in the marsh. The curses were uncreatively repetitive, but heartfelt.

Then I massaged my fingers for several minutes until they could move again. They made soft cracking sounds when I flexed them, and I couldn't close them all the way to a fist, but it didn't feel like there was permanent damage.

I checked that I could still hold the violin bow. I could.

I checked that I could still hold a ferocious grudge against Hakoore. I was on top of that too.

Then I started the walk back home.

"Should I Commit male or female?" I shouted at a red-winged blackbird. It flew off without answering. Sometimes the gods visit Earth in the form of birds, but this one just seemed to be a dumb animal.

"Male or female?" I called to a garter snake trying to hide from me in long grass. The snake didn't budge a scale.

"Male or female?" I asked a squirrel on an upper branch of an elm. At least the squirrel made eye contact with me. I took this as an encouraging sign. "You see, it's Commitment Day morning," I explained, "and I should have made up my mind by now."

The squirrel decided my problems were too big for its brain . . . not surprising since a squirrel's brain is about the size of a ladybug. With a sudden leap, the squirrel scrabbled up the elm tree and out of sight.

"Thanks a lot!" I called after it. "Consider yourself a fur scarf if I ever catch you!"

The squirrel didn't seem impressed. A fine Patriarch's Man I'd make if I couldn't even intimidate a tree-rat.

Not that I wanted to be Patriarch's Man.

Although it might be amusing to get Bonnakkut alone with the mechanical hand for five minutes. Find out if his talk about Cappie was all hot air.

No. Not the Patriarch's Man. Not the old snake's *disciple*.

And if I Committed female, Hakoore couldn't claim me. His threat to make my life hell if I became a woman gave me chills, but at least I wouldn't have to spend more sessions with him and the hand. Unfortunately, Committing female meant facing all the promises my sister self made to Cappie . . . including that promise to become the next Mocking Priestess.

Male or female: Patriarch's Man or Mocking Priestess.

The gods were conspiring to give me a future in theology.

When I reached town the streets lay empty, though the sun hung well above the horizon. What other evidence could you want that Commitment Day was a holiday? Cows needed milking and chickens clucked for feed, but other chores would wait till tomorrow. The perch boats wouldn't go out. The blacksmith's forge would stay cold. Water ran down the races at our sawmill and grist mill, but the wheels were locked, frozen for the day.

Even the women, cooking late into the night for the afternoon's feast, would take it easy for an hour now; their preparations were mostly over, and their men were home to watch the children. Fathers were eager to tend the children on Commitment Day—one last lump-in-the-throat chance to see the boys and girls before they became girls and boys.

Thinking about that made me walk faster toward Zephram's house. Waggett would take his first trip to Birds Home today. When he came back—when *she* came back—how long would it take her to notice how things had changed in her diapers? Over the years, I'd laughed at parents lurking near their children so they'd be present for the moment of discovery . . . but I fully intended to do the same with Waggett, to catch that look of surprise and curiosity on her face when she saw she'd been transformed.

Outsiders sometimes worried children would be traumatized by the change: former boys wailing that they'd lost something, former girls shocked by the sudden dangly addition. Not so. The reaction was always fascination and delight . . . or rather, fascination followed by delight as inquisitive fingers discovered interesting sensations when the new architecture was poked and prodded.

Outsiders worried about that too: parents smiling fondly as they watched their children play with themselves. Frankly, outsiders worried too much.

I could smell bacon frying even before I opened Zephram's kitchen door. I could hear it too: not a hot sizzle, but the soft whish of summer rain falling through birch trees. Zephram stood at the stove making dramatic gestures with his spatula, all to impress Waggett who sat giggling at the table. The boy's expression didn't change when he saw me—no cry of "Da-da!" even though he'd spent the night without me. Oh, well. I'd left after Waggett was asleep, and had changed him during the night, so he probably didn't realize I'd been gone.

That's what I told myself anyway.

"So the great vigil's over," Zephram croaked cheerfully. He always croaked these days until he had his first cup of dandelion tea. It was his only sign of age—over sixty and he still had all his hair, with no gray to mar the curly dark brown. Perhaps he'd grown a little roun-der, perhaps he walked a little slower . . . but to me, that wasn't aging, that was just becoming even more Zephram-like than he'd been before.

"How did it go in the marsh?" he asked.

"More interesting than I expected." I laid my violin on the sideboard and gave my knuckles a discreet rub. "How were things with you two?"

"Waggett went the whole night without changing," Zephram answered proudly. "The boy has a bladder of steel."

I ruffled Waggett's hair affectionately. Finally, he deigned to smile at me and try to grab my hands. "Bah-kah!" he said . . . which may have been his version of *bladder*, *daddy*, or *bacon*. For that matter, it may have been his version of *Let's play a violin duet*—Waggett invented his own words and the onus was on grownups to figure them out. I picked him up, kissed him on the forehead . . . then remembered that the last time I'd played with my son, Female-Me had sidled in to take over my body. Women love playing with babies, and who can blame them? But I didn't want to do anything that might encourage her to come back. My sister self had caused enough trouble already.

Reluctantly I eased Waggett back into his chair. To turn my thoughts a different direction, I asked Zephram, "You ever know someone in the cove named Steck?"

His back was to me. I saw it go rigid.

"Steck?" he croaked. "Where'd you hear that name?" He didn't turn around . . . as if the bacon would take advantage of his inattention and jump out of the pan.

"Leeta," I replied, picking the first person who came into my head.

Given my oath, I couldn't tell Zephram the truth. "Leeta roped me in for a solstice ceremony last night. She mentioned that she once had an apprentice named Steck."

"I thought you weren't supposed to talk to anyone on vigil."

"The Mocking Priestess stands outside the rules."

"How do I get her job?" He poked the bacon sharply with his spatula.

"So you *did* know a Steck?"

He sighed . . . the way people sigh when they're trying to decide whether to admit to something they'd rather keep hidden. "Yes," he finally said, "I knew Steck."

"Steck who Committed as Neut?" I asked.

"Leeta *was* chatty, wasn't she?"

I waited.

"Steck was here the first year I was," Zephram said at last. "Fall, winter, and spring."

"And that summer, Steck went Neut."

"She did."

"So Steck was a girl that last year?"

"I wouldn't use the world 'girl,' " he replied distantly. "I know the cove considers you a boy or girl until you Commit permanently. But Steck was twenty; to me, she was a woman."

"Oh." By which I meant *Uh-oh.*

That was all either of us said for a while. The bacon continued to hiss like summer rain.

"I blame myself," Zephram said.

Breakfast was on the table now, the slabs of bacon beautifully browned. My foster father never burned food, no matter how much weighed on his mind.

"What do you blame yourself for?" I asked.

"Steck turning . . ." He stopped, as if he couldn't say the word. Suddenly, he blurted, "You call them Neuts, but they aren't neuter. Neuter means sexless, and they're perfectly hermaphroditic. They can even have children: father them or mother them, both ways work."

"How do you know about Neuts?"

"Steck wasn't the first of her kind—you know that. I met another down in Feliss City, almost forty years ago. A manwoman named Qwan. Qwan missed Tober Cove a little, but still thought getting exiled was the best thing that ever happened to her. Or him."

"*It,*" I said pointedly.

"Qwan wasn't an It. Qwan was a contented father of three, and just as good a mother. And don't make faces like you're going to be sick,'' Zephram snapped. "Half the people in this village have been both mothers and fathers.''

"Not at the same time.''

"Neither was Qwan: married to a woman for ten years, widowed, then married to a man. Both marriages were happy, believe me.''

"And you told that to Steck?''

Zephram sighed. "Yes. I told that to Steck.''

"You *are* to blame.''

"So I said.'' He poked at his bacon with a fork . . . probably just to shift his attention to something that wasn't accusing him. "I told Steck about the bad parts too. Qwan had two happy marriages, but she sometimes ran into trouble walking down the street. Boys shouted insults . . . mothers pulled their children out of the way . . . there were a few close calls with drunks . . . I told Steck about those things too, but she must have thought it would be different for her. And Steck could never resist a melodramatic gesture. She was the sort of person who had crazy impulses, thought about them a long time, then surrendered to them anyway.''

Zephram's tone of voice suggested he wasn't just thinking of Steck's decision to Commit Neut. "What kind of impulses?'' I asked.

"Well . . . me.'' He kept his eyes on the bacon. "She was a stunning twenty-year-old beauty, while I was a middle-aged outsider, half-dead with grief. What could she possibly see in such a shattered wreck of a man? Most folks in the cove thought it was my money. I thought so too for a while—it was a motive I could understand. Then I wondered if she just wanted to shock people . . . or if she looked on me as a charity case, with herself as Sister of Pity, bringing me back to life with fleshly mercy. But I've had twenty years to think about Steck, and I've rejected all the easy answers. She met a withdrawn, far-from-enticing stranger and the idea just popped into her mind: 'Wouldn't he be unlikely!' I imagine she wrestled with the notion for weeks. In time, she succumbed to the idea . . . and I succumbed to her.''

I could barely hold my stomach down. My foster father and a Neut? But of course, Steck hadn't been Neut back then: just a normal girl, a good-looking one if Zephram could be believed. Then again, by the time you're sixty, every woman you've slept with must turn beautiful in memory. Beautiful, or else hideous; when you're sixty, why waste your memories on anyone in between?

"So you and Steck were . . .'' I let my voice trail off rather than say a word that would make me cringe.

"Lovers?'' Zephram finished for me. "Depends on your definition. I was a needer rather than a lover. I needed someone in the nights, and I needed someone in the days too. Steck saved me from smothering under grief. As for what was in it for her—I don't know if she loved me or needed me, but some impulse made her *claim* me." He suddenly picked up his knife and briskly chopped his bacon into pieces. "Let me tell you about meeting Steck," he said.

And he did.

The Silence of Mistress Snow settles over the village with the first snowfall every winter. By tradition, no one speaks a word from the first sight or touch of a snowflake until dawn the next day. This isn't the Patriarch's Law—Leeta thinks it goes way back to monkey times, when the coming of snow stopped our ancestors jabbering in the trees and reduced them to watching the world coat up with white. There's something about the quiet of snow, especially when it comes after sunset and descends like a million ghosts slipping from the skirts of Mistress Night: you *have* to hold your breath. You stand silent in the open doorway, with no thought of how hard winter will be, no worry whether you've put up enough preserves or stored enough hay for the cattle. What's done is done; you're ready or you're not, and either way, the snow is too beautiful to care.

So Tober Cove falls silent when the snow arrives, as mute as an initiate in prayer. Even the children understand. Parents hug them to show it's all right, but keep a finger to their lips until they get the idea. Chores get set aside to let the hush settle in deeper; many people sit on their front steps or in their windows, with no lamps cheapening the blackness.

Then, around midnight, the Council Hall bell rings once: the Cold Chime, rung by Mistress Snow herself. Sure, it might be the mayor who pulls the bell-rope, but it's Mistress Snow who carries the sound through the village, her fingers so fuzzed with frost that they muffle the tone. The chime signals people in town to make their Visits . . . Visits which are promises, sealed by Mistress Snow, that you'll help another household through the winter.

A Visit is simple. You get a small piece of burnable wood and carry it to someone else's home. Every front door is open, if only by a crack. You walk in without a word, add your stick to the fire, then go, closing the door tight behind you. The closed door shows that this house has been placed under your protection—others who might come by should Visit elsewhere, looking for a door that's still open to the wind. One by one, the doors are closed; and so the people of Tober Cove silently promise that no one will face the winter alone.

You don't break promises made to Mistress Snow.

Zephram had lived in our town almost a month by the time snow came. He couldn't say why he hadn't left while there was still time before winter. "I'm bad with explanations," he told me. "Now and then I believe I understand why things happen . . . but then I always think better of it."

People had seen the snow coming long before it arrived: a bundle of bleak clouds advancing across Mother Lake from the northwest. The clouds had the feathery gray look of mourning doves, and they closed off the afternoon as they drew in. Every perch boat came back to harbor early. Down at the Elemarchy School, the teacher let her children out at two o'clock so they could scurry home to help with last-minute chores.

Zephram happened to be near the docks when the boats started to come in—"All right," he admitted, "I was sitting half-numb on the pier, watching the clouds choke the sky"—but he fought off his gloom and roused himself to help unload the day's catch. That's when he heard about the Silence of Mistress Snow, and the other Tober traditions associated with winter's coming. The men were divided on what Zephram himself should do at midnight: whether he should make a Visit of his own or keep shut behind a closed door. Both sides of the discussion meant well. Some thought it would be good for Zephram to participate in community traditions, while others said it would be easier on him not to get involved. After all, if Zephram made a formal Visit at midnight, he was committing himself to stay in the cove until spring. Was that what he wanted? The trip down-peninsula wasn't easy in winter, but a few sleighs made the journey every year—supposedly to buy supplies, really just for something to do once the harbor froze. Zephram could catch a ride down to Ohna Sound any time he wanted . . . but not if he promised Mistress Snow to see someone else through the hard cold season.

After the fish were unloaded, Zephram went to ask Leeta whether he should or shouldn't make a Visit when the snow came. That shows how much Zephram already knew about being a Tober—a true outsider might have gone to Hakoore and received a flat no. Leeta, on the other hand, gave a typical Mocking Priestess answer: Zephram had to decide for himself. If he wanted to remain an outsider, he could stay home, keep his door shut, Visit no one. If he wanted to be part of the community, he had to leave his door open and choose someone to help.

That was Leeta, all right: "You have a completely free choice, and never mind that there's only one decision a decent person would make."

*   *   *

Zephram said the snow arrived around sunset—not that anyone could see the sun with the sky smothered by those gray-feather clouds. I could imagine the way the snow sifted down that evening, bleaching away the world's color. Gray and gray, white and white. No sound from any house—even the sheep and cattle subdued as they huddled in barns that were tautly insulated with hay.

Night nestled down into hours of muted blackness. Zephram's house, called the Guest Home back then, had always been quiet—it stood apart from the rest of the village, separated by a big stand of trees—but on Mistress Snow's night, the normal quiet turned to thick granite silence. No dogs barked. No hammers tapped and no saws rasped, now that people had set aside their usual carpentry work. Many couples choose Mistress Snow's arrival as a time to make love . . . but even that goes slow and silent, voiceless as an iced-in pond.

Zephram sat alone in darkness; and as the snow on the window thickened flake by flake, he too thought of making love. The silence of snow was not a tradition in the South, but people still felt it and held each other as winter floated in. Zephram thought about his fresh-lost Anne, how they had watched and loved many snowfalls together. What would she want him to choose tonight? An open door or a closed one?

Easy question.

When the chime rang, he pulled on his boots and went out into the snow. Behind him, his door was propped open with a block of pristine pinewood he'd always intended to whittle into a bust of Anne. (Even as he told me this story, he still had that block, untouched, sitting on his work table amidst the shavings of owls and beavers that actually did get carved.)

Zephram cleared out of the house fast because he was shy of meeting whoever visited him. He had no doubt that someone would come; on the docks that afternoon, several men had dropped hints they wouldn't let an ignorant city-gent freeze to death. Most Tobers wouldn't mind lending Zephram a little help and a lot of advice—telling your neighbors what they ought to be doing has always been the cove's chief pastime in winter—but Zephram didn't want to see people coming to give what he regarded as charity.

(In that, he showed he *was* an outsider. No Tober thinks of our silent Visits as charity: it's something you do because the alternative is just too mean.)

Once Zephram was clear of the house, he slowed his pace. Snow still fell, but not much; the air was damp and windless, with the kind of cold that freshens rather than chills you. The night was fine for walking . . . and Zephram took his time, letting the native Tobers go about their

Visits without him. He had no one special he wanted to claim as his responsibility, no person or family he was closer to than any other. Instead, he intended to give the real villagers first choice of whom to support, then take the house left over. He had some idea that people would resent him intruding, or become annoyed if he "adopted" the family they wanted to claim themselves. Zephram thought it more polite to let the others sort themselves out. It meant, of course, that he would end up visiting someone unpopular, or perhaps a family so needy no one else dared commit to their well-being; but Zephram could afford both unpopularity and expense.

Or so he thought.

He ambled quietly along the edge of the forest for perhaps twenty minutes—ample time, he thought, for the rest of Tober Cove to settle who was going where. Then he aimed his feet toward the Council Hall steeple: the center of the village and a natural place to start looking for an open door. Most of the houses he passed were dark already, all lamps extinguished and the hearths damped down. People in the cove almost never stayed up to midnight, so they were quick to do their business and get back to bed . . . though not necessarily to sleep. In time, however, Zephram found one house still lit, with three stubby candles on a stand outside the open door.

Steck's house.

He knew Steck vaguely, just as he knew almost everyone in the village by now. Zephram had nodded to Steck that afternoon when he visited Leeta; Steck had been puttering with herbs on Leeta's kitchen table, making mint-scented packets for unknown priestess purposes. To Zephram, Steck was just Leeta's apprentice, a keen-eyed girl of twenty who carried herself like a spear, even if she was seven months pregnant with Master Crow's child.

Zephram approached the door with a flush of bashfulness, embarrassed by the boldness of walking unan-nounced into someone else's house . . . a young woman's house at that. It seemed indecent, a middle-aged man becoming this girl's "protector"; and now that he thought about her, she grew imposing in his mind—not just a girl, but a beautiful one, alarmingly so. Wasn't it disloyal to his late wife to "claim" a girl like Steck so soon after Anne's death? But he knew what Anne would say about that. *You're being an ass. Do what's right and don't invent complications.*

Even so, he found himself hoping Steck was still out on her own Visit, so he could scurry in, toss a stick on her fire, then rush away into the night.

She was home: seated on a rocking chair in front of the fireplace, tucked under a down coverlet that came up to her throat. Her jaw was clenched as if she was fighting the shivers. Zephram didn't think the cabin felt cool, but Steck was pregnant and might suffer chills more easily. Without thinking, Zephram closed the door behind him to shut out the cold. When he turned back, it struck him, *I'm alone with her now*; then he mentally kicked himself and set about fulfilling his new commitment to take care of her.

He made tea.

She watched him with firelight reflecting in her eyes, the expression on her face unreadable. Several times Zephram was on the verge of speaking, to ask if she was all right, and whether the jar of apple-scented flakes was really tea or just potpourri; but he remembered Mistress Snow's Silence and held his tongue. The only sound was the soft crackle of the hearth, with Zephram's split of wood atop the flames. He took his time hanging the kettle on its hook above the fire—he knew that once it was put in place, he'd have nothing else to do but avoid Steck's gaze until the water boiled.

And yet he had to look at her eventually: her fire-flickered eyes, her mouth set as if she were trying not to let her teeth chatter. When he summoned what he hoped was a comforting smile, she didn't smile back; she only nodded toward a chair on the other side of the hearth. Zephram took the hint and sat.

The chair was angled to look directly at the girl rather than the fire. This would be Leeta's seat, he realized, when the priestess came over to bestow wisdom on her apprentice—Leeta was the sort to aim herself face-on to anyone she was talking with. Zephram had no choice but to aim face-on too . . . and Steck stared back in the midnight hush, with snow drifting down outside.

He found himself prickling with the hope she would make love to him . . . that she would throw off the coverlet to reveal she was naked underneath, and that she would rise from the chair with unashamed deliberateness, she would walk slowly to him, and in the thick silence of the night . . .

("Hey!" I said from the other side of the breakfast table, "do I need to hear this?"

"What's wrong?" Zephram asked. "One reason I like Tober Cove is how open you are about sexual feelings."

"Yeah, but . . ." It was one thing for *me* to talk about my fantasies, and quite another for my *father* to blather away.

"I'm not trying to upset you," Zephram said. "I only wanted . . . it was the first time since Anne died that I had thoughts about another woman—"

"Just tell what happened," I interrupted, "and skip the daydreams. Unless Steck actually took off the coverlet and things got . . ."

"No," my father answered. "She was shivering cold and seven months pregnant.")

Zephram might have allowed himself to imagine the touch of Steck's soft skin, but that was only a tiny chink in his armor of mourning—Anne was still too much with him. After a time, he found he could superimpose his lost wife over the reality of Steck's eyes and the fantasy of her body . . . so that when he pictured making love with this girl, he was actually remembering Anne at the same age, and the sweet honeymoon caresses of long ago.

Soon enough, Steck's kettle boiled. Zephram stirred himself to find mugs—good clay mugs fired in the local kiln—then set one filled with steeping tea on a small table beside the girl. Steck took the mug immediately and pulled it under the coverlet . . . cradling it in her hands, Zephram supposed, although the cup was burning hot. Perhaps Steck rested it on the roundness of her stomach, where the heat would flow to the child within; perhaps that felt soothing to her. Zephram didn't know what pregnant women found comforting: he and Anne had never managed to have children.

While his own tea steeped, Zephram poked up the fire and slid in another piece of wood. Now that the cabin door was closed, the room was warming up: warm enough that he would soon have to decide whether to take off his coat or just go home. He didn't want to leave while Steck still looked close to freezing, but he also didn't want to outstay his welcome. The houses outside lay dark now; all the other Visits were clearly finished, and the visitors gone back to bed. He wondered if the cove's etiquette required Visits to be as short as possible . . . especially since talk was forbidden till dawn. Zephram was preparing himself for a conversation with Steck, spoken entirely with silent gestures—*Shall I go? Will you be all right?*—when the girl slipped off the coverlet and stood up.

She wore pure white: a white pleated dress so long it touched the floor, and a white wool sweater knit as fine as a spider's web. The clothes were impractical for life in the cove—sure to get dirty, hard to clean—and the bottom hem of the dress was already soggy from traipsing through snow outdoors. Steck must have worn this outfit when she went on her own Visit . . . as if she were pretending to be Mistress Snow Herself, come to bring cold serenity to the world.

The girl still held the mug of tea in her hands. She lifted it and sipped, her eyes on Zephram. With anyone else, the gesture might have been coy or seductively blatant—when I was female, I used that move myself—but Zephram assured me Steck was simply using it as a "thank you": wordlessly showing she was grateful for his efforts. He took this as a cue to leave and gave her a good-bye nod; but she held up her hand and motioned him back to his chair.

Zephram sat—the wary way you sit on the edge of your seat when you don't know what's happening and some part of your mind wants the option of retreat. Steck walked back to her bed and knelt beside it, giving Zephram a twinge of sexual panic . . . or perhaps hope. But she was only crouching down to pull out something stored under the bed: a violin case.

(When Zephram said that, it jolted me. Yes, Steck had played violin in the marsh; I'd thought, however, that the Neut had taken up music during Its time down south. If Steck had already been a violinist twenty years ago in Tober Cove . . .)

Zephram watched as Steck carefully took out the instrument and tuned it—not sounding the notes with the bow or even pizzicato plucks, but with delicate rubs of her finger that barely set the strings vibrating. The sound would never carry outside the house, which was obviously the girl's intention; Zephram didn't know if Mistress Snow's Silence applied to violins as well as voices, but Steck clearly didn't want to be heard rippling the quiet.

When she was happy with the tuning, Steck came back, pulled the rocking chair close to my father—close enough that their knees touched—then she settled down to play. She didn't tuck the instrument under her chin; instead, she held it like a guitar, resting it on the gentle roundness of her stomach. Steck let her eyes lock with Zephram's for a moment . . . then she bent her head and softly stroked the strings.

The tune was "Lonely Hung the Clouds," a song I knew well myself. Wherever I played, you could count on the song being requested at least once a night . . . partly because the melody was dreamy and beautiful, partly because the sentiment struck a responsive chord in many listeners. The first half of each verse describes how the singer has "lived with empty hands" and held "many a conversation with cold bare walls"; the rest of each verse is a surprised and grateful confession that everything has changed—presumably because she has found someone to love, although that's never said explicitly.

> *Lonely hung the clouds*
> *But now the light has come.*

Cappie sometimes sang the piece to me when she was a man . . . not that she was ever directly lonesome, but in her male years she brooded about the future possibility. I could imagine Zephram listening to the same tune in the stillness of Steck's cabin: each note brushed out of the strings so softly it barely had the strength to cross the small gap between Steck's body and his. Notes whispered in the still and magic dark. The entire world shrank to a man and woman, their knees touching in the firelight.

I didn't need to hear any more of the story; I could guess how the rest unfolded. Nothing would happen that night—Steck was too pregnant, and Zephram too burdened by the memory of Anne to abandon himself immediately. In a few months, the child in Steck's belly would be born. In a few months, the wound in Zephram's heart would heal to the point where his pulse could race again. They would be lovers before spring . . . and remain together until summer solstice.

When Steck Committed Neut.

When she was exiled from the cove.

When Zephram had no choice but to adopt Steck's newborn child.

"I was the baby," I said. "Steck's baby, right? That's why you're telling me this?"

"Of course," Zephram answered. "Of course."

TEN

An Assembly for Father Ash and Mother Dust

"My mother is a Neut?" The words choked out of me.

"Your mother was a woman," Zephram answered. "A troubled woman with a desperately caring heart. Not that anyone realized how vulnerable she was, except me and Leeta. Steck was too independent for Tober Cove to understand her. There was a reason she was living alone in one of those log cabins that are supposed to be for couples. I've always hoped she had an easier time down south."

Zephram hadn't heard Steck spilling out resentment beside Leeta's campfire: "Driven down-peninsula to cities we don't understand, where we're despised as freaks. Shunned by friends, separated from my lover and child . . ." No, Steck hadn't had an easier time. Being a Neut and being so chip-on-the-shoulder "independent" had killed all chance of a welcome from strangers.

"And when Steck left," I said, "she didn't take me with her?"

"She tried," Zephram answered, "but there was a mob on her heels. They ripped you out of her arms, then drove her off. The Warriors Society harried her through the forest and mounted a guard to make sure she didn't come back. She tried once anyway and got speared in the stomach; the Warriors wouldn't say whether she was dead or not, which means she got away. If they'd actually killed her, they would have paraded her head through town. But that was the last anyone saw of Steck."

"You never tried to find her?"

Zephram shook his head. "I had to take care of you. It was Hakoore's ruling—yes, I'd be allowed to stay and yes, I could adopt you, but only if I swore never to remove you from the cove. You're a Tober, Fullin, and a child of Master Crow; Hakoore refused to expose your god-given blood to the 'materialistic contamination' of the South. The vicious old bastard made me choose between you and Steck . . . and I knew what Steck would want. Her own parents were dead. If I didn't take you, you'd go straight into the hands of the people who exiled her.''

''And no one ever told me the truth.''

''People thought it would be kinder not to. They were eager to be nice to you after the hysteria died down—after the evil Neut was gone and they began to think about what shits they had been. They twisted themselves double pampering you, so I'd tell them that what they'd done wasn't so bad.'' Zephram sighed. ''I'm not a man who can hold a grudge, Fullin. Heaven knows I tried, for Steck's sake; but I couldn't stay angry with them, not as long as I should have. I let myself go along with the lie.''

He closed his eyes tight, fighting with something inside him. Guilt? Anger? In a moment he pushed the feeling down and spoke rapidly. ''So. Steck was gone and the whole town decided to tell you your mother was a paragon of virtue—accidentally drowned and nothing more.''

A question popped into my head: ''Does Cappie know about this?'' It surprised me that I could care what she thought, but I did.

''She shouldn't know,'' Zephram answered. ''All the children were supposed to be told the same story—otherwise, they might spill the truth to you. It's possible her parents told her when she was old enough to keep a secret . . . but why would they? The town just wanted to forget.''

He pushed his chair away from the table, though he'd hardly touched his breakfast. Taking his plate, he began to stash the uneaten food in the ice chest. ''I suppose,'' he said without looking at me, ''Leeta decided to mention Steck to you because it's Commitment Day. She's always regretted that she couldn't protect her apprentice. Leeta brought up Steck's name, but didn't tell you the truth?''

''No.''

''She must have lost her nerve—wanted to tell you the whole story before you Committed, then couldn't do it. That was always Leeta's problem: she thinks a Mocking Priestess should be defiance personified, but it just isn't in her.'' His voice was less accusing than his words; Zephram wanted to be outrage personified, but that wasn't in *him*.

''Maybe after you've Committed,'' he said, ''we'll go south together to see if we can find her. Steck was a good woman, Fullin, she really was. The rest of the town were intimidated by her—even before she Committed—but Steck was a good gentle woman.''

A good gentle woman who had tried to kill Cappie and me with a machete. Of course, before she attacked, she'd asked if either of us was named Fullin . . . and what would have happened if I'd answered truthfully? Would she have fallen on my neck with slobbery Neut kisses? *Oh my baby, I've come back to see your Commitment!*

That had to be her reason for coming to the cove on Commitment Eve. She'd kept track of the years; she knew this was my time. I could imagine she had spent every second of her exile plotting how to return for this day. Attaching herself to a Spark Lord for protection. Persuading him to come to the cove to observe the Commitment ceremonies. Did Rashid even know why Steck had brought him here? Or had she manipulated him to the point that Rashid thought this was his own idea?

Suddenly, I felt an irresistible need to pick up Waggett and hold him close. My son. When I took him in my arms, he snuggled against my chest out of reflex, not needing me, just making himself comfortable because comfort was his due. Only a few minutes before I had resolved not to get carried away with cuddling, but I couldn't help myself. I wanted to protect him. I don't know if I wanted to protect him from Steck, returned to the cove like the corpse of a murder victim seeking revenge . . . or if I wanted to save him from what happened twenty years ago, when a child was ripped from its mother and both became lost.

Trying not to hug him too fiercely, I nuzzled Waggett's sweet-smelling hair. He ignored me, as if his life would always be so full of kisses, there was no need to acknowledge every one.

The Council Hall bells rang. Both Zephram and I looked toward the clock hanging above the fireplace: a silver-embossed treasure with black metal hands shaped into crow feathers. Zephram had commissioned the piece from a clockmaker down south, in honor of Master Crow. Hakoore pouted for a while when the clock arrived, saying it verged on blasphemy . . . but even Hakoore realized he was being childish.

The hour was only seven o'clock, far too early for the usual Commitment Day festivities. Still, the bells kept ringing—calmly, not the fast *clang-clang-clang* used to warn of danger—so we had to conclude that the mayor was calling an impromptu town meeting.

"What's going on?" Zephram asked. He didn't expect an answer, so I didn't invent one. The mayor's summons could only be something to do with Steck and Lord Rashid; why else would Teggeree disrupt the usual Commitment Day schedule?

"You'd better go down to the hall and see what's happening," I said to Zephram. "I'll finish up here."

He looked at me in surprise. "What needs finishing up?"

"Cleaning . . . you know." I waved my hand vaguely.

"You've never volunteered to clean anything in your life," he said. "Not unless you were trying to get out of something worse. Do you know something about this meeting?"

"No."

"And you aren't curious?"

"Sure I am." I tried to think of anything I could say that wouldn't sound suspect. *Truth is, Dad, my Neut mother is in town and I don't want to meet her.* "It's just that . . ."

My voice trailed off.

Zephram rolled his eyes. "It's just that you want the house to yourself so you can search for the Commitment Day presents I bought you. Isn't that right?"

I immediately put on a sheepish look, as if Zephram had hit the nail on the head. He laughed and gave me a playful swat. "You don't find out till noon, boy. Now let's go see what's up."

Acknowledging defeat, I moved toward the door while hefting Waggett into a better carrying position . . . then I stopped. If I walked into the town square carrying the boy, Steck would see him. Steck had to know I had a child—all Tobers do by the time they reach Commitment Day. Did I want a Neut touching my boy? Could Steck have some demented plan to kidnap "her grandson"? Who knew what crazy ideas went through a Neut's head?

"Here," I told Zephram, "why don't you carry Waggett for a while?"

"That sounds more like you," he said. With a smile, Zephram took Waggett from me. The boy gave him a small hug—more recognition than *I'd* gotten. With a twitch of jealousy, I almost asked Zephram to give my child back . . . but it was better for Waggett if Steck didn't know he was mine.

Half the town got to the meeting before Zephram and me: mostly men and children, the people who could pick up and go as soon as the bells rang. The women came in their own time, after pulling pies out of the oven or running the iron over a few more pleats. Several older ladies never showed up, either because they were still working on last-minute details or because they thought they were—Tober Cove had its share of people who made themselves busy, busy, busy, no matter how little they had to do.

The interior of the Council Hall was big enough to hold the adult population of the village, but in good weather, meetings were held outside so that people weren't cramped together. Speakers stood up on the steps where they could be seen; the rest of the crowd filled the square, leaning against the hitching rails or sitting on the grass in the shade of what we called Little Oak. The tree had received its name almost two hundred years ago, back when there was a Big Oak too. Big Oak dropped in its time, getting sectioned into tabletops for half the homes of the village, and now Little Oak had a trunk so thick two men couldn't join their hands around it . . . but it was still called Little Oak and would keep that name until the centuries pulled it down.

That tells you something about Tober Cove.

Steck and Rashid weren't in sight. Mayor Teggeree stood at the top of the steps, smiling cheerfully at the crowd as he waited for latecomers to straggle in. Hakoore hunched beside him, glowering at the world, and Leeta leaned against the banister two steps lower down the stairs.

Since Cappie wasn't with the priestess, I looked around the square until I spotted her in a huddle with her family. They had oh-so-casually arranged themselves in a protective circle around her, and although I could only see the top of her head, I knew she must have dressed in male clothing again. Otherwise, her sisters and brothers wouldn't make such an effort to shield her from the village's eyes.

Why was she dressed like a man today? Last night it had just been the solstice dance, but now . . . did she *want* to shock people? Yes, I could believe that she did. I could believe she got out of bed, ran her fingers through her chopped-off hair, saw the male clothing scattered around the room and said, "Why not? Show the village I don't give a damn."

Either that, or she was dressed that way because she thought I liked it. Moment by moment, you could never tell whether Cappie was going to be defiant or clingy.

Heaving a sigh, I headed toward her. On the morning after the night before, a gentleman knows his duty: submitting himself to all that awkward "How are you?" "No, how are *you?*" that women need as confirmation that Something Indeed Took Place.

Sometimes, it's a pain knowing how women think.

Cappie's sister Olimbarg spotted me first. Olimbarg was fourteen and had a permanent crush on me. This year, the crush disguised itself as haughty annoyance, making her blurt out adolescent insults whenever I came into view. I put up with it because kids will be kids; and the insults didn't bother me as much as her behavior the previous year. Then, Olimbarg had been a thirteen-year-old boy while I was a nineteen-year-old girl. Picture a pubescent drool-monster getting underfoot every time Cappie and I wanted privacy.

It didn't help that Olimbarg was one of those rare people whose female self was almost an exact twin of her male. Now that she had begun filling out with adolescence, there was a little more variation from year to year; but still, when I looked at her face, I sometimes had an uncomfortable jolt, thinking I had a male Olimbarg infatuated with Male-Me.

"Here comes Fiddle-fingers!" Olimbarg called when she saw me. "Did the gods send you a duck, Fullin? Or did they decide you deserved a skunk?"

"Happy solstice to you, too," I told her. I kept it civil, because Cappie's whole family had turned to look at me. Some smiled; some didn't. Her father, for example, wore the expression of a man with nerves as taut as bowstrings, skittish for fear someone would notice Cappie wearing his clothes. His name was Nunce, and he dreamed of becoming mayor when Teggeree stepped down. If you ask me, he hadn't a chipmunk's chance of getting elected—his strategy for winning public favor was an obsessive concern with appearances, and it made him compulsively dodgy. Nunce had never quite decided how a man with leadership potential should hold his hands. He seldom spoke to any member of his family except in sharp whispers, telling the children, "Stand straighter," or, "Stop that, people are watching."

In another family, Nunce's constant fretting would have produced a pack of rebellious brats, going out of their way to make themselves embarrassments. Fortunately, Cappie's mother Jewel had a counterbalancing talent for making children civilized. She was a big blond woman, tall and wide, proud possessor of a cheerful no-nonsense approach to dealing with everyone except her husband. Jewel fiercely believed Nunce was an important man, a thinker and philosopher. I can't tell you what his philosophy might have been—he never shared it with the village. Rumor suggested that Nunce was writing a book which would explain everything in the world so easily a child could understand it . . . but most Tobers believed the rumor had been started by Nunce and Jewel themselves. I'd visited their house almost daily since I was born, and had never seen anything that looked like a manuscript.

"Happy solstice," Nunce said as he fidgeted to keep Cappie out of public view. "Did you have a pleasant vigil?"

"A gripping one," I replied. "Just thought I'd check how Cappie was doing."

"Fine," came a tentative answer from behind Nunce's back. "How are you doing?"

"Fine. Just fine."

I'd been trying for an ambiguous tone of voice—not post-love creamy, but not a hard-edged "Sorry, babe, the dew has dried" either

... something cozy enough for Cappie's peace of mind, but detached enough for mine.

Okay: it's a lot to expect from three words.

Cappie stuck her head over her father's shoulder; she must have been standing on tiptoe. Her expression was balanced right on the divide between happiness and fury, ready to swoop down the slope in either direction if I gave her cause. "Your note said you went back to vigil."

"Good thing I did," I replied. "Hakoore came to see me."

"Leeta said he might."

"Really?" I asked. "How would Leeta know?"

"The Patriarch's Man discusses lots of things with the priestess."

That surprised me. I couldn't imagine Hakoore discussing anything with anyone. "Did Leeta tell you why Hakoore wanted me?"

Cappie nodded. "But you told him you couldn't, right? That you had other plans?"

"I said no as clearly as I could," I assured her . . . which wasn't really what she was asking, but I hoped sounded like an answer anyway. Thank heavens women seldom resort to direct questions. "I refuse to be anyone's *disciple*."

"You'd be Leeta's disciple," she said. "Unless you intend to weasel out on what we agreed last night."

"I'm not a weasel!" I snapped.

She pushed her father out of the way so she could confront me face to face. "Look me in the eye, Fullin, and tell me you'll keep your promise."

"Um . . ." Looking her in the eye was tough for more than the usual reasons: the male clothes were even more interesting on her in full daylight. They made her look excruciatingly feminine—the slight definition of her breasts under that white shirt, the short-cropped hair framing her delicate face. At that moment, I wished I had more visceral memories of our lovemaking the night before . . . something juicier than the secondhand recollections of what my body had done while my sister self was in charge. "At this moment," I said with all sincerity, "I'm tempted to reopen negotiations. If you go male, I'll never see you look like this again."

She stared back, her eyes judging me. "What, Fullin?" she finally asked. "Are you actually feeling something, or are you just horny again?"

"Oh, *please!*" Olimbarg moaned. She thrust herself between Cappie and me, planting a hand on each of our chests and pushing us both back. "No one wants to hear this!"

On the contrary, Cappie's whole family was listening with avid interest. Her mother wore a hopeful smile; her younger brothers and sisters had their hands over their mouths to stifle giggles, but were crowding close to make sure they didn't miss a word; even her father was paying attention, temporarily forgetting he wanted to hide his daughter from the neighbors. Cappie, however, took advantage of the distraction and stepped clear of everyone: Olimbarg, me, the rest of her family.

"Look," she said, to them as much as to me. "The meeting's ready to start. We'll talk later, okay? Okay, Fullin? We'll really talk?"

"Sure," I said. "We'll talk. We will."

If the Patriarch's Hand had been fastened on me at that second, I don't know if it would have taken my words as truth or crushed me for lying. Part of me had suddenly decided to want Cappie again. A different part would rather kiss a snapping turtle than "really talk" with her.

"Good morning, friends!" Mayor Teggeree called from the top of the steps. "You have other things to do, so I won't waste your valuable time. Permit me to announce that we'll have a dignitary among us today: Knowledge-Lord Rashid of Spark!"

Rashid emerged from the interior of the council hall, while the assembled village favored him with gasps, chatter and hasty applause. Under the noise, I whispered to Cappie, "Didn't he want to keep his presence a secret?"

"Absolutely," she whispered back. "And I'm sure he thought he could blend right in with us Tobers . . . except that he's a complete stranger wearing bright green armor."

Cappie had a point: Rashid carried his helmet under his arm, but he still wore the rest of his green plastic suit. The glossy shell reflected the sun like an emerald mirror, flashing glints in all directions as he stepped forward. In the full light of day, it was obvious the armor was far finer than anything owned by even the greatest nobles down-peninsula. If Feliss nobles wore armor at all, it was only a steel breastplate that went over a chain mail tunic. Rashid wouldn't fool anyone by claiming to be some visiting Southern Duke—the only people in the world who might encase themselves in OldTech plastic were the Spark Lords.

And Master Disease, some upstart voice whispered inside my head. But I refused to feel sheepish about my mistaken assumption—Rashid's tear gas had hickoried my brain, so how could I be expected to think clearly?

"Ladies and gentlemen," Rashid said warmly, "boys and girls—or vice versa—I'm delighted to come here for your Commitment Day and would like to thank your Council of Elders for graciously inviting me."

Cappie made an outraged choking sound. Her mother patted her on the back and asked if she had a tickle in her throat.

"I'm especially pleased to be here," Rashid went on, "because it's a Knowledge-Lord's duty to learn as much as I can about every society on our planet; and frankly Tober Cove has a pretty interesting one, don't you think?"

Many people smiled, but Cappie only snorted. Her mother placed a hand on Cappie's forehead and offered her a barley sugar.

"Now I'm just here to observe," Rashid was saying, "and I don't want special treatment. A lot of places I go, people start talking the way they think lords talk, using big words, rolling their Rs, quoting obscure old poets . . ."

Cappie took the barley sugar, popped it into her mouth, and ground her teeth against it.

"But I don't hold with such top-lofty behavior," the Spark Lord said, "and neither should you. Just do what you'd do on any other Commitment Day, without putting on a show for me. I know you don't get many Spark Lords here—as far as I can tell, you've *never* had a Spark visit, although your Patriarch came to see *us* long ago—so some of you might want to chat with me . . . shake my hand . . . have me kiss your baby . . . something you can drop into conversation the next time you go to Wiretown."

I heard a crunch as Cappie bit clean through the barley sugar; and just for the record, Jewel's homemade candy was only a hair softer than quartz. Zephram called it "barely sugar"—he liked it enormously.

"Don't worry," Rashid said, "I'm happy to give everyone a few minutes. But that's not what Commitment Day is about, is it? It's not about catering to lords, it's about your children going to meet Master Crow and Mistress Gull. That's worth celebrating and I don't want to get in the way."

Cappie gripped my arm and made a show of digging in her fingernails . . . as if she were desperate enough to kill Rashid or herself any second now. I just shrugged. She might mistrust him, but everyone else in the crowd clearly took him at face value. Why shouldn't they? From birth, we'd been taught to revere the Sparks as our protectors, our line of defense against the scheming traitors who sold out to the star demons four hundred years ago. If Cappie and I had met Lord Rashid under different circumstances: without Steck, for example . . .

My mother . . .

Where *was* Steck anyway?

"That's all I have to say," Rashid finished. "I wish everyone a good celebration and thank you for giving me such a . . . robust welcome so far.''

Mayor Teggeree surged forward with his hands high in zealous applause. The rest of the village joined enthusiastically—most of them anyway. Neither Leeta nor Hakoore put much energy into their clapping, although Leeta at least had the grace to wear an expression of determined courtesy. Hakoore didn't so much as smile, and his ovation was restricted to three constipated claps.

"It's an honor to have you with us, my lord," Teggeree boomed out when the applause eased. "And while the Council of Elders has already welcomed you . . ." (he didn't mention that it happened in the middle of the night) ". . . I want to make sure you receive the full offer of hospitality you deserve.''

Cappie inhaled sharply. "He wouldn't!"

But the mayor was already gesturing into the crowd. "Father Ash? Mother Dust? Are you willing to come up here?"

Heads nodded approval all around as people near the stairway nudged back to form an open space. Into that space, Bonnakkut and the other members of the Warriors Society helped two people as thin as skeletons: Father Ash and Mother Dust, the oldest man and woman in Tober Cove. Their names were ceremonial titles, given when their predecessors died; I had known them by other names before, but it was disrespectful to use those names now. When this Mother or Father died, the next oldest in town would rise to the position, losing whatever human name he or she might have and becoming what we called a Doorkeeper to the Gods.

As Father Ash and Mother Dust moved to the bottom of the stairs, everyone in the crowd knelt. You did that when the Mother and Father came together—going down on your knees wasn't just a tradition, it was an automatic response. No matter how foul-tempered or foolish the two might be as human beings, Father Ash and Mother Dust commanded respect.

They were the true masters of Tober Cove. Outsiders might think the mayor and Council of Elders spoke for the town, but they were only in charge of mundane matters: setting the price of fish and collecting taxes to pay the schoolmaster. Hakoore kept the town true to the Patriarch's Law and Leeta stood for woman's wisdom, but neither Patriarch's Man nor Mocking Priestess had final word over what went on in the cove.

That right belonged to Father Ash and Mother Dust. They almost never took a stand . . . but when the mayor said one thing, Hakoore said another, and Leeta said a third, Father Ash and Mother Dust were there to adjudicate between the squabbling children. Zephram called them figureheads, but he was wrong—they were our spiritual leaders, raised by venerability above Hakoore's legalistic theology and Leeta's milk-weed dances. Father Ash and Mother Dust were the tiny nuggets of holiness that remained after you got past the rules and rites of religion. "Father . . . Mother . . ." Teggeree called from his knees. "I beg you to extend the hospitality of Tober Cove to Lord Rashid."

"And to my Bozzle, of course," Rashid said offhandedly.

Steck stepped out of the Council Hall doorway, sliding in behind Rashid like a shadow. I doubt if most people in the crowd even noticed—everyone knew Spark Lords had such aides to handle secretarial chores and other menial details. The town's concentration was centered on Rashid, Father Ash and Mother Dust. Perhaps Cappie and I were the only ones to give the Bozzle a second glance.

Overnight, Steck had become female . . . at least to outward appearance. The beard was gone and the carelessly shaggy hair had been trimmed into the practical style worn by many farm wives: efficiently short but feminine, in a hearty way that fit Steck's broad-shouldered physique. I wondered if the mayor's wife had done the haircutting. Certainly, she had donated the clothes Steck now wore—I recognized the long but billowy dress of forest green, and the lighter green overshirt with enough of a V neckline to show a hint of cleavage. As a forty-year-old woman, Steck actually had a remarkable body . . .

. . . then it struck me I was ogling a Neut, not to mention my mother. I shuddered with a sudden case of the icks.

Get over it, I told myself. *Pretend Rashid's Bozzle is just some Southern woman, not worth a second thought.* I had sworn I would keep Steck's secret, and besides, I didn't want to remind the town of my scandalous parentage. It wouldn't hurt to think of Steck as a woman, at least for a day.

She looked enough like a woman, didn't she? The face was not one hundred percent female, but it would pass. In a way, seeing that ambiguous face made me want to know what Steck looked like when she was my mother. She wouldn't have been the same, I knew that. Except for flukes like Olimbarg, people's male and female selves seldom resembled each other more than brother and sister; Neuts were supposed to be different again. There was little chance anyone would recognize Steck as a Neut they'd seen briefly twenty years ago . . . especially now, when all the people had turned their attention to Rashid.

Father Ash and Mother Dust were sizing up Rashid just like everyone else. We were lucky this Father and Mother both had clear wits—not always the case, when the sole criterion for gaining the position was being older than anyone else. The elderly man and woman squinted up at the lord with thoughtful expressions on their faces, while Rashid returned their gaze calmly. He didn't make the mistake of trying to charm them with a politician's smile, but I thought he looked pleasant enough: a good-natured man, well-groomed and respectful.

Mother Dust whispered something to Father Ash and he whispered back. I found it hard to believe they were seriously discussing the option of denying hospitality to a Spark Lord—more likely, this was only a token gesture to assert their independence from the Sparks, the mayor and everyone else.

Then again, it was possible they really were talking it over. Offering the town's hospitality to Rashid and Steck was almost like making our visitors official Tobers; it was a sober commitment, an honor that had only been bestowed once before in my lifetime (to Governor Niome of Feliss). Furthermore, Ash and Dust were above trying to curry favor with *anyone*: they were close enough to the embrace of the gods that worldly blessings had lost their shine.

That's what we were taught anyway. And since Father Ash and Mother Dust had been taught the same things ninety-odd years ago, they believed in their own impunity.

"All right," Mother said in a whistling voice. "You have our hospitality."

"Both of you," Father added.

On her knees beside me, Cappie shuddered. I wondered what bothered her more: that Rashid had been granted full access to our Commitment Day ceremonies, or that Steck had been officially welcomed back to Tober land. The hospitality of Father Ash and Mother Dust had the legal force to override the decree of banishment imposed twenty years ago—my mother was no longer an exile. And the hospitality had not been won under false pretenses; Ash and Dust surely knew who Steck really was. I couldn't remember if they'd been present for the council meeting in the middle of the night, but Teggeree would never request their indulgence without making sure they had the facts. Our mayor had a knack for his own expedience, but there are some lines you just don't cross.

"What's done is done," I told Cappie, "and they knew what they were doing."

"Sometimes," she answered, "nobody knows what they're doing." And she got to her feet so fast, for a moment she stood tall while the rest of the town stayed crouched on their knees.

ELEVEN

A New Name for Steck

Mayor Teggeree dismissed the assembly. The result was a general milling about, with some people trying to push their way through the crowd in order to rush home, but many others staying to chat with neighbors, or shuffling in search of their closest cronies so they could jabber about the Knowledge-Lord. The talk all amounted to, "A Spark here in the cove . . . well, well, well!" but everyone felt compelled to offer his or her variation on that theme. People who've heard surprising news are like wolves staking out their territory—they have to piss on it to prove it's theirs.

From where I stood with Cappie's family, I couldn't see Zephram and Waggett, but I assumed they were tied into one of the knots of people babbling about our distinguished visitor. Eventually they'd come looking for me, and I didn't want that—not if Steck was in a position to connect me with my son.

"Olimbarg," I whispered to Cappie's sister, hanging close at my heels while pretending complete indifference to me. "Can you do me a favor?"

"No," she answered automatically.

She didn't mean it. "Can you tell Zephram to take Waggett back home without me? There's something I have to do here first."

"What do you have to do?" Olimbarg asked. "Paw up my sister?"

"Don't be jealous. You can be nice to have around when you aren't jealous."

That was true . . . not that I'd ever seen her keep the jealousy in check for more than a minute at a time.

"Who's jealous?" she said with unconvincing haughtiness; then she went to give Zephram my message, walking with a flouncing swing of her hips because she knew I was watching her. I couldn't tell if she intended her walk to be sexy or belligerent . . . but then, she was fourteen and likely didn't know which she wanted either.

It took a full ten seconds for me to pull my gaze from Olimbarg—not because I felt lustful urges toward a bratty kid, but because I wasn't eager to turn back to Cappie and her family. If Cappie wanted to "really talk" right away, which part of me would be ready to speak? The part that liked the curve of her breasts under suspenders, or the part that lied and evaded as easily as scratching an itch?

I finally took a deep breath and wheeled around with words tumbling out of my mouth, "All right, if you want to talk, we should just—"

Cappie was gone. In the distance, her father was bustling her away, with the rest of her family still clustered close to hide her clothes and hair. I don't know why she didn't resist them; maybe she'd had a tweak of nerves and was suddenly not so eager to thrash out our problems either.

I watched her go . . . and out of the corner of my eye, I saw Dorr, Hakoore's granddaughter, watching me. She must have seen me when I spun around, talking to thin air. Dorr's expression was more than curious; her eyes had a focused astuteness, as if she knew everything about Cappie and me, as if she could see clear as a soap bubble into my mind.

It made me wince. Dorr always had a witchy, watchy way to her, especially around me. When I was a fourteen-year-old boy, and she was a nineteen-year-old girl, I sometimes noticed her lurking in the woods outside the house where I lived with Zephram. I told myself then I should be flattered that an older woman had a crush on me . . . but after a while, I found it more creepy than pleasing.

Now I turned toward Dorr so that she wouldn't think she could shy me off. "So," I said, "a Spark Lord. What do you think of that?"

She only shrugged and turned away. Dorr didn't talk much in public.

The square began to empty as people headed back to whatever last-minute preparations remained for the festivities. Nothing formal would happen before noon, when Master Crow and Mistress Gull came to take the children away; nevertheless, there would be small celebrations in homes all over town, private gift-giving or special breakfasts, that sort of thing. Every family had its own traditions. Still, a few folks remained in the square, moving closer to the steps rather than walking away: children, teenagers, and others without immediate duties, all of them crowding up to talk with the Spark Lord.

"Have you ever fought a demon?" "Can you really ride lightning?"

"How much do you have to study to be a Knowledge-Lord?" The questions piled on top of each other, exactly the things I'd be asking too if I didn't have a horror of looking gauche in front of a Spark. Perhaps Rashid groaned inwardly at such questions, the way Tobers groaned at outsiders who wanted to know male/female things; but he paid attention anyway, easing himself down to sit on the steps and answering the questions he chose to hear amidst the barrage. I listened for a while in spite of myself—yes, he had fought demons, although he preferred to call them "extraterrestrials," and they weren't all as bad as the stories claimed. . . .

When I finally pulled my attention away, Steck was no longer standing on the Council Hall steps.

Perhaps she had retreated into the Council Hall itself. There was little risk of people recognizing her after twenty years—as I said, she looked completely female, and with a different face than when she was a woman living in the cove—but maybe she was playing it safe by staying out of sight. Quietly I drew away from the pack around Rashid and circled to the hall's side door.

Don't ask me why I wanted to see where Steck was. If she'd suddenly appeared before me, I wouldn't have known what to say. How do you speak to your mother, when she doesn't feel like your mother at all? My mother was still a corpse drifting among the reeds of Mother Lake: a woman who might be illusory but who had lovingly held my hand through childhood bouts of loneliness. I had prayed to my drowned mother; I had seen her in dreams; I had occasionally dressed as she must have dressed, and worn my hair in the way I imagined she wore hers. That fictitious woman was my mother, even if she never existed. Steck was just a Neut who gave me birth.

And yet . . . I went looking for her, even when I would have flinched to meet her.

She wasn't in the Council Hall—there was nothing in the building but the smell of varnish, since the big meeting table had been recently refinished. Steck must have left through the same side door I'd come in; and she must have left soon after the welcoming ceremony finished.

Where would she go in such a hurry?

The natural answer was she wanted to find me, her beloved child. But I had been standing in plain sight near Little Oak; if she wanted to shower me with maternal kisses, she knew where I was. Steck had bustled off in a different direction . . . and I asked myself why. What other business did she have in Tober Cove? Whom else could she want to see apart from me?

When the answer thumped into my mind, I wanted to smack myself in the forehead. Zephram. Her old lover. Of course she'd recognize him and want to talk with him. And like an idiot, I'd let him carry Waggett so Steck wouldn't take an interest in the boy. Even now the damned Neut might be chucking my son under the chin and talking to him like a proud grandma.

I stormed out of the Council Hall and ran toward Zephram's home. He'd lived there since his earliest days in the cove—Steck would know where to find him. She might even catch him before he got to the house. As I've said, Zephram's place stood apart from the rest of the village, with a good stand of birch and poplar between the property and its nearest neighbor. For some reason, it seemed more sinister if Steck caught up with my father and Waggett on the path through those trees. I could imagine her standing athwart the trail like a toll collector . . . maybe even with her knife drawn.

Twenty years had passed since Steck and Zephram had been to-gether—twenty hard years for Steck, and who knows what crazy re-sentments she might have developed? Maybe she had talked herself into believing everything was Zephram's fault; after all, he was the one who told her about that other Neut who lived "happily" in the South. Had Steck come to Tober Cover for revenge against my father? And what would she do to the boy Zephram was carrying?

I ran faster.

As I entered the woods between the town and Zephram's home, I slowed to a quiet trot. If Steck really was up to no good, it might be better to catch her by surprise.

The trail wound as all trails wind on Tober land, shifting in response to the ledges of limestone that slab up out of the earth. The ledges seldom rose higher than my waist, but combined with the shimmering leaves that drooped down from the trees, there were places I could scarcely see a dozen paces in front of me.

That's why I didn't notice the body until I was almost upon it.

It lay near the halfway point of the woods, curled into a fetal position on the path. The back was toward me; I could tell it was a man but not who it was. Not Zephram, at least—my father didn't have any sleeveless shirts, and this man, whoever he was, had muscular arms bare to the shoulder.

Before I approached the body I froze and listened. The breeze rustling a forest full of leaves hissed up enough background noise to cover any quiet movements of threat nearby. I couldn't see anyone in the neigh-borhood, and there wasn't anywhere within ten paces that someone could hide . . . unless the killer was lying behind one of the low rock ledges, waiting for the moment I turned my back . . .

Don't do this to yourself, I thought. After thirty more seconds with no sign of trouble lurking, I slipped warily toward the unmoving form.

It was Bonnakkut: our First Warrior. A slash across his throat dribbled blood onto the dirt. Red blobs low down on his shirt showed he had taken some gut jabs too, but the throat gash had all the finality a man required. I didn't need to take his pulse or check for breathing.

The ground was scuffed, but it didn't look like there'd been a major fight. Bonnakkut's beloved steel ax still gleamed sharp and unused, secure in the leather housing that Bonnakkut had made himself—a sort of hip holster which allowed him to whip out the ax in a split-second. Either he hadn't had time to defend himself . . .

. . . or he'd decided to pass up the ax in favor of shooting his attackers with his brand-new Beretta.

I didn't see the gun anywhere. Not in his hands. Not on the ground nearby.

"This is not good," I whispered. Much as I hated Bonnakkut having a firearm, he wasn't the worst type of owner: the worst was someone who'd *kill* Bonnakkut to get the gun.

Suddenly, I had a twitch in the small of my back—the queasy feeling of someone dangerous right behind me. I spun around, but there was no one . . . just shimmering leaves, stolid rock, and a dawdle of insects flicking through the pockets of sunshine that penetrated the tree cover.

Whichever way I turned, I felt there was someone just a hair behind me.

"Help!" I shouted. "Hey! Anyone hear me? Help!"

Ten seconds later, Cappie came running from the direction of Zephram's house. She still carried my spear, and she held it ready for trouble.

What was she doing here? I thought she'd gone home with her family.

"Fullin," she said, "why are you making all that . . . oh." She stopped. She had seen Bonnakkut.

"I didn't do it," I told her.

Cappie didn't answer. Her gaze was on the corpse.

"He was like this when I found him."

"Don't be so defensive," she said, but there was no snap in her voice. She looked quickly left and right; I don't know what she expected to see. Oddly enough, the twitch in my back had disappeared the moment Cappie showed up. We were alone now—I could feel it.

"His gun's missing," I told her.

"Why doesn't that surprise me?"

She squatted in front of the body, an unladylike pose made decent only because she was wearing pants. Her hand reached out toward Bonnakkut's slashed throat, but I grabbed her wrist in time. "Don't be crazy," I said.

"I'm not a woman yet," she answered.

"Bonnakkut might not care." Everyone knew that a woman should never touch a man's corpse, just as a man shouldn't touch a woman's. If Bonnakkut's spirit hadn't left his body yet, it would be lonely and maddened; one touch from Cappie and he would suck her soul into his corpse to be his death-wife. Some Elders claimed that was impossible— before Commitment, we couldn't marry, either in life or in death. But I didn't trust Bonnakkut dead or alive, and I didn't let go of Cappie's hand until she shrugged and eased back from the body.

"We should tell someone," she said.

Her eyes met mine. I don't know what she was looking for, but her face had a focused seriousness that I found beautiful in its intensity. After a few seconds, I asked, "Do you want to stay with the body or shall I?"

She actually smiled faintly. "Thanks. Trusting me for once." She drew a breath. "I'd better be the one to stay. I've got the spear."

As I ran back to the center of town, my brain rattled with questions. Who killed Bonnakkut? That was my top concern. And my top suspect was Steck. Someone callous enough to Commit Neut was callous enough to commit murder . . . but I couldn't see a motive. Bonnakkut was only five years old when Steck left Tober Cove; she shouldn't have any longstanding hatred for him. Anyone else might have killed Bonnakkut to steal his gun, but Steck had no reason to do that. Working for a Spark Lord, she could have any weapon she wanted, just for the asking.

It was possible there might be a criminal hiding nearby; as I've said, fugitives occasionally came up-peninsula to hide from the Feliss Watch. It was also possible one of the muscle-brains in the Warriors Society had decided to take the Beretta for himself. It was even possible someone else in town hated Bonnakkut enough to do the deed . . . but I had trouble believing it.

We were Tobers. We didn't ambush other Tobers in the woods and kill them. The only homicide in my lifetime was fifteen years earlier, when a man named Halsey killed his brother in a drunken fight. A town like ours didn't get cold-blooded murders. Especially not the morning of Commitment Day.

I told myself the killer couldn't be a Tober. Better for it to be Steck or a fugitive—some outsider.

But I didn't just think about the murder; I thought about Cappie too. She had come from the direction of Zephram's house . . . so what was she doing there? Just returning my spear? Or had she come for that talk with me?

For a guilty moment, I felt glad about Bonnakkut's murder—even Cappie couldn't expect me to discuss our future with a corpse at our feet.

And I thought about more immediate questions: whom should I tell about the murder? Officially, the Warriors Society kept the local peace, but with Bonnakkut ready for worm-fodder, it was a joke to think of turning to Kaeomi, Stallor or Mintz. Mayor Teggeree was no better; he was good for speeches and organizing storage of our spring wool, but not for surprise crises. Leeta was dither-headed, and I refused to go to Hakoore. Father Ash and Mother Dust? They would pronounce sentence when the time came, but you didn't just run up to them shouting, "Help me, help me!"

Which only left one choice.

Lord Rashid still sat on the steps of the Council Hall. He stood when he saw me running toward him—they say Sparks have an instinct for recognizing trouble.

The Knowledge-Lord didn't ask why I wanted him; he told the people around him, "Sorry, I have to go," and waved away the few who tried to follow. It was only when we were out of the square that he murmured to me, "Problem?"

I nodded. "A murder."

"Damn!" he whispered. "And I bet that girl Cappie is right on the spot to say, 'I told you so.' "

"Cappie won't—"

"She will," he interrupted. "She went on about my very presence provoking . . ." He stopped. "I don't suppose she could have done it? Just to prove her point?"

"Never! Never . . ."

Rashid looked at me curiously. I didn't speak, but I admit, I suddenly wasn't as sure about Cappie as I wanted to be. Fighting last night in the creek, she'd shown how well she could manage the spear, even if she was female; she might be able to take Bonnakkut, especially if she caught him by surprise. I couldn't imagine why she'd want to—but now that I thought about it, Bonnakkut *had* made those leering insinuations about wiving her. If he saw how good Cappie looked today . . . if he had talked her into meeting him in the woods, then tried to force her into something she didn't want . . . I could believe Cappie might slash him in the heat of the moment. Then she might run up the trail, wipe Bonnakkut's blood off the spear head, and wait for someone to discover the body . . .

. . . whereupon she arrived in response to my calls, playing innocent as a crow.

Last night I'd believed Cappie was possessed by devils. Since then, I'd let go of that theory, but now I wasn't so sure.

Rashid knelt beside Bonnakkut's body. The Spark Lord's armor wasn't quite flexible enough for him to lean in for a truly close look, but he did his best.

"This is exactly how you found him?" Rashid asked.

"Give or take a few ants," I replied. The insects had begun to take an interest in the corpse, scurrying over Bonnakkut's bare arms as if he were no more than a log.

"Did he have any enemies?"

"Steck," said Cappie.

Rashid looked at her sharply. "Do you have any solid reason to suspect Steck?"

"Bonnakkut tried to shoot her last night," Cappie shrugged. "Maybe Steck decided to return the favor."

The Spark Lord shook his head. "My Bozzle had no grudge against this man . . . and even if she did, she wouldn't act on it before Master Crow and Mistress Gull get here. Steck has been pining for this day too long to mess things up so quickly. All she can talk about is showing me how the children go off to Birds Home . . ."

I bit my lip.

"No," Rashid said, "my Bozzle has her faults, but if she really wanted to kill someone, she'd have the self-restraint to hold off until the festivities were over."

"Suppose it was Bonnakkut who wouldn't hold off," Cappie suggested. "He tried to kill Steck last night. Suppose he gave it another shot and she fought back."

"Then she wouldn't run afterward," Rashid answered. "The Patriarch's Law recognizes self-defense, doesn't it?"

"Certainly," I said.

"So Steck would walk straight into town and announce she filleted a man who tried to kill her. She's not the sort to be shy about that."

Rashid said that with the rueful ghost of a smile.

"It's not funny!" Cappie told him.

"I know." Rashid stood up, his armor clicking over itself as he re-adjusted his position. "What happened to the gun I gave him?"

"Gone."

"Any chance he just left it at home this morning?"

Cappie and I gave him "Who are you kidding?" looks.

"All right," he grumbled, "it was worth asking." He glanced around at the woods. "Tree trunks are too thin here to hide behind. The killer couldn't just leap out and take this man by surprise. Unless . . ." Rashid looked straight up. "No, the trees aren't sturdy enough to support a man's weight. You couldn't wait up there, then jump on your victim."

I looked at the trees myself. The Knowledge-Lord was right: poplars and birch are the herons of the tree world, with spindly stems and limbs. Even someone as slender as Cappie couldn't climb one or hide behind a trunk. "So what are you saying?" I asked Rashid.

"The victim knew the killer," he replied. "Otherwise, Bonnakkut wouldn't have been taken by surprise. After all, if you met a stranger with a knife coming down this path, would you let the guy get within throat-slitting range?"

"Bonnakkut might," Cappie said. "He was a cocky fool."

"Mmm."

Rashid sounded dubious. Loyalty demanded I back Cappie up. "If Bonnakkut ran into a fugitive," I said, "he might try to take the fellow single-handed. That was Bonnakkut's style. He'd draw that gun and say, 'Surrender or die.' "

"And if the fugitive tried to knife him," Rashid replied, "Bonnakkut would fire, wouldn't he? You'd hear the shot all over town."

Cappie gave him a look. "Provided the gun worked."

"It worked flawlessly last night," Rashid answered in a wounded tone. "So unless the idiot forgot to take off the safety catch . . ." He waved his hand dismissively. "It's possible, but I don't like it. Too convenient. Anyway, I need to take a closer look at the cuts . . . but we should call your Town Watch before I start playing with the body. I don't want to tread on official toes. You do have a Town Watch, right?"

"You're looking at it," Cappie answered, gesturing toward the corpse.

"Oh. Right. Then again, it gives me a free hand, doesn't it? You," he pointed to Cappie, "bring me your local Healer. Expert medical advice." There was only a trace of irony in his voice, just enough to suggest our Healer was a country bumpkin who couldn't tell her ankle from her adenoids. "And you," he pointed to me, "find Steck. I don't want her wandering too far away with killers on the loose."

Cappie and I exchanged looks, but an order from a Spark could not be ignored. She headed into the village to get Doctor Gorallin. I went the other direction, hoping Steck wasn't at Zephram's house but certain that she was.

Steck sat with my son on her lap. Her Neut lap. Zephram was nowhere to be seen.

"Where's my father?" I asked.

"Busy," she answered. "You'll have to make do with your mother."

I stormed forward and pulled Waggett roughly away from her. She made no effort to prevent it. Waggett made a soft bleat of surprise, but decided not to be scared. When I clutched him to my chest, he snuggled in complacently.

"He's good-tempered," Steck observed.

"What do you want here?" I asked.

"Honor thy father and mother," Steck said. "It's the Patriarch's Law, Fullin."

She continued to sit in the chair as if nothing was wrong. *My* chair, the one I had sat in for years before my legs were long enough to touch the floor.

"How can I honor my mother," I asked, "when she chose to Commit as Neut?"

"You might think of it as a brave choice rather than a stupid one."

"It's more than stupid, it's blasphemy."

"Then why did the gods put it on the menu?" she asked calmly. "You haven't Committed yet, Fullin. You've never faced Commitment Hour and heard that voice ask, 'Male, female, or both?' There's no sneer in those words, none at all. There's no suggestion the gods think 'both' is only an option for heretics. People may have decided that Neut is bad, but the gods are more broad-minded."

"The Patriarch said—"

"Fuck the Patriarch," Steck interrupted. "A depraved old zealot who perverted everything Birds Home stood for. Before him, there were plenty of people like me in the cove: people who believed that 'both' might be the answer most gods wanted to hear . . . that the tired old stereotypes of male and female were too deeply embedded in the monkey brain, and the only way out was becoming something new. But the Patriarch was too insanely jealous to allow the best of both worlds. Not only did he anathematize those who refused to restrict themselves, he regimented male and female roles far beyond anything you find in the South."

"Southerners can't choose," I answered. "We can. If we choose male, we choose the male role, period. Same with female. It would be ridiculous if we Committed male, then still acted female."

"What does it mean to act female?" Steck demanded. "Both sexes eat. Both sexes sleep. Both sexes sweat on a hot summer's day. I shouldn't have to tell you how similar they are, Fullin—you've *been* both. You've felt both. Were they really that different? No. No difference, except the way people treated you and the jobs they told you to do."

"You obviously don't understand anything," I said, "which is why you're a Neut. There's no point discussing it further."

"This was a discussion, was it?" She gave me a look. "Here I thought we were having a fight . . . and I was blessing the gods for my luck, not to have missed your adolescent rebellion phase."

"Is that what you came here for?" I asked. "To make up for twenty years when you couldn't nag your kid?"

Steck didn't answer right away. It seemed as if she thought deeply before words came out. "I came here for a lot of things," she said at last, "like the off chance that I'd look at you, you'd look at me, and something would happen. Something besides disappointing each other for being the wrong kind of people." She stood up; she was as tall as me. "What's your son's name?"

I hesitated, then decided to show I was well brought up. "Waggett."

"Amazing—that's what Zephram called him too. I wondered if you'd lie to me. About my own grandson."

"Rashid wants you," I said. "On the trail back to town."

"He's probably found some kind of beetle he's never seen before."

"Not quite," I told her.

She turned away, then abruptly turned back. "I'll make you a deal, Fullin. Spend the morning with Rashid and me, until you have to go to Birds Home. Do that and I'll stay away from Zephram and Waggett."

"I won't be your son," I said.

"You are," she replied, "and for twenty years, I've told myself that means something. I won't talk you into Committing Neut, if that's what you're afraid of. You're my child, and I want you to have every freedom to choose who you want to be. But this is our only time together, Fullin. A single morning for the rest of our lifetimes. Years down the road, this day will be as important to you as it is to me. Even if you decide you hate my guts, at least you'll *know*. Trust me, not knowing hurts to the bone."

I hate it when adults say, "Trust me." It's not that I think they're lying—it's that they're telling me I'm too green to appreciate some great truth they've learned from experience. The more painful the experience, the more mysteriously profound they believe the truth must be ... when most of the time, it's as plain as dung in the street and they've just been too thickheaded to notice. "You only want to spend time with me?" I asked.

"That's all," Steck replied.

"And you'll leave Waggett and Zephram alone?"

"I'll leave Waggett alone," she said, "and I won't seek out Zephram. If he comes to me, that's his choice."

I thought about it. I didn't like the picture of my father deliberately approaching a Neut (my foster father seeking out my mother), but if he had ghosts he needed to lay to rest, I could hold my nose and suffer through. After all, Steck wanted me close by her side, didn't she? So I'd be there to keep things platonic if Zephram came calling.

"All right," I told Steck, "you've got a deal. Give me a minute to talk to my father."

"He's in the back."

For some reason, I bowed to her slightly before leaving the room ... but I took Waggett with me.

Zephram was in his bedroom with the door open. He wasn't doing anything—he was sitting fully dressed on the bed, staring bleakly into space.

"Maybe," I said, "I should have warned you she was here."

After a silence, he answered, "That would have been nice."

"I swore an oath to keep it secret. On the Patriarch's hand."

"Oh, well then ..."

He didn't finish his sentence.

Eventually, I said, "It must have been a shock."

"Yes."

"Did you recognize her yourself, or did she approach you after?"

"I recognized her, Fullin. Even though I'd only seen that face once, twenty years ago ... I recognized her. No one else did—I looked around the crowd and they didn't seem to see her at all. They had worked so hard to put her out of their minds. I never understood why anyone would want to forget something ..." He shook his head. "No, I guess I understand."

"Are you going to be all right? I need you to look after Waggett."

"Can't you do it, Fullin? Today of all days ... I'm not so good all of a sudden."

"Look," I said briskly, "you need something to take your mind off Steck. And she's promised to leave you and Waggett alone if I go with her." I plunked Waggett down in Zephram's lap. Dully, as if it was a great effort, my father put his hands on either side of the boy's small ribcage to hold him in place.

"There you go," I told him. "You'll have fun together. And you know what to do—you saw me through all my Commitment Days."

"I'm feeling old today, Fullin."

"Children make people feel young," I answered. "Everyone says that. You be a good boy, Waggett." I gave him a quick kiss on the forehead, then left before Zephram could argue more. Frankly, I couldn't see why the old man was making such a fuss. He only had to babysit a well-behaved toddler. I was stuck with the Neut.

"How's Zephram?" Steck asked when I came back into the front room.

"You rattled him," I said. "If you cared about him, you shouldn't have given him such a shock."

"Things are simple for you, aren't they, Fullin?"

"No. Things are just complicated for everyone else."

Steck sighed. "I hoped you'd grow up like Zephram. Instead, you grew up like me. I've never believed in heredity before, and I don't like it."

She stood up, smoothing her dress and overshirt self-consciously; it must have been a long time since she'd worn such aggressively feminine clothing. I found myself peering at that V neckline again, and forced my gaze away. Next thing I knew, I might be staring at her crotch.

"Are you ready?" she asked.

"Sure, Steck."

"Call me Maria—Rashid thinks it would be better if I use a Southern name today. Heaven forbid that my presence ever remind the town of ugly deeds twenty years ago."

"So you don't want me to call you Mother?"

She looked at me pensively. "If you ever call me Mother," she said at last, "I'll know you truly hate me."

"Then let's go, M—" But I couldn't finish the word. "Maria," I substituted.

Steck gave a tiny smile. "Show me where Rashid is. We have a full morning ahead."

TWELVE

A Kiss for Dorr

I had no chance to watch the look on Steck's face when she saw Bonnakkut's body—the path through the trees was too narrow for us to walk side by side, so I was obliged to take the lead, with my back to the Neut.

Approaching from this direction, we could see the murder scene from twenty paces off. Not that we could see the corpse itself: Rashid knelt on the ground in front of it, conducting an examination of the wounds. As we drew closer, I saw he had snipped off Bonnakkut's bloody shirt to provide a clear view of the belly injuries. Rashid's nose was only a finger away from the body as he peered through a magnifying glass at the slashes.

"Not a beetle after all," Steck said behind me.

I turned. She wore a guarded expression, very contained. It could be the look of a person who was clamping down on real shock; it could also be the look of someone who'd been preparing for this since committing the murder.

"Do we know who did this?" she asked.

"No."

"Definitely a surprise attack," Rashid said without looking up. "No defense wounds."

"What's a defense wound?" I asked.

Steck answered. "Cuts on the hands or arms from trying to block the blade. You see them in almost every knife attack . . . unless the victim was dead before he knew what was happening."

"You two have seen a lot of murders?"

"Enough. When someone important like a Governor or Elemarch gets killed, it's best if a Spark conducts the investigation. More impartial."

"And that's what they do down south—kill Governors and Elemarchs?"

"If 'down south' means Feliss," Steck said, "the answer is no. Feliss is a bourgeois little province that's too self-satisfied to indulge in assassination. But there's more to the world than Feliss."

"I know that." Theoretically, I was supposed to have memorized all the provinces and their capitals—Tober Cove had a good Elemarchy School that taught such things. But even if I'd never gone to the trouble of learning the list myself, I'd heard Cappie recite it enough times when her father demanded. Two hundred and fifty-six provinces; Earth was a big planet.

"The stabs in the belly were likely made after death," Rashid announced suddenly. He straightened up and brushed hair out of his eyes. "The throat slash came first: one slice, that was it. Hard to be a hundred percent sure without any real equipment, but that's my guess."

"Sounds like a crime of passion," Steck said. "The victim's dead on the ground, but the killer still wants to stick him a few more times."

"Either that," Rashid agreed, "or someone wants us to jump to that conclusion." He turned to me. "Do people read OldTech mysteries in this town?"

"People read all kinds of things," I answered. "We have a library."

"With almost fifty books," Steck added disdainfully.

"Hundreds of books," I retorted. "The cove has come a long way since you lived here."

"So much outside information," she marveled. "It must drive Hakoore wild."

I didn't answer . . . but I couldn't help remembering what the old snake said about prosperity corrupting our people.

And now we had a murder.

Voices sounded a short distance in front of us. Moments later Cappie appeared, leading our Doctor Gorallin. Gorallin was a steely woman: steel gray hair and steel gray eyes, with a spine as rigid as metal and fingers of unforgiving iron when she was probing your body for hernias, lumps, and other offenses to propriety. She had been brought up in Tober Cove, but educated at a real medical college down south, one that had worked hard for four centuries to preserve everything the OldTechs knew about the human body. The cost of Gorallin's training had come out of town taxes, as she never ceased to remind us. "Your grandparents sacrificed their hard-earned silver so I could tell if your cervix is healthy, and by damn if I'll let them down because you play shy!"

Yes, there were some things I *did* remember clearly from my female years.

The instant Gorallin saw the corpse, she roared, "Which one of you did this?"

"Person or persons unknown," Rashid answered.

"I found him," I volunteered. "Then Cappie came along and I went to get the Knowledge-Lord."

"Hmph." She tromped up to Bonnakkut and gave him a healthy nudge with her moccasin. When he didn't respond, she announced, "He's meat. That's my official medical opinion."

Lord Rashid cleared his throat. "We were hoping for more in the way of forensic analysis."

"You think I wasted time with forensics when I was in school?" Gorallin snorted and gave the rest of us a "Who is this fool?" look. "Tober Cove didn't pay me to waste time learning things I'd never need. I took pediatrics! Obstetrics! Those were my electives. Around here, we care about kids, not carcasses."

"So you can't say anything about the cuts . . ."

"Cuts are made by sharp things," the doctor snapped. "Like the girl's spear. Your Bozzle's machete." She gave me a half-second loo-kover. "The boy's not carrying anything, but he could grab a kitchen knife at his father's place, not thirty seconds away."

Rashid raised his eyes briefly to heaven. "I really think we should move on from the idea that any of us is the killer."

"Why?" Gorallin replied. "You're the only ones here."

"In our experience," Steck said tightly, "murderers often run away from the scene of the crime."

"In my experience, they don't," Gorallin growled. "I've lived here fifty-five years, less the time I spent south learning my trade. Seen three murders, and every one, the killer was right with the body. Wife who hit her husband too hard and was crying with him in her arms, pleading for him to take her in death-marriage. Husband who caught his wife in bed with her best friend, chop-chop-chop, murder-murder-suicide. And a drunk who knifed his brother . . . hell, I found him trying to sew up the chest wound to make it all better. Had a spool of the cord he used to mend fishnets. Not bad stitching, given how soused he was—the man could have been a surgeon. Or a devil-be-damned forensic pathologist."

With that she wheeled about and strode down the trail toward the center of town. Rashid took a step after her then restrained himself. "It must be an experience," he said, "when she tells you to turn your head and cough."

"Oh, yeah," answered Cappie, Steck, and I in unison.

*   *   *

Ten useless minutes later, Rashid said, "There's nothing more I can learn from the body. What's the custom now? Notify the next of kin?"

"He's male," Cappie answered. "The Patriarch's Man takes custody of the corpse. But someone should tell Bonnakkut's mother and . . ."

She didn't finish her sentence. Bonnakkut had a six-year-old daughter named Ivis. Till the end of her life, maybe the feasting and celebration of Commitment ceremonies would remind Ivis of the day her daddy died.

"Speaking to next of kin is priestess work," Steck said. Her voice had suddenly fallen soft. "If a mother has to hear bad news, it should come from someone who can comfort her."

"You're right." Cappie gave Steck a keen look, and I could understand why. It was easy to forget that Steck had been a hair away from becoming priestess herself—that Leeta had chosen Steck as someone with the brain and heart to prop up the women of the cove. Things may have soured inside my mother, but bits were still intact. I caught a glimpse of Rashid, and he was looking at Steck too: smiling fondly, the way men do.

It occurred to me, he might have been glad for an excuse to dress Steck as pure woman.

"Do you want to take care of that, Steck?" Rashid asked. "You and Cappie?"

For a moment Steck paused; then she shook her head. "The mother will want to see faces she knows. Not strangers."

"I'll get Leeta," Cappie said. She gave Steck a little smile, but the Neut only responded with a nod. I realized it was hard for Steck, turning down a chance to do priestess work after so many years.

My mother is sad, I thought; *my mother is a sad woman.* I couldn't help remembering how Zephram had visited her during the Silence of Mistress Snow. Out of all the doors in the village, Steck's was the last one for someone to enter.

Cappie went to pick up Leeta. Together they would break the news to Bonnakkut's mother, Kenna.

As for me, I got conscripted to escort Rashid to Hakoore's, while Steck stayed with the body. I expected Steck to protest, but she didn't. She seemed subdued, possibly thinking how she had lost the chance to become comforter to the women of our village . . . possibly thinking something completely different. I couldn't read my mother's mind.

It was only a minute later, as I was leading Rashid up the trail, that it occurred to me Steck might be happy for a chance alone with the body . . . if she'd had anything to do with the murder. She could check to make sure she hadn't left behind any clues.

"You know she's my mother," I said to Rashid.

"Who?"

"Steck. Maria. Whatever you want to call her. She's my mother."

"You're joking."

"She's from Tober Cove. She has to be *someone's* mother."

Rashid stopped walking. "I never thought of that. You all have children, don't you?"

"Yes."

"No exceptions?"

"Some girls turn out to have medical problems. But Steck wasn't one of them."

"And you're her . . ." He didn't say the word. "Is that why she wanted to kill you last night?"

"It was why she went to the marsh to find me—she knew it was my year to be there. The knife fight was just an impromptu thing."

"Because you tried to kill her first."

I shrugged. "Cappie overreacted."

"For a quiet little village," Rashid said, "Tober Cove has a wicked taste for blood."

"We're fine when Steck's not around."

"Don't speak ill of your mother." He paused. "She's really your mother?"

"Steck didn't tell you?"

He didn't answer. He didn't have to.

I'd never met anyone as important as Rashid, but I'd heard plenty of stories: official ones taught in school, as well as campfire talk at sunset. Bozzles weren't supposed to keep secrets from their masters. There should be a lake full of trust between Bozzle and master, with no one quietly peeing when the water's over your waist. Too much of that starts killing the fish.

Cappie once told me I should stay away from metaphors.

"I just wanted you to know," I told Rashid, "Steck had an ulterior motive getting you to come here."

"To watch her child Commit," Rashid answered after a pause. "That's no crime, Fullin. It's an important day in your life, isn't it?"

"The most important."

"What kind of mother would she be if she didn't want to see you? Perfectly understandable . . . perfectly natural." His voice was getting stronger, more definite. "This shows quite a positive side to Steck's character."

"You're making excuses for her," I said. "Is she your lover?"

Rashid coughed. "Where I come from, boys don't ask that about their mothers."

"Where I come from, they do. Do you love her?"

"You tell me," he answered. "How do *you* feel about her? One minute you're screaming, '*Kill the Neut*,' and the next I can see you thinking she's not so bad."

"One minute she acts hateful, and the next she lets on she might be a human being."

"That's Steck," Rashid admitted. He started walking again, the plastic soles of his boots clicking when they touched any pimples of limestone poking up through the soil.

I fell in behind him. "My father still loves her," I said. "At least I think he does. Or maybe it just pains him she's lonely."

Rashid murmured, "Sometimes that kind of pain passes for love."

I couldn't argue with him. My mother seemed to have the same effect on a lot of people.

The village streets had come alive with children and parents. Breakfast was finished, and everyone wanted to squeeze in some playtime before the gods arrived at noon. The most popular game had to be Catch: Catch with bright rubber balls bought down-peninsula, or floppy homemade pouches stuffed with dried corn kernels. Mothers threw easy lobs straight to their children's hands, while fathers made the kids run, work for their successes. But all the parents were watching with keen bright eyes—trying to memorize how their boys and girls used their bodies, because it was all about to change.

I've already mentioned how my female half felt awkward in my male body the night before. The same thing happened every year at the solstice switchover ... except that it was more confusing when you were only five or six. Your hands were bigger or smaller, your eyes weren't the same height above the ground, and it always looked like your feet weren't the right distance away. It was worse come puberty: the presence or absence of breasts, the difference in how your weight sat around your hips, and of course, the variations in sheer muscular strength and stamina—not that your male half always had the physical advantage. Female-Me went into a growth spurt at thirteen, and Male-Me didn't catch up until sixteen. My two halves had a full head difference during those years, and that meant embarrassing clumsiness for weeks after each transition. Parents found that kind of awkwardness amusing and endearing ... which is why they made a point of testing their kids' coordination just before changeover and would repeat the same games when the children came home again.

The kids checked themselves out just as thoroughly after each change. You just couldn't help staring at yourself. A whole year had passed since you had occupied your other self, and even if the body had just been sleeping in Birds Home, it had still been growing—changing—while your eyes and brain had been living elsewhere.

You heard a different voice echoing in your head.

So you marveled at your arms: they had hair or they didn't, and all the moles and freckles you'd been used to were now replaced by a different set, ones you vaguely remembered from a year ago but which seemed darker or bigger . . . more noticeable anyway, and you thought all the other kids would gawk at these strange marks on your skin.

And my oh my, your skin . . . especially once you hit puberty. You couldn't help touching your skin. It was skin exactly like the skin you lusted after just days before. I don't know why my skin had such an effect on me. Of course, there were also the overtly sexual body parts, and yes, a lot of teenagers (including yours truly) held solitary Orgasm Derbies every day for a week after each gender swap; but for me, having different skin was always the most arousing change. Male in a male body, I might find myself remembering how my female half had longed to stroke a boy's chest or thighs, to feel muscles close beneath the skin, the hard warmth . . . and female in a female body, I still recalled the pure lust that boiled in my brother self at the sight of a mere bare shoulder . . .

You felt sexy. That's the simple truth. You looked at your skin, your legs, your body, and you *knew* you were sexy. You knew how the opposite sex burned in your presence. And for a few weeks, until you got caught up in your own new burning, you knew you were wonderfully, powerfully desirable.

In those few weeks, lovemaking was always lazily relaxed—enthusiastic to be sure, because you'd slept for a year and were juiced up now with the urge to take your newly regained equipment for a ride. But for a while, you never asked, "Does he like me? Does she want me?" You possessed a comfortable confidence, knowing you had what your bedpartner craved.

Doubt only surfaced later: when the sweat-sheen dried and the whispers in the dark strayed into topics beyond, "Isn't this great!" When you had to deal with each other as people instead of bodies. When, "Of course he wants me!" gained the tag, "But does he want me the right way?" When your sweetheart wanted to set a definite time to get together and you preferred to play it by ear.

When being who you were stopped being a delicious novelty, and settled back into a snarled tangle of normal humanity.

Suddenly, the realization struck me: after today, I'd never experience that golden self-wonder again. I'd be myself, day after day, locked into a single identity till I died.

Feeling that, I knew the real reason why parents came out into the streets to play Catch with their children: to remember when they thought they'd never stop being new.

Hakoore and Dorr lived in a house of gray flagstone, meticulously preserved since OldTech times. No doubt it had taken a few tumbles in the four hundred years since OldTech civilization committed suicide . . . but when a flagstone wall collapses, you can just stack the stones again, using fresh mortar and timber framing. Wood houses rot, and bricks erode one pock at a time; Master Stone, however, gives his children a chilly permanence, so they can last to see the Great Arrival at the culmination of all things.

Dorr came out even before we had set foot on the porch. I don't know what she had been trying to do with her hair—mere minutes ago in front of the Council Hall, it had been combed to ignorable anonymity. Now one side was clumped like a haymow, while the other was frazzled to the consistency of a bird's nest that's been gale-whacked out of its tree. It was the kind of mess a seven-year-old girl makes when she discovers the principle of "teasing," then loses her patience halfway through. Surely Dorr was past that stage . . . although now that I considered it, I couldn't remember her ever coifing herself beyond the minimal limits of neatness. Most of the time she let her hair go about its independent business, as if she were loath to burden it with her own expectations; I wondered what had sparked this sudden change.

Did she want to impress Lord Rashid? But here she was now, meeting him nose-to-nose on the porch steps of her house without a flicker of emotion crossing her face.

She said nothing, waiting for Rashid to speak first. Rumor whispered that Hakoore once told her she had an ugly voice, and she'd used it sparingly ever since; but sometimes I wondered if Dorr had started the rumor herself so people would hate her father. Whatever the cause for her silence, I'd seldom heard her talk over the past years . . . even during that odd period when Dorr just happened to be lingering outside our house every time I headed to the marsh for violin practice.

Rashid eventually realized Dorr would not bubble out effusive welcomes, so he accepted the conversational duties himself. "Hello. We're looking for the Patriarch's Man." He spoke slower and enunciated more clearly than usual. Perhaps he thought Dorr was wrong in the head . . . not an unnatural conclusion for anyone looking at her semi-threshed hair.

"We have to see Hakoore," I told her. "You could say it's official."

Dorr raised an eyebrow.

"Nothing to do with his visiting me in the marsh," I said hastily. "Something else that's come up."

She shrugged and held out her hand. To me. The gesture was surprising enough that I put my hand in hers without thinking. She closed her fingers carefully, as if worried about causing me pain—evidence that she must know what Hakoore did to me in the marsh—but after a moment, she gripped me warmly and pulled me forward up the stairs.

This was strange behavior, even for Dorr. Yes, she'd had that crush-smush on me when I was fourteen, but that had vanished as uneventfully as it first arose. These days when I played violin for weddings and such, I still noticed her watching me with glittering intensity . . . but Dorr was glittering and intense about everything she did.

Besides, I was used to people ogling me as I performed. The price of talent.

Had Dorr been oiling a torch for me all this time? Maybe letting it flare brighter, now that Cappie and I weren't cooing with domestic bliss? Had she made an effort to gussy up her hair to catch my eye—one last kick at the can on the day I would choose a sex for the rest of my life?

And had she thought of this on her own, or had Hakoore put her up to it?

Oooo. Ugh.

I could just imagine the old snake whipping into his daughter, hissing about her duty to the Patriarch. "Granddaughter, go *influence* that young weasel." Dorr would diligently set about prettifying her hair, and just as diligently sabotage the whole effort in submerged protest against Grandpa's dictatorial ways. It had nothing to do with me—she might still find me attractive, even as she beat her hair with a whisk to scare me off. Somewhere in the quirks of her mind (maybe the same place where her unsettling quilt designs got hatched), she might even be drawn by the idea of submitting herself to her granddad's disciple, the same way she submitted to Hakoore himself.

The Patriarch's Man was forbidden to marry, but he was definitely allowed to dally. Way back when, the Patriarch had supposedly sampled all the women in the village—with their flattered permission, of course. Hakoore was now too old for fleshly urges—at least I hoped he was, because the idea of him tangling sheets with a woman made my stomach churn gravel—but in his day (I had it on good authority), he besported himself in accordance with the Patriarch's outreach-to-the-masses example.

Would that be my life if I became Hakoore's disciple? And was Dorr now holding my hand because the idea baited some hook in her mind? Maybe Hakoore didn't need to pressure her more than a nudge . . . not if she'd been waiting all her life for an excuse to approach me.

Or maybe I was reading too much into simple hand-holding. This might just have been her unschooled attempt at being a good hostess . . . or perhaps sympathy for how her grandfather had bruised my knuckles at dawn.

Sometimes I wish the gods had given us the ability to read each other's minds. Alternating genitalia each year is nice, but there are questions it doesn't begin to answer.

The interior of Hakoore's house smelled of Dorr's dyes: dampish plants from onions to bloodwort, some fresh, some crinkling their way into the late stages of decomposition. I knew she kept her mixings in the basement—during my female years, I sometimes bought dyes here rather than make my own—but the odors barged their way out of the cellar with the determination of a drunkard, settling thickly into the cloth oversheets that covered all the furniture.

Those oversheets were densely embroidered: a few with Dorr's work (slanted horses stretched like taffy, winged spirits burying their faces in leaves), but mostly with the work of her mother. Dorr's mother had been a meticulous needleworker; or more accurately, an obsessed one. From dawn to dusk, she filled her days with French knots, lazy daisies, and countless cross-stitches . . . literally filled the day, with no time spent on cooking, cleaning, or even getting dressed.

No one ever told me what caused the mother's compulsion—whether a friend had betrayed her, a lover died, or the gods spoke to her in voices that drowned out the rest of the world. Perhaps Hakoore had traumatized her with the Patriarch's Hand, crushing her under its grip whenever she misbehaved. Whatever the reason, Dorr's mother simply stitched with all her strength until the day Dorr turned twelve; then the mother went to the basement, drank a jugful of her most poisonous dyes, and choked her life away with smeary rainbow vomit. ("She must have dreamed of that death for years," Zephram told me. "She must have dragged it along like a weight tied to her ankle, until it started dragging her.")

All of this may explain why Dorr seldom spoke, why she made the quilts she did, and why she passively submitted to her grandfather's will . . . but I'm suspicious of glib hindsight analysis. It was too easy to say

Dorr had slipped helplessly into her mad mother's shoes. Dorr was not buffeted by irresistible winds in her mind; she just *liked* the role of someone shadowed by insanity. It shielded her. It excused her from small talk, and from her Great-Aunt Veen dropping hints that she wasn't getting any younger. When Dorr's baby by Master Crow died in a four-month miscarriage, Tober Cove accepted the death as the sort of bad luck that happened to Dorr.

(Cappie actually slapped me when I whispered Dorr might have tried a sip of the plant dyes too. Tobers aren't supposed to know there are vegetable extracts which can spill a fetus out of the womb before its time.)

With all these thoughts running through my head, I found myself staring at Dorr more intently than I intended . . . and suddenly she turned, meeting my gaze with hers. She studied me for a moment, as if debating whether to break her silence and ask that most female of questions, "What are you thinking?" I saw no madness under that mad hair—simply a woman of deep and silent privacy, *in* the world, but not *of* it. Her lips parted and she took a breath to speak; but at that moment, a cough sounded across the room and Hakoore shuffled in through the doorway.

"What now?" he snapped.

I had broken eye contact with Dorr the moment I heard Hakoore coming, but I still felt as if I'd been caught in some guilty act. "Bonnakkut's dead," I blurted. "Murdered."

The fingers of Dorr's free hand brushed lightly across my wrist. It seemed more like a caress than a gesture of shock at the news. "Will you take possession of the body?" I asked Hakoore.

"Bonnakkut?" the old man said, with a tone so sharp he obviously thought I was lying. "Bonnakkut's been murdered?"

"I'm afraid so," Rashid answered. "On a trail through the woods out . . ." He waved his hand in the direction of Zephram's house.

"Who murdered him?" Hakoore asked.

"We don't know," Rashid said.

Hakoore looked at him with narrowed eyes. "Where was that Bozzle of yours?"

"With my father," I said immediately. I don't know if I was defending Steck because she was my mother or because I was her son.

"With your father," Hakoore repeated. "With her old . . ." He hissed in disgust. "Are there any devils left in hell, or have they all come to Tober Cove today?

Rashid looked to me as if he expected an explanation of what the old snake meant. I ignored him. "You should take possession of the body now," I told Hakoore. "It's already attracting insects."

"Hmph." Hakoore was obligated to collect the body as soon as possible, and he didn't like it. Our Patriarch's Man preferred to make other people dance to his tune; he had a reputation for hating deaths and births, because they came at odd hours and forced him into someone else's schedule. "Has the doctor looked at the body?" he asked.

"She says the man is dead," Rashid answered dryly. "Her interest doesn't extend further."

"Hmph," Hakoore said again. He must have hoped to gain a few minutes by sending for Gorallin. "All right. If it has to be done. Woman!" he growled at Dorr. "Let go of that fool boy and get the stretcher. Wait, wait, where's my bag?"

Dorr pointed. The Patriarch's Satchel, containing unguents and totems used in last rites, hung on the back of the front door. I'd seen it hanging there every time I visited the house—Hakoore must have known exactly where it was and just wanted to shout at someone who wasn't a Spark Lord.

While the old snake busied himself taking the bag off its hook, Dorr went for the stretcher . . . but she didn't let go of my hand. Rather than make a scene trying to detach myself in front of the Knowledge-Lord, I went along with her: down the cellar steps and into the basement, where the smell of dyes increased to vinegar proportions.

Since there were small glass windows high up one wall, we didn't need a candle for light. Still, the large cellar workroom had an earthy dimness to it, with piles of shadow heaped up in clots wherever the sun didn't reach through the windows. It struck me that maybe this faint darkness wasn't the best place to have a witchy older woman clinging deliberately to my arm.

"Fullin," she whispered.

Uh-oh.

"The stretcher is over here," she finished.

She guided me to the gloomiest corner of the room, where the stretcher was propped against the wall. It was nothing fancy, just ordinary sail canvas slung between two carrying poles. Dorr gestured toward it and released my hand so I could carry it; she didn't offer to help. I bundled up the load and hefted it off the floor, wishing the poles weren't quite so heavy. Of course they had to be good stout wood, to bear the weight of the cove's plumpest citizens without breaking. Still, the whole package made an awkward armload that took several readjustments before I finally had it under control.

That's when Dorr kissed me. Soft hands clutching my shoulders, then lips pressed against mine and her tongue slipping briefly inside before she stepped back a pace.

"Dorr, don't," I said in a low voice.

"Wasn't that what you were expecting?" she whispered. "What you thought I was going to do?"

"Well . . . yes."

"You thought I'd kiss you, so I did," she said. "Heaven forbid you could ever be mistaken in reading a person."

"I was that obvious?"

"You're always obvious," Dorr answered. "That's why you're interesting."

Not the kind of interest I ever wanted to provoke. "We should take the stretcher upstairs," I said.

She slipped back to give me room and motioned toward the steps. "Go ahead."

I adjusted my load again and moved forward. As I passed her, she darted forward again: hands, lips, tongue. It was over in the blink of an eye, and Dorr eased away with a triumphant look on her face. "The first kiss was yours," she said. "The second was mine."

THIRTEEN

A Wife for the Dead Man

The parents playing Catch in the street knew what it meant when the Patriarch's Man walked through town with his stretcher. They fell silent and still, even as their children called, "Throw the ball! Throw the ball!" People looked at me or Dorr, their eyes asking, "Who?" No one had the nerve to speak the question out loud: no one until we passed the house of Vaygon the Seedster, and his wife Veen planted herself in front of us with the air of a woman who won't budge until she gets an answer.

Veen was Hakoore's older sister; or rather she had been his older sister when Hakoore was a runny-nosed boy, and his older brother when Hakoore was an idolizing little girl. If anyone in the village was unimpressed with Hakoore's hissing snake act, it was Veen.

"Last rites?" she asked loudly. She had a surprisingly deep voice for a woman, even though old age had shrunk her body like moss drying on a rock. "Who's dead, Hakoore?"

With any other woman, the Patriarch's Man might have snapped, "No concern of yours!" A pity for him that wouldn't work with his sister; she'd be completely comfortable raising a scene, a harangue that would be recounted and inflated by gossip for weeks to come. "Bonnakkut," Hakoore told her in a low voice, though he must have known that whispering wouldn't keep the secret.

"Bonnakkut!" Veen repeated, as naturally loud as thunder. At least four other people were standing close enough to hear, all of them wearing "I'd never eavesdrop" expressions that didn't fool anybody. Within fifteen minutes, the whole town would know the news.

"What did the fool boy do?" Veen asked. "Shoot himself with that gun?"

Even though she was his sister, Hakoore hissed. No one was supposed to know about the gun, or about whatever other bribes Rashid doled out to the Council of Elders. Still, what did Hakoore expect? Veen's husband was Vaygon, and Vaygon was an Elder; it went without saying Veen knew everything that happened behind the Council Hall's closed door.

If I'd been Hakoore, I'd have let Veen think whatever she wanted; but I suppose the Patriarch's Man didn't want the town to go wild with rumors about firearms. "Bonnakkut didn't die from any gun!" Hakoore growled.

"Then what happened?" Veen asked.

Hakoore should have known the question was coming, but he had no ready answer. Veen always had that effect on him—he just couldn't think fast enough in her presence.

Sometimes I'm glad I'm an only child.

Smoothly, Rashid spoke up for the tongue-tied Hakoore. "This isn't the place to discuss details," the Spark Lord said. "No doubt there'll be a public announcement in due course." Putting an armored hand on Hakoore's shoulder, he gave the gentlest of nudges and the old snake quickly spurred himself forward.

Veen didn't move from the middle of the street. Hakoore was forced to skirt around her, giving her a wide berth like you'd keep your distance from a porcupine. Dorr, on the other hand, murmured, "Auntie," as she passed Veen, and planted a vigorous kiss on the old woman's cheek. It seemed to surprise Veen as much as the rest of us.

When we reached the murder scene, Steck was sitting on a low limestone outcrop, carefully stripping the greenery out of an oak leaf to get down to the bare leaf skeleton. As far as I could tell, Bonnakkut's body was exactly how we'd left it. (For a moment, I contemplated what would happen if Steck touched the corpse. Could Bonnakkut suck in a Neut soul to serve as his death-wife? Just imagine the dead Bonnakkut's reaction when he saw what he'd done!)

Rashid asked, "Everything all right, Maria?"

Steck nodded. With the possible exception of Dorr, we all knew the Neut's real name . . . but I suppose Rashid *liked* addressing his Bozzle as a woman. "Okay—" the Spark turned to Hakoore "—do what you have to."

The Patriarch's Man lowered himself stiffly beside the body and blinked at it. Then he touched his hand to Bonnakkut's throat and stroked the bloodied flesh, running his fingers along the length of the death cut. I couldn't tell if this was part of the last rites or mere curiosity—I'd never seen the last rites ritual before. Funerals, yes: I'd attended many funerals up on Beacon Point, swatting mosquitos in summer and blowing on my hands in winter. But last rites were held in private, seldom attended by more than the priest and the corpse.

Hakoore lifted his fingers to his nose. I suppose the old snake enjoyed smelling the blood on them. Then he turned to me and hissed, "Get over here, boy. Watch and learn."

Rashid and Steck turned to me with curious expressions on their faces. Dorr smiled to herself. I didn't want to explain and I didn't want to take part in the rites, but I also didn't want to stir up a hornets' nest by refusing Hakoore. Reluctantly, I set down the stretcher and went to kneel by the corpse.

"Can you explain what you're going to do?" Rashid asked. He had the sound of a man who wanted to jot notes, but was restraining himself in deference to the solemn occasion. Hakoore didn't answer so I had to hold my tongue too. Surprisingly, it was the usually silent Dorr who finally spoke up.

"Bonnakkut's soul is a child in the womb," she said in a voice barely above a whisper. "It doesn't want to leave the comfortable enclosure of his body. But the body can no longer see, hear, or feel. That makes the soul isolated and lonely. It seeks a death-wife."

"A death-wife," Rashid repeated. "Oh, I *like* that name. What is it?"

"A completion—the dead man's missing half. When we are born, we are each male and female, both in one. At Commitment, the male or female half of our soul is absorbed back into the body of the gods. Except those who keep both halves." Her eyes were on Steck . . . which meant she knew Steck was Neut, and Hakoore was no better at keeping secrets from his family than Vaygon the Seedster. I doubted that he actually shared confidences with his granddaughter, but I could easily picture him throwing a tantrum about the presence of a Neut in the cove. He'd do that in front of Dorr with no more thought about her than a piece of the furniture.

"So," Dorr continued in her half-whisper, "a dead man longs for a death-wife, just as a dead woman longs for a death-husband. The half-soul wants to become whole again. If I were to touch Bonnakkut now, he would seize my spirit like a lover and lock me to him in the deep forever blackness. We would lie together in that decaying flesh, feverishly coupling till the end of time . . . all in a futile attempt to crush ourselves into one complete being."

She looked at me. Her eyes gleamed. It could have been a kind of desire . . . but I told myself she was just baiting me.

"So," said Rashid, "males should avoid touching female corpses and vice versa. Fascinating." His fingers played with the pouch on his belt where he kept his notebook; clearly, he wanted to whip the book out. "And you're about to perform a ritual that makes the body safe?"

"My grandfather will entice Bonnakkut from his body by offering him a proper death-wife: one of the gods."

"A god. Really."

I could tell Rashid had to make an effort to sound impressed rather than amused.

"The gods are great," Dorr replied. "They may take any number of husbands or wives. Think of Mistress Leaf, for example." Dorr gestured to the woods around us. "Mistress Leaf fills the trees here, and in the forest beyond, and in all the forests of the Earth, and all the forests of all the planets from here to the edge of the Glass. If she chooses Bonnakkut, she has ample abundance to be his wife forever, and wife to every other she may take for her own. Do you think a mere man would ever be disappointed with her? She's beautiful and sweet . . . maybe not clever, but Bonnakkut will do well if she accepts him."

"And what other gods are available if, ah, Mistress Leaf decides Bonnakkut isn't Mr. Right?"

"Mistress Water, Mistress Night, Mistress Deer . . ."

"Mistress Want," Steck suggested from her seat on the rock.

"Who's Mistress Want?" Rashid asked.

"Not all the Tober gods are happy and woodsy," Steck replied. "Mistress Want is a symbol of poverty. Starvation. Despair. She's usually depicted as a skeleton, creeping invisibly past your hut at night."

"And she can be a death-wife too?"

"If no one else will take you," Steck said. "Most other gods have standards—I don't imagine Mistress Leaf wants anything to do with a bear-fart like Bonnakkut. But Mistress Want will wrestle almost anyone into her bed. As will Master Disease."

Steck smiled at me, teasing. I glared back at her.

"This is quite an elegant system," Rashid said with too much patronization in his voice. "Bad people obviously suffer a hellish afterlife with Mistress Want or Master Disease, while good people are taken into bliss with one of the other gods. And since you have a lot of benevolent gods, people with different tastes can all have something to look forward to. A woodsman might be happy with Mistress Leaf, a sailor with Mistress Water . . ."

"Don't get it backwards!" Hakoore hissed. "The gods do the choosing, not the mortals. Right now, there may be a dozen gods standing among us, talking over which will take Bonnakkut for a husband."

Dorr gave me a look. Obviously, we both doubted that Bonnakkut would have so many takers.

"How do we know which gods are nearby?" Rashid asked.

"We don't," Hakoore snapped. "It's none of our business, who's here and who isn't. We just have to persuade Bonnakkut to come out of his body. If he takes even the tiniest peek into the world at large, he'll see the goddess who's chosen him and it will be love at first sight."

"Even if it's Mistress Want?"

"She's still a goddess," Dorr answered. "With a great and terrible beauty that will pull Bonnakkut like a rope. If she's his best wife out of all the other gods, he'll spill himself with lust when he sees the snow-pure whiteness of her bones."

Steck made a soft choking sound. Even Hakoore chose not to look at his granddaughter for several minutes thereafter.

Last rites aren't intended to be showy. People are generally sent away while the Patriarch's Man plays matchmaker for the corpse's soul . . . but Hakoore wanted me there as his "disciple" and it soon became apparent Rashid had no intention of leaving while we practiced our "indigenous cultural ways." Hakoore made a half-hearted attempt at getting rid of Steck, but she just laughed. Dorr was the only one he had a chance of ordering around, and he didn't say a word to her.

Therefore, we were all standing close as he opened his embroidered satchel and began to pull out the elements for the ritual: a gold pin, an OldTech shaving mirror, a small wineskin . . .

"What are these things for?" Rashid asked.

Hakoore plunged the pin into Bonnakkut's arm. "First things first," he answered. "Test that the man's really dead."

Rashid pointed to the throat wound. "Isn't that obvious?"

"I don't cut corners," Hakoore hissed. Placing the nozzle of the wineskin into Bonnakkut's ear, he gave a good healthy squeeze. Clear fluid squirted out, bounced against Bonnakkut's eardrum, and splashed onto the ground. "It's only water," Hakoore said before Rashid could ask. "But if a person doesn't react to a spritz in the ear, odds are the person is past reacting."

Rashid turned to Steck. "Don't you just love folk wisdom?"

"You can find the same in any OldTech medical text," Steck replied.

"But when it happens in the middle of a forest, it's quaint. I must say . . ."

He stopped and looked toward the village. I had already heard the sound of feet running toward us, and the slash of leaves as someone swiped at a branch that lay too close to the path. A moment later, the remnants of the Warriors Society stormed into sight, all three of them breathing heavily.

It's an odd thing about bullies: they seem so ridiculous in the abstract. From a distance, I thought of Kaeomi, Stallor and Mintz as bumbling oafs—Bonnakkut's pack of yappy little terriers. I always managed to forget how imposing they were face to face. How quick and muscular Kaeomi was. How Stallor's barrel chest loomed at the level of my head. How Mintz had the just plain mean expression of someone who wouldn't stop hitting you merely because you'd fallen unconscious. Our three warriors weren't quite as bad as the Southern murderers and rapists they had to track down, but they were all men who'd sneer and call you weakling for playing the violin.

"Get out of here," Hakoore snapped at the three of them. "I'm performing last rites."

"So?" Mintz kept advancing and the other two followed with barely a pause. "People are saying that Bonnakkut . . ."

He stopped, looking down at the First Warrior's corpse. Stallor and Kaeomi stepped up beside him, making a wall of muscle. Since I was kneeling beside the deceased, the warriors towered above me as tall as firs.

"Who did it?" Kaeomi asked. I had the feeling he was talking to me, though he wasn't looking in my direction.

"We don't have any suspects yet," Rashid answered. "I've barely started my investigation."

"It's *our* investigation," Mintz snapped. "We're the Warriors Society."

Dorr let out a derisive snort. Mintz wheeled on her. "What was that?"

She met his gaze silently, her expression just short of outright mockery.

"Investigations are up to the First Warrior," Hakoore hissed irritably. "Not you three."

"One of us will be First Warrior soon enough," Kaeomi said.

"And how does that work?" Rashid asked pleasantly. "Do you hold an election? Tests of skill?"

"Traditionally," Steck answered, "each warrior spends the next few weeks being an officious pain-in-the-ass and alienating the entire village. When Father Ash and Mother Dust get fed up with all that posturing, they appoint one of the candidates more or less at random . . . unless they secretly go behind closed doors and compare penis size, which is what it's really about anyway."

All three warriors turned angrily toward the Neut, their hands bunching into fists. I was glad their attention was focused on my mother, so they couldn't see me trying not to laugh.

"You!" Kaeomi's face reddened as he pointed his spear toward Steck. "You're the prime suspect here!"

"Why?"

"Because you're a—"

"Cherished guest, officially granted hospitality?" Steck suggested.

"We know what you are," Mintz glowered. "And hospitality or not . . ."

Dorr made a soft gasp and gave Mintz a sudden shove. For a second I couldn't believe it; then I heard a thunk and saw a knife hilt sticking out of a tree beside my mother's head. Mintz must have drawn the blade stealthily and only Dorr's quick eyes had noticed. Her shove had knocked off Mintz's throw.

"Bitch!" Mintz growled at Dorr. He lashed out, a straightarm swing that slammed across her chest and propelled her backward. By Mintz's standards, it was almost a love-tap: just pushing her out of the way, with no intention to do real damage. Even so, it knocked the wind out of Dorr's lungs and she stumbled back, sucking air as she struggled to keep her balance on the uneven ground. Back she came toward me . . . and that meant toward Bonnakkut's corpse, still hungry for a death-wife. Kneeling there, I had no choice—I threw myself across the dead man, trying to cover his body to protect Dorr from touching it.

A second later, Dorr tripped and fell on top of me.

I was facing the ground so I didn't see exactly how she came down. She must have twisted around somehow, because she fell front first rather than on her back. Her hand thrust out to catch herself; I heard the dull *chud* of bone snapping as something broke in her wrist. Then her weight crushed down onto me.

Breath huffed out of my lungs. Somewhere close by, Hakoore growled with outrage, but neither Dorr nor I had enough air for sound. We lay there, me pressed hard against Bonnakkut's corpse, my nose actually digging into his cooling cheek; and Dorr above me, flat against my back. I could feel her breasts squashed into me . . . and I could also feel . . .

I could feel . . .

Pressing into me, the unmistakable feel of . . . pressing into my rump . . .

I've been a woman. I know what it's like when a man comes up fondly behind you and snuggles his crotch against your butt.

Thank the gods, at least Dorr wasn't erect.

*　　*　　*

There was a fight . . . or maybe it only deserves to be called a scuffle. Steck drew her machete, its blade glinting at the edge of my peripheral vision. Then Rashid shouted something I couldn't hear because of Dorr's pained panting in my ear.

Whatever Rashid said, it had to be a threat—Spark Lords had a strict scorched-earth policy when it came to protecting their own. I don't know if Rashid even drew a weapon . . . but that armor of his might have concealed an arsenal of guns, death beams, any of the thousand and one lethal gadgets you hear about in campfire tales. Even Mintz was smart enough to realize he'd gone too far. In a moment, I could hear feet pounding away into the distance, our brave warriors running off through the trees.

And I scarcely paid them any attention.

Dorr was a Neut. I could feel a woman's breasts and a man's groin, tight against me, *touching* me except for our clothes.

Feverishly, I tried to crawl my way out, away from being sandwiched between a corpse and a Neut. I didn't know which appalled me more.

"Hold still!" Hakoore hissed, and he slapped my shoulder. "Dorr's hurt."

Hakoore. The Patriarch's Man. He had to know about Dorr. How could he not know? He lived in the same house, for heaven's sake. Wouldn't she have to shave several times a day to keep her face looking female? Maybe not—I'd heard that some Neuts were naturally smooth-faced like women. But even so . . .

He'd have to know. The Patriarch's Man. And he protected her.

Oh, I could imagine how it all happened. If anyone in the village had the self-destructive defiance to Commit Neut, it was Dorr. She might have done it simply to rebel against Hakoore, or to make an artistic statement in the same vein as her taffy-stretched horses. Then again, Dorr might have chosen it as the only escape from her grandfather's tyranny: guaranteed banishment to a new life in the South.

Except that she must have looked too much like herself.

When people come back after Commitment, no one asks them to drop their pants to prove they aren't Neut. It's assumed everyone will just know—if you return from Birds Home and you don't look like your male or female self, you have to be Neut. But suppose Dorr was like Cappie's sister Olimbarg: suppose the Neut version of Dorr wasn't so different from the female. Dorr's last year before Commitment had been spent male . . . so when she came back from Birds Home, no one had seen her female body since the summer before. If her Neut body looked enough like her female self that no one immediately cried foul . . .

Back Dorr went to Hakoore's house. Probably delighted with herself.

She'd never openly confronted the old snake, and wouldn't do so now—no stripping naked to exhibit what she'd become. But in her passive defiant way, she'd soon make sure Hakoore found out: leaving the door to the commode ajar as she urinated standing up, something like that. Only Hakoore never kicked her out in disgrace. He didn't set her free. Our Patriarch's Man hadn't denounced her. Maybe he didn't want to lose face in front of the community; maybe he refused to let Dorr slip from his grasp; maybe he had some actual affection for her, hard as that was to believe. He kept her home and kept her under his thumb.

I tried to remember how many times I'd seen Dorr out of the house without Hakoore keeping a milky eye on her. Not often. And it suddenly occurred to me why Dorr seldom spoke, and then only in whispers: her Neut face might be close to her old one, but her voice had changed. Her voice must have deepened and Hakoore bullied her into keeping that a secret.

For a moment, I almost felt sorry for her . . . for It. Then I remembered those two kisses in the basement, and I almost retched. My lips had touched a Neut. Been touched by a Neut. Had that *thing* been pining for me all these years? *No*, I told myself, *no*. This was all Steck's fault. Dorr had only grown brash at the sight of another Neut, an unashamed Neut with no sexual scruples . . .

"Let me help you up," Steck said from close by. She was talking to Dorr, and there was a soppy tenderness in her voice. Another person might have taken this as simple gratitude—Dorr *had* saved Steck by throwing off Mintz's aim—but I thought I heard more in my mother's tone.

Recognition? Approval? It wouldn't surprise me that Neuts could identify each other in some creepy way we normal people wouldn't understand.

Dorr's weight eased off me. "Did you touch the corpse?" Hakoore hissed. "Do you know who you are? What's my name?"

"Bonnakkut didn't take me for his death-wife." Dorr spoke in her usual half-whisper, but I could hear the strain in it. "Fullin saved me."

"Don't mention it," I mumbled as I rolled off Bonnakkut's corpse. Partly to avoid meeting anyone's eye, I carefully started brushing ants off my clothes.

"I'm sure," Dorr said, "you would have done the same thing, Grandfather, if Fullin hadn't reacted first."

Hakoore inhaled sharply. Dorr watched him, her eyes glittering as they silently accused him of cowardice.

*   *   *

"Are you sure you aren't hurt?" Rashid asked.

Dorr didn't speak. I was the one who finally answered, "She broke her wrist."

"Nonsense," Hakoore hissed. "It was just a little fall."

But Steck lifted Dorr's arm and examined it closely. "It's swelling," she said. "We'd better take you to the doctor."

Dorr shrugged. "I can go myself."

"We're taking you." There was a finality in Steck's voice. "You too, Fullin."

"I'm fine," I said.

"She fell on you pretty hard," Steck insisted. "You should be checked out."

"No thank you."

"Fullin . . ." Steck began.

"Traditionally," Rashid nudged me, "this is where a headstrong young man would say, 'You aren't my mother!' "

Steck's mouth closed abruptly. The Spark Lord looked at her, his face the picture of innocence.

"Get out, the lot of you," Hakoore growled. "Bonnakkut's mortal soul is in an empty hell, suffering torment every second until he's released. Leave me alone to my job."

"Come on," Steck said to Dorr, putting an arm around her shoulders as Dorr supported her own injured wrist.

"Yes, let's go to the doctor," Rashid told me, "just to humor my dear Bozzle. Maria can be such a handful when she doesn't get her way."

I glanced at Hakoore. Gruffly, he waved me off. So why had he decided he didn't want his "disciple" here after all? Guilt that I had saved Dorr from eternal damnation while he did nothing? Or was it something else? Cappie claimed my face was perennially obvious; maybe something about my expression had betrayed what I learned about Dorr as she lay on top of me.

Well, Hakoore needn't worry about me blurting the truth to the world—not when I could hold it over his head until he reconsidered this "disciple" business. I would never stoop to blackmail; but what was wrong with two gentlemen agreeing to exchange favors?

For the first time since dawn, I could smile.

FOURTEEN

A Gift of Blood for Master Crow

Doctor Gorallin's home had been on the verge of collapsing for most of my lifetime. She had the idea she would be a great renovator, handier with tools than anyone in the village because she had surgical training . . . so whenever someone offered to reshingle the roof or shore up that corner where the foundation was sinking, Gorallin would growl in her suffer-no-fools way and swear she intended to do it herself.

She never did. When I was ten, Zephram persuaded me to fake a desperate stomach ache to drag Gorallin out on a prolonged house call. That gave a squad of barnstorming carpenters enough time to dash into her place and repair the parts closest to total disintegration. They said they'd done a perfect job of concealing the work they did, but it wasn't good enough to fool Gorallin's steely gaze. The moment she saw her home, her eyes narrowed; then she turned around and came directly back to Zephram's house saying, "I've reconsidered. When a boy is as sick as poor dear Fullin, he deserves a thorough enema."

Sigh.

In Gorallin's waiting room, we found Cappie pacing, her face pale. "Weren't you supposed to be finding the priestess?" Rashid asked.

"I did," Cappie answered. "Leeta decided she'd rather visit Bonnakkut's family alone. And she told me I'd better bring Pona . . . my daughter . . ." Her voice broke off.

"Pona's giving the Gift?" I asked. Cappie nodded.

Tentatively I held my arms open. After a moment's pause, she slid in against me. I even made an effort not to look down the loose front of her shirt—Cappie had helped me through the previous year when I brought my son to give the Gift, and I believed in repaying my debts.

"What's happening?" Rashid asked, his voice too chipper and intrusive. "What's does it mean, giving the Gift?"

"At this moment," Cappie replied, "the doctor is cutting a hole in the back of my daughter's neck."

"She's . . ." Rashid stopped himself. "Cutting a hole. Well, well. How extraordinary." He turned to Steck, who was helping Dorr settle into a chair to wait. "When you told me about Tober Cove, Maria, you didn't mention anything about giving a Gift."

"It's stupid superstition," Steck replied airily. "Beneath a scientist's notice."

Cappie pushed herself out of my arms to confront Steck. "You think I'd let the doctor cut my daughter just for superstition?"

Steck shrugged.

"You know this is crucial," Cappie snapped. "Without the Gift, the gods won't accept Pona when she goes to Birds Home. She'll be Locked her whole life."

"Really?" Rashid's voice had just shifted from idle curiosity to something more intense. "Tell me about this Gift."

Neither Steck nor Cappie answered—they were too busy glaring at each other. Finally, Dorr spoke in her half whisper. "The first year of a child's life, the gods don't take the baby to Birds Home; traveling is hard for infants, and their mothers can't come along to nurse them. Instead, the gods accept a symbolic substitute for the child: a Gift of blood and bone that's carried to Birds Home in place of the actual baby."

"And the doctor's taking such a Gift right now?" Rashid asked. "I really must see this."

"That isn't a good idea," I piped up, but Rashid was already pushing his way through the door that separated the waiting room from the much larger surgery beyond. Cappie rushed after him and I hurried behind . . . which meant I was just in time to have Gorallin shout at all three of us.

"What the devil do you think you're doing?"

"Ahh . . ." said Cappie. She had stiffened at the sight of blood on the doctor's hands.

Gorallin had many granite-hard rules about practicing medicine, and one of them was, "Never let parents see the taking of the Gift." When I'd brought in my son the year before, I waited outside, shuddering in Cappie's arms until it was all over. It only took ten minutes, and if Waggett had cried or wailed, I hadn't heard a peep. When Gorallin brought the boy out of surgery, the incision at the back of his neck was no more than a nick, neatly closed with a single stitch. Within months, the scar was scarcely visible . . . and in a few months more, I had calmed down enough to stop looking at it every night.

However, when we barged in on Pona's Gift-giving, there was no closed incision, no neat stitch, no baby skin carefully cleaned to hide all trace of what happened. Pona, six months old and naked, lay belly down on Gorallin's operating table. A generous wash of blood had spilled down the sides of her throat, dribbling onto the table's iron surface; and in the middle of the bloody cut at the back of her neck, the red-smeared white of bone peeked out.

"Fascinating," Rashid said.

"I don't need an audience," Gorallin roared. She held a scalpel in one blood-specked hand.

"Sorry," Rashid told her, with no apology in his voice, "but I'm a Knowledge-Lord. I live to learn new things. How does this work exactly?"

Gorallin glared at him. Like many people that day, she must have been debating whether she could tell a Spark to go to hell . . . perhaps trying to judge how much luck she'd have throwing him bodily from the room. Then she grimaced with acceptance of the inevitable—no one has ever stopped the Sparks from doing what they want, and it's a waste of time to try. "Just watch," she muttered, "and if you have stupid questions, save them till after."

She turned back to Pona and began to deposit tiny scraps of baby flesh into a test tube.

Cappie closed her eyes when Gorallin started scraping out picks of Pona's bone. I didn't, but I wished I could close my ears.

Scrape-pick.

Scrape-pick.

Scrape-pick.

"The Gift is taken from the spinous process of the sixth cervical vertebra," the doctor suddenly announced. I suppose even Gorallin had the sensitivity to know what the sound was doing to Cappie's nerves. "That's the prominent nub of bone at the back of your neck."

"Why there?" Rashid asked.

"Because that's what the gods want," Gorallin snapped. "There are alternate sites if there's a medical reason why the Gift can't be taken from the standard spot, but I never have to use them."

"And what exactly do you take?" Rashid clearly wanted to lean his face right down over the doctor's work but was holding himself back.

"Blood and bone," Dorr murmured. When she'd seen that Gorallin wasn't going to kick us out of the surgery, Dorr had silently entered too. "The gods require us to give blood and bone as a token of our obedience. It is the only price they accept."

"Actually," the doctor said, "I take bone and a bit of muscle tissue. Skin too. The blood comes for free, but I don't go out of my way to get any."

"And who taught you what was needed?" Rashid asked.

"My predecessor . . . who learned from her predecessor, and so on back to the first doctor in Tober Cove. She was taught by the gods themselves."

Steck made a disdainful sniff. She had come in with the rest of us, but was making a show of dismissive boredom. No one paid her any attention.

"And you seal all the tissues in a test tube," Rashid said, "which you send off to Birds Home?"

"That's right." Gorallin laid down her scalpel and picked up a fine needle for stitching the wound closed. Baby Pona didn't move; she lay breathing quietly, pacified by an anaesthetic the doctor had given before we arrived.

"The gods must think this Gift is very important," Rashid mused, "if you have to slice into every baby. Don't you worry about doing permanent damage?"

"I know what I'm doing," Gorallin bristled. "Babies heal quickly."

"But suppose a child is sick," Rashid said. "That must happen occasionally. If a baby is so sick that this surgery would risk its life . . ."

"Then I tell the parents it's too dangerous to take the Gift," Gorallin answered. "I'm a *doctor*, you . . ." She stopped herself in time. "I don't harm my patients," she finished grimly.

"You just carve up their necks," Steck said.

"A tiny cut!" Gorallin growled. "And given the alternative . . ."

"What's the alternative?" Rashid asked quickly.

"Becoming Locked," Dorr told him. "Spurned by the gods. Cursed to remain the same sex forever."

"So if you don't send a test tube for a child this year, the child can't change sex next year?"

"That's why the Gift is important," Gorallin said. "You think I bleed babies for fun?"

Cappie took a deep breath. "I wouldn't let her do this to Pona if it weren't necessary. What kind of savages do you think we are?"

"All over the world," Steck sneered, "people mutilate their children and say it's necessary. The greater the maiming, the more they claim it's a sign of civilization."

"Excuse me," Rashid said, "while I have a private word with my

Bozzle." He crossed the room in two strides, grabbed Steck by the arm, and almost shoved her into the waiting room. As the door closed, I heard his harsh whisper. "So you want to take the moral high ground, do you? When you forgot to mention they take tissue samples from the children and . . ."

Gorallin looked at the rest of us and rolled her eyes. Cappie, Dorr and I all nodded. Outsiders were inherently crazy: unbalanced at best, and often insane. If spilling a few drops of Pona's blood saved her from that blinkered confusion, the price was worth it.

Cappie helped Gorallin swab blood off Pona's body. It mopped up easily; in less than a minute, the baby's skin was back to its clean soft pink, and the black-stitched incision just an inoffensive line no longer than my fingernail. As Cappie slipped Pona into a new diaper and her summer smock, the doctor ran through a set of instructions that she must have given dozens of times over the years: how to care for the cut as it healed, how to check for signs of infection. Cappie nodded carefully as Gorallin spoke . . . and I noticed that Dorr, standing silently in the corner, nodded too.

I wondered how Dorr felt: to be childless in a village where almost everyone else had borne a life. Suddenly, I felt guilty for thinking she might have guzzled some herbal concoction to abort her baby. Suppose Dorr's miscarriage had been perfectly natural; suppose it was the pain of that loss which unhinged her enough to Commit Neut.

Quietly, I left Cappie listening to the doctor and went to Dorr. "Are you okay?" I asked softly. "How's your wrist?"

"It hurts." Her glittering eyes turned toward me. "You know Bonnakkut wouldn't have taken me as his death-wife."

"Dorr . . ."

"I know you know. You had to be able to feel what I have . . . and I just lay there. Because my wrist hurt and because I suddenly found myself tired and angry about hiding. Do you know what I did while I was lying there?"

"No."

"I touched him," she whispered. "Bonnakkut. You weren't covering his whole body. I reached under you and laid my hand on Bonnakkut's bare arm . . . and nothing happened. Even a dead man doesn't want me."

"Hakoore had started the last rites—"

"Don't be stupid," she interrupted. "I carry the stretcher whenever my grandfather attends to a corpse. I know how the rites go; I know when the body is and isn't safe. But it seems I don't have to worry."

Hesitantly I suggested, "Maybe with the corpse of a woman . . ."

Dorr gave me an exasperated look. "It's not that I *want* to marry a corpse, Fullin. Do you think I'm just looking for a boyfriend? I've got—"

She stopped. Cappie and Gorallin were looking at us.

"My wrist hurts," Dorr said; and like a stone sinking in muddy water, the emotion vanished from her face. She must have had years of practice making her feelings go away.

"All right," Gorallin said, "let's have a look." She glanced at Cappie and me. "In private."

Cappie picked up the still-sleeping Pona and I opened the door for her. With a glance back at Dorr, I wondered why she'd confided in me. Merely because I knew her secret? Because she'd once had a crush on me? Because she recognized me as a woman who would sympathize with . . .

Recognized me as a *woman*?

Oh. It seemed I'd become female again.

Rashid and Steck fell silent as Cappie and I entered the waiting room. For the first time it struck me how handsome Rashid actually was. His long black hair made him look dashing, even rakish, but his eyes had a poetic sensitivity to them, like a man who has always been too intelligent to feel at home among the people he meets. I could understand how he'd fallen for Steck—both of them fish out of water, a Spark and a Neut, distanced from the common crowd.

"So the operation's over?" Rashid asked Cappie. He was trying to sound casual, as if he and Steck hadn't been fighting. "How's the little girl?"

"She'll be fine." Cappie turned to me. "I'd better take her back to my mother now. Do you know where you're going to be?"

"I promised 'Maria' I'd stay with her until the gods come at noon."

"Why don't you and Steck walk me around town?" Rashid suggested. "We'll talk to people. Investigate Bonnakkut's death." He sighed, as if the murder had been committed purely to spoil his day. "We can always hope a witness saw someone sneaking behind Bonnakkut with a knife." The Spark Lord turned to Cappie. "If Tobers noticed something suspicious like that, whom would they tell?"

"The neighbors," she answered drily. "But eventually they'd go to the mayor."

"Then we'll go to the mayor ourselves," Rashid said. "Ask if he's heard anything."

Cappie nodded, then leaned in and gave me a quick kiss on the corner of my mouth. "After I drop off Pona," she murmured, "I'll meet you at Mayoralty House. We'll find a place to talk."

Then she was gone.

Dorr told us not to wait—Gorallin agreed that the wrist was broken, and now had to go through the chore of mixing plaster to make a cast. Rashid was keen to get moving and Steck wisely didn't try to cross him. I didn't understand why Rashid was annoyed at her for not telling him about the Gift, but he clearly thought she should have mentioned it to him earlier. Steck had forced herself to couch down into meek acquiescence with Rashid's mood . . . although as we walked to the door together, she did stop to look at me.

"You're sure you don't want the doctor to examine you?"

"I'm fine," I told her.

"You're walking oddly."

"There's nothing wrong with me."

"Oh." She stopped for a moment and gave me an appraising look. Suddenly, a smile seeped across her face. "What sex are you, Fullin?"

The question caught me off guard. I answered, "Male, of course," but I knew I didn't sound convincing. Even Rashid could tell something was amiss.

"Male, of course?" he asked.

"Of course." I still didn't sound convincing.

Steck patted me on the cheek, her face preening with an "I've got you" smile. "Don't lie to your mother," she said.

"So you think he's female?" Rashid asked. "What's going on?"

"Are we going to the mayor's or not?" I snapped. Without waiting for an answer, I headed out the door and down the doctor's front steps. Rashid followed quickly, still looking back and forth from Steck to me for an explanation.

"It's something no one talks about," Steck said, tracking along on my heels, "although as far as I can tell, it happens to everybody. I certainly switched several times on my Commitment Day. Leeta once told me she'd had plenty of women confide that it happened to them too. But most people do their best to keep it a secret. Why, Fullin? Do you think it's indecent? Or just too private to bring out into the open?"

"Too tricky," I replied. It surprised me that I spoke the words out loud; but then, I had been thrown off balance by what Steck said. This happened to everybody?

"What's going on?" Rashid demanded.

"In the day leading up to Commitment," Steck told him, "Tobers go through short bouts when they feel as if they're the other sex. Their other sexual selves. Right now, I have the feeling Fullin's male body is occupied by the personality that usually takes charge in his female years. Isn't that right, Fullin? Isn't that why you're watching your feet a little too much while you're walking?''

That was precisely what was going on . . . but I immediately lifted my eyes from my feet and focused them straight ahead. I didn't fool anyone—I could feel myself blushing, which surely showed on my face. "Can we change the subject?" I mumbled.

"No," Rashid answered, and turned back to Steck. "You say this happens to every Tober?"

"That's my guess."

"In the day leading up to Commitment?"

"It would make sense," Steck said.

"How so?" Rashid asked.

"As a reminder!" I suddenly blurted out.

Steck and Rashid looked at me.

"You're right, it *does* make sense!" I said, thinking it through for myself. "It's been a year since I was female . . . distant enough to forget what it's like. The different priorities I have. The different weight of memories. So the gods are giving me a chance to recall who I was. Who I am. To make sure I have a clear idea of both my male and female selves before I choose between them."

"Good thinking by the gods," Rashid agreed. "You don't usually expect that much foresight from a deity."

"So there's nothing to be ashamed of, is there?" Steck said to me. "It's ridiculous how Tobers all think they're abnormal and bottle it up."

I didn't answer; I was too busy thinking about Cappie. She must have been switching back and forth between male and female too. Was that why she had worn male clothes this morning, even though they were no longer needed for the solstice dance? Which soul was she wearing when she sang to me in the marsh? During the fight with Steck . . . when she punched me and stole my spear . . . as we made love . . .

Who the hell had I been with when?

"What surprises me," Rashid said, "is that Tobers don't discuss this openly. If it happens to everybody, why treat it as a shameful secret?"

I thought of Tobers back through the years, most of them living in relationships by the time they reached Commitment Day, and most of them intimidated by the permanent repercussions of the choice they were about to make. They had enough complications already without having to confess they were occasionally not who they appeared to be.

"It might not be shameful," I said, "but it *is* secret. That's not such a bad thing; that's not such a bad thing at all."

*   *   *

The path from the doctor's office to Mayoralty House led around the mill pond, where a single mallard floated peacefully in the center of the water. The bird was lucky; our miller, Palph, was a good archer, and any other day, a duck on the pond had a good chance of becoming Palph's dinner. No Tober, however, would dare kill a bird on the morning of Commitment Day—that was an insult to Master Crow and Mistress Gull.

I said as much to Rashid. He nodded, but didn't answer; his mind was obviously elsewhere. After a moment, he spoke without looking at me. "What's going to happen today at Birds Home?"

"Rashid," Steck began, "I've told you everything . . ."

"You didn't tell me the doctor took tissue samples," he interrupted. "So I'd like to hear what Fullin has to say."

I looked back and forth between the two of them. Of course, Rashid would have quizzed Steck long before coming to the cove—about our way of life, how switching sexes affected us, what the gods did in Birds Home. And because he was infatuated with her, he had believed what he heard: he thought he knew everything she did. Now, however, something had stirred a freckle of doubt; now, he wanted to check her version of the facts.

Steck's face flushed with emotion. Anger? Hurt? I couldn't tell—it disappeared in an instant, replaced by a hard-edged stoniness, as if she didn't care whether he believed her or not. "Go ahead," she said grimly to me. "Tell him whatever he wants to know."

"There's not much to tell," I mumbled, embarrassed for her. Embarrassed for my mother. "At noon, Master Crow and Mistress Gull arrive from Birds Home and land on the lake. The children go with Master Crow; the people ready for Commitment go with Mistress Gull."

"Go with," Rashid repeated. "That means you get inside."

"Yes, we boat out and get inside Mistress Gull and Master Crow," I said, wondering why he had decided to be obtuse. "There are chairs inside. We sit in the chairs and the gods fly us north to Birds Home."

"What happens there?"

"The children are taken into Master Crow's nest. They climb out of Master Crow and wait in a special area until they are touched by the gods. Then everyone falls asleep."

"Gas," Steck murmured. "Knock-out gas."

I shrugged, not wanting to argue about how the gods did what they did. It felt awkward, being questioned by Rashid to see if my mother had lied to him; I just wanted to get it over with. "After a while, the children wake up and find they're the opposite sex. They get back inside Master Crow and fly home.''

"That's the children,'' Rashid said. "What about the candidates for Commitment? You and Cappie.''

"Mistress Gull takes us into a different nest, her own. I don't know what happens there because it's a holy secret—no one who's gone through it is ever supposed to reveal the details. But the gods will come to us in the Commitment Hour and ask, 'Male, female, or both?' We tell them our choice, and that's our Commitment.'' I looked at him sharply. "Good enough?''

Rashid hesitated, as if considering whether to grill me further: to keep pushing to see if my story matched whatever my mother had told him. He glanced at Steck, but she wasn't looking at either of us. She had picked up a stone and was staring at the duck in the mill pond. Her fingers rolled the stone back and forth across her palm.

"All right then,'' Rashid muttered. "I was just checking. It's always possible that something changed in the twenty years since you Committed, Steck.''

She made a scoffing sound, but her face lost some of its grimness. When she threw her stone, she aimed well clear of the duck. The rock landed in the water with a light plop, scarcely rippling the pond at all.

Mayoralty House lay at the base of Patriarch Hill, in the shadow of the OldTech radio antenna that speared into the sky on the heights. Zephram claimed the big ramble-faced building must have been a hotel back in OldTech times. It had more than two dozen rooms, all the same . . . or at least they had been the same before years of rain, snow and termites took their toll.

By the time the Patriarch came to power a hundred and fifty years ago, much of the old hotel had collapsed. He ordered it rebuilt to his own specifications, calling it the Patriarchal Palace. After his death, there had been a fierce political struggle between the mayor and Patriarch's Man of that day, fighting over which would get the house. Somehow, the mayor had won—possibly by making generous financial concessions to the Patriarch's Man—and the old hotel had been residence for every mayor since.

To the mayors, it must have been a mixed blessing. A house that size needed constant expensive upkeep. Even worse, the summers boiled insufferably hot in that area, thanks to a huge expanse of OldTech asphalt that bordered the building on front and sides. ("The hotel parking lot,'' my father said.) Four hundred post-Tech winters had churned that aging pavement like taffy, but fractured and crumbling, there was still enough old blacktop left to drink up every drop of sun and fill the air with the fierce smell of baked tar.

On the front edge of the asphalt, an OldTech horseless cart had been crisping its way to rust for four centuries. The exterior body was completely gone, shredded partly by weather and partly by Tober children prying off souvenirs to stash in dresser drawers and other hidey-holes. Earlier generations must have had it easy; by the time I came along, the only parts left were solid and heavy, almost impossible to break off. Cappie had won himself a quick close-lipped kiss for chiseling off a piece of the underframe and giving it to me on my ninth birthday.

As soon as the cart came into sight Rashid made a beeline for it, his plastic boots making sticky sounds as he crossed the sun-soft blacktop. Leaning over the remains of the engine, he tried to wiggle various components. I could have told him he was wasting his time—anything with a hint of wiggle had been worried off by children long ago.

Steck nudged me and murmured, "All his life he's been looking for a car that's still in running order. We've found plenty that look good on the outside—preserved by eccentric collectors, that sort of thing—but the engines are always seized up. Even with a heap like this, Rashid has this insatiable optimism that he might find good spare parts."

"This one doesn't have any parts," I said. "It's rusted into a solid whole."

"I know that," Steck replied. "You think I didn't try to pull pieces off that pile of junk when I was—"

She stopped. Rashid had just reached down into the motor, a look of triumph on his face. He bent over farther and farther, straining to get at something until his feet were almost off the ground.

"What is it?" Steck called.

Rashid's voice echoed from the cart's metal belly: "Something I've never seen in all my years looking under the hood."

Steck gave me a "let's humor him" look and we both moved forward. Rashid pulled his head out of the machine long enough to take a short metal cylinder from a pouch on his thigh; when he twisted one end of the cylinder, the other end suddenly shone with light like a lantern. He turned the yellow beam toward the engine and aimed it down into the rusted guts. "See that?" he asked.

Steck and I looked. The beam of Rashid's lamp was centered on a palm-sized box of black metal, attached to a hunk of rust-slathered steel. Of course I'd noticed the black box before, back when I was young enough to care about getting a piece of the cart. I'd hammered the box with a rock, poked it with knives stolen from our kitchen, even held a candle under it to see what happened. "It doesn't come off," I told Rashid. "It's just a black lump."

"A black lump that shouldn't be there," he replied. "Ask Steck how many engines I've examined since we've been together."

"And the engines have all had their idiosyncrasies," Steck told him. "I admit I haven't studied cars like you have, but you've taught me yourself there were hundreds of different types. Dozens of companies manufacturing dozens of models each, and every year they made changes and improvements . . . not to mention that individuals sometimes whipped up customizations of their own. Why is it surprising there are engine thingummies you haven't seen yet?"

"Because I'm the Knowledge-Lord." He leaned into the cart again, trying to give the black box a jiggle.

"It doesn't move," I told him. There was no shade here on the asphalt, and the sun pressed down hard. The last thing I wanted was to stand around baking while a Spark Lord picked away at something that died four hundred years ago.

"Aha!" Rashid said, his voice muffled. "An antenna!"

"What?" Without thinking, I glanced up to the antenna on Patriarch Hill. This cart had nothing remotely like that. I supposed there might be different types of antennas, but our schoolteacher had never mentioned the possibility. She had been hard-pressed to tell us much about radio at all: she called it a baffling OldTech technique for sending sounds from one place to another. Almost every town on the peninsula had at least one antenna, usually rusted and toppled by wind; but all such antennas were long and thin and exposed, not hidden in the motor of a cart. "What are you talking about?" I asked Rashid.

"This box has a wire antenna running tight against the engine block. Camouflaged to match the metal. And there's another wire running to . . . I'll bet those are photoelectric cells. Solar collectors. This thing may still have juice." Rashid lifted his head and grinned at Steck. "Still think it's just a normal engine thingummy?"

Steck put a hand to her mouth and faked a yawn. "The OldTechs had a saying," she told me. "Something about boys and their toys."

I nodded, amused that Steck had decided to play the age-old part of the long-suffering woman when she was half man herself. Then again, how could *I* talk? Male outside, female inside . . . and sweat-drippingly bored with black boxes. "How much longer?" I asked Rashid.

He grinned impishly at me. Men get a kick out of being an aggravation to women; my brother self delighted in teasing anything female, especially by exaggerating the most juvenile tendencies of being male. A long time ago, some bastard invented the phrase "boyish charm," and since then the whole gender has believed the way to a woman's heart is behaving like an eight-year-old.

Then again, we women still believed the way to a man's heart was playing hard to get. Why did the gods have to make both sexes so calculatingly stupid?

"Just one more thing to check," Rashid said. He pushed his shinelight cylinder back into its pouch and drew out a hand-sized plastic box. "Radio receiver," he said. With his thumb he rolled a dial on the box; the little machine began to make a raspy noise, like waves washing up on a gravel beach.

"Nothing but static," Steck said.

"You think it's just static?" Rashid asked. Slowly he moved the radio receiver toward the black box on the engine . . . and the volume of the sound increased, as if the waves on the beach were churning up, peaking, getting blown into whitecaps.

"See?" Rashid told us, patting the black box fondly. "This little baby is transmitting something. Using the whole car as an antenna."

"Why would the OldTechs do that?" I asked.

"They didn't," Rashid answered. "If I didn't know better," he looked at me, "I'd say someone from a long way away has been planting bugs in Tober Cove."

His eyes turned thoughtfully toward the sky.

FIFTEEN

A Predictable History for the Patriarch

Mayor Teggeree had heard nothing about the murder—no one had even told him Bonnakkut was dead. That didn't surprise me; the news was still in the bubbling gossip stage, and people wanted to share it with others quickly. Mayoralty House just wasn't close enough to the rest of town for people to pop in on a moment's notice. Under normal circumstances, it would be the First Warrior who hurried across the hot pavement to pass word to Teggeree. As it was, we were the ones who got to see the mayor's jaw drop when we reported the bad tidings.

For one second Teggeree was caught by shock. Then he opened his mouth and said, "How tragic." A mayor's phrase: the position was talking, not the man. In a way, I admired Teggeree for that. "How tragic," he repeated. "But at least we're fortunate in having a Knowledge-Lord to seek out the truth. That is, if it's not an imposition on Your Lordship's time . . ."

"No, no," Rashid answered, "I've already started investigating. That's why I came here—I'm told that anyone with relevant evidence will report it to you."

"Just so," Teggeree nodded. "Let me ask my family if anyone has come by already." He turned to me. "Fullin, perhaps you'd show Lord Rashid to the Patriarch's Hall where he can wait in comfort?"

"Sure." I had to smile; every child in the cove was marched through the Patriarch's Hall at least once a year, and I had never imagined it could be described as comfortable. Our mayor simply wanted to impress the visiting dignitary. Don't ask me why Teggeree hadn't dragged Rashid into the hall as soon as the Knowledge-Lord arrived last night—

Rashid must have dodged the mayor's clutches somehow. *A temporary reprieve only*, I thought. *You're stuck with the full tour now.*

Then again, the Patriarch's Hall was dusty, self-important and largely irrelevant. It might be exactly Rashid's cup of tea.

"This old place!" Steck said with disgust. But her gaze traveled sharp-eyed around the room, as if reminding herself of all the things she had missed the chance to despise during her banishment.

The hall was the Patriarch's memorial, and crammed with keepsakes from his era: some mounted in formal displays, others just stacked where there was available space on shelves or the floor. This was my first visit here since I'd graduated school at fourteen, and the room seemed to have shrunk in the intervening years . . . not to mention the air growing more stifled and close, as dust accumulated on the so-called "treasures." It occurred to me that mayors might regard this place more as a junk heap than a shrine—somewhere to stash things they couldn't throw out but didn't want cluttering up the rest of the house.

Take, for example, the collection of glass jars filling up three long shelves—the same sort of jars all Tobers used for fruit preserves, but this batch contained ashes from the execution pit on Beacon Point. They had no labels: no way to tell whether a given jar contained the incinerated remnants of a scientist, a Southern trader, or a Neut. Knowing the Patriarch, some of the jars might just hold clinkers pulled out of his bake stove—the old tyrant had no qualms about inflating his reputation with a few false urns. Then again, if the Patriarch thought his shelves looked too empty, he might simply accuse another Tober of uttering heretical thoughts; preferably someone well off, whose goods could be confiscated for the public coffers.

The public coffers administered by the Patriarch, of course.

Looking around the room, I was struck by how he had spent that money on personal indulgences. Paintings of himself. Fine clothes and trinkets brought from the South. Still-corked wine bottles that probably contained nothing but vinegar.

Supposedly, my violin dated back to those times. Leeta claimed the old tyrant had paid a master violinist to come up-peninsula and settle in the cove, so that the "palace" would always have music. Such an extravagance was typical of the Patriarch—killing innocent Southern peddlers to "cleanse" the cove, then immediately importing a Southerner of his own because it suited his pleasure.

Still, I shouldn't complain: I was descended from that hired Southern musician . . . as was Steck.

Neither she nor I spent much time looking at individual items in the hall; it was more a matter of absorbing the whole ambience, letting our attention wander from the Patriarch's tooled leather saddle to his "coat of many colors" constructed by the Hearth and Home Guild at his dictatorial command. I blanched at a tapestry showing a couple making their marriage vows on the Patriarch's Hand—unbidden, my mind conjured up the image of that hand suddenly coming to life and grabbing the woman by the throat as the Patriarch hissed, "Do you love him? *Do you?*"

But I put that out of my mind; I had promised Cappie to Commit female and become priestess. To hell with the Patriarch and all his successors.

Spinning away from the sight of the tapestry, I nearly bumped into Rashid. He had planted himself in front of a wall-sized painting of the Patriarch during the Harsh Purification: a fierce white-haired man with a blazing torch in his hand. The artist, no doubt working under the Patriarch's eye, had painted the ghost of a halo around the old tyrant's head. The painter had also placed three blackened figures in the background, burning their last in a well-fueled pyre.

After a long moment contemplating the scene, Rashid turned to me. "What do you think of that, Fullin? About the burnings and the Patriarch and all? Just doing what the gods demanded?"

I hesitated. "You remember I'm female at the moment?"

"What does that have to do with it?" Rashid asked.

Steck snorted. "What do you expect? Men and women have completely different opinions about the old bastard."

"How can that be?" Rashid said. "When Fullin changes from man to woman, how can his opinions suddenly change? Are Tobers all multiple personality cases, or do they just—"

"My opinion on the Patriarch," I interrupted, "is that he should have died when he was a baby . . . like everyone thought he would."

Rashid frowned. "He was an unhealthy baby?"

"Too sick to give the Gift of Blood," I replied, "so he was Locked male all his life. Everything else follows from that."

"Tell me," Rashid said.

Steck and I met each other's gaze. Perhaps my mother and I didn't have much in common, but I could see that for the moment we were thinking like two women.

And women who spend time thinking all have the same opinion of the Patriarch.

May he rot forever in the death-grip of Mistress Want.

*　　*　　*

The Patriarch (who erased all record of his real name) was born two hundred years ago—a child of Master Crow and always prick-proud how his parentage made him one half divine. Leeta told all the girls in Hearth and Home that the Patriarch despised people fathered by normal men: whenever he needed to make an example of someone, he chose someone of "thin human blood" to be whipped.

But that was after he came to power. The Patriarch's story started only a few months after he was born: a baby boy who got sick just before summer solstice. High fever, vomiting, convulsions . . . when Hakoore preached his annual sermon on the Patriarch's life, he took morbid delight in hissing out the list of symptoms. Hakoore loved to label the illness as the work of devils who wanted to kill our Redeemer before he could save the world; but when I told this story to Rashid, I steered away from mentioning devils.

I'd come to feel sheepish on the devil issue.

Anyway, there was no question the infant Patriarch suffered extreme sickness, whatever the cause—the doctor of that day believed the baby wasn't strong enough to give the Gift. Yes, the child would be Locked male all his life . . . but, "Male is better than dead," as the doctor told the Patriarch's mother.

("I'd have to agree," Rashid said.

Steck and I exchanged "isn't that just so typical" looks.)

So the Gift was never taken. In time the baby recovered (". . . through sheer force of will!" Hakoore preached). The infant even traveled to Birds Home the following summer with all the other children. That was common practice—whether or not the boy had given the Gift, the gods might decide to switch his sex anyway. They were gods; they could break their own rules.

But they didn't. (They never did.) The Patriarch went out a boy and came back the same way. At that age, he didn't understand why it broke his mother's heart.

He must have found out soon enough. I didn't grow up with any Locked kids, but I can imagine how Tober children would have treated someone who was so creep-ily handicapped—with an inconsistent mix of cruelty, pity and indifference, changing from hour to hour depending on the whim of the schoolyard mob. When a boy receives that kind of treatment, the outcome is determined by how he reacts: if he makes himself likable, the other children soon forget he's different; if he tries to make himself likable but isn't, he becomes the school goat or perhaps class clown; and if he fights back verbally or physically, he becomes hated, taunted, and shunned . . . in other words, a pariah.

Guess which option the Patriarch took.

A big-muscled pariah turns himself into a bully; a small one becomes the brat who steals and tells lies to get everybody else in trouble. The Patriarch tried the bully route for a while, picking on kids weaker than himself, but in Tober Cove, little kids often have big brothers (or big sisters with all the instincts of big brothers). The young Patriarch soon realized he couldn't make a success of bullyhood, at least until he became a teenager and could match big brothers in size. Therefore he went the other direction—becoming a weasel, as Hakoore might put it, although the Patriarch's Man never used that term when speaking of our Revered Redeemer. ("The other children spurned him because they were shamed by his inner radiance.")

Time passed. The boy grew crafty. He learned to ingratiate himself to adults, who were (then as now) easier to manipulate than children. Leeta liked to tell us he had a knack for wheedling perks and privileges out of grownup women—he always had a ready tale of woe, how he felt deprived by never knowing the joys of femininity. It may seem naïve that they believed him . . . certainly in light of how he treated women later on. But you have to understand that no one was used to a child like this. No one back then had ever dealt with a boy who never became a girl.

It's hard for me to imagine what it's like to have a single, unified soul. When you're just one person, everything that happens in your life can only happen to *you*; it's always immediate. With most of us . . . well, when I was a girl of five, I decided I didn't like oatmeal. I don't know why—kids sometimes get attacks of the Stubborns, and then it becomes a matter of honor: no oatmeal would ever pass my lips. I tried to tell Cappie that oatmeal was poison . . . some complicated tale about the Mishi pirates crossing wheat with poison ivy and getting oats. No doubt I drove poor Zephram to distraction; not to mention, it was all empty pigheadedness after the first few days, just an obstinate refusal to admit I was making a fuss over nothing.

Then summer solstice came, I turned male, and my old pointless obstinacy seemed like someone else's problem. I had different areas of stubbornness—that was when I began *plink-plink-plinking* at my mother's violin—but fighting about oatmeal just wasn't worth the headaches. Yes, I could remember that it was important to me only the day before; but I felt as if my sister self had *told* me it should be important, not that I really believed it myself.

So I started to eat oatmeal. And by the time I turned female again, it was all a dead issue.

You see how it works? When you're two people, some of your extreme rough edges get rounded out. Hates, loves, frights . . . my male half's fear of snapping turtles used to be much worse. He used to be paralyzed with terror at the thought of going down to the dock where he saw the girl get bitten. But the next year, I wasn't so afraid—the fear wasn't so immediate. I worked up the courage to go to the waterfront now and then; and by the time I turned male again, I could draw on my female experiences of sitting on the docks with nothing bad happening.

Only one version of me had the truly intense fear. The other could cope . . . and the first one could learn from the coping.

The Patriarch never experienced that restful kind of distancing. His fears always clutched him; his resentments stayed hot at the boil, like a kettle that never gets taken off the stove; his loves (if he had any) never got the chance to mellow and rearrange themselves.

He was a violin that always played the same tune . . . and his only possible variation was to play louder and louder.

The Patriarch's mother made a token effort to expose him to women's culture: sent him now and then to talk with the priestess, for example. It didn't work. "He saw the falseness of women's ways," Hakoore preached . . . which probably meant that he felt out of place surrounded by girls and made a fierce nuisance of himself until the priestess told him to leave. He never learned womanly skills like cooking, sewing, and tending the sick: skills aimed at helping other people more than yourself.

But the most crucial lack in the Patriarch's life was that he never gave birth. He never felt a life emerge from him, never felt the needy sucking at his breast soften into contentment.

Zephram tells me there are plenty of good fathers in the South: men who have always been male, but still cherish and keep their children with loving devotion. I hope that's true. Still, a voice in my mind whispers that Tobers are different. Every father in the village has also been a mother. Every father *knows*.

You take bullies like the Warriors Society: even Mintz, the meanest of the bunch. In his last year as female, Mintz wasn't a model mother, but he gave it a genuine effort. He nursed his son; he changed diapers; he sang self-conscious lullabies when the baby wouldn't sleep, and screamed at the doctor, "Make him better!" when the boy picked up a case of the sniffles. Mintz Committed as male because he knew he wasn't cut out for nurturing . . . but he still cared for his child in a haphazard way. A few times in the previous year, on my way to the marsh for violin practice, I'd met Mintz and his daughter out searching for medicinal herbs—she'd got the idea she wanted to take over as Healer when Gorallin retired. And Mintz, who wouldn't know a medicinal herb if it cleared up his eczema, was out with his kid to make sure she didn't drown in a sinkhole and to let her know, "Yes, I believe you're smart enough to be a doctor."

No one, not even Hakoore, could imagine the Patriarch getting his shoes muddy for the sake of a child's dream. So ask yourself what a man like that might do in a town where everyone else *does* have a fierce concern for children.

There's an old saying that children are "hostages to fate": dependents who make any parent think twice about stepping out of line. And when the person who draws the line is an angry man who doesn't give a damn what happens to kids . . .

. . . you've got the secret of the Patriarch's success.

The rest of the Patriarch's story you can fill in yourself. Or you could see it in the paintings on the walls of the Patriarch's Hall. The Patriarch taking the oath of office as mayor (after a campaign of bribery and intimidation had eliminated other contenders). The Patriarch posing with his cadre of hand-chosen warriors (stupid teenaged boys who liked seeing fear in adult eyes). The Patriarch being blessed by Father Ash and Mother Dust (while somewhere not shown in the picture, warriors held the Father's and Mother's families in "protective custody").

But those things are all Male History: public events, with public reactions recorded and private consequences ignored. The facts of Male History are only important if you want to know the exact number of people the Patriarch killed in his efforts to gain power and keep it.

Numbers like that must have been of great interest to the Patriarch himself. He was that kind of man.

"Sounds like you detest him," Rashid observed.

"That's what it sounds like," I agreed.

"And all Tober women feel the same way?"

"Fullin's opinion is stronger than most," Steck answered, "but the majority of women have similar feelings. Not that they usually waste the time to think about it."

"And the men?" Rashid asked. "Men who were also women for half of their youths?"

"They say it isn't worth getting excited about. The laws aren't so bad, so why tear them down?" Steck grimaced. "And in a way, the men are right. You know what the Patriarch really did to Tober society? In the long run, nothing. He seized power, he ran the place for thirty years, and he laid down laws about the proper 'roles' for each gender . . . but the instant he died, our village waffled back to comfortable ground. Fullin," Steck turned to me, "has Tober Cove burned anyone since the Patriarch died?"

"No."

Steck turned back to Rashid. "See? People swear oaths on the Patriarch's Hand now instead of Master Stone, and Hakoore is called the Patriarch's Man instead of the older title of "priest" . . . but how much more of the Patriarch's heritage is left? Take the Council of Elders. Before the Patriarch, both men and women sat on the council; afterward, it was men only plus the priestess. But in Tober Cove, that has less effect than you might think. People who are attracted to politics know they have to Commit male, so they do. Same thing with laws like *Only men can work the perch boats*. If you like fishing, you Commit male; if you like cooking, you Commit female."

"I never thought of it that way," Rashid said, his brow furrowing. "When I think of laws that dictate men have to do this, women have to do that, my natural reaction is to ask, 'What if a woman wants to be a warrior? What if a man sets his sights on caring for children?' But in Tober Cove, you just decide what you want to do in life and base your gender choice on that. Of course, if you want to be a warrior *and* you want to be a woman too . . ."

"The Mocking Priestess has a saying," I told him. "You can get what you want most in life; not even the gods can guarantee you get your second choice too."

Footsteps clunked on the floor outside. A moment later Teggeree entered, walking uncomfortably in city-bought boots rather than moccasins. As far as I knew, he had only worn the boots once before, back when Governor Niome of Feliss had made a "diplomatic visit" (two hours of diffident talk about trade, followed by three days of enthusiastic hunting and looking at our fall leaves). Still, our mayor managed to retain his dignity, even in those unaccustomed shoes; he moved with slow composure, like a boat taking its time as it entered an unfamiliar harbor.

"Any news?" Rashid asked. "Witnesses to the murder?"

Teggeree sighed. "One man has arrived, claiming to have evidence . . ." The mayor glanced at me. "It's Embrun."

"Wouldn't you know," I grimaced.

Embrun was a strange case, even for Tober Cove. His female half got kicked in the head by a horse when she was five, and had never been right afterward—moody and slow, subject to falling fits at least once a month. Her problems were bad enough to drag down her brother soul too; he had a normal brain, but only got to use it every other year.

Other children went to school each fall, and learned their lessons whether they were boys or girls . . . but poor Embrun could only make progress in class when he was male, so each year he fell farther behind the kids his age. After a while, he stopped trying. Embrun became the cove's hard luck case, even after he Committed male and shed the weight of his ill-fated sister self. He was forever dropping in just before supper to see if you had any errands you'd pay him to run, but could always find a conflicting commitment when someone offered him a real full-time job.

I could just bet Embrun had evidence to report about the murder. He'd ask Rashid how much such information was worth, but if the Spark Lord actually shelled out some crowns, Embrun would only have useless things to tell: some story about an indistinct figure seen in the distance, or vague rustling sounds he heard near the time of Bonnakkut's death. Embrun wouldn't trump up a tale to implicate someone specific—he was never deliberately vicious—but he would try to make himself seem like an important witness, especially if someone would pay him to talk.

"Let's see this man by all means!" Rashid said. "I'd love to wrap up this murder investigation before Master Crow and Mistress Gull arrive."

Teggeree gave me another look. I could tell he wanted me to warn the Spark Lord about Embrun—Teggeree couldn't do it himself because it was indelicate for a mayor to accuse a voting citizen of being a conniving opportunist. Before I could speak, however, Cappie quietly appeared in the doorway—slim, almost frail, as she stood beside Teggeree's great bulk.

"Can we talk now?" she asked quietly.

Her words stirred up the urge to run away, but her fragility made me want to wrap my arms around her, to protect her from the world and herself. I realized I was male again—changed in the heartbeat of seeing her. Or maybe changed long before and I just hadn't noticed: the boundary between my two selves was blurrier than I'd once imagined.

Steck looked quickly between Cappie and me, then said, "Yes . . . you two stay here and talk. Rashid and I can question this Embrun on our own."

Embrun had only been a toddler when Steck left the cove. She didn't know what he'd become.

Teggeree gave me one more look, a glance that might have been pleading in someone less self-composed. But Rashid moved toward the door and gestured for the mayor to take the lead. "Show us to this witness, if you don't mind, Your Worship. Embrun, did you say? I suppose he's a reliable sort?"

The mayor cleared his throat. "Perhaps I should tell you about our Embrun," he murmured.

Teggeree continued to talk as Rashid and Steck followed him out of the hall. Cappie and I were alone.

She had changed back into women's clothes: a simple summer dress, styled for loose-fitting comfort and coolness. Maybe Cappie's family had prevailed on her not to scandalize the village; maybe she'd had enough of me "being obvious" as I ogled her in men's clothing.

Or maybe, I thought to myself, *her female body has a male soul inside and he's hiding under a feminine masquerade.*

The thought made me sick—not that it might be true, but that I had a mind which found it so easy to imagine Cappie was trying to deceive people. What was wrong with me?

She took a step into the room, then stopped and suddenly looked around: at the paintings, the dusty mementos, the jars of cremated heretics. "Someone should burn this place," she muttered.

"It's a memorial to the Patriarch!" I said, shocked. "Even if you don't like some of the things he did, you have to respect the history."

"Do I?" She lifted one of the jars of ashes and shook it. The feathery gray flakes inside flew around like snow. "Rashid's going to be disappointed when he talks to Embrun."

I was glad for the change of topic—partly because I had no urge to argue about the Patriarch, partly because it meant Cappie was afraid of coming to the point, just like I was.

"Rashid is only investigating the murder out of duty," I told her. "The mystery he really wants to solve is Tober Cove. Master Crow and Mistress Gull. How it all works. You know what I mean?"

She nodded. "Maybe the Patriarch had a point when he started burning scientists." She shook the jar again. "Since Rashid arrived, I've been seeing the cove through outsider eyes, and it all looks so ... clumsy. Like we've made everything up and are just pretending to believe what we say. About the gods and Birds Home, about everything. I'm afraid he'll see through it somehow, have a mundane explanation for the things that make us special."

"Rashid won't explain away anything," I said to Cappie. "Before the Patriarch, other scientists came to the cove. They blustered about, got in everyone's way, and still went home mumbling."

"None of the other scientists were Spark Lords," Cappie replied. She turned the jar upside down and watched for a moment as the ashes filtered down like sand in an hourglass. "You know the Sparks have dealings with people or things off-planet. Rashid has more resources than any normal scientist.''

"Still, what can he find? The way we change sex really is the work of the gods. Right?''

She didn't answer.

"Right, Cappie?'' I repeated.

After a pause, she sighed. "Fullin, you *are* the one who should become priestess. And Patriarch's Man, for that matter. You have more faith than I do. Or you ask fewer questions.''

"You think Rashid might find something?''

"I think you were raised by a Southerner, Fullin. A kind-hearted Southerner who didn't want to step on Tober toes, and bent over backward never to cast doubt on our gods.''

"And you were raised by your father,'' I replied, "who has all kinds of strange notions that he calls philosophy.''

"True.'' Abruptly, she set the jar of ashes back on its shelf. "This isn't what I want to talk about.''

"Oh.'' I felt my scalp prickle with dread at what might happen in the next few minutes. "Okay,'' I told her. "Talk.''

She didn't answer immediately. Instead, she lowered her eyes and suddenly reached out to finger the sleeve of the Patriarch's coat of many colors. The dyes had faded over the years, and the cloth seemed as thin as a spiderweb.

"I just want the truth,'' Cappie said softly. "Soon I have to make the most important decision of my life, and I need to know the truth. No holding back. If you don't love me . . . I don't know, maybe it'll be a relief to hear you say it. Probably not, but still. Being hurt and angry will go away little by little. But if you let me Commit without telling me the truth . . . that's wrong, Fullin, you know it's wrong. I don't deserve that from you.''

I let out my breath slowly. She was right—a gentleman can't leave a lady hanging forever. "Okay,'' I said. "The truth. The absolute truth. As I understand it.''

Her hand tightened into a fist, crushing the fabric of the coat's sleeve.

"The truth,'' I said hurriedly, "is that my female half loves you. Loves your male half anyway. Loves you for real. Last night when we . . . that was her. Me. You know what I mean. Steck says that in the time leading up to Commitment Hour, the gods send our other selves to take over for . . . well, haven't you been possessed by your male half in the past twenty-four hours?''

"Yes,'' she said.

"When?''

"You're the one who's talking, Fullin."

"Okay. I guess we'll get to that. Later." I couldn't meet her gaze; but when I looked away, there was nothing to see but that painting of the Patriarch, poised with his burning torch. "So my female half... *me* ... even if I became Mocking Priestess and couldn't marry you, my female half would like to stay with you forever."

"There's a way that can be arranged," Cappie said.

"How?"

She shook her head. "Later. Tell me what your male half thinks. What *you* think. Of me."

"I think..." Feeling suffocated, I had to take a deep breath. "It hasn't been a good year for us. And men are ambitious, they want to make something of themselves..."

"They want to play violin down-peninsula and fuck any woman who makes herself available."

I couldn't answer that. By the strict definition of sexual intercourse, I had never actually cheated on her... but rationales like that sound good in your own head, then wilt like old spinach when exposed to air.

"If you want me to tell the truth," I said, "don't make it hard for me to speak it. I'm just saying that as male... as a man, I'm not sure what I want. For one thing, I don't know about becoming priestess: I look at Leeta and ask if she's what I want to be for the rest of my life. To be perfectly honest, she's a little ridiculous with the milkweeds and the bear claws... and her whole point of view—as if dancing in the forest could affect the rotation of the Earth. I believe in the gods, you know I do, but those priestess rituals... what can I say? Not that I want to be Hakoore's disciple either."

"Forget that, Fullin." Cappie suddenly leaned in close. "All I need to know is whether you want to belong to me. Can you let yourself be *mine*? Male or female, that's the thing I never feel from you. I know when you want to bed me. I know when you're glad for my company. I know how you're happy to live with someone who'll do most of the chores, because you've convinced me it's important you have time to play your music. But are you ready to be mine? Whether or not we can be married. You say you love me... or at least your female half does. But can you give yourself to me? Can you let yourself go without hiding behind anything?"

I didn't answer.

After a while, Cappie said, "I'm going to Commit female, Fullin. My male half needs you too much."

She opened her hand to let go of the Patriarch's coat. The sleeve fell—limp cloth, worn and faded.

"Just so you know," she added, "in case I end up as the next priestess . . . Leeta says there's an unwritten law that the priestess and Patriarch's Man must secretly get married. The Patriarch saw it as a sneaky way to 'subjugate' women under male command. That's the Patriarch for you. But Hakoore and Leeta have been happy with each other over the years. I hope the next Patriarch's Man, whoever he is, won't be someone who makes me feel so cryingly lonesome."

Without looking back Cappie strode away, disappearing out of the hall and out of Mayoralty House.

SIXTEEN

A Dish for the Traitors

I intended to wait five minutes—give Cappie plenty of time to leave, even if she ran into the mayor, or Rashid and Steck. But the atmosphere of the Patriarch's Hall oppressed me: the cloying smell of dust, the pointless faded finery, the picture of the couple swearing their love on the Patriarch's Hand. When I was young, this room seemed full of treasures; now I realized it was a place that adult Tobers sent their children but never went themselves. After only sixty seconds, I fairly ran away from the ominous mementos, as if ghosts were chasing me—down the corridor and out to the wide front steps where Rashid and Steck sat with Embrun in the sunshine.

Steck looked at me quizzically when I arrived, as if she could claim some right to ask what had happened between Cappie and me. She couldn't; by my age, boys didn't confide in their *real* mothers, let alone Neut strangers. If we had been alone, Steck might have pressed me . . . but Rashid was interrogating Embrun, and showed no sign of acknowledging my return, let alone allowing the conversation to be diverted to my personal life.

From the sound of it, Embrun's information about Bonnakkut hadn't taken much time to tell. Rashid's questions had already shifted to his real interest, learning more about Birds Home and the Tober sex change process. For that, Embrun could actually be helpful—he had Committed the previous summer, so the memory was still fresh in his head.

"And it's a disembodied voice?" Rashid was saying. "Asking, 'Male, female, or both?'"

"Right you are, master," Embrun replied. He had sprawled himself on the house's cracked concrete steps in an effort to look casual, as if he talked to Spark Lords all the time. I noticed though that he seldom looked in Rashid's direction. It wasn't humility; he was just devoting his attention to Steck, ogling her in that deepcut neckline.

I could have punched him in the nose.

"So," Rashid said, "if it's not too personal, could you tell me why you chose male?"

Embrun glanced at me with the look of someone trying to decide if he can get away with lying. Finally he decided to tell the truth. "I didn't have much choice, did I?" he answered. "My female half got kicked stupid. I couldn't live like that."

He proceeded to tell about the accident and its consequences, embellishing details here and there, because he seldom got a chance to share his story with newcomers. The way I originally heard it, Girl-Embrun had been teasing the horse when it kicked her—poking it with a stick. In the tale Embrun told Rashid, however, his female half's motives were far more noble: trying to pull out a thorn that had speared the horse's rump, making it bleed.

Off the top of my head, I couldn't think of any local vegetation with thorns growing as high as a horse's flank. In fact the stupid animal had nowhere to pick up a thorn at all, unless it decided to sit on the mayor's rose bushes. Still, I couldn't see the harm in letting Embrun glamorize himself, provided he didn't go too far.

Besides, it was interesting to hear him describe what it was like to be . . . well, brain-damaged. Not that he could remember much from his female years: just moments of emotion, pain at touching a hot stove, or fear and confusion one time when she got lost in the woods. Mostly, those years had just disappeared from his memory, like muddy dreams that are gone when you wake.

As Embrun continued, Rashid took on the expression of a man mulling over a profound revelation. When it was over, he murmured, "You received the injury as a five-year-old girl. You switched to a boy at six and poof, you were fine—except that you couldn't remember much of the past year. Then when you returned to being a girl at seven, you were . . . disadvantaged again?"

"That's right, master," Embrun nodded enthusiastically. "I'm not lying, am I, Fullin?"

"Not on that," I agreed. "His girl half truly had her brains jarred loose by that kick. Her body kept growing after, but her mind stayed stuck where it was."

"So your female body was damaged, but your male body wasn't," Rashid said. He turned to me. "Is it the same for everyone else in Tober Cove? I mean, injuries to your female body don't affect your male, and vice versa?"

"Of course," I said. Holding out my arm, I pointed to a pale pink scar just above my wrist. "That's a gash I got as a kid, exploring a half-collapsed house on the other side of town—I didn't see a nail sticking out of a board. My male body has the wound, but my female one doesn't."

"This is amazing!" Rashid said.

"Oh, that's nothing, master," Embrun told him. "What about Yailey the Hunter? She's got my head-kick beat."

"Who's Yailey the Hunter?"

"Eight years ago now," Embrun answered, "Yailey drowned. He was sixteen—out diving ropeless with a bunch of other boys off some rocks up the coast. Tried some fancy dive he'd read about in an OldTech book, and fucked the . . . I mean, he made an awful mistake. Hit his head on the way down. And the thing was, he'd gone off a ways from his friends so's he could practice the dive without them laughing at him. By the time they came to check on him, Yailey was face down and floating.

"The other boys were in tears as they carried him into town," Embrun went on. "I remember that much, even if it was one of my dull years. Scared me, all that wailing. Anyhow, the drowning happened in late spring. Then solstice came, the children headed off to Birds Home, and when we came back, guess who was tagging along with us? Girl Yailey."

"You mean," said Rashid, "her male body died, but a female version of her came back at solstice?"

"That's what happened," I assured him. "Yailey herself lit the funeral pyre for her male body. Hakoore delayed the cremation until he found out whether Yailey came back from Birds Home—apparently this has happened before."

"Where is this Yailey?" Rashid asked, ablaze with enthusiasm. "I must talk to her."

"Sorry, master," Embrun said, "she's hard to find. Dying like that upset her—not that she remembered it. Everything went black the moment she hit her head. But it still nettled under her skin."

"And knowing Tober Cove," Steck muttered, "people treated her like a monstrosity."

"I don't remember anyone ragging on her," Embrun said—untruthfully, because he himself called her names in the schoolyard: *Hey, Corpse-girl! Mistress Want!* "But Yailey turned more and more edgy as time went on. Especially close to the next solstice."

"Hakoore decided to get dogmatic," I put in, "and declared she'd have to go to Birds Home when the time came."

"It wasn't just Hakoore," said Embrun. "Yailey was only seventeen; she hadn't even had her child by Master Crow. A lot of people thought she should go back to Birds Home and do everything right. But Yailey was afraid she'd get there and come back dead . . . or Neut or something else. On Commitment Eve, she ran off into the forest and she's been out there since. That's why they call her Yailey the Hunter. Now and then she sneaks back to her parents' house to trade meat and furs for things she needs. Officially though, Hakoore has declared her unwelcome in town."

Steck snorted. "Because she refused to follow his nasty little orders."

Embrun looked surprised at Steck's anger. "Hakoore just doesn't want kids thinking they can avoid the proper switchover. Hell, there were sure times *I* didn't want to go to Birds Home. When I was boy, thinking how the gods would make me back into a girl with my brain all clotted—some days, I felt like hiding so I'd miss the trip. And the year I knew I'd come back pregnant . . . that terrified me. Not for myself, you understand, but for the baby. My female half couldn't be a proper mother, could she, master?"

I doubted that Embrun really worried about the baby more than himself, but he still had a point: switching sexes could be a scary thing. In the weeks before my pregnancy solstice, I considered haring off down-peninsula—becoming a traveling minstrel rather than a mother. The thought of my body harboring some alien little being, like a parasite inside me . . . and suffering all the pains of pregnancy, the dangers of labor . . . yes, I contemplated taking the easy way out. The idea must have crossed a lot of people's minds.

Maybe Hakoore had a point when he took an inflexible stand against Yailey. The cove's way of life depended on a tough Patriarch's Man who ensured that teenagers didn't dodge their commitments.

It made me wince. I was making excuses for Hakoore. I was arguing for the necessity of the Patriarch's Man.

Who was secretly forced to marry the Mocking Priestess. To become *hers*.

Why was everything so complicated all of a sudden?

Rashid declared he had run out of questions for Embrun. "Stay here," he told Steck and me. "I'll just walk our friend a little way back to town."

He and Embrun started across the parking lot, Rashid's boots making more sticky sounds on the hot pavement. As soon as they were out of earshot, I asked Steck, "What's Rashid up to?"

"He plans to give Embrun some money," Steck replied, "and he doesn't want to do it where the mayor or I can see. He's afraid we'll think he's a sucker for paying off such an obvious little worm . . . and he's right."

"So Embrun didn't have any real evidence about Bonnakkut's murder?"

Steck shook her head. "Just that his dog had some kind of barking fit about the time Bonnakkut was killed."

"Embrun's dog has barking fits five times a day," I told her. "The poor animal liked female Embrun a lot more than the male version; it's missed her dreadfully since Embrun Committed."

"Speaking of Commitment," Steck said, "how did it go with Cappie?"

I should have expected the question—Steck trying to play the attentive mother. "Cappie and I have our troubles," I muttered.

"Would it help if you talked to Zephram?" Steck asked. "I know we agreed you'd stay with me, but if you wanted to talk to . . . your father . . . if you wanted to talk to him alone . . ."

"It wouldn't help," I said, mostly out of stubborn pride. "Thanks for the offer though."

"If you need to talk to anyone . . ." Steck didn't finish the sentence. "When you face Commitment Hour, it's best not to have conflicts weighing on your mind."

"Is that what happened to you?"

"I made a choice," Steck said. "That's all. A choice to be new."

"What do you mean by that?"

She glanced at me but looked away again quickly. "Zephram said he told you how we got together: in the Silence of Mistress Snow. Did he tell you that no one else in town chose to visit me?"

I nodded.

Steck shrugged. "There were reasons for that—reasons I was living alone in my final year before Commitment. I hadn't gone out of my way to make myself popular. Things were better when I was with Zephram, but I couldn't imagine he'd stay with me long. I convinced myself his feelings were . . . oh, just his way of mourning, I guess. He was vulnerable because he missed his wife. Once he got past the worst of his grief, he wouldn't need me anymore—that's what I thought. That he'd wake one day and wonder why he was spending time with a girl who couldn't give . . ."

Her voice trailed off.

"You couldn't have been that bad," I said. "Leeta wanted you as her apprentice."

"Leeta only took me because I badgered her," Steck replied. "I'd got the idea that if I became priestess I'd suddenly *mean* something. It's hard to feel worthwhile when you're a teenager with no friends . . . girl or boy, it made no difference. Leeta accepted me out of pity; or maybe she thought she could mold me into a real person somehow. Either way, she didn't *like* me. I wasn't likable, male or female. And on Commitment Day, I thought maybe if I picked the third option, things would be different.''

"You thought people would like you more as a Neut?" I asked. "Not in Tober Cove."

"I thought maybe I'd like *myself* more. A new body, a new personality. Leaving behind all the stubborn habits that made me . . . difficult. I wanted things to change for me. Inside."

"But you knew you'd be banished!"

"Did I care? What was so attractive about Tober Cove?"

"Me."

She sighed. "I know, Fullin. But I thought I could take you with me. I'd leave Tober Cove with my baby . . . and Zephram would go with me, back to the South . . . where he told me Neuts and normal people could live as husband and wife . . ." She shook her head. "And I'd be a new person. I wouldn't make the same mistakes. I'd stop being . . . oh, the kind of woman Zephram would hate as soon as he came to his senses."

Women say such things for only one reason: to have a man tell them they're mistaken. *No, no,* I was supposed to say, *Zephram loved you for yourself.* And I think he did; when he spoke to me at breakfast, his voice had been full of fondness, not "What was I thinking?" embarrassment. Still, it was hard for me to treat this Neut, my mother, as a normal woman who wanted reassurance. A wall of awkwardness loomed between us . . . and before I could speak, Rashid reappeared at the far end of the pavement.

As before, he stopped at the rusting OldTech cart. For a moment, he leaned into the engine again, presumably to look at the black radio box. Then he suddenly straightened up, and lifted his eyes to the hill behind Mayoralty House. His face broke into a jubilant smile.

"Damn," Steck whispered.

"What?" I asked.

"He's figured it out. He's figured it all out."

She suddenly flinched, as if she hadn't intended to speak those words aloud. Before I could ask what she meant, Rashid started running toward us.

*   *   *

Rashid's feet slapped the pavement like waves clapping against a boat's hull. His smile gleamed with excitement. Long before he reached us, he called out, "On top of the hill . . . that antenna . . ."

"It's an OldTech radio tower," I told him.

"The hell it is," he answered. "Have you had a good look at that dish assembly on top? The OldTechs never built anything close." He stopped in front of me, panting lightly. "Quickly, O Native Guide—show us the fastest route up the hill."

Steck put on an irritable expression as she got to her feet. "What's this all about?" she asked.

"Radio relay," Rashid panted, pointing back to the rusted cart. His finger swiveled around to point to the antenna on the hill. "Main receiving station. That's got to be the answer."

"What answer?" I asked.

"Take me up the hill and I'll show you."

The top of Patriarch Hill was a patchwork of bare limestone ledges alternating with scrubby clumps of brush and buttercups. Paper birch and poplar ringed the area, like hair around a man's bald patch; the trees even had a distinct lean to them, as if the prevailing westerlies had tried to comb them over to hide the bareness.

The antenna squatted on limestone in the center of the open area, with three wrist-thick guy wires strung out and anchored into other sections of rock. Kids occasionally climbed a short way up those wires, going hand over hand until they got high enough to scare themselves; but I couldn't remember anyone climbing the antenna itself. Its base was enclosed by a rusty chain-link fence, topped with barbed wire and big signs showing pictures of lightning bolts. That meant you'd get hit by lightning if you touched the tower itself . . . and heaven knows, the antenna must have had enough lightning to discharge because it got hit a dozen times in every summer thunderstorm.

Neither the fence nor the signs fazed Rashid. In fact, he gave the chain-link a quick look-over, then turned back to me with a gloating expression on his face. "When you were a young boy, didn't you ever go places you weren't supposed to?"

"Sure," I answered, "there was one time we found this garbage dump—"

"But," the Spark Lord interrupted, "I've never seen an OldTech fence in this perfect condition." He threaded his fingers through the links and gave a yank; the fence barely yielded. "With any other fence," Rashid said, "local kids would have pulled up the bottom to crawl under, or made dents crawling over."

I pointed to the nearest lightning sign. "We didn't want to get zapped."

"Come on," Rashid scoffed. "In four hundred years, kids never dared each other to give it a try? And what about wild animals? You'd think a bear would have pushed in a section while using it as a scratching post, or maybe a big deer hit the fence in the dark."

"Tober Cove prides itself on its hunting," Steck told him. "Bear and deer know better than to come this close to town."

"Still," Rashid answered, "OldTech fences don't survive this well." He gave it another tug; no response but a small rattle. "Proof it's not OldTech at all."

"If it isn't OldTech," I said, "what is it? We Tobers didn't build it."

"No," Rashid agreed, craning his neck back to stare at the arrangement of gadgets high up the aerial. "You probably don't need a maser array that can squirt several hundred terabits of data every millisecond." He waved his hand to stop me before I could ask what he meant. "The details aren't important. Just trust me: the OldTechs never reached the technical sophistication of those dishes up there. They've got more bandwidth for sending and receiving than the communication systems for an entire OldTech city."

I turned to Steck and whispered, "Bandwidth?"

She patted my arm soothingly. "Most of this is going over my head too."

I didn't believe her. Rashid shouldn't have either, but he was too excited to pay attention. "We won't learn anything standing out here. In we go."

He reached toward the hip of his armor. As he did, a section of the green plastic slid back and a small holster pushed out of the armor's thigh. The holster held a green plastic pistol: very flat and compact, with none of the chunky menace of the Beretta he'd given to Bonnakkut.

"Laser," Rashid said, drawing the gun.

"Heat ray," Steck explained, pulling me away from the line of fire.

Rashid aimed the gun's muzzle at the fence and made an easy sweeping motion, starting high, ending low. The air filled with the tangy smell of metal, and billows of smoke drifted up into the hot summer day. Rashid put his glove against the chain-link to give it a tentative push; when he did, a whole section moved inward, severed from the adjoining links along a sharp-cut line. "At least the wire's not laser-proof," he muttered. The gun swept across the fencing two more times, shooting no visible bullets or beams . . . but when Rashid planted his foot against the wire and shoved, a door-shaped section of chain-link fell away, sliced off precisely where the gun had pointed.

He turned back to Steck. "After you, my dear."

Steck gave a mock curtsy and slipped through the gap. A moment later, Rashid and I followed.

Rashid bent in close to examine the antenna's metal frame. It looked like normal rusted steel, with red-orange corrosion dusted like thick powder over every metal strut. After a moment, the Spark Lord huffed out a single heavy breath, the way you do when you want to fog a mirror. He watched the metal a few more seconds, then murmured, "Very convincing."

"Why do you keep talking like the tower's not real?" I asked.

"Oh, it's real," Rashid replied. He tapped one of the tower's struts with his gloved finger; the metal *tink-tinked* exactly the way you'd expect. "It's just not what it appears to be."

He pointed his green pistol at the strut he'd just tapped. With two quick pulls of his trigger finger, he sliced out a small section of metal, leaving a gap about as wide as my thumb. "Now watch," he said. "See if this is an ordinary OldTech tower."

I waited a few seconds. "I don't see anything."

"Patience," he said. He bent and picked up a small twig that had blown off one of the nearby trees. Carefully, Rashid slipped the twig into the gap he'd just cut in the steel.

The process was almost too slow to see; but gradually, the gap in the metal began to narrow . . . as if the two freshly-cut ends were steel teeth closing in on the twig. Soon Rashid could let go of the little stick—the gap had closed enough to clamp the twig in place. As I watched, the teeth continued to bite into the wood. The twig bent . . . then broke . . . then dropped in two pieces as the antenna completely closed over the cut Rashid made.

"The metal is self-repairing," he said. "And it would have to be, wouldn't it, to survive four centuries."

"I don't understand," I told him, trying not to sound unsettled by what I'd just seen.

"This antenna isn't OldTech steel," Rashid replied. "The whole damned tower must be solid nano. Smart metal camouflaged to look rusty."

I stared at him blankly.

"Think of it as a machine," he answered with the air of a man who doesn't want to explain himself to a country bumpkin. "Solar powered.

Probably can store energy from lightning strikes too . . . or get power beamed down from orbital collectors. It must need a lot of juice.''

He glanced back over his shoulder. ''The fence must be nano too. That's why it's still in such good shape. Let's leave before our way out seals itself shut.''

Steck looked up at the collection of dishes on top of the tower. ''Don't you want to check out the transmitter array?''

''How?'' Rashid asked. ''If we try to climb this tower, I bet it has defenses . . . like struts that break off while we're standing on them. It may even get mad at us for just hanging around here. We'd better leave.''

He gave my shoulder a nudge to start me moving toward the gap in the fence. I rolled away from him. ''No.''

''No? No, what?''

''No, I'm not leaving until you explain what's going on.'' I reached out and grabbed one of the metal struts, just to let him know I wouldn't be moved.

With a cry, Steck leapt forward and knocked my hand clear of the tower. ''Don't touch that, you idiot!''

I looked at her in astonishment. Rashid gave a thin smile. ''Fullin,'' he said, ''I think your mother has a better understanding of this antenna than she'd like to let on.''

''If it's nano, it's dangerous,'' Steck said sullenly. ''I don't know any more about the tower than you do.''

''Will someone please explain . . .'' I started.

''Yes,'' Rashid interrupted. ''Once we're safe. Come on.''

''You want the truth?'' Rashid asked. ''You really want it?''

''Yes,'' I said.

We were standing outside the fence, watching the section of chain-link that Rashid had cut out and pushed down onto the ground. The chain metal had lost its solidity; it had turned into a gooey black liquid as thickly viscous as molasses. Slowly, very slowly, the liquid was flowing across the dirt.

How could such a thing happen? Not that I wanted an explanation of the science or magic that could turn steel into this tarry fluid; how could this fence and this antenna, perched on Patriarch Hill my entire lifetime and for centuries before I was born, be made of such otherworldly stuff?

Tober Cove was my home. I thought I understood it.

''What's going on?'' I asked . . . and for some reason I turned to Steck. ''Is this just some trick you've set up to scare me?''

She closed her eyes for a moment, then shook her head. ''Sorry,

Fullin," she murmured. "I know it's hard when you realize things aren't the way you thought." She opened her eyes again. "It really might be best if we walk back to the town square and pretend you haven't seen a thing."

The black chain-link fluid had pooled into an oily puddle directly under the rest of the fence. Now the liquid began to flow straight upward, like a waterfall in slow reverse, inching up to fill the hole Rashid had cut.

"I want to know," I said. "Please."

Steck turned to Rashid. He shrugged. "All right. You know why OldTech civilization collapsed?" he asked me.

"Because demons came from beyond the stars—"

"Not demons," he interrupted. "Aliens. Extraterrestrials. The League of Peoples."

"Inhuman creatures," I said. "And they offered exotic riches to anybody who wanted to leave Earth. Enough people went with them that things fell apart."

"Close enough," Rashid said. "And then?"

"Then the Sparks restored order and organized the planet into the Spark Protectorate."

"Don't make it sound like it happened overnight," Rashid chided. "When the League of Peoples came to Earth with their proposal, the only humans who accepted were those with nothing to lose: people facing starvation or war, not to mention patients with terminal diseases who thought they could be saved by League medicine. They went off; then they came back two years later looking healthy and driving FTL starships, saying no, there really weren't any strings attached to the League's offer. A few more people left . . . then a few more, and a few more, with each wave coming back to tell friends and family, it's wonderful, we have a clean new home planet, we have unbelievable high-tech gadgets, we have peace. There were plenty of doubters, but there were also plenty of people who decided to take the plunge."

"Traitors," I said.

"You don't know how terrible things were in the twenty-first century," Rashid replied. "Toward the end of OldTech times, most of the human race was poor and hungry. The planet was damaged—the air, the water, the soil—and there were so many conflicting factions claiming they knew how to solve the world's problems that no one could rally enough support to get any recovery plan started. Twenty years after the League's first offer, more than seventy percent of the Earth's human population had decided it was better to start over than stay on a sinking ship."

"Traitors," I repeated.

"So speaks the descendant of someone who stayed home . . . and in a part of the world that was affluent and not too polluted. Anyway, so many people left that OldTech culture couldn't sustain itself . . . and it took forty more years before my Spark ancestors managed to reestablish equilibrium. You know what happened in those forty years?"

"High Queen Gloriana of Spark battled the star demons into subjugation and forced them to pay her tribute." Why was he asking me this? Every child on Earth learned history.

"Well," Rashid answered with a wry look on his face, "it's more accurate to say that Gloriana came to an accommodation with the League of Peoples. In exchange for certain, uh, considerations from my family, the League granted us sovereignty over the planet . . . as well as a supply of high-tech goodies that would help us convince the struggling dregs of humanity to accept us as their rulers."

"The word 'puppet' was never used," Steck put in.

Rashid glared at her. "You know nothing about the League," he snapped. "They didn't need Earth as a vassal; they just felt bad for disrupting Terran society so badly. The League decided Gloriana was the best bet for ending decades of violent anarchy."

"What does this have to do with the antenna?" I asked. "And the fence." The tarry fluid had climbed to the height of my knees now—like a paper-thin black curtain stretched across the hole. Second by second, it continued to climb. I wanted to touch it; I didn't dare.

Maybe it would feel greasy like butter. Maybe the slightest touch would burn like a spider bite.

"This antenna," Rashid said, "almost certainly dates back to the forty years between the OldTech collapse and Gloriana's hands-off treaty with the League. During that time, Earth was officially a free zone—open to any League members who cared to drop by. Nonhumans mostly weren't interested, but humans . . . they'd got their hands on all kinds of nifty technology from the League, and they were itching to play god with the poor benighted barbarians who'd stayed back on Earth."

I didn't like his choice of phrase: "play god." My face must have shown my resentment. "I'm sorry, Fullin," Rashid said, "but that's what they did. Certain humans from the stars returned to Earth to set up experiments. They treated their old home planet as one big laboratory filled with guinea pigs who had *chosen* to be backward . . . who had irrationally refused to go into space. So the star-siders came back to test their lovely new gadgetry on us. Brain/machine interlinks. Clever tricks to work on genes. Nanotech . . ."

He gestured toward the fence. The black sheet of goo had risen to cover the hole completely now. There was no more fluid on the ground; it had all seeped upward to bond with the rest of the chain-link.

"They usually set up their experiments in abandoned towns," Rashid said. "Often, they built societies from the ground up—starting with infants they kidnapped from elsewhere on Earth, or even with baby clones of themselves. They'd invent religions, customs, ways of life, all carefully taught to the kids . . . because these projects were meant to be *demonstrations*, Fullin. Demonstrations of social theories. Nice little rustic utopias. And they thought they were doing us a favor; they really did. To them, life here on Earth was a violent, ignorant hell. Forcibly imposing new social structures on us was nothing more than kindness."

"And that's what you think Tober Cove is?" I asked. "Some project built by traitors who came back from the stars?"

Rashid nodded. "The OldTechs were obsessed with gender differences, Fullin: which traits were innate, which were just a result of training. In the years after OldTech civilization collapsed, it's not hard to believe that some of the star-siders set up a research program here—to see what happened when people had the chance to be both male and female . . ."

"Or both," Steck added.

"Indeed," Rashid said. "An experiment to see what differences persisted even when people saw both sides of the gender gap . . . and could straddle the middle if they wanted."

The sheet of blackness covering the gap in the fence was beginning to tatter. Holes opened in the goo as other regions began to thicken— a crisscross pattern congealing slowly into the familiar diamonds of chain-link. Red specks appeared on the black surface: simulated dots of rust. The underlying black changed color too, fading to metallic steel gray.

It had only taken a few minutes. Rashid had cut out a section of fence . . . and the fence had healed itself. I couldn't even see where the cuts had been made.

"This is just some sort of machine?" I asked.

"Actually millions of tiny machines," Rashid said. "Bonded together to look like a fence. Same with the antenna."

"All just machines."

I thought of the Patriarch's Hand—another machine. And Hakoore had slyly told me, "Maybe the hand is older than the Patriarch, dating back to the founding of the cove." Another high-tech toy, brought to Earth by those who created this fence. I could imagine how traitors from the stars would love to give such a gift to their priesthood: a lie detector for keeping the rabble in line.

"So if Tober Cove is an experiment," I murmured, "or a demonstration . . . are they still watching us now?"

"No," Rashid said. "When the Sparks signed their treaty with the League, the star-siders were all obliged to leave. Since Master Crow and Mistress Gull still show up every year, I assume the whole process is mechan-ized. Computer-controlled, continuing to run itself on autopilot—"

"Wait a second," I interrupted. "You think that Master Crow and Mistress Gull are part of this too?"

"It's all the same package," he replied. "Master Crow and Mistress Gull are just airplanes, aren't they? Robot-driven planes that pick the Tober children . . ."

I let out a sigh of relief. Airplanes. The airplane argument. That familiar old refrain.

It put everything else in perspective.

Listen: Tobers know about airplanes. We've seen their pictures in OldTech books. And when someone from down-peninsula says, "Hey, your gods are just planes," it's hardly the complete refutation of all our beliefs that outsiders seem to think.

Yes, Tober children flew to Birds Home in airplanes. Mundane aircraft. Machines.

But why should that matter? Everything belonged to the gods. Machines were no less god-given than a stone or a leaf. And the planes weren't the *real* Master Crow or Mistress Gull—they were just tools held by divine hands. The real gods wore the planes' metal and machinery like unimportant clothing.

If that was true for the planes, why not for everything else? For machines like the Patriarch's Hand, the self-healing fence, and everything. Why not even the star-siders who might have founded Tober Cove? The gods could use people just as easily as they used machines. They could send a duck to tell whether they wanted you to Commit male or female, and they could send traitors from space to set up a town where people could live sane lives.

If the gods were behind it, who cared about the apparent physical cause? Getting distracted by such issues was just Hakoore's materialism, wasn't it? Thinking that the gods weren't in the picture just because the cove had a surface explanation. But the gods *were* in the picture; I refused to doubt them.

Damn, I hated when Hakoore was right.

"Lord Rashid," I said, "the Patriarch once preached that a scientist will cut a gull into pieces, then be astonished none of the pieces can fly. That's what you're doing here. You may be happy you've cut all this to pieces, but you haven't got the truth of Tober Cove. You haven't seen a drop of it."

The Spark Lord looked at me curiously. "You're all right with this? The fence, the antenna . . ."

"Why should I care about the antenna?" I asked. "It's just a big tall thing up on a hill. You haven't even suggested it has a purpose."

"It's a collector," he answered, watching me to see my reaction. "This whole peninsula must be covered with radio relays like the one hidden back in that car's engine. The relays gather low-powered local radio transmissions, and forward them to the array on this tower. This antenna amplifies the signals and sends them on a tight beam to another site—"

"Wait," I interrupted. I was actually smiling, even if I didn't understand half of what he said. "What local radio transmissions? No one has a radio in Tober Cove."

"Oh. That."

Rashid reached into a belt pouch and pulled out his little plastic radio receiver. When he turned it on, it made the same waves-on-gravel sound it had made before.

"More static," Steck muttered.

"No," Rashid told her. "Just a type of transmission that's too complicated for my receiver to decode. And guess where it's coming from."

He touched the receiver to my forehead. The noise of the static went wild.

"See?" Rashid said. "Radio Fullin is on the air."

SEVENTEEN

A Barrel for the Bereaved

Rashid offered no explanations. "You don't like me speaking like a scientist," he said.

Steck wouldn't clarify things for me either. She contended she didn't see the significance of what Rashid had discovered. He refused to believe it. "I've taught you enough science," he told her. "You can figure out the whole setup. If I were a suspicious man, I'd say you knew how Tober Cove worked long ago. You only pretended it was a great mystery because you wanted me to bring you here for Fullin's Commitment."

She wrapped her arms around him. "What's wrong with caring about my son?"

"Nothing. But you could have told me the truth. Did you think I wouldn't find out when we got here?"

Steck shrugged. She looked like a woman preparing for lovey-dovey apologies and kiss-kiss "Ooo, don't hate me!" manipulations. That was something I did *not* want to see ... partly because she was my mother, partly because she was a Neut, and partly because I didn't want to know that a Spark Lord could be taken in by such obvious sugar-spreading.

"Were we going to leave?" I asked loudly.

They looked at me. Rashid gave Steck a lurid wink. "We'd better cool off," he said. "No hanky-panky in front of the kids."

She laughed.

I spun away from them and stormed down the hill.

By the time I reached the town square, Rashid and Steck were walking beside me ... and I made sure to keep between them so they wouldn't be tempted to hold hands.

I wouldn't be the first son in history to shove himself in as his mother's chaperon.

As we rounded the Council Hall building, I saw Kaeomi, Stallor and Mintz rolling a black-painted water barrel toward the center of the square. The paint was fresh—as the barrel rolled across the council lawn, its sticky surface accumulated a litter of grass cuttings, pebbles, and even an unlucky worm flattened to a gooey ribbon by the barrel's great weight.

I'd seen black barrels often enough. This one told me Bonnakkut's body had been put on display under the branches of Little Oak. All our dead spent a day on a bier at the base of the tree; and when people came to pay their respects, they dipped a cup of water out of the black barrel and shared a last drink with the deceased. Most people just lifted the cup in a toast before drinking . . . but a few would place the cup to the corpse's lips and spill a little there before taking their own sip.

Doctor Gorallin made sure that people all drank from separate cups.

A group of Tobers had already gathered around the body—an outer ring of onlookers, plus an inner ring with Hakoore and Leeta accompanied by Bonnakkut's immediate family: his daughter Ivis and his mother Kenna. Dorr was there too, her arm in a sling that seemed very white against her tanned skin. She was the only one of the inner circle who looked in our direction as we approached. Hakoore and Leeta supervised the three warriors as they manhandled the barrel closer to the corpse. Ivis and Kenna did nothing. They both wore lost, slightly ashamed expressions on their faces, as if they felt they ought to be helping in some way but couldn't figure out how to contribute.

The mother's eyes had the reddened look of recent crying. The daughter's didn't. At six years old, she should have had some understanding of death, but the blankness on her face said she was too full of shocked confusion for any other emotion to surface.

As we approached, Ivis decided to be scared at the sight of strangers. She ran to her grandmother and wrapped her arms around Kenna's waist. Kenna hugged the girl's shoulder while Leeta hurried up to Rashid. "Do you have to be here?" she asked in a low voice.

"Is there a problem?" Rashid replied.

"Bonnakkut's dead!" Leeta snapped. "Murdered because of that gun you gave him."

"How do you know that's the reason?"

"The gun is missing, isn't it?"

"Yes," Rashid admitted, "but that doesn't mean the killing was purely because of the pistol. Someone may have wanted Bonnakkut dead for some other reason. I got the impression from Fullin that—"

He broke off with a glance at Ivis and Kenna, then lowered his voice. "The deceased was not the most popular man in the village."

Leeta's soft old eyes took on a hard edge. "And it's just coincidence he stayed healthy for twenty-five years, then died twelve hours after you arrived?"

"Yes," said Dorr, "it's just coincidence."

I hadn't even heard her coming up behind me—living in Hakoore's house, she had learned to move without making noises that might disturb the old snake. Dorr said, "Bonnakkut's death had nothing to do with the outsiders."

We all turned to look at her. She reached to her belt and pulled out the knife from her hip-sheath: the knife I had seen her holding in Cypress Marsh, when she had just cut off a wad of dye plants. In the marsh, the blade had been clean except for a gleam of sap from the reeds. Now the metal was splashed with rusty brown stains.

"Dorr . . ." Steck began.

"Quiet!" Dorr snapped. It was the first time in years I'd heard her raise her voice; and the voice was deep, unwomanly. "This is my time," she told Steck. Then she lifted the knife above her head, blade pointing to the sky. "See?" she shouted. "Everybody see? I killed him!"

With a fierce motion, she swung down the knife and rammed it deep into the wood of the black barrel.

No one moved. It wasn't shock or surprise; we were frozen with embarrassment, as if Dorr was an unliked little girl who was telling lies to get attention. Even with blood on her knife, no one took her seriously. This was Dorr, granddaughter of the Patriarch's Man. She wasn't a killer, she was just crazy and desperate.

Dorr looked around at our faces; she must have seen our pitying disbelief. "I really did it!" she said angrily. "Because he was a pig."

"Dorr . . ." Steck began again, at the same time Leeta said, "Shush, Dorr! His family's here."

"My granddaughter is out of her mind," Hakoore declared loudly. He jabbed a bony finger in her direction. "Go home, woman."

"You know I'm not a woman," Dorr said. And reaching down with her good arm, she pulled her simple cotton dress high above her waist.

She was wearing underwear—a tight white girdle at crotch level, probably intended to smooth the outline of her groin . . . binding the bulge of penis and testicles. Under a dress, the camouflage worked, but exposed now in the bright summer sunlight, the tell-tale contours were plain for all to see.

Hakoore made a choking sound. Leeta looked toward him, concern filling her eyes. *They really are lovers*, I thought. Hakoore must have told Leeta about Dorr long ago. Now our priestess was more worried about the old snake than about his crazy granddaughter.

Dorr let go of her dress. It fell haphazardly about her thighs, and she made no effort to smooth it. "Bonnakkut knew about me," Dorr told the crowd. "He came to our house now and then to discuss law with my grandfather. He must have seen something about me that made him suspicious."

Sure, I thought. *Just by chance.* I could imagine Dorr tormenting her grandfather whenever Bonnakkut came over . . . dropping veiled hints about her true gender just to give the old man shudders. She might have "accidentally" sat with her knees a little too open, or maybe scratched herself like a man, and eventually Bonnakkut caught on.

"He didn't do anything right away," Dorr said, "but when Lord Rashid and his Bozzle arrived . . . something about their presence infuriated Bonnakkut. He decided to take it out on me."

I looked at Steck. Her face was stricken with dismay . . . and rightly so, I thought. Bonnakkut was just the sort to boil with rage over a Neut he couldn't fight; so he turned his anger on Dorr, a Neut who didn't have a Spark Lord for protector.

"He followed me into the woods and grabbed me," Dorr went on. "He said he'd tell everyone my secret unless I . . ." She stopped; her gaze moved to Ivis, who was listening in mute bewilderment, as if this had nothing to do with her father. "He threatened me," Dorr said in a lower voice. "And I got very very angry. Bonnakkut must not have known how angry I could get—he actually turned his back on me while we were talking. That was when I . . ."

She reached toward the knife, still stabbed deep into the lid of the barrel. Her fingers stroked its hilt.

"And you took his gun?" Rashid asked.

Dorr looked at him, silent for a moment. "Yes. I took his gun."

"What did you do with it?"

"I threw it away."

"Where?"

"Just away." She turned back to the knife. "Tober Cove doesn't need guns."

Rashid gave an unreadable look to Steck; Steck didn't return it. My mother's eyes were downcast, guilty. One Neut precipitating the ruin of another.

The Spark Lord turned back to Dorr. "So you killed Bonnakkut because he threatened to expose you. But here you are, only an hour later, voluntarily telling the whole village . . . when no one has accused you, or even questioned you about the murder.''

She looked at him, then shrugged. ''The truth would come out eventually. I didn't feel like waiting.''

''So you're saying you killed him,'' Mintz suddenly said.

''I slit his throat like a hog.''

Mintz's spear lay near him on the ground. He snatched it up and leveled it at her; but Rashid moved quickly in front of Dorr, blocking any attack with his armored body. ''Let's not do anything hasty,'' he said. ''Tobers believe in fair trials, don't they?''

''For Neuts?'' Dorr laughed as if the idea was genuinely funny. ''Neuts get beaten and banished merely for existing. When one has actually committed murder . . .''

She looked at Mintz and the other warriors expectantly, but they showed no stomach for tangling with a Spark Lord twice in one day. Mintz let the tip of his spear sink until it touched the ground.

''Good,'' Rashid nodded. ''We'll all be smart about this.''

''Too bad,'' Dorr said to the warriors. ''You had your chance.''

Her free hand darted into the sling wrapped around her other arm. She pulled out a wineskin, its top already open, and squirted a stream of brown fluid into her mouth. Steck leapt forward, but Dorr had already swallowed.

She smiled as if she was pleased with herself.

Steck grabbed Dorr under the armpits and kicked her legs out from under her; Dorr's eyes widened in surprise, but her mouth stayed closed as Steck set her down roughly onto the grass. ''Open up!'' Steck yelled, trying to force her fingers past Dorr's lips. ''Open your mouth!''

Dorr shook her head, teeth clenched tight.

''What goes down can come up again,'' Steck replied. ''If you don't let me stick my finger down your throat, I'll punch you in the stomach.''

Dorr tried to cover her mouth with her hand.

''Fullin!'' Steck snapped. ''Help me.''

I knelt and held Dorr's head steady as Steck tried to pry her jaw open. Dorr was still smiling, even as she resisted. Her eyes glittered, as if she were laughing at us.

''Don't hurt her!'' Hakoore cried. ''You're hurting her.''

''Not her,'' Mintz sneered. ''*It*.''

Steck glared at him in fury, then suddenly slammed the heel of her palm into Dorr's belly. Dorr gasped; her jaw loosened for a split second, and I got my fingers into her mouth. Her teeth clamped down on me . . . not hard, but enough to show she could do damage if she wanted.

The look in her eyes was easy to read—if I didn't pull my hand out, she'd bite with all her strength.

Carefully, I drew my hand away. She actually gave a coy lick to my fingers as they slid out.

I remembered her kissing me.

"Yes," Dorr murmured, her old half whisper. Perhaps only Steck and I heard. "Your father would never forgive me if I hurt you . . . your violinist's hands."

"Let us help you, Dorr!" Steck cried. "This is such a waste."

Dorr lifted her hand and cupped Steck's cheek. "Take good care of him. You've always been . . ."

She suddenly gagged, as if she were going to throw up without our help. The sound turned into a cough, then a convulsion. I found myself holding her with all my strength, somehow believing she would be all right if I could stop her shaking.

Rashid leaned over me. "Can you guess what she took?"

I shook my head. "She knew a lot about vegetable extracts. She learned from her mother."

Hakoore groaned. Leeta stood beside him, holding his hand.

Dorr lasted another twenty minutes. Eventually, we did make her vomit . . . after she was too weak to fight us. By then, her convulsions were coming every few seconds: long, shuddering spasms with all her muscles tightening, bucking, nearly bending her double.

It was not an easy death.

Toward the end, someone pulled me away from her body: Veen, Hakoore's sister, stone-faced as she watched her grandniece die. "There's nothing you can do," Veen said. "And you don't want to become her death-husband, do you?"

I didn't know if a Neut could have a death-husband. But for Dorr's sake, I hoped one of the gods would accept her.

EIGHTEEN

A Chicken Foot for Zephram

Rashid carried Dorr's body into the Council Hall where the last rites would have some privacy. He said he didn't worry about touching the corpse; his armor would protect him.

Hakoore and Leeta went to conduct the rites together. From the look on their faces, they didn't want spectators. Rashid, Steck and I quietly slipped out the side door.

The sunlight outside was bright enough to make your eyes tear up.

Steck let out a long breath. "Shit," she said.

"Shit indeed," Rashid nodded. "Hands up, anyone who believed that woman's confession."

"What do you mean?" I asked.

"There was no reason for her to do it," Rashid replied. "She wasn't backed into a corner; no one even suspected her. And she didn't sound like someone driven to come clean out of remorse."

"Maybe she was proud of doing it," Steck said.

"Why?" Rashid asked. "Because Bonnakkut was obnoxious? People need more motive than that."

"She said Bonnakkut was threatening her," I said. "He wanted her to . . ."

I didn't know how to finish the sentence.

"What did he want?" Rashid asked. "Dorr tried to suggest it was something sexual. Is that really likely? Considering how he reacted the night before, do you think Bonnakkut would lust after a Neut?"

"Sexual attacks aren't about lust," Steck answered. "They're about rage and frustration. Bonnakkut was enraged over my presence, and frustrated he couldn't do anything about it. With me out of his reach, maybe he settled for venting his anger on another Neut . . . *raping* another Neut . . .''

"I won't say it's impossible,'' Rashid replied, ''but it's strange. Why this irresistible urge to molest Dorr at . . . what was it, seven thirty in the morning? Couldn't he wait till nightfall when there'd be less chance of getting caught? And couldn't he pick a better place than that path? I assume people use the path all the time, right, Fullin?''

"Only my . . .'' I stopped. ''Actually, yes, a lot of people use the path.''

"See?'' Rashid asked. ''Too many things that don't add up. So you have to ask, why would Dorr lie? Is there anyone in town she'd die to protect? Someone who might be the real murderer?''

He was looking at me. I gave what I hoped would look like a careless shrug. ''Maybe her grandfather . . . but I can't imagine he killed Bonnakkut. Hakoore can barely walk on his own, let alone kill a top warrior and run away before anyone came on the scene.''

"He gives that impression,'' Rashid admitted, ''although it's wrong to take anything for granted. Still, even if Hakoore can secretly sprint like an ostrich, this isn't his kind of crime. He strikes me as subtle. He'd try to make it look like an accident, or blame it on someone he didn't like. Who else could Dorr be protecting? Did she have a lover?''

"Not Dorr,'' I answered quickly.

Rashid looked at me with curiosity.

"Hakoore kept her on too short a rope,'' I explained. ''He wanted her all to herself.''

"Lovers usually find a way,'' Rashid said. ''But if you don't know of anyone . . .''

Above our heads, a bell rang from the Council Hall steeple. It was a high soprano chime, the smallest bell of the four that hung in the tower.

"What's that?'' Rashid asked.

"An alert,'' I answered. ''One hour till Master Crow and Mistress Gull arrive . . . assuming they haven't been scared off by everything that's happened today.''

Rashid and Steck met each other's gaze. ''Maybe we'd better get going,'' the Spark Lord said.

"Going?'' I repeated. ''I thought this is what you came for.''

"We'll watch from someplace with a better view,'' Rashid replied. ''Maybe Beacon Point. That way we can see where Master Crow and Mistress Gull come from.''

I stared at them suspiciously. ''Are you two up to something?''

"How often do I have to say we aren't going to interfere?'' Rashid asked. ''Go. Get ready. Have a good Commitment.''

I could have argued; but the truth was I had other things on my mind, and I needed time to myself. "All right," I said. "You'll still be here when I get back?"

"What kind of a mother would she be," Rashid asked, "if she didn't want to know how her son Committed? I must admit I'm curious myself."

"That makes three of us," I told him.

"Good," Rashid said, "keep us guessing. Now kiss your mom, and we'll be off."

Steck elbowed him. She and I settled for shaking hands.

I avoided the square—it would only be full of people babbling about Dorr and Bonnakkut. Instead, I took the route Steck must have taken herself when she left from the side door of the Council Hall and went to Zephram's house.

Along the path where Bonnakkut died.

Of course, I had lied to Rashid; the trail wasn't frequently used. It only went to Zephram's; no one walked that way except people going to visit him.

Why would Bonnakkut have been out there?

Dorr said the First Warrior had been following her. Rashid thought her whole confession was a lie, but suppose it wasn't.

That only changed the question: why had Dorr been heading for Zephram's?

I thought back to the days when I was fourteen, and she was forever lingering outside the house. Especially at times when she knew I would be heading to the marsh for practice.

Suppose she wasn't waiting for a glimpse of me, or to tag along and eavesdrop on my playing.

Suppose she had been waiting for me to leave.

And in the past few years, when I had been living with Cappie down by the waterfront, Dorr could visit Zephram almost any time. No one would notice, if the two of them were discreet.

Dorr could move so quietly when she wanted to.

When she was dying, she'd said, "Your father would never forgive me if I hurt you . . . your violinist's hands." And to Steck: "Take good care of him. You've always been . . ."

You've always been what? Zephram's true love?

Had Dorr killed herself because she thought Zephram would leave her for Steck?

I didn't know; but I urgently needed to confront my foster father.

*   *   *

Zephram sat at the table where we had breakfast. Tears dampened his cheeks.

"You know about Dorr?" I asked.

He nodded. "I was taking Waggett down to the square when I heard."

"Where's Waggett now?"

"Cappie was in the square too; I left him with her. He knew something was wrong. Maybe I was even crying, I don't know. It scared him. So I thought it was better..."

"Cappie will take care of him," I said. "What about you?"

He shrugged dully.

"So you and Dorr..." I couldn't finish the sentence.

"Yes. Me and Dorr."

Neither of us said anything for a while.

"How long?" I asked.

"Years," he said. "Since before she Committed." He gave a sad laugh. "It's pathetic, isn't it? An old man and a young woman."

"A young Neut."

"Stop right there, Fullin. I don't want you sneering at Neuts. Not today."

I didn't fight him. "Which of you started it?"

"No one ever starts these things," he said. "Dorr always liked talking to me about life in the South. Even as a young teenager, she probably intended to run away once she Committed: to get out of that house. By the time she was nineteen, she was coming here almost every day. We both pretended she was just picking my brains about being a merchant in Feliss City, but... then it went beyond that. Dorr was the first person in Tober Cove who actually wanted to hear the things I knew about business, and I was the only person who could speak three words to her without worrying what Hakoore would think."

"And what *did* Hakoore think?" I asked. "Did he know about you two?"

"He knew. She made sure he knew. Dorr loved getting under her grandfather's skin. And he wasn't as upset as she thought he'd be. It's easy to picture Hakoore as heartlessly rigid, but he lost his own daughter to madness, and when it came to his granddaughter... even as he lectured Dorr about 'godless outsiders' I think he was secretly pleased she wasn't as lonely and isolated as her mother. Close to Commitment Day, he even suggested he might allow a marriage..."

"Oh gods!" I groaned, "how brainless could he get?" I wanted to bury my face in my hands. "Accepting Dorr's relationship with you? Suggesting you get married . . ."

"What's wrong with that?" Zephram protested.

"Dorr didn't want to get married!" I snapped at him. "She wanted to get out! Out of the cove, away from Hakoore. Marrying you would just be another tie to keep her here. It was a threat, not a concession. Hakoore practically held a knife to her throat and *forced* her to raise the stakes. To Commit Neut."

"No," Zephram murmured. "Dorr did that to please me."

"To please *you*?" I repeated. "Don't tell me you gave Dorr the happy story about your Neut friend down south! You couldn't be that stupid . . . not after the trouble with Steck."

"I never talked to Dorr about Neuts," Zephram replied. "Not before she Committed. But Dorr was five when Steck . . . made her choice. Dorr was old enough to remember some of what happened, and young enough to have it all confused. She got the idea . . ."

He waved his hand as if groping for the right words.

"That you had been Steck's lover after she turned Neut?" I suggested. "That you liked Neuts?"

Zephram ran his fingers through his hair; the hair was damp, soaked with sweat. He said, "Maybe I *should* have talked to her about Neuts before she Committed. But I wanted to stay clear of the topic—to avoid influencing Dorr like I influenced Steck. Once or twice, Dorr even brought the subject up . . . and I avoided it. It seemed like the right thing."

Sometimes there is no right thing, I thought to myself. Aloud, I said, "And when she Committed Neut?"

"I stayed with her," my father replied. "Of course I did. She was the same person. And I wasn't about to abandon her when she . . . for my sake . . ."

"Okay, sure." I didn't want to hurt him by pursuing my thoughts aloud, but I wondered about Dorr. Had she really thought Zephram would prefer her as Neut? Or had she Committed Neut to horrify her grandfather, then invented a second story to tell Zephram? Maybe she was afraid Zephram would turn her away unless he thought it was his own fault.

No way to know. Dorr was dead. Poor cryptic Dorr, who spent twenty-five years trying to do something crazy enough to break herself free of her grandfather.

I suppose it wasn't coincidence she had fallen in love with a man the same age as Hakoore.

* * *

"So about Dorr and Bonnakkut," I said. "Did she really kill him?"

Zephram nodded.

"Do you know that for sure?" I asked. "Rashid thinks her confession doesn't make sense."

"He's right; her confession was a lie. But she did kill him. I was there."

"What happened?"

He told me the story with his eyes closed, as if he was seeing it all in his mind . . . or perhaps because he didn't want to look at me or the rest of the world for a while.

Everything had started, of course, at the gathering where Tober Cove welcomed Rashid. Zephram had sat on the grass with Waggett in his lap, both of them calm and content in the early morning sunshine. The day ahead would be so pleasant—sending me off with Mistress Gull at noon, then feasting cheerfully with the adults of the village until the children returned at nightfall. Zephram could meet a Spark Lord, spend time with Dorr . . .

Then Rashid's Bozzle appeared on the Council Hall steps.

The long-lost Steck had returned.

As soon as the gathering broke up, Zephram headed for his house—running away, really, though Steck would know where to find him. Since he was carrying Waggett, and since he was over sixty, Zephram only got partway home before Steck caught up with him . . . on that path through the woods where everything happened.

They talked. Awkwardly. About each other. About me.

Then Bonnakkut arrived, gun in hand. He had kept an eye on Steck, thinking the time might come when she strayed from the protection of Rashid's "force field." Our First Warrior hadn't seen Steck sneak out the side of the Council Hall, but he guessed where she would go: to find her old lover. (Bonnakkut was five when Steck was banished; like Dorr, he remembered. I suppose the day of Steck's exile was the high point in Bonnakkut's life: a Neut in the village and a chance to throw stones.)

If Bonnakkut had pulled the trigger as soon as he arrived, Steck would have died. Our proud First Warrior would have dragged her corpse back by the hair and proclaimed his triumph from the Council Hall steps. But fortunately for my mother, Bonnakkut couldn't resist the chance to gloat while holding Steck and Zephram at gunpoint.

Enter Dorr.

How did Dorr feel, now that Zephram's old lover had returned? Zephram couldn't tell me. "She didn't seem upset," he said. "It was almost as if she was *liberated*. As if she could pass me to Steck and start her own life.''

I thought about Dorr as I had seen her when I went to fetch Hakoore for last rites. Dorr trying to restyle her hair. Kissing me twice out of sheer mischief. If she believed she was free of Zephram, her last tie to Tober Cove finally cut . . . but maybe it was just giddiness after the murder—and before the suicide she was already contemplating.

But that came later in the morning. Before the murder, Dorr was simply walking through the woods because she wanted to visit Zephram—presumably to talk with him about Steck's return. She must have heard Bonnakkut's taunts and threats while still some distance away. Quietly, she stole forward until she could see everything: the gun . . . my father and Steck in danger of being shot . . .

Dorr drew her knife and used it. Bonnakkut had his back to her; he was dead before he knew she was there.

''And then she ran off,'' Zephram said. ''She called to Steck and me, 'Be happy together,' and ran into the woods. I thought she might be heading down-peninsula, just like that. But apparently she decided she had to invent a story; she decided she had to protect me.'' He shook his head. ''I never understood her, Fullin. Not really. I don't know why she stayed with me, and I don't know why she left.''

He bowed his head and covered his eyes.

How do you comfort your father?

Pat his shoulder? Murmur sympathetic words? Hold him till he stops crying?

Of all the people in the universe, your father is the one person you can't touch when he grieves.

I leaned against the kitchen counter, not knowing what to do with my hands.

Eventually he spoke again, no more than a whisper. ''It's a pity Dorr ran away—if we all just walked straight to the center of town and announced that Dorr had killed Bonnakkut to protect Steck and me . . . maybe Father Ash and Mother Dust would have declared the killing justifiable. Probably the truth about Dorr and me would have come out, and maybe about Dorr and Steck both being Neuts. I don't know. Without Dorr there, Steck and I couldn't make the decision for her. We just tried to confuse things, so no one could piece together a clear interpretation. Steck stabbed Bonnakkut a few more times in the belly. I took his gun . . .''

''What did you do with it?'' I asked.

"It's here. In the root cellar."

"You have to get rid of it."

"I know," he nodded. "Tonight I'll throw it into the lake."

"And what if someone sees you? What if Rashid finds out about you and Dorr before then and comes to search the house?"

"How would he find out?"

"Hakoore knows you and Dorr were lovers," I said. "That means Leeta too. Maybe other people—Tobers know a lot about each other's business. If Rashid wanders around the feast this afternoon, asking questions . . ."

"So what should I do?"

"Give me the gun. I'll get rid of it."

He looked at me with his reddened eyes. "You wouldn't keep it for yourself, would you, Fullin?"

"No," I snapped, "and I'm not going to shoot anyone either, if that's what bothers you. Just get the gun."

Stiffly, he forced himself out of the chair and toward the cellar steps. When I was sure he was steady enough to be left alone, I hurried to my old room at the back of the house. There, laid proudly on my bed, was my Chicken Box.

I've already mentioned that everyone going to Commit at Birds Home carries a chicken foot, symbolizing the Patriarch's Hand. In recent years (as the cove succumbed to Hakoore's "materialism"), the fashion had sprung up for parents to give their children gold-painted boxes reminiscent of the box that contained the real hand. The parents also filled the box with presents, sometimes so many gifts they could barely fit in the requisite chicken foot. Supposedly, the presents went to Birds Home for "blessing" by the gods, but really they were just trotted out so neighbors could see the display of wealth.

Zephram had known what was expected of him as father of a Committing child—a box chocked with trinkets that must have been purchased down-peninsula. I didn't even look at them as I tossed them out on my bed; I was just glad the box was big enough to hold a Beretta.

By the time Zephram returned from the cellar, I had brought the box to the kitchen table. "You're going to take the gun to Birds Home?" he asked.

I nodded. "My offering." It was tradition to leave something at Birds Home as an offering to the gods. Usually people left a token of the soul they were giving up. If you were Committing female, you might leave your spear to show that you were setting aside male ways, or if you were going male, you might give a sample of your last menstrual blood.

"I don't know what it means to give the gods a gun," I told Zephram, "but it will be safer with them than with anyone here."

"And you'll make sure no one looks in the box before you get to Birds Home?"

"People will wonder what extravagant Southern gifts you bought me," I told him, "but there's no rule I have to show them."

"Well, then . . ." He held the pistol cradled in both hands, as if it was as heavy and precious as gold. Last night, I'd only seen the gun by starlight; now, with sun streaming through the kitchen windows, the weapon gleamed with sly eagerness. We stared at it for a moment, then Zephram sighed. "I've put the safety on," he said, "so it won't go off accidentally. You should make sure it's still on before you take it out of the box. Do you want me to show you how?"

"I know all about the safety," I answered. "Steck explained everything to Bonnakkut last night; I watched too. But how do *you* know anything about guns?"

"A merchant friend of mine was a collector. He had nearly a hundred OldTech firearms of various types . . . only two of which were preserved well enough to fire. What he wouldn't give for a gun like this. . . ." Zephram shook his head. "But then, he's probably dead. It's been twenty years. Twenty years since I've seen anyone I used to know down south."

I looked at him: an old man, tired to the bone. Tober Cove had been hard on him. He'd been trapped up here by snow that first winter, and frozen in place ever since.

"Rashid and Steck will be leaving in a day or so," I said. "Maybe you'd like to go south with them."

"Steck told me she's with Rashid now."

"Even so . . . you wouldn't have to worry about bandits if you traveled with a Spark Lord, and maybe you could use some time away from the cove."

"I know you, Fullin," he said with a weak smile. "You just want to claim my house for your own."

I smiled back. "That's it exactly. Never mind that you deserve a vacation after putting up with me for twenty years."

"Well," he said. "Well." He looked around the kitchen with the air of a man who isn't trying to see anything. "If I decided to go south," he murmured, "I'd just go. Throw some stuff in the wagon, hitch up the horses, and leave. Pick a sunny afternoon when the sky was clear and I could make a good start before nightfall." He took a deep breath. "Best choice would be a big summer holiday when Tober farmers weren't working their fields; that way, no one would see me on the road. Just go, with no good-byes.''

He looked at me with a question in his eyes.

I nodded. "Sure. That'd be nice. No good-byes.''

After a while, my father set the Beretta carefully into the box. I had already put in a towel as padding, so the gun wouldn't slide around. Zephram picked up the chicken foot lying on the table and moved to put it into the box too; but I stopped him. "Keep it," I said. "A Commitment Day present for you.''

"Don't you have to take it to Birds Home?''

"No one checks," I said, "and the gods will understand.''

"So, a Commitment Day present," he repeated. "You want me to have a symbol of the Patriarch?''

"It's the only thing I have to give," I told him. "Everything else, you bought me.''

He smiled. "I bought you the chicken foot too.'' But he took it and patted my hand.

NINETEEN

A Pair of Fleas for Mistress Gull

No one in the town square knew how to behave.

There were two black barrels under Little Oak now, and two bodies on the bier—Dorr and Bonnakkut, side by side but arranged head to toe (partly for the sake of decency, and partly because they fit together better that way on the bier's narrow surface). Hakoore and Veen stood mutely beside one barrel while Kenna and Ivis stood beside the other. Almost no one had thought to bring two cups with them from home; people had to decide which corpse to toast now, promising to come back for a second toast when they got another cup.

On the other hand, it was Commitment Day—folks had looked forward to this for months. Every kitchen swam with the smells of food for the afternoon feast: pork roasts, crayfish chowder, and wild blueberry pie. Little boys and girls all sported new Blessing outfits made specially for the day . . . or at least new decorations on old clothes, embroidered or smocked by lamplight over the past few weeks. The day before, a dozen people had asked me, "Fullin, you'll play a few tunes before you go, won't you? Good dance tunes?" And I had said yes, because I never imagined Bonnakkut would get killed and Dorr take her own life.

Tober Cove wanted to sing and dance. As I made my way through the square (my fiddle case under one arm and Chicken Box under the other), I felt longing eyes stare at the violin. A child's voice in the crowd piped up, "Oooo, is he going to play?" That brought a chorus of adult shushes; there'd be no jigs or reels in front of the mourners.

And yet . . .

It was hard for people to contain themselves. The youngest were puddly with excitement that soon they'd be flying over Mother Lake . . . and soon too they'd wear another body, start fresh again, find out what had happened to their brother or sister selves over the year. As I passed two teenaged boys, I heard one whisper to another, "I just know I'm going to have breasts. They were starting to come last year. I'm going to have great breasts now, *perfect* ones, and I swear I'll go into the woods and rub my nipples for hours!"

Typical Tober thinking. I remember embarrassing Zephram terribly when I was a fifteen-year-old girl about to become a boy. "One thing I'm going to do," I announced at the breakfast table Commitment Day morning, "I am definitely going to learn not to come after only, like, two seconds. Don't you think boys ought to learn that? It can't be difficult; I'm sure it just can't be that difficult."

And parents were excited too . . . wistful, yes, because the quiet times of baking bread together were going to change into spear practice with the Junior Warriors, but as the old saying goes, "You aren't losing a daughter, you're gaining a son."

I'm told that means something different down-peninsula.

Everywhere I went, people would catch sight of me, smile and open their mouths as if to shout, "Happy Commitment!" . . . then they'd remember the corpses a stone's throw away and speak the words softly enough not to disturb the bereaved: "Uh, Happy Commitment, Fullin." A few would nod at my violin and say, "I hope you don't intend to leave that as a gift to the gods in Birds Home. Whether you Commit male or female, we'll always be glad to hear you play."

"No," I told them all, "I'm just taking it to get blessed." And they nodded, still worried. As I mentioned earlier, a person Committing female might leave her spear with the gods to show she would no longer be male; but a spear's too big to hide in a Chicken Box. When someone headed for Birds Home with spear in hand, it was traditional to say you were taking it to be blessed. Sometimes the words were even true—the person would come home male, with spear still in hand. But most people in the square seemed to think I intended to leave my violin with the gods.

The opposite was true. I was carrying my instrument because I didn't want to abandon it. After my night in the marsh, I'd left the violin at Zephram's for the morning. If I didn't bring it with me now, I'd have to go back for it when I returned from Birds Home . . . and I didn't want to do that. I doubted that I'd ever enter that old house again.

When people asked me where my father was, I always waved vaguely at another part of the crowd and said, "Talking to someone over there."

In time, I made my way to the waterfront. The atmosphere was more bubbly there—out of sight of Little Oak and its two black barrels. Kids sat on the docks and dabbled their feet in the chilly water, snapping turtles be damned. Mothers stood nearby chatting with each other, occasionally shouting an unnecessary, "Don't fall in!" to their children. Fathers pretended to talk about the repairs they needed to make on their perch boats, but were actually watching the children too . . . probably trying to memorize the look of a smile or the sound of a giggle, because it would never be quite the same again.

Cappie sat on the beach with her sister Olimbarg, my son Waggett safely between them and playing in the sand. They all looked up as I approached.

"How's Zephram?" Cappie asked.

The old reflex to lie twitched in my brain; but I crouched in front of her and said in a low voice, "He's leaving the cove. Probably on the road already. Please don't tell anyone."

"He's leaving?"

That came from Olimbarg, who seemed to find the idea incomprehensible. Cappie only nodded, as if she'd expected something like this. Maybe she knew about Zephram and Dorr; Leeta might have told her, priestess to apprentice. But all Cappie said was, "I'll miss him."

"Yeah." I gave Waggett a small pat on the knee. He was too young to understand the conversation, but there'd soon come a time when he wanted to see his grandfather. Then what would I tell him? "Olimbarg," I said, "are you going to look after Waggett on the trip up to Birds Home?"

"Not my job," she answered in her snotty kid sister way. "I'm only fourteen." Traditionally, the chore of tending first-time infants went to nineteen-year-olds when they rode with Master Crow. We twenty-year-olds, Cappie and I, flew separately with Mistress Gull.

"Just keep an eye on him," I said. "He knows you. And if he asks about me or his grandfather . . ."

I found I didn't know how to finish my sentence. She put on a bratty "I'm waiting" expression.

Then someone yelled, "Master Crow!" and pointed to the sky.

The gods came from the north—Master Crow visible long before Mistress Gull, because he was so much bigger. Master Crow had room for almost three hundred children, far more than any generation Tober Cove had produced. Mistress Gull, small and white and delicate, could only carry a maximum of twenty. This year, she would just transport Cappie and me . . . plus the Gifts of Blood and Bone taken from the babies of our village. Doctor Gorallin had already left the Gifts in a metal carrying-chest at the end of the main dock.

All the bells in the Council Hall steeple began to peal in jangly clatter—no matter how many bodies lay under Little Oak, the arrival of the gods meant clanging and prattle and excited shouts as people moved from the square to the waterfront. Children old enough to outrun their parents crowded onto the beach and the docks; younger kids were turned over to the care of older siblings, or other designated babysitters. As I was still trying to persuade Olimbarg to take Waggett, a cheerful nineteen-year-old farmboy named Urgho came up to volunteer. "Let me, Fullin," Urgho said. "Good practice for when I have one of my own."

I didn't know the farm country Tobers as well as I knew people who lived right in the village, but Urgho and I had been friendly enough in Elemarchy School. He was right too—this year, he would come back pregnant from Birds Home, and a little practice with kids wouldn't hurt. I bent down beside my son and said, "Do you know Urgho, Waggett? This is Urgho."

Urgho crouched on his haunches and gave my boy a friendly smile. "Remember me, Waggett? You and your dad's friend Cappie came out to our farm last spring. Remember when you saw the sheep?"

I vaguely recalled Cappie telling me she'd gone to some farm to buy wool from the spring shearing . . . but Waggett clearly had a much more vivid memory of the event. "Baaaaaaa!" he called out immediately. "Baaaaaaa!" He giggled at his own voice. "Baaaaaaaaaaa!"

Urgho winked at me as he lifted the boy into his arms. Waggett kept baa-ing happily, unafraid of being taken away by a stranger.

The gods flew toward us, unhurried. Master Crow left a drifting trail of white behind him—he was so holy that even in the heat of a summer's day, his breath turned to steamy cloud. Mistress Gull, always more demure, simply flew without leaving a mark . . . in contrast with real gulls, who left plenty of marks, all over the waterfront.

For a moment, I glanced at Beacon Point, checking if Rashid and Steck were up there watching. They weren't in sight, but I could imagine them on the grass in front of the old lighthouse, maybe staring at the gods through an OldTech telescope.

Rashid would be talking about airplanes and trying to identify what kind he was looking at. I wondered whether my mother had got muck-mired in that same mindset . . . or if, perhaps, she could still look up at the sky and think, "gods," not, "aircraft."

Steck had wanted to be priestess once. She must still have some tiny bit of faith. Or was I just trying to believe good things about my mother?

*   *   *

Master Crow—or perhaps I should say Master Crow's airplane disguise—sped over Mother Lake in a long low glide that suddenly ploughed up a furrow of water as he skimmed down onto the surface. Unlike mortal crows, the god always landed on the lake: he had special feet shaped like skis which could buoy him up, no matter how many children he held. He came to a stop perhaps two hundred paces from shore.

I don't want you thinking he was an OldTech seaplane like you see in books. For one thing, he was much, much bigger than any antique seaplane; my father had once toured a partly preserved seaplane in a Feliss museum, and Zephram assured me it was tiny compared to Master Crow. Furthermore, Master Crow looked more birdlike than a common OldTech plane—he had a sharp black beak, and sly shiny eyes in place of the windows that OldTech pilots peered out.

Master Crow didn't need a pilot. He was a god, guided by his own wisdom, flying by divine power. Even on solstice days crackling with thunder, he speared his way safely through the storm.

Mistress Gull, smaller and quieter but no less strong, *splish-splashed* her way to a landing two minutes after Master Crow. She rode low on the waves, like a real gull—pristine white in the sunshine, as calmly beautiful as a new mother sleeping. Looking at Mistress Gull, I suddenly wanted to hold Cappie's hand; but after our talk in the Patriarch's Hall, I was sure Cappie wouldn't want to hold mine.

By the time Mistress Gull settled comfortably, Master Crow had already sent out his "chick": a boat with a hull of black rubber, as if an OldTech cart-tire had been stretched big enough to hold twenty children. The boat moved quickly over the waves, giving off a smoke that smelled like hot asphalt. Kids always curled up their noses at the stench; ten-year-old boys made fart jokes, and when they couldn't think of actual jokes, made fart sounds with their armpits. (To ten-year-old boys, any notable odor reminds them of farts.)

Children began to line up on the main dock, with the older teenagers maintaining order and safety. This was a point of pride for our generation: the adults remained back of the line of sand where the beach began, while we "youngsters" took care ourselves. We needed no final sermon from Hakoore . . . no muddled good wishes from Leeta. Of course, the parents looked on with a keen watchfulness—just as I refused to take my eyes off Urgho and Waggett—but this was the children's responsibility. Our *moment*.

I say "our" . . . but Cappie and I remained on the sand while the others organized themselves on the dock. We were not adults yet, but we were not Master Crow's passengers either. We would never ride between his black wings again.

"How are you doing?" Cappie suddenly asked.

I looked at her; she'd been watching me. After so many years, growing up together, she knew me so well she could almost read my mind.

"It's strange not being out there with them."

"Yeah." Her eyes met mine for an instant, then turned quickly back to the dock. "Waggett looks happy enough with Urgho."

"Waggett's a happy boy."

"Do you wonder what he'll be like as a girl?"

"Of course."

"He'll be happy," she said. A moment's silence . . . then: "Whatever happens between us, Fullin, will you let me visit him once in a while? I've watched him grow up this far . . ."

"It's a small village," I told her. "He'll always be just around the corner." I gave a tentative smile. "You can visit Waggett and I'll visit Pona."

She nodded. We continued watching our child.

It took the black boat four round-trips to carry all the children to Master Crow. Waggett and Urgho went with the second group. I sighed with relief as they climbed the steps from water level and vanished into Master Crow's interior. It was always hushed inside there, where the feathery padding on seats and walls soaked up the edges of sound. I could picture the older teenagers patiently buckling seat belts around the smaller children, just as it had been done for generation after generation back through the centuries.

As the last boatload left the dock, I felt Cappie tense beside me. Mistress Gull had lowered her own chick—smaller than Master Crow's but similar. A boat of white rubber.

My stomach was full of butterflies. The lake was calm, but I suddenly worried that the rocking of the boat might make me sick.

"Well," Cappie said, "shall we?"

She stood. In one hand, she carried her spear ("just taking it to be blessed"). Under the other arm, she lugged her Chicken Box . . . bigger than mine and intentionally so. Nunce didn't want his daughter to be shown up by an outsider's child. I lifted my own load—Chicken Box, violin—and we waddled together to the end of the dock.

People shouted, "Happy Commitment!" after us. I imagined I could hear Zephram among them, but I knew it wasn't true.

*　　*　　*

Cappie emptied her arms before boarding the boat, then I passed her all our baggage: spear, violin, and the two Chicken Boxes. The butter-flies in my stomach took an extra flurry as I handed her the box holding the gun, but she stowed it under a seat without comment and turned back to me for the final piece of our load—the metal case containing blood and bone.

"Careful," she said.

I gave her a wounded look ... but then, Cappie was just being a mother, concerned for her child's welfare. In a sense, Cappie's baby was inside the case: the Gift that would let Pona live a normal girl/boy childhood. *I care about Pona too*, I wanted to say; *I've changed Pona's diapers on occasion.*

Rare occasions. Too rare.

Was that thought just sentimentality, or was I becoming female again? I couldn't tell, and maybe it didn't matter. Carefully, I passed Cappie the case and waited for her to stow it securely.

When I was ready to board the boat, she held out her hand to help me. I took it.

Mistress Gull's boat made the same smelly fumes as Master Crow's, but to me the odor was more nostalgic than unpleasant. (Fullin the near-adult: finally past the, "Ooo, fart!" stage.) Water rocked gently beneath us as we slipped away from the dock. The sun sparkled. A light breeze played with Cappie's hair; even cut short like a man's, her hair was lush and silky. I thought of her as priestess, dancing the solstice dance with daisies curled around her ears ...

"Why are you looking at me like that?" Cappie asked.

"Picturing you taking over from Leeta."

"Really?"

"Really." It surprised me too. I'd told her the truth as if it was an easy thing—as if my habit for lying had fallen asleep with the gentle motion of the boat. "So how long have you and she been discussing that you'd ..."

"Just a few days. Leeta only got the bad news from Doctor Gorallin last week."

"And you'll still have time to learn everything?"

Cappie shrugged. "Leeta thinks so. There aren't that many rituals. Last rites, birth-naming, solstices and equinox ..." She paused. "If *you* have the urge to be priestess instead of me, you could pick it up easily ... provided you decide it isn't a ridiculous Anti-Patriarch heresy after all."

"It *is* a ridiculous Anti-Patriarch heresy," I told her. "That's its charm."

She smiled—a smile that neither believed nor disbelieved me. A "summer day on the lake" smile.

The boat docked at a small landing stage that extended from one of Mistress Gull's feet: "pontoons" as Nunce called them. Cappie scrambled up and we began to unload, beginning with the case that contained the blood-gifts. When I handed it to Cappie, she went straight up the steps into Mistress Gull—no leaving it on the landing stage where a sudden wave might tip it into the lake.

While she was gone, I simply waited: smelling the wet rubber of the boat, watching the sun dance on the water...

Something moved. Something under the surface.

Working on the perch boats, I'd seen fish brush the surface many times. The biggest were muskies—as long as your arm or even your leg.

The thing I'd just glimpsed was bigger...a huge dark shadow.

I held my breath. The sunlight on the water made it hard to see anything below. Like any fishing village, Tober Cove had its share of campfire tales about monsters lurking in the deeps—giant snakes or squid or octopi. "Myths," my father had said. "Maybe in the ocean but not Mother Lake." And yet...

Cappie's spear was in the boat. I reached for it slowly and eased it into attack position, ready to stab down into the water if I saw another hint of motion.

"What the hell are you doing?" Cappie asked. She'd come back out to Mistress Gull's doorway. "If you spear a hole in that rubber, you're going to regret it."

"There's something in the water," I answered in a strained voice. "Something big."

"Probably just a school of fish," she said. "When they're all swimming together, they can look like one big creature." But as she came down the steps she kept her gaze trained on the lake. "Let's just get the stuff on board and...shit!"

I snapped my head up. She was staring wide-eyed at the shadowed patch of water between Mistress Gull's pontoons.

"See something?" I whispered.

She held her hand out. "Give me the spear."

"Are you sure..."

"I'm not a helpless woman, Fullin! Give me the damned spear."

Reluctantly, I placed the spear shaft into her outstretched hand. She immediately swung the tip of the weapon into position for a downward jab.

"Now you handle our gear," she said. "Get everything inside Mistress Gull."

"What are *you* going to do?"

"Stand guard. Whatever it is, maybe it's only curious about Mistress Gull. If it's just having a look, I won't provoke it. But if it decides to attack . . ."

She readjusted her grip on the spear handle.

Trying not to make noise, I leaned over the side of the boat and laid our remaining cargo on the landing stage: the Chicken Boxes and my violin case. As I clambered out myself, I glanced back toward the land. All of Tober Cove had clustered on the beach, shading their eyes and peering at us, no doubt wondering what we were up to. If they got worried enough, a few fishermen might venture out in a boat to ask what was wrong . . . but that was a last resort. People past the age of Commitment were forbidden to approach Mistress Gull, for fear of scaring her off forever.

Holding my violin case by the handle, I wrestled with the Chicken Boxes until I had one under each arm. Cappie remained as still as a cat watching a mouse, spear at the ready. Now that I was on the landing stage, I could see what she was looking at: a dark blob as big as a man below the surface of the water. In the shadows beneath Mistress Gull, the blob was greener than the water itself.

The butterflies in my stomach fluttered furiously. I had a nasty suspicion what I was looking at.

"Get on board," Cappie ordered grimly.

Weighed down by the Chicken Boxes, I plodded up the steps to the entry. Mistress Gull's interior was a smaller version of Master Crow's, tinted white instead of black: rows of plush chairs covered with a feathery padding that muted sounds to a whisper. I stashed the Chicken Boxes under a pair of seats and belted my violin securely into a seat of its own. The quiet emptiness of the cabin had an eerie quality to it—in my previous years, traveling with Master Crow, there were always the other children, rustling and shuffling, chattering in subdued voices.

I went to the door and called down, "Ready."

Cappie glanced at me and nodded. Then suddenly she raised her spear high. I had time to shout, "No!" before she thrust with all her might at the dark blob in the water.

Violet flame exploded upward. The head of the spear must have vaporized instantly—hot gas blew from the lake's surface like a geyser. By then, however, the violet fire had continued up the spear shaft, incinerating wood to ash in the blink of an eye. Cappie screamed as the blaze ripped into her hands, burning bright purple for a lightning flash. Then the flame faded and she crumpled to the deck, her hands black and smoking.

With one jump I leapt down beside her, grabbing her arms by the elbows and thrusting her hands into the water. Steam curled up lazily. Cappie's eyes flickered toward me, then slipped shut. Her whole body slumped, fainting from pain.

"Damn," I whispered. "Damn."

I had seen many cremations up on Beacon Point: all the Tobers who had died in the twenty years of my life. The bodies were wrapped in winding sheets before they were put on the pyre . . . but sometimes the sheets fell open, exposing a bare arm or leg to the flames. I had seen skin turn brown and tight like a roast, sizzling until it split.

Cappie's hands were worse than that.

In front of me, a green helmet broke the lake's surface. Moments later, a second head appeared close by: Steck wearing a glass-faced swimming mask. She had metal tanks strapped to her back and a mechanical contraption thrust into her mouth—no doubt an OldTech scuba device, like you read about in books. Rashid had nothing like that; presumably his armor, supplied to the Sparks by traitors from the stars, had its own air supply.

"Why did she do that?" Rashid demanded. His voice boomed hollowly inside the helmet. "Couldn't she guess it was us?"

"Perhaps," I answered bitterly. "But I think she decided you needed a lesson. Don't you know it's blasphemy, trying to interfere with Mistress Gull?"

"I'm not interfering!" he growled. "How often do I have to say I'm just here to observe?"

"Tell that to Cappie. Or Bonnakkut or Dorr."

"She was the one with the spear," he protested. "And she knew about my force field—she saw it on the river bank."

"But she didn't see it later, when it vaporized all those arrows. She didn't know what it could do."

I hadn't told her. When I talked to Cappie about what happened in the woods, I'd spent all my time describing how quickly Bonnakkut had taken the gun as a bribe—jealous backbiting, instead of telling Cappie what she needed to know.

Steck pulled the scuba gadget out of her mouth. "The people on the beach have seen us," she said, pointing. "They'll be putting out boats in a minute."

I turned around. Men were running down the docks, heading for the perch boats. It wouldn't take long for them to slip the mooring lines and grab the oars.

Rashid grabbed the edge of the landing stage and heaved himself out. "We were just going to ride the pontoons," he said, "but it looks like we'd better head inside."

"You want to ride in Mistress Gull!"

"Yes," he snapped. "We'll see this through all the way."

"No!"

"Don't be stupid," Steck said to me. She pulled herself up on the landing stage too; since I'd last seen her, she had abandoned her green dress for a skintight suit of green rubber. "If you wait for the boats to get here," she said, "they'll *all* try to spear Rashid. Is that what you want?"

"And the best thing for Cappie," Rashid put in, "is to get her to Birds Home. Look at her hands, Fullin! Even my brother the Medicine-Lord couldn't repair that damage. But if she Commits male or Neut, she'll be all right. Uninjured and whole."

I wanted to scream curses at them both; but I gritted my teeth and said, "Fine—come to Birds Home. Straight to the sanctuary of the gods. Let them decide what you deserve."

TWENTY

A Mechanical Welcome for Rashid

Steck and I carried Cappie up the steps into Mistress Gull. Cappie was not entirely unconscious; her eyes were closed, but she groaned as we gingerly tried to maneuver her into a seat. I strapped her in, then took the place beside her.

"You'll be all right," I whispered to her. She merely grimaced, either because she disbelieved me or because she was too lost in pain to hear.

"What happens next?" Rashid asked, flumping into the seat behind me and unscrewing his helmet. "Do we push a button to show we're ready to take off?"

"Mistress Gull knows when we're ready," I told her.

"Then why isn't she moving?"

"Fasten your seat belt," Steck murmured.

"Oh."

I heard the click of a metal buckle. Immediately, the entry door slid shut. Outside the window, the rubber boat partly deflated itself and slipped into a housing in one of the pontoons. Although I couldn't see the other side of the plane, I knew the landing stage would be retracting back into the other pontoon; Mistress Gull gave a tiny shudder as the platform locked itself into place.

"The fishing boats are still coming," Rashid observed.

He pointed out his window. Four perch boats slashed through the light waves, each rowed by six men. The men had their backs toward us ... but I didn't have to see their faces to know they were blazing with fury. Spark Lord or not, Rashid had violated the most sacred moment in the life of our village. Tober Cove would not forgive.

"They're too late," Steck said. She had taken off her swimming mask and now unbuckled the scuba tanks. Just the buckles on her left—rather than take the tanks off completely, she slipped the strap off one shoulder so she could swing the tanks around to one side. It didn't look like a comfortable position—she could only sit halfway back in her seat. Still she muttered to herself, "Good enough."

Even as Steck spoke, Mistress Gull began to move. The motion was so smooth, I didn't feel it; I could only tell we had started by looking out the window, seeing the perch boats fall back even as the men continued to row with angry strength. Water skipped beneath us, the waves streaked with spills of noon sun ... and then we were airborne, angling up into the sky.

Rashid put his hands to his ears and began swallowing hard. "What are you doing?" Steck asked.

"Getting ready for the pressure change."

"There is no pressure change," Steck told him. "This isn't some rinky-dink OldTech plane—the League of Peoples made it perfectly pressurized."

"Damn!" Rashid said. "All my life, I've been waiting for a plane ride, and my ears don't even pop?"

The expression on his face suggested he was telling a joke, or at least trying to lighten the mood. I didn't want to be lightened. Turning back to Cappie, I stroked her arm soothingly, trying not to look at her blackened hands.

She whimpered.

We flew north, faster than any mortal bird. Quickly we passed the litter of tiny islets that dribbled out from the end of our peninsula ... over Manitou's Island ... over the great north channel and on to the rugged timberlands: trees and lakes and rocks, a region barely penetrated even in OldTech times.

"Good place for a secret installation," Rashid whispered to Steck. "Do you think anyone lives down there?"

"A few," Steck answered, "but not many. OldTech times lasted just long enough for the local people to forget how to live off the land. They got used to hunting with guns instead of arrows. Then, during the Desertion, most old-timers decided to pack up to unpolluted territory out in the stars. The rest came south after the collapse."

"How do you know all this?"

"I traveled up this way after getting banished from Tober Cove."

"Looking for Birds Home yourself?"

Steck shrugged. "Just wandering. I wasn't having such a great time in the South."

"Poor girl." Rashid patted Steck's hand. I turned sharply away.

* * *

"Fullin," Cappie whispered. "Fullin . . ."

I laid my hand on her cheek. "I'm here."

"What happened?" she asked.

"It was Rashid under the water. His armor defended itself."

"I didn't know . . ."

"Shh," I said. "Just rest."

She tried to lift her hands and winced immediately.

"What . . ."

"Shh," I repeated. "You got burnt. Very badly. You understand? It would be a terrible idea to Commit female because your hands are burnt."

"But I was going to . . ."

"It's your decision, Cappie, but you're very, very hurt. I can't imagine the damage will ever heal. Just look."

Her eyes opened slowly. She looked at her hands, lying limply in her lap. After a while, a tear rolled down her cheek.

"I'll have to Commit male, won't I?" she whispered.

"You'll be fine as a man. Whole."

"But I wanted to be a woman, Fullin. I was going to be priestess . . ."

She let her breath slip out in a sigh.

"You would have been a great priestess, Cappie."

I put my arm around her; she laid her head against my shoulder. She made no sound as she cried.

For a short time, I thought I was female; then I suspected I was male; then I didn't care. Cappie fell asleep, still leaning against me. I listened to her slow breathing, to make sure that it continued.

The burns weren't the greatest danger . . . not in the short run. Not when Cappie could claim a new body within an hour or two.

But every year, Doctor Gorallin had come to our school to teach first aid classes, and she never failed to warn us about shock. *Clinical shock comes with any major injury. Your body doesn't know what the hell has happened to it; it doesn't know where to send blood, and sometimes it skimps on the brain.*

I watched as Cappie's face gradually drained to wood white. But at least she continued to breathe.

Rashid was the first to notice we were descending. He pulled Steck over to look out the window; slowly, the forest beneath us got closer as we approached a lake among the trees. It was no different from any of the thousand other lakes in the timberlands—a gleam of blue surrounded by pine woods and bare rock outcrops . . . hard cold rock, not like the friendly waterpocked limestone of Tober Cove.

Just before touchdown we whisked over Master Crow, already floating majestically on the lake; then water sprayed in clear sheets around us as Mistress Gull skimmed down to her landing.

I heard the click of a seat belt unbuckling—Rashid, eager for whatever came next.

"Wait," Steck said, laying her hand softly on his wrist. "There's nothing for us to do till the planes go into their hangars."

Planes. Hangars. I shook my head at her choice of words, and turned my attention out the window. Master Crow was easing unhurriedly over the water. It seemed so sad for me to be watching from the outside, not sharing the delight of the children as they quivered with the excitement of being so close to Birds Home. I still had my butterflies, but they'd lost their exuberant flutter. Now they were only flying out of worry for Cappie.

Master Crow adjusted his course to point his beak at a tall cliff of granite forming one shore of the lake. He continued forward ponderously, the air crinkling with heat around his wings. Just as slowly, the wall of granite began to sink into the lake, revealing a mammoth chamber beyond. Lights, electric lights, sparked themselves inside.

"Master Crow's hangar," Steck murmured to Rashid.

"His *nest*," I corrected her.

By the time Master Crow reached the entrance, the wall of granite had completely disappeared under the lake surface. Master Crow continued to sail forward, his wings just fitting through the opening.

"Doesn't look like there'll be room for us in there," Rashid said.

"We go elsewhere," Steck answered, pointing to another granite wall part way around the lakeshore.

"So we won't see what happens to the children?"

"There's a rocky area in the back of Master Crow's nest," I told him, "where everyone sits on the floor. They'll sing hymns until the gods put them all to sleep."

Master Crow was completely inside his nest now. The granite wall began to rise out of the lake again, water streaming down its stone. I caught myself biting my lip—Waggett was in there. *Urgho*, I thought, *you know you have to set the babies down on the floor, don't you? Because if you're holding a child on your lap when the gods make you fall asleep, you might slump over on top of him . . .*

But Urgho knew how it all worked—he'd gone through it many times before. And the older teenagers would remind each other what they had to do.

The granite wall closed behind my baby. Mistress Gull began to move.

Since I had been closed up with Master Crow in previous years, I had never seen Mistress Gull head for her own nest. For that matter, I only had the vaguest idea of what would happen next; Zephram couldn't tell me, and as I'd explained to Rashid, other adults in the village called it a holy secret that I had to learn for myself. It wouldn't surprise me if Cappie's mother had told her the details of what to expect—mothers had a way of breaking secrets to their children when the rest of the world was close-mouthed—but I had only picked up a few hints let slip by adults over the years.

Still, I had my mother right here with me . . . and she had already broken the holiness of the secret by telling Rashid about Birds Home. Why shouldn't she tell me too?

"So what happens to us?" I asked Steck. "Same thing? Get out and fall asleep?"

"No," Steck answered. She turned to Rashid. "No knock-out gas," she said in a mock whisper, as if I wasn't supposed to hear the words. Then she turned back to me. "You'll be met by robots . . . by servants of the gods. One for you, one for Cappie, one for the Gifts of Blood. They'll take you to the place where you make your choice."

"Meanwhile, Steck and I will tour Birds Home," said Rashid, his voice burbly with expectation. "Do you think it's very big?"

"Probably," Steck answered. "It wouldn't surprise me if the installation stretched for miles under the rock."

In front of us, a second granite wall had begun to lower into the lake. I couldn't see much with Mistress Gull's beak in the way, but the chamber beyond looked much smaller than Master Crow's nest. Slowly we slipped inside, into a space that seemed stifled and dark after the bright sun, even though the ceiling was striped with long electric lights.

"Wonder how they get the power," Rashid said. "Probably a hydro dam somewhere in the area. And did anyone spot a receiving antenna as we landed?"

Steck and I shook our heads.

"Well," Rashid shrugged, "the antenna wouldn't be hard to hide in the forest. With a million trees in the area, who'd notice one that was a little taller and had a dish assembly?"

The granite wall closed behind us. As the last wedge of sunlight squeezed shut, Mistress Gull's entry door slid open. Rashid bounded to his feet immediately. Steck did too, slipping the scuba tank strap back over her shoulder and buckling it into place. "You want to help Fullin with Cappie?" she said to Rashid. "I'll hold your helmet."

"Who's the lord here?" he grumbled. But he handed her the helmet and moved forward to my side. Together, we eased Cappie out of her seat and into the aisle. "Can you walk?" Rashid asked.

"Yes," she replied weakly.

"Doesn't matter," I told her. "We're carrying you."

She didn't even try to object.

The chamber outside smelled of chilly damp, like the tiny caves along the shore of Mother Lake where you can still find patches of snow hiding in summer. Of course, the damp came from the lake-filled part of the chamber: Mistress Gull's nest was mostly water, edged on three sides by a U-shaped floor of rough-cut stone.

Rashid and I struggled onto solid ground with Cappie slung between us, while Steck made two trips back into the cabin to fetch our baggage. As she laid the Chicken Boxes at our feet, I thought of the gun inside mine; but Steck showed no curiosity about what the boxes contained. Instead, she immediately set out prowling, pacing along the edge where the rock floor met the lake water.

"Looking for something?" Rashid asked her.

"Just wondering," Steck called back. "They have to do maintenance on these planes, don't they? It would be easier if they could drain the water until the plane was sitting on dry land. But I don't see anything that would suggest . . ."

"Here we go!" Rashid said loudly.

A hidden door had just slid open in the stone wall close to us. Three creatures emerged from the gap: human-shaped but with the heads of great birds. Huge eyes perched above huger beaks, faces brightly colored but not plumed—their skin had the glossy finish of plastic rather than flesh. The bird-creatures wore feathered robes that belled out from their bodies, making it impossible to tell whether the figures were male or female.

"Greetings," they said in unison. The voices were identical, and pitched in the middle between man and woman. Their beaks scarcely moved when they talked. "Welcome to Birds Home," they went on. "You are honored guests. We will serve you on behalf of the gods."

They spoke with an unfamiliar accent—not Tober, and not like any Southerner I'd heard. The accent of heaven.

The bird-servant in the middle stepped forward. Its colors were blue, white and black, like a jay. "I will take the Gifts offered by your infants," it said. "Please give them to me." It held its hands out stiffly—normal human-shaped hands, but the skin was a whorl of blue and white plastic.

I bent quickly and picked up the metal case Steck had unloaded. "Here," I said, hurrying forward and placing the case in the creature's arms.

"Thank you," it answered, with a small bow. Cradling its arms around the case, the bird-servant turned and walked off through the doorway in the wall.

Another bird stepped forward. This one was bright red with black facial markings—a cardinal. "I will serve as guide for the woman Cappie. Please come to me."

I nudged Rashid; we helped Cappie forward. As we approached the cardinal, it said, "Only Cappie please."

"She can't walk," I answered.

"Only Cappie please," it repeated.

"Not very sophisticated programming," Rashid muttered.

"I can walk," Cappie said. "I can, Fullin. Please."

Rashid eased away from her. Reluctantly, I did too. She took a deep breath and forced herself to totter the last two steps toward the bird-servant. For a moment, I thought she was going to pitch forward against its chest; but it reached out and steadied her with an arm around her shoulders. "Hello, Cappie," it said.

She didn't speak; she just nodded.

The third bird stepped forward: white with tufts of gray, like a snowy owl. "I will serve as guide for the man Fullin. Please come to me."

Taking a deep breath, I picked up my violin and the Chicken Box. "I'm Fullin," I said. The butterflies in my stomach didn't stop me from moving to the creature.

"Hello, Fullin," it said. It put its arm around my shoulders, the same way the other was supporting Cappie.

"You will now sleep," the two birds said in unison.

Rashid's head snapped toward Steck who was still at the far end of the chamber. "You said there was no knock-out gas!"

"Sorry," Steck answered. She lifted the breather of her scuba tank and placed it into her mouth. With Rashid's helmet still tucked under her arm, she hopped into the water under Mistress Gull's wing. In a moment, Steck's head disappeared beneath the surface

Rashid ran to the edge of the water, then stopped. He turned back to me; the color had drained from his face. "Gas," he said. "She knew my force field doesn't protect against gas."

He sat down abruptly on the stone floor, his face stricken.

A great sleepiness washed over me. The bird-servant's arm tightened around my shoulders to keep me from falling.

I woke on the hard stone floor. My cheek hurt from pressing against the rock, but otherwise I was intact.

You couldn't say the same for my owl bird-servant. The body of my Commitment guide lay on the floor to my right; its head lay to my left. Wires dangled from the head's severed throat, but the cut looked very clean. It had to be the work of Rashid's pistol, the one that shot invisible beams.

Why would anyone destroy my bird-servant? But of course, the killer wasn't just "anyone"; it had to be Steck.

Still woozy, I dragged myself to my feet and looked around. How long had I been unconscious? My mouth was as dry as sand; I must have been out four or five hours. Maybe longer—there was no way of telling except by the stiffness in my bones.

Cappie and her bird-servant were gone. Closer to the edge of the water, Rashid lay on the stone floor. He no longer wore his armor—nothing but a light cotton undershirt that came down as far as his knees. I wondered if he'd actually been wearing that under his armor or if Steck had put it on him . . .

. . . after she'd taken his suit. No one else would dare to steal Spark armor—campfire tales said it could defend itself, even when the wearer was asleep, but Steck must know how to get around those defenses. How to make them her own.

"Rashid!" I called to him. When he didn't move, I knelt and shook his shoulder. No response. At least he was still breathing.

I shook him several more times without success. He looked deeply unconscious. Perhaps Steck had done something to him, some anaesthetic injection like the one Doctor Gorallin used to put children to sleep before taking the Gift of Blood and Bone. Whatever the reason, Rashid showed no sign of waking up soon.

Now Steck had his armor. And his force field. And the beam-shooting pistol that she used to kill my bird-servant. She must have hidden in the water until the gods put the rest of us to sleep, then come out again for . . .

For what? What did my mother intend to do in Birds Home?

A shiver rippled through me. Whatever Steck wanted couldn't be good.

I went back to the headless bird-servant. My Chicken Box lay on the floor nearby, but my violin was gone. Stolen by Steck.

Why? Why would she want my violin? But then, it had originally been hers, hadn't it? My violin, my sheet music, the instructional books that taught me how to play . . . all Steck's. A gift of music, given by my mother.

I swore that when I got back to the cove, I would buy a different instrument. I would never so much as touch the bow that had belonged to Steck.

"And you took the wrong thing, Mother," I said aloud. "You should have taken the Chicken Box."

I opened the box. The Beretta still lay inside. I checked; it was fully loaded.

"Mother," I whispered, "watch out."

Then I headed into Birds Home to find her.

TWENTY-ONE

A Coffin for Fullin

Beyond the open door lay a corridor sloping slightly downward. There were no lights—only the glow spilling from the hangar area behind me. After a time, I tucked the gun into my belt at the small of my back and walked with one hand brushing the wall. The stone was cold and weepy with moisture.

My moccasins whispered on the floor—not quite as silently as Dorr could move, but even with echoing rock walls, the sound wouldn't travel far. If I could catch Steck while she was busy with something . . .

But what would she be busy with? What did she want to do? She must have been planning this for twenty years—somehow meeting the Knowledge-Lord, persuading him to come here at this particular moment, lying to him about the "knock-out gas" so he wouldn't interfere with whatever she intended . . .

I just couldn't imagine what she wanted. Even wearing Rashid's armor, what could she do against gods?

But the gods used machines as tools—machines like the bird-servant, with wires dangling from its severed head. She had dealt with that machine easily enough.

Sacrilege didn't stop Steck for a second. I wondered what would.

As the light from the hangar faded behind me, I became aware of a glow far ahead. Good—I'd been worried that the gods and their servants didn't bother with lights because they could see in the dark.

Soon I could tell I was heading for a large chamber, lit to dim melancholy by gray-blue electric light-tubes. Holding my breath, I pressed tight against the corridor wall in case someone in the chamber might see me; but there was no motion out there, no sound. After a minute of listening, I moved forward cautiously.

The room was at least as big as Tober Cove's town square . . . and like the square it contained bodies. Bodies in glass coffins.

Every coffin was smashed and every body was dead.

I moved to the closest. Tears stung my eyes—Urgho, poor Urgho. It looked like he had been sleeping peacefully inside the coffin; then someone had hammered against the glass until it broke. Before the boy could wake, the killer sliced Urgho's throat with one of the broken glass shards: up, across, down. Urgho's blood had sprayed in gushers against the inside of the coffin until the flow gurgled to a stop.

Steck had done this. My mother. Then she went on to the next.

The next was Thorn, one of the noisy neighbors living in the cabin next to Cappie and me. She had been female over the past year, but this was her male body—dead, killed like Urgho, blood running down the walls of the glass casket and pooling in the bottom.

I moved on: Chum, Thorn's lover. Chum's male body, dead.

And in the next coffin . . .

The next coffin . . .

"Oh, Cappie," I whispered.

Cappie, the brooding male Cappie, drenched in his own blood.

She was supposed to Commit male, I thought. *Her hands were burnt, so she was supposed to Commit male.* But that half of her was dead.

I reached through the broken glass and laid my hand on his cheek. It occurred to me I had never touched her this way, male me, male her. "Cappie," I whispered.

The corpse was beginning to cool.

I forced myself to pull away. There was nothing I could do here—nothing but look, memorize why Steck had to die.

Cappie had been sleeping: the way all our souls slept in Birds Home when they weren't needed. His body was naked . . . and as I looked more closely, I saw tiny tubes and wires stretched out from the bottom of the coffin, reaching into Cappie's body from head to toe. *Feeders*, I thought. A mother bird brings food to her nestlings; and here in Birds Home, the gods supplied Tobers with food too, as we slept. Food, water, whatever care a body needs . . .

But these coffins were too frail to stand up to deliberate homicide. I could picture Steck in Rashid's armor, slamming her mailed fist against the glass, reaching in to cut a throat—Cappie's throat.

I moved to another coffin. The room contained dozens of the glass caskets, laid out in rows: first row, the oldest of our generation, Cappie and the nineteen-year-olds; next row, the eighteen-year-olds, all their male bodies; next row, the seventeen-year-olds . . .

Oh god . . .

I began to run, past the teenagers, past the children, to the coffins at the far end of the chamber. The youngest, the infants.

Waggett. His first time at Birds Home.

His last time at Birds Home.

Steck had killed him like all the rest—her own grandson. She had smashed through to his defenseless little body and cut him, spattered his blood.

I seized the Beretta and crashed its butt down on the coffin, bashing again and again until I had battered a big enough hole to pull out my son's body. He was so limp. I cradled him in my arms and he just lay there, his little hands floppy, his face slack.

The last time I had seen him alive, he had been happily making sheep sounds. "Baaaaaa!"

I lowered my head to his bare stomach and wept.

After a while, I laid him back in his coffin. There was no better place to put him.

I took the time to check every other coffin in the room. Perhaps Steck had slipped up with someone; perhaps she hadn't cut deep enough and one of the children was still alive.

But they were all dead—the male selves of every child in Tober Cove, slaughtered. Olimbarg. Cappie's other brothers. Even the male half of Ivis, throat cut just as her father's throat had been cut by Dorr.

All dead.

I took a ragged breath. Of my whole generation, I was the only male that Steck had allowed to live. Such love for her baby boy . . . but it didn't extend to Waggett.

Damn her, I prayed. *All you gods, damn her.*

Nothing happened. Here, in the home of the gods, they allowed such a thing to happen, and did nothing.

Opposite the door I'd come from was a second door . . . or rather an open entryway leading into another unlit corridor. Part of me was afraid of going there—I already suspected what I would find next. But the alternative was staying where I was in that silent bloody room, with Cappie at one end and Waggett at the other.

No. Forward.

The new corridor wasn't as long as the first. As soon as I entered it, I could see what was at the other end: another large chamber, similar to the first, filled with more glass coffins. I willed myself forward, though I knew what I would find: our female halves.

Our dead female halves.

Again, Urgho was closest to the entrance—a husky female Urgho, all freckles on creamy skin . . . except that the freckles were now mingled with blood flecks spattered from her throat.

One of Urgho's limp hands lay across her bare belly: a belly just starting to swell with the first signs of Master Crow's child. The child would never be born now. Urgho had wasted his time, "getting a little practice" by taking care of Waggett.

Poor Urgho. Poor Waggett.

This time, I went straight to the far side of the room, to the coffin in the same position as the one that had held my son. This one contained a little girl: a perfect little girl, with perfect baby skin and soft brown curls that had never been cut. There was nothing to indicate this was Waggett's female self, but I knew it was—a parent knows. I reached through the broken glass to smooth the hair off her forehead.

Just one touch. I wanted that. But I let her lie peacefully.

She was dead. Quite dead.

I moved methodically back through the room, checking for signs of life. The one-year-olds, the two-year-olds . . . all dead. I had seen them all so recently on the dock in Tober Cove. Ivis, Olimbarg, all the rest.

Cappie . . .

Cappie too. Her thin familiar body . . . the body I had made love with so often . . . the spring when I was fifteen, she had taken my female virginity, and later that summer, I had taken hers . . .

But her hands were seared to charcoal, and I had betrayed her many times. I don't know why those seemed part of the same thing.

I wanted to bend in and kiss her, but it would mean breaking more glass. Anyway, I wasn't sure I had the right to kiss her anymore.

Placed alongside Cappie was one extra coffin, one where there had been no coffin in the other room.

This coffin's lid was intact. Inside I saw myself.

I was still breathing.

My female half was alive. Steck couldn't bring herself to kill me.

Wielding the pistol butt again, I knocked in the glass—carefully, carefully, so I wouldn't cut her. First came a hole just above her feet, tapped out delicately, crack by crack. Then I worked upward, rapping the glass hard enough to star it without breaking through, then levering my hand underneath and lifting up so that the glass pushed out instead of in. I had to force myself not to speed up or cut corners; but at last I had cleared away the whole top, enough so I could reach in without fear of cutting myself.

"Wake up now." I gave her a light touch on the cheek. Her skin was warm and soft—I remembered how often I had been intoxicated by the feel of my own skin. For a strange moment, I looked down at her, my own naked body, my own breasts, and hips, and legs . . .

"This is sick," I muttered. With a mental slap to myself, I placed both hands on her shoulders (warm, bare shoulders) and gave her a gentle shake. "Wake up. Come on, wake up."

Her eyes fluttered, then opened. She smiled thinly, then reached up and touched a finger to my lips. "Cappie's right," she said. "You *do* look obvious."

Wires and tubes pulled away from her body as she sat up in the coffin. They left no mark.

"Good," she said.

I didn't understand. "Good what?"

"Good that they didn't leave any marks. I can hear what you're thinking."

"I can't hear you."

"So it's a puzzle," she shrugged. "Maybe Rashid can explain it."

"Rashid's out cold."

"I know. I know everything that's happened." She looked grimly toward Cappie's body. "I suppose it's like always—while I'm sleeping in Birds Home, the gods send me your thoughts. It's like I'm seeing it all in a dream."

"You aren't sleeping now."

"No, but I'm still . . . receiving. It's strange—as if I'm looking out my own eyes, but I can still see ghosts of what you're seeing too. And feel ghosts of what you're feeling." She slipped her leg over the side of the coffin and heaved herself out. "Give me your shirt."

"Why?"

"Because looking at my body is distracting you, and that distracts me. It's hard enough to concentrate as it is."

I wanted to protest; but before the words were even out of my mouth, she gave me a look that said I was wasting breath. They say you can't lie to yourself. With a sigh of resignation, I pulled my shirt over my head and tossed it to her. She shinnied into it, then smoothed out the wrinkles. It was long enough to reach halfway down her thighs, covering her most "distracting" parts.

She caught my eye and winked. "I'd better be careful—I know how much you like women in men's clothing."

"This is unfair," I protested. "If you keep ragging on me because you know what's in my mind . . . we're supposed to be on the same side, aren't we?"

"We are," she replied. "On most things anyway. Like Steck."

"Right." The thought sobered me. "Steck."

"I don't suppose you'd let a mere woman carry the pistol?"

I shook my head.

She said, "You know bullets won't go through the armor's force field."

"I know. But I want to try anyway."

She nodded, then gestured toward the door at the far end of the room. "Let's go."

Another corridor led further into Birds Home. We walked it together, my sister self and I. Part way along, she slipped her hand into mine. I didn't even know I'd been longing for that, for a little human contact in the face of so much death . . . but she knew.

I suppose she felt the same need. We were the same person, weren't we?

Ahead lay a third chamber, with more glass coffins. As before, we stopped to listen before entering . . . but this room was as silent as the first two. Wherever Steck was, she must have gone deeper into the stone reaches of Birds Home. My sister and I exchanged a look, then moved forward to the first coffin.

Urgho again—a Neut version. Hairless face and womanly breasts. Penis and testicles. And just behind the scrotal sac, delicate labial lips.

The coffin's glass was intact. The Neut Urgho was alive.

"I'll check Waggett," my female self cried. She ran, and I was right on her heels. We crossed the room and skidded to a stop beside a coffin containing a pink-skinned Neut infant. It wasn't exactly like Waggett, either the boy or girl version of him, but the Neut's face was similar, like a brother-sister.

The child's chest rose and fell with slow, healthy breathing.

"It's got your nose," I said to my female self. I didn't want to cry in front of a woman.

She didn't care. She put her hands against the coffin lid, as if she could touch our baby through the glass; and tears streamed down her face.

We agreed to leave Waggett where he was. ("He," not "it.") As far as we could tell, he was safe and well cared for inside the coffin; better to leave him there until we had settled the score with Steck.

There was yet another corridor leading forward . . . but before we moved on, we made a circuit of the room to check the other coffins.

Neut versions of everyone else, all alive.

Strangely, we found no Neut version of me—the coffin was missing. But there was a Neut Cappie, breathing, asleep. The Neut's body was slim like the female Cappie, but taller, beefier around the shoulders. The face was not so bad. You could get used to a woman with that face.

"Not a bad face for a man either," my female half put in, though I hadn't said anything aloud. "Are we going to fight over him?"

"Her," I answered.

We both smiled.

"He deserves a shot at Steck too," Female-Me said. "Steck killed his male body."

"They all deserve a shot," I replied. "Urgho, Chum, Thorn . . . they'd all help us."

"Help us how? Throw themselves bare-handed at the armor's force field?" She shook her head. "Anyway, they don't know what's been going on. Cappie does."

I nodded, as if I agreed with her logic. Of course, Cappie couldn't help us against the force field any more than anyone else. But I wanted her here with me, to make sure she was all right, to have her support . . .

"To show her how manly you are when you kill Steck?" Female-Me suggested.

"Will you stop doing that?" I asked.

She pointed to Cappie's coffin. "Just break the glass."

Cappie woke groggily. When she saw what she was, she screamed.

We held her hands. After a while, the scream faded to a whimper.

"Fullin," she breathed, "I didn't choose this!" Tears streamed down her face. "I didn't make any choice! I didn't!"

"I know," my sister and I answered in unison.

"They said I'd hear a voice, 'Male, female, or both.' But I didn't get to make a decision!"

"Shh." Female Fullin and I stood on opposite sides of Cappie's coffin. We reached out together to caress Cappie's cheek.

"Why are there two of you?" Cappie asked. She looked back and forth between my sister and me. "How can you both be here at once?"

"It's hard to explain," I began . . . but I stopped, lifted my head, listened.

Music came playing from the entryway in front of us . . . soft violin music. The tune was "Don't Make Me Choose": the song Steck had played in Cypress Marsh.

Calmly she emerged from the unlit corridor—wearing Rashid's armor, but with the helmet off so she could tuck the violin under her chin. As soon as she saw us, she stopped and lowered the bow. "Well," she said, "so this is it. Commitment Hour at last. And here I can see all three choices: male, female, and both. Two Fullins and a Cappie?"

If I'd been holding the Beretta, I would have shot her without a moment's hesitation; but I was holding Cappie's hand, with the pistol once again stuck in my belt at the small of my back. Cappie's grip had tightened unconsciously when she heard the music . . . and rather than free myself from her, I decided to let her hold me, draw whatever strength she needed.

Now was not the time for shooting anyway. I'd never fired a gun before. Books said they were hard to aim, unless you were standing at point-blank range. Did I want to start the bullets flying with so many children in glass coffins between me and Steck?

And Steck didn't know I had the Beretta with me. If I shot now and missed, I'd lose the element of surprise. Better to wait until my target was closer.

Female-Me nodded silent agreement with my decision. She turned toward Steck. "So your hands are steady enough to play," she said, "after killing a hundred children in cold blood."

"I didn't do anything that wouldn't have happened anyway," Steck answered. "You've seen the other rooms: male, female, and Neut versions of every child in Tober Cove. Think about what happens when you Commit. You, Fullin," she pointed toward me with the violin bow, "let's say you Commit male. What happens to your female half?" Steck turned to my sister self. "What happens to you . . . my pretty baby girl?"

She waited for us to answer: anyone, Male-Me, Female-Me, Neut-Cappie. Finally, it was my sister who spoke. "If he chose male, I suppose I never would have left my coffin."

"Right," Steck said grimly. "Committing to one version of yourself means killing the other two. *Killing.* I've been to the lab next door— there are machines getting ready to render the rejected bodies down to basic nutrients. Feed for the other bodies.

"If I hadn't intervened," Steck went on, "one of you two Fullins would be dead by now. You're both healthy, you both could live long lives, but the machines would dispassionately stop one of your hearts.

That's the dirty secret of Birds Home. That's how much the gods of Tober Cove really love you.''

Cappie let go of my hand. Slowly, deliberately, she climbed out of the coffin and picked up a long glass splinter from the litter that had fallen to the floor. She held the splinter like a knife. ''Steck, I'd rather believe in the gods than you.''

''Careful with that,'' Steck pointed to the sliver. ''If you attack me while I'm in this armor, you'll burn your hands again. And this time, you've run out of replacement selves.''

''I never had any replacement selves,'' Cappie said. ''I'm a single person, that's all.''

''Like Fullin?'' Steck asked, pointing the violin bow toward me. ''Or the other Fullin?'' Steck shook her head. ''Cappie, I thought the same as you once. I thought the gods could work miracles. And every summer solstice, Master Crow waved his wings to reshape my body by magic— boy shimmering into girl, girl shimmering into boy. But then I was exiled. I went to the friendless South, where freaks get beaten, or raped, or shunned to the point of starvation. It was sheer luck that I stumbled into an enclave of scientists who were willing to feed me and teach me what they knew in exchange for studying my anatomy. Eventually, word about me spread from the enclave to the Science-Lord . . . and by the time Rashid came to see the astounding hermaphrodite for himself, I'd learned enough about science that I didn't believe in magic anymore. Or gods.''

''Your loss,'' I said.

''True,'' Steck agreed. ''My loss. Who wouldn't like to believe be-nevolent deities took an interest in the world? But the only ones at work in Birds Home were busybodies from the stars who treated the people of Tober Cove like lab rats. There aren't even people here anymore— it's all run by machines. But we lab rats are still running through the maze.''

''How do you know?'' I demanded. ''Have you talked to the gods? Have you been to Birds Home before?''

To be honest, I didn't care about her answers. But I wanted to get her talking. She would try to justify herself; she would try to explain, and as she did, I would slowly reach for the gun tucked in at my back.

''No, I haven't talked to the gods,'' Steck admitted. ''And I haven't been to Birds Home since my own Commitment Hour. But I've thought about this, Fullin. I've thought about it every day for the past twenty years. It took a while to learn enough science to figure out the tricks, but I deduced it all before I got here, and I've seen enough in Birds Home to confirm my guesses."

My hand touched the butt of the pistol. The metal was warm from lying against my skin.

"You want to know what's really going on?" Steck continued. "How the tricks work? It starts with the Gift of Blood and Bone that's taken from every baby. When those tissue samples are delivered to Birds Home, some very clever machines go to work extracting the DNA—the seeds that eventually grow into a human being. The machines give those seeds a little twist: swap an X chromosome with a Y, change a girl seed into a boy seed, or vice versa. And since they take the replacement chromosome from someone else rather than deriving it from your own chromosomes . . . no, never mind, I'm just showing off. I've spent twenty years accumulating the knowledge to understand Tober Cove, and you're the only people I may ever be able to tell. I have to do this right. The machines made a seed for boy Fullin by starting with the seeds of girl Fullin and adding a tiny boy-bit from some other person. Which is why your boy self doesn't look exactly like your girl self."

"My sister Olimbarg looks the same, boy or girl," Cappie said.

"The wonders of genetics," Steck answered. "Flukes happen. But the people who made Birds Home had a lot more control over genes than the OldTechs did. The machines here can work with the tissue samples taken at a baby's first solstice, and by the next summer produce a child of the opposite sex who looks a year and a half old. Don't ask me how they accelerate the growth—there's a laboratory next door, but I don't understand a tenth of the equipment."

I had my fingers wrapped around the pistol grip now. Slowly, I eased the gun out of my belt. It made a soft sticky sound as it slipped away from my sweat-damp back.

"And cloning isn't the only trick," Steck went on. "There's also the memory transfer. When your son Waggett arrived here, Fullin, there was a female version of him waiting, constructed from the tissue sample taken the previous year. But the girl-Waggett was a blank slate; her whole life she'd been dormant under glass, so she had an empty brain. No, that's going too far; her brain wasn't *completely* empty. Some time in the past year, the machines had placed a communications implant in her head . . . and as soon as the original Waggett arrived, they put a similar implant in his."

The muzzle of the gun was free of my belt. I kept my eyes on Steck, as if I had nothing on my mind but listening.

"I watched that implant process," she said, "and you wouldn't have liked it, Fullin. A robot feeds a tiny wire through the back of the baby's neck and straight up into the brain. The wire goes through the hole made by the Gift of Blood and Bone, so there won't be a second scar. Isn't that clever? I always wondered why they took the damned tissue sample from the spine instead of someplace less gruesome; the Old-Techs could get DNA just by swabbing the inside of your mouth. But the scar at the back of the neck gives a camouflaged entry point for injecting nano-transmitters.''

Slowly, I eased my other hand behind my back. The next part would be difficult, especially to do without looking. The safety mechanism was a sort of slide that had to be moved to the right position before the gun would shoot. Steck herself had demonstrated how it worked last night, as Bonnakkut and I watched. Bonnakkut had practiced a few times; I had never done it before.

"Once the transmitters are implanted," Steck said, "they download—copy—everything from the original Waggett's brain into the clean-slate clone. I watched that happen too, Fullin; the lab next door has video displays to monitor the copying process. Bit by bit, I saw the little girl Waggett clone acquire all the original Waggett's thoughts and personality.''

"Before you killed her," I said. I was blindly pushing and pulling parts of the pistol behind my back, but nothing wanted to slide.

"Before I killed that particular body," Steck corrected. "But Waggett is still alive in a Neut body . . . because the machines make hermaphrodite copies of children as well as opposite sex bodies. The child in that coffin," Steck waved in the direction of Neut-Waggett, "may look different from your son, but in his head, he's everything the original Waggett was. A perfect mental copy.''

"And what about later?" my sister self asked. "My male half got copied from my brain," she said, pointing to me, "but that was when we were one year old. We've stayed connected for years.''

Steck nodded. "After the first body switch, you have three copies of the same person, all with communication implants in their heads. The implants are like a million tiny radios in your brain—although they're biological, powered by your own metabolisms. Remember Rashid picking up radio waves from your head, Fullin? Every second of every day, you broadcast low-powered encodings of your mental state. The signals get picked up by relay stations like that one in the car's engine . . . and there must be hidden relays all over the peninsula to cover you whenever you leave home. The relays transfer your broadcasts to that antenna on Patriarch Hill, which transmits everything up here to Birds Home. Moment by moment, the two dormant bodies receive transmissions from the body that's walking around in Tober Cove . . . so the sleeping versions experience everything the active version does."

"So this past year," I said, "I was the sender . . ."

"And I was the receiver," my sister finished. She gave me a veiled look. Of course, she was receiving even now—that's why she could pick up my thoughts and feelings. She must know exactly what I was doing with the gun.

Did Steck know we were still linked?

"How come it sometimes reverses?" I asked Steck. "How could my sister get into my head when she was asleep up here?"

Suddenly I felt a part of the pistol begin to slide under my hand. I had to force myself not to smile.

"That's part of the grand design of the star-siders who set up this experiment," Steck answered. "From what I've seen in the lab, the communication implants make it possible to override one personality with the other. Basically, they set the male Fullin to receive, then set the female Fullin to transmit . . . and turn up the volume so loud that the female drowns out the original male. I think this happens on Commitment Day so that both personalities can have input into the final decision. Other times, the reversal only kicks in under extreme stress. For all I know, it could be some kind of overload—one personality goes into shock and the communication system goes out of whack. I don't know if it's intentional or not."

"The gods arrange it so that one soul can help the other," I said.

"Oh come on, Fullin," my sister suddenly snapped, "the *gods*? Haven't you been listening? The gods have nothing to do with this. Traitors from the stars made Birds Home. It's all an experiment . . . except they got bored and walked away when we stopped being amusing."

I stared at her in shock. My hand froze on the gun, the safety slide only partly moved to the right position.

"Well it's true, isn't it?" my sister self said to Steck. "They had some notion about men and women getting along better if we knew how the other half lived?"

"Yes," Steck nodded. "It was an experiment. Although I don't know if it was just about men and women. Remember that everyone has a Neut version too. I think the designers considered hermaphrodite the best choice: combining male and female in one body."

"You *would* believe that was best," Cappie said bitterly.

"But think about it," Steck told her. "Your Neut self slept through the male and female years of your childhood. That makes the Neut more impartial than the other two. When you're male, your female life seems distant and secondhand; when you're female, your male life is the dream. But the Neut sees both halves as childhood ghosts; the Neut can wake at the age of twenty, and start life in equilibrium.''

"Is that why you killed the male and female children?" I asked. "Because you thought being Neut was a *gift*?"

I yelled the word "gift." My voice covered the click as I slid the safety catch all the way.

Steck sighed. "Before the Patriarch came along, Neuts were accepted. But like all tyrants, the Patriarch had to demonize someone and he could only get so much mileage out of scientists. He taught everyone that Neuts were devils; he even burned them as blasphemies against the gods. We aren't blasphemies, Fullin. We're just people. Aren't we, Cappie?"

Cappie's eyes narrowed. She was squeezing the glass splinter so tightly, a bead of blood trickled out where the sharp edges had begun to cut her palm. "I never had a problem with Neuts like Dorr," she said. "*You're* another story."

"Neuts like Dorr," Steck repeated. "Poor, crazy Dorr. Committing Neut was an act of desperation for her . . . or defiance, I don't know which. It shouldn't have to be that way. People should be able to choose Neut because it's right for them. Healthy. It oughtn't to be some forbidden attraction . . . some last resort of lonely people who can't stand a normal existence. What's wrong with deciding you want to be whole? Not stuck in the rut of one gender or the other, but free?"

"And that's why you killed the boys and girls," my sister self said. "You want Neuts to be accepted again, and you think when the Neut children go home, Tober Cove will be forced to take them in."

"Exactly!" Steck answered. "The cove will be faced with an entire Neut generation—their own beloved children. Hakoore may hiss and howl, but even he can't force parents to exile their babies. You tell me, Fullin: how do you feel about a Neut Waggett?"

I glared at her. My anger felt powerful—the gun was ready to fire. "I love Waggett," I said, spitting the words at her. "I love whatever he is. And I hate you for taking away his choices."

"I'm giving the cove *back* its choices," Steck replied. "Everyone will spend time with Neuts; everyone will see they aren't innately evil. The next generation will know that Committing Neut is just as good as male or female."

"The next generation?" Cappie asked. "Are children really going to visit Birds Home again? You've smashed up the place—"

"The machines repair themselves," Steck interrupted. "By this time next year—by the time your daughter Pona is ready to come here—

Birds Home will be back in business. I've had time to look at the control room next door. The equipment is already gearing up to replace the broken coffins. And Pona's tissue samples are turning into a male Pona, even as we speak."

"You see?" Female-Me said to the rest of us. "It isn't as bad as you think. The children are still alive . . . one version of them anyway, which is all that ever survives. And Birds Home will continue the same as ever."

"Why are you apologizing for Steck?" I demanded. She *knew* I had the gun ready; she was linked to my mind. Yet she was suddenly sticking up for . . .

"Our *mother*," my female self snapped. "Our mother was just trying to help. To open our eyes." Female-Me turned back to Steck. "What about the Neut version of us? There must have been a Neut Fullin. Where is he?"

"*It*," I said.

"We've really got to get some new pronouns," Cappie muttered.

"Where's Neut Fullin?" Female-Me asked again.

Steck looked at her, then at me. Finally, she said, "I killed him."

"You what?"

She sighed, then let her hands fall to her side. The violin, still in her left hand, made a light four-stringed twang as it tinked against her armor.

"I killed him," she said. "My Neut child." Steck closed her eyes as if she could see it all in her mind. "I opened his coffin, said, "Wake up, it's all right!" . . . and the stupid bastard attacked me. Just screamed and came at me with his bare hands. Must have been picking up someone else's hate."

She looked at me as if she expected me to confess something. I didn't; I tightened my grip on the gun. "So," Steck went on, "the idiot hurled himself at my throat . . . even though he must have known about the force field. If I could have stopped the damned field from turning itself on I would have—he couldn't have hurt me, not through this armor."

Steck shook her head sadly. "But the armor has a mind of its own. It realized that he wanted to hurt me and reacted accordingly. The force field came up; Fullin burned. I could smell him: his flesh cooking, his hair in flames. His hands were on fire and he just kept after me, trying to get his fingers around my throat. By the time he passed out from pain, he was so burnt . . . his arms, his face, all down his bare chest . . ." She squeezed her eyes tight shut. "I had to shoot him with the laser: drill a hole through his brain. He was charred completely black."

I glared at her, wondering whether to believe her story. If a copy of me had died, wouldn't I have felt it? No. All three of us Fullins had radios in our heads, but I was the only one transmitting. My poor Neut self spent Its entire life in a glass coffin, passively receiving my sister and me.

"Where's the body?" I asked.

"One of the bird-servants took it," Steck answered. "How do you think I learned that unneeded bodies are broken down into nutrients? I saw my own burnt child dumped into a vat and slowly turned to mush. . . ." She inhaled raggedly. "Soon there was nothing left but the smell of charcoal in the air. My own child."

"No," Female-Me said softly, "*I'm* your own child." She moved forward. "I'm the original, aren't I? The others are just copies."

"Stop this!" I cried to my sister. "Don't give her sympathy! She's Steck! The Neut who killed Waggett—who cut Waggett's throat!"

"There's one version of Waggett still alive," my sister replied. "He's not gone. None of them are gone."

"She cut his throat in cold blood!"

"Drastic times require drastic measures."

Cappie made a disgusted sound. "There's nothing drastic about these times . . . or there wasn't until Rashid and Steck came along. Maybe it *was* unfair what Tober Cove did to Neuts, but we could have changed that without killing babies. With me as priestess and Fullin as Patriarch's Man . . . I mean the male Fullin . . ."

Her voice trailed off. She looked down at herself—the unfamiliar Neut body that would never be priestess now.

"Would you really be able to change things?" Female-Me asked. "Would you have thought it was worth the effort? No," she shook her head, "I know you and I know my brother. Mumbly good intentions, but no real commitment. Not like Steck. Do you think this was easy on her? Killing all those children? Her own grandson? But she did it to break the Patriarch's curse on Tober Cove. And she succeeded. The next generation will be free." She turned and walked toward Steck with open arms. "Thank you, Mother. At least one of us knows you did the right thing."

That was when I whipped the gun from behind my back and fired at my female self.

Maybe I was just too angry to shoot straight . . . but then, it was the first time I'd ever pulled the trigger and my sister had moved most of the way across the room. The gun kicked in my hands. A bullet ricocheted off a rock wall and zinged who knows where as the boom of the shot echoed through all of Birds Home.

Cappie dove to the ground, screaming, "Stop, you'll hit the children!" She was right—I had to get close enough so I wouldn't miss again. I started running; don't ask me whether I intended to shoot my sister or mother, but one of them was going to die.

Female-Me dashed toward Steck, shouting, "Help me, Mother!" Steck spread her arms wide in a welcoming embrace. My sister threw herself forward, the way Waggett sometimes threw himself into my own arms, diving toward sanctuary. She collided with Steck's armored chest, and pressed in tight, hugging the green plastic. I fired, and by now I was close enough that the bullet was right on target . . .

Violet light erupted at the point of impact, bright as staring into the sun. It left a scorched hole in my vision; but around the edges I could see my traitor female half nestled snugly against Steck, both of them safe within the crackling violet protection.

"Put the gun down," Steck yelled at me. "You'll only hurt yourself."

"That's what I'm trying to do," I answered. I fired at my sister half again.

"Stupid!" Steck cried as another burst of violet blazed the bullet to slag.

"You almost hit the violin!" Female-Me shouted in indignation. She reached out and lightly pulled the instrument out of Steck's hand, then hugged it to her own chest for protection. As an afterthought, she took the bow too . . . as if she might actually decide to play a ballad while I was shooting at her.

I fired. Point-blank range. Violet flame burnt the bullet to smoke.

"This is futile," Steck growled. "You can't get through the force field."

"True," my sister said in a hard, quiet voice. "But I'm already inside."

And she rammed the point of the violin bow into Steck's unprotected eye.

The point was not very sharp; but it was sharp enough.

My sister had gripped the bow in her fist, with four inches of the tip end showing. All four inches speared into Steck's eye and on into her brain, driven by the force of sheer hatred . . . driven by the gods and the souls of dead children. Steck gave nothing more than a surprised grunt; then she was falling, dragging my sister with her as Steck's arms spasmed and locked Female-Me in a bear hug.

When they hit the floor, the force field was still active. Violet flame broke against the rock underfoot, a flash explosion that seared an armor-sized patch of granite into a sheen of smoking lava. The explosion had enough force to bounce Steck and my sister partway up again; then they fell once more, bounced, fell, bounced, like a fiery violet ball taking its time to settle.

When they finally came to rest, the force field continued to burn, smelting its way into a trench in the bare rock floor. Steck's legs jerked with dying convulsions. My sister, still holding the bow, pushed it deeper into Steck's brain, as blood spilled out of the eye socket and onto her hands. Steck gave one last shaking shudder . . . and then the breath sighed out of her for the last time.

Gradually, the violet flame subsided. The suit was smart enough to realize it was fighting a lost cause.

Cappie and I helped my sister up, making sure she didn't step on the red hot rock that surrounded the fallen armor. ''I thought you had turned traitor,'' I mumbled to my female self.

''You should know better,'' she answered. ''I'm you, aren't I?'' She looked at me, then Cappie. ''Steck had to die, didn't she? She had to.''

Cappie stared down at the body. ''In her own mind, Steck had done nothing wrong. As she said, the children are all alive—Neut versions of them anyway. And the way things work in Birds Home, two versions of each person die anyway. Steck didn't do anything that wouldn't have happened eventually . . . but yes, she had to die. Even if it all balances out, some things can't be forgiven.''

TWENTY-TWO

A Prayer for Us All

When Rashid arrived, I was debating whether to pull the violin bow out of Steck's eye. I didn't want to touch it, but as the heat of the moment cooled, I began to hate the sight of my mother, disfigured by the protruding murder weapon. My sister self may have been having the same thoughts—she was me, wasn't she?—but she didn't reach for the bow either.

Cappie stood in shadow farther down the unlit corridor. Now that the excitement was over, I think she'd become painfully aware of her nakedness . . . or painfully ashamed of her Neutness.

"Hello," Rashid said to the three of us. "Where's Steck?"

My sister and I pointed to the floor. Rashid's mouth tightened. He came forward far enough that he could see past the glass coffins to the corpse.

"Dead?" he asked.

We all nodded.

He lowered his head and let his breath out slowly. "I suppose I should thank you—if you hadn't killed her, I would have been forced to do it myself."

"Why?" I asked.

"Family policy: no one walks away from betraying a Spark." He looked down at Steck's bloody face. "Stupid rule." He took a deep breath. "But if I didn't enforce it, my brothers and sisters would. Steck was the one who killed those children in the other rooms?"

"Yes."

He looked at the corpse again. "Sometimes you can't tell if a person is Iago or Desdemona." He sighed. "With Steck, it always had to be both."

*   *   *

After a while, Rashid asked, "Did Steck have a reason? Did she tell you why she did everything?"

We explained as best we could. It took all three of us, Cappie, sister Fullin and I, to piece together everything Steck said about the workings of Birds Home. Even then, Rashid had questions we couldn't answer: questions about technical details that Steck hadn't mentioned, either because she thought we were too stupid to understand, or because she didn't understand them herself. Rashid might have continued the talk about chromo-this and DN-that until the rest of us dropped from brain fatigue . . . but he was interrupted by the sound of approaching footsteps.

Cappie, farther up the corridor than the rest of us, spun immediately to face whatever was coming. She still held the glass splinter; now she raised it like a dagger, and waited . . . then lowered it again. "Just a bird-servant," she said.

A moment later, I could see the figure for myself—the bird-servant colored like a cardinal, although its brilliant red was muted to charcoal gray in the shadowy corridor. It passed Cappie without a glance and stepped coolly over Steck's corpse.

"Not interested in us," Cappie observed.

"Not programmed to be," Rashid replied.

The cardinal went straight to the nearest coffin . . . which happened to hold Waggett. My sister and I tensed as the lid of the coffin swung open. The bird-thing reached in and lifted out my son with expert care: supporting the head, snuggling the child's small body in red plastic arms. I took a step forward, but Rashid caught me by the shoulder. "Easy. Let it do its job."

The bird adjusted Waggett's weight until my son was securely cradled against the creature's chest. Then it turned and walked back the way it came, ignoring all of us as if we were part of the stone walls.

"Where is it taking him?" my sister demanded.

"Back to the hangar," Rashid answered. "On a normal Commitment Day, the children wake up near the plane in Master Crow's nest, right? The bird-servants must carry them there."

Even as he spoke, four more bird-creatures strode out of the darkness: a hawk, a goose, the jay, and a mallard. Their movements were unnaturally smooth, every step measured like honey. Silently, they gathered four more children and carried them out of the room.

"This is a good sign," Rashid said. He kept his voice low, as if he didn't want to disturb the birds as they passed. "Despite all the damage," he went on, "the machines have obviously figured out what to do—send the Neut children back to Tober Cove, because they're the only ones left alive. It's nice to know the programming for Birds Home is smart enough to deal with this situation.''

My sister self continued to stare into the darkness, watching the bird-servants disappear. ''We should follow them,'' she murmured.

''The robots won't harm the children,'' Rashid told her.

''But the children will soon wake up, won't they? And when they see what they've become, someone should be there to calm them. To tell them it's okay.''

''The new priestess,'' Cappie said. ''You.''

My sister met Cappie's gaze. Neither of them spoke for a moment. Then Female-Me said, ''I'm ready to be priestess if you don't want the job. But you have first claim to it.''

Cappie shook her head. ''A Neut priestess? The cove has enough to swallow already. They'll accept the Neut children because they have to; but given a choice between a Neut and a true woman, I know which would make Tobers more comfortable. Isn't that a big part of the priestess's job—comforting people?''

''All right,'' my sister said. ''But we'll do what we discussed last night—work as a team. Even if I'm the official priestess, we'll make our decisions together and . . .''

''No,'' Cappie interrupted. ''I'm not going back to the cove. Not right away.''

''What?'' I blurted. ''Not going home?''

''Someone has to stay here,'' she said. ''Make sure that Birds Home really can repair itself.''

''I'll do that,'' Rashid answered immediately. ''I owe you that much, considering I was the one who brought Steck here. And there's so much I can learn in a place like this. I want to understand the cloning process . . . the exact way thoughts are transferred . . .''

''While you're doing that,'' Cappie said, ''could you use a second pair of hands?''

''Probably,'' Rashid nodded. ''It so happens I have an immediate opening for a new Bozzle . . . and there's a precedent of filling the position with a person of dual gendership.''

Cappie glared at him with steely eyes. ''If you think you're going to start up with me the way you were with Steck . . .''

''No!'' Rashid said sharply. It was the first time his self-control had broken since he found Steck dead: the first time he sounded like a man instead of a Spark Lord. ''I'm standing here with a corpse at my feet— her corpse! Do you think I'm so inhuman I can just . . .'' His voice choked off. ''No,'' he said with a catch in his throat, ''I'm really just looking for an assistant, Cappie: a second pair of hands, as you put it.

It'll be a long time before I . . . never mind. You help me here in Birds Home, and after that, I'll see you get back to Tober Cove. If that's what you want.''

She looked at him for a moment more, then nodded. "It's a deal." Cappie turned back to my sister self. "Can you take care of Pona for a while?"

"Of course."

"I'll be back when I'm ready," Cappie added hurriedly. "I promise. It's just . . . I knew who I was when I was male and when I was female. Now that I'm neither one . . ." She shrugged.

"So you're trying to find yourself," I said. "But why can't you do that in Tober Cove? We need you there."

"Why? So you Fullins can fight over me?"

"We won't fight over you," I protested.

"In a few weeks, you might be fighting over who gets stuck with me. I know," she said quickly, "that's unfair. But it was just a few hours ago that you couldn't give yourself to me; not the way I needed. Has anything changed? Have you suddenly fallen in love with me because I'm a Neut? Not likely." She gave us the ghost of a smile, trying to take the sting from her words. "You may feel fond and sentimental about me right now, but that's not enough. There's too much pity in it—pity because I'm not male or female, and you think that's a tragic loss. Maybe it is, I don't know. But I need time to decide for myself."

"Then take the time," Female-Me told her. "Pona will be all right. And when you're ready to come back, I guarantee Tober Cove won't have a law about banishing Neuts."

"To make changes like that, you'll need help." Cappie smiled. "You'll need help from the Patriarch's Man."

She turned to me. "How about it? Will you say yes to Hakoore? For the good of the cove?"

"Patriarch's Man?" When I said it, the title sounded so sadly pompous—a relic of some long-dead tyrant, one more thing that should have gone on that junk heap in Mayoralty House. The Patriarch's Man was a self-deceiving fool with a book of laws and a machine that looked like a severed hand. "I don't know if I believe in the position," I said. "After everything that's happened in Birds Home . . ."

"You mean you've lost your faith in the gods?" Rashid asked. "This is so typical. I've bent over backward not to utter a word against your faith, but you're going to say I raised doubts—"

"I still believe in the gods," I answered quietly. "But not the Patriarch's Law."

"Then change it," Cappie said. "The Patriarch has been an ugly sore, festering on the face of the cove for a hundred and fifty years. Get rid of him.''

"By becoming Hakoore's 'disciple'?''

"Yes . . . if that's what it takes to make things right.''

A fire burned in her eyes. It felt strange to have someone believe in me.

"Do you agree?" I asked my other self. "If Hakoore puts the squeeze on me with that damned Patriarch's Hand . . .''

"I'll support you," she said. "Make sure your head stays straight.'' She laid her fingers lightly on my arm and smiled. "Two weasels together can beat a snake.''

I smiled back. "All right—I'll do it. Patriarch's Man.''

My commitment.

"Of course, you remember," Female-Me added, "there's a special *arrangement* between priestess and Patriarch's Man.''

I raised my eyebrows. She was looking at me with cool appraisal. I returned her gaze evenly.

"This could get interesting," Cappie murmured.

"What?" Rashid asked. "What's this special arrangement?''

"Tell you later," she answered.

"And in the meantime," I said to Rashid, "can you do something about this radio in my head? I refuse to match wits with someone who can hear everything I think.''

"Yes," my sister agreed, "please stop him transmitting. It's so embarrassing to know the second he gets horny for me.''

"Me? Horny for you?''

"Silence, peasants!" Rashid commanded with mock severity. "Whatever you're arguing about, I don't care—I've had my fill of cultural observation for one day. Let's find the damned lab so I can get back to the hard sciences. I'm longing for things that make sense.''

The lab was gigantic—far larger than all three coffin chambers put together. The front part held five large glass windows, showing words and numbers and graphs painted in colored light. There was also a corridor slanting upward, no doubt leading to Master Crow's nest. But what caught my interest most was the rear part of the room: a single wide aisle down the middle with banks of arcane machinery on either side. Even the height of OldTech culture couldn't have created such equipment. Glistening steel vats with pipes sprouting out in all directions. A tall pillar from floor to ceiling, with an exterior of black matte plastic and an interior of who knew what. Gray metal boxes that breathed out warm air through grilles, and faceless things with inhuman arms, delicately jiggling test tubes of red fluid.

"Glory be!" Rashid cried with delight. "Home at last!"

"This looks like your home?" I asked dubiously.

He ignored me, moving to a nearby window-glass and punching at a row of buttons beneath it. Immediately, the picture in the window changed to a list of names—all the children of Tober Cove.

"Amazing," Rashid said. "How could they find out your names? Unless they can analyze the thought transmissions as they're coming through and extract specific information. But that would mean they understand the actual encryption of mental data in the brain . . ."

"Can you turn off the transmitter or not?" I asked.

"Hard to say," Rashid answered. "If I find a nice simple data screen with a button that says, CLICK HERE TO TURN OFF FULLIN'S TRANSMITTER, then we're fine. Otherwise, it may take months to figure out the trick. This setup is far more complicated than I expected, and I don't want to monkey with things I don't understand."

Footsteps sounded from the up-slanting corridor. A moment later, the bird-servants appeared: all five walking in lock step, their arms empty. They paid no attention to us as they proceeded on toward the Neut chamber.

My sister self gave me a look. "We'd better get up to Master Crow's nest before the children start waking."

I nodded, then turned to Cappie. "Are you going to be all right?"

"Helping a Spark Lord in the home of the gods? You can't get safer than that." She stepped forward quickly and gave me a hug. "Don't worry about me." She gave another squeeze and turned to my female half. "I'll be back for Pona, trust me."

"Sure." My sister self closed her eyes as Cappie embraced her. "I'll miss you," she whispered.

Cappie gave her a light kiss on the nose. "You'll have each other," she said with a laugh. "I'll come back to the cove just to see how that works out." She grabbed my sister and me by the arm and gave us a slight shove toward the door. "Now get out of here. You both have work to do."

We nodded. My sister had already turned toward the door when I stopped. "One last thing." I reached behind my back and pulled out the gun; sometime after Steck's death, I had shoved it into my belt again without thinking. "This stays here," I said, checking the safety before I laid the pistol on the floor. "And Rashid . . . next time you bring presents to Tober Cove, try a fruit basket. Something harmless."

"Next time I come to Tober Cove," Rashid answered, "I'll bring Cappie. Is she harmless?"

My sister laughed . . . then slipped her arm into mine, as if she were taking possession of me. I didn't push her away.

As we began the climb up the slope to the hangar, Rashid cried, "Aha! Just what we were looking for. We look under Fullin's name, cross-match his personal transmission frequency, type in the numbers under DEACTIVATE, and . . ."

Everything suddenly went black.

"Fullin . . . Fullin . . ."

Someone was patting my face. I turned my head away.

"Come on, Fullin, wake up. Come on."

I opened my eyes. Cappie, the Neut Cappie, stared down at me.

"What?"

"Wake up, sleepyhead."

Groggily, I rolled up onto one elbow. I felt the weight of breasts on my chest as they shifted position. Was I the Female-Me? But I could feel . . . down at my crotch . . .

"Oh gods," I groaned, looking at myself. "I'm the Neut."

I let myself slump backward. I was lying inside a glass coffin.

Cappie stroked my cheek soothingly. "It's a shock, isn't it?"

"All this time I thought I was the male version . . . no, he was transmitting and I was just receiving." Suddenly I sat up. "Steck said the Neut Fullin was dead. Burned black as toast."

"And you believed her?" Cappie said. "Steck had better control of the armor than that. When your male self started shooting and your female self ran to Steck for protection, the force field didn't flick on until your woman half was safe in Steck's arms. Steck could keep the force field turned off when she wanted . . . so I knew she wasn't telling the truth."

"But why did she lie?" I asked.

"We'll never know. Maybe she didn't trust the male and female Fullins—she might have thought they'd hate a Neut version of themselves. This might have been a way to keep you safe from them. Or perhaps Steck just wanted to stash you out of sight until everyone else left Birds Home. It would give her time alone with her child: the one version who might truly understand her. Whatever the reason, she wheeled your coffin into the back part of the lab and hid you among the machines."

I looked around; I was indeed surrounded by machines. Off to my right, a gadget with a large metal drum whirled faster than a spinning wheel; something liquid gurgled inside. "So you were just exploring and stumbled on me here?"

"No, idiot. I started looking for you as soon as your other two selves left. Why do you think I wanted to stay in Birds Home?"

"You stayed for me?"

"Yes." She leaned over the edge of the coffin and kissed me. Hard.

"But I've been such a bastard . . ." I started.

"No, not you," Cappie interrupted. "That was the other two Fullins . . . with the other two Cappies. When I think of all the bad things that happened between us—those are like dreams from a previous life. I remember, but I'm not scarred by them. Isn't it the same for you?"

I thought back . . . and I could remember all the times I took advantage of her, the times I cheated or told lies; I could even remember the rationalizations I used to justify myself. But it was all secondhand, half-lost in haze; stories someone else had told me, dreams that meant as little as dreams always do. Only a few memories felt real and vivid: giving birth to Waggett (with Cappie holding my hand); my first kiss (with Cappie); my first time making love (with Cappie) . . .

Carefully, I climbed out of the coffin and wrapped my arms around her. Two newborn Neuts, warm against each other. The gods had never given me an opportunity to choose my gender, but they had still left me the chance to decide my future.

The choice was easy. "Happy Commitment," I whispered in Cappie's ear.